"I liked this book.... Stirling is a master of world building. This series has gone a long way from its point of departure, but still keeps a horde of fans wanting more."   —SFRevu

"Fans will remain enthralled.... The tale is filled with action, strong characters in conflict, vivid descriptions of a battered, dying land trying to come back to life two-plus decades since the Change, and a great cliff-hanging climax."
—*Midwest Book Review*

"Stirling has crafted a complex follow-up to *The Sunrise Lands* that vividly describes the political landscape.... Rudi's character is satisfyingly multifaceted, deeply troubled by his visions as he searches for answers at the risk of his life in a world gone awry."   —Monsters and Critics

The Sunrise Lands

"Brilliant action."   —*Booklist*

"Combines vigorous military adventure with cleverly packaged political idealism ... Stirling's narrative deftly balances sharply contrasting ideologies.... The thought-provoking and engaging storytelling should please Stirling's many fans."   —*Publishers Weekly*

"Fast-paced."   —*Futures Mystery Anthology Magazine*

"Stirling has his world firmly in hand.... All those who were on board for *Dies the Fire*, *The Protector's War*, and *A Meeting at Corvallis* should jump on this ride as well."
—*Contra Costa Times*

"A master of speculative fiction and alternate history, Stirling delivers another chapter in an epic of survival and rebirth."   —*Library Journal*

continued ...

A Meeting at Corvallis

"[A] richly realized story of swordplay and intrigue."
—*Entertainment Weekly*

"Stirling concludes his alternative history trilogy in high style. . . . [The story] resembles one of the cavalry charges the novel describes—gorgeous, stirring, and gathering such earth-pounding momentum that it's difficult to resist."
—*Publishers Weekly*

"A fascinating glimpse into a future transformed by the lack of easy solutions to both human and technological dilemmas."
—*Library Journal*

"Grand and resonant . . . exciting and suspenseful. . . . Blending elements of Arthurian and Tolkienesque romance with down-in-the-muck details of birth and death, farming and herding, building and politicking, Stirling manages to fashion a narrative that acknowledges that humanity is a creature of both soul and body, heart and mind, lust and sacrifice, much in the manner of Poul Anderson. . . . Stirling has blazed a clear comet trail across his postapocalyptic landscape that illuminates both the best and the worst of which our species is capable."
—Science Fiction Weekly

"The ensuing maze of intrigue, diplomacy, and battle (with a wonderful variety of weapons ingeniously exploiting archaic technology) comes up to Stirling's highest standards for pacing, world building, action, and strong characterizations, particularly of women . . . a major work by an authentic master of alternate history."—*Booklist* (starred review)

The Protector's War

"Absorbing."   —*The San Diego Union-Tribune*

"[A] vivid portrait of a world gone insane . . . it also has human warmth and courage. . . . It is full of bloody action, exposition that expands character, and telling detail that makes it all seem very real. . . . It is the determination of its major characters to create a safe and loving world that makes the book so affecting."
—*Statesman Journal* (Salem, OR)

"Reminds me of Poul Anderson at his best.... Against a colorful, action-filled background, Stirling shows characters who've solved the problems of immediate personal survival and can now focus on their legacies."
—David Drake, author of *When the Tide Rises*

"Rousing.... Without a doubt [*The Protector's War*] will raise the bar for alternate universe fiction and shows all of S. M. Stirling's hallmark ability to tell a stirring tale with vivid characters."
—*New York Times* bestselling author John Ringo

"The characters are distinct and clearly drawn with a lovely sense of humor.... Very readable."　　　　　—SFRevu

"Villains of the darkest hue are matched by average men and women grown into heroes of Arthurian stature and complexity. The action streaks across the page like an avenging blade.... When you're finished reading, you'll beg him for more." —John Birmingham, author of *Final Impact*

Dies the Fire

"*Dies the Fire* kept me reading till five in the morning so I could finish at one great gulp. It's an alarmingly large speculation: How would we fare if we suddenly had the past 250 years and more of technological progress taken away from us? No more electricity. No more internal-combustion engines. No more gunpowder or other explosives. All gone, vanished in the blink of an eye.... Don't miss it."　　　—Harry Turtledove

"Gritty, realistic, apocalyptic, yet a grim hopefulness pervades it like a fog of light. The characters are multidimensional, unusual, and so very human. Buy *Dies the Fire*. Sell your house; sell your soul; get the book. You won't be sorry."
—John Ringo

"A stunning speculative vision of a near-future bereft of modern conveniences but filled with human hope and determination. Highly recommended."　　　—*Library Journal*

"S. M. Stirling gives himself a broad canvas on which to display his talent for action, extrapolation, and depiction of the brutal realities of life in the absence of civilized norms."
—David Drake

THE
SCOURGE of GOD

A NOVEL OF THE CHANGE

S. M. STIRLING

A ROC BOOK

ROC
Published by New American Library, a division of
Penguin Group (USA) Inc., 375 Hudson Street,
New York, New York 10014, USA
Penguin Group (Canada), 90 Eglinton Avenue East, Suite 700, Toronto,
Ontario M4P 2Y3, Canada (a division of Pearson Penguin Canada Inc.)
Penguin Books Ltd., 80 Strand, London WC2R 0RL, England
Penguin Ireland, 25 St. Stephen's Green, Dublin 2,
Ireland (a division of Penguin Books Ltd.)
Penguin Group (Australia), 250 Camberwell Road, Camberwell, Victoria 3124,
Australia (a division of Pearson Australia Group Pty. Ltd.)
Penguin Books India Pvt. Ltd., 11 Community Centre, Panchsheel Park,
New Delhi - 110 017, India
Penguin Group (NZ), 67 Apollo Drive, Rosedale, North Shore 0632,
New Zealand (a division of Pearson New Zealand Ltd.)
Penguin Books (South Africa) (Pty.) Ltd., 24 Sturdee Avenue,
Rosebank, Johannesburg 2196, South Africa

Penguin Books Ltd., Registered Offices:
80 Strand, London WC2R 0RL, England

Published by Roc, an imprint of New American Library, a division of Penguin
Group (USA) Inc. Previously published in a Roc hardcover edition.

First Roc Mass Market Printing, September 2009
10 9 8 7 6 5 4 3 2 1

To Alfred Bruce Stirling, father and inspiration

ACKNOWLEDGMENTS

Thanks to my friends who are also first readers:

To Steve Brady, for assistance with dialects and British background, and also with bugs, birds and plants.

Thanks also to Kier Salmon, for once again helping with the beautiful complexities of the Old Religion, and with local details for Oregon. And for the use of BD!

To Diana L. Paxson, for help and advice, for insights into a certain Person, and for writing the beautiful Westria books, among many others. If you liked the Change novels, you'll probably enjoy the hell out of the Westria books—I certainly did, and they were one of the inspirations for this series.

To Dale Price, for help with Catholic organization, theology and praxis.

To Brenda Sutton, for multitudinous advice.

To Matt Miller, for answering questions about the lovely Silver Creek area of Idaho, which he has helped to preserve.

To Melinda Snodgrass, Daniel Abraham (loved that suggestion about cues!), Emily Mah, Terry England, George R. R. Martin, Walter Jon Williams, Jan Stirling and Ian Tregellis of Critical Mass, for constant help and advice as the book was under construction.

Special thanks to Heather Alexander, bard and balladeer, for permission to use the lyrics from her beautiful songs which can be—and should be!—ordered at www.heatherlands.com. Run, do not walk, to do so.

Special thanks to Kate West, for her kind words and permission to use her chants.

Special thanks also—I have an infinite fund of them—to William Pint and Felicia Dale, for permission to use their music, which can be found at www.pintndale.com and should be, for anyone with an ear and with salt water in their veins.

And to Three Weird Sisters—Gwen Knighton, Mary Crowell, Brenda Sutton, and Teresa Powell—whose alternately funny and beautiful music can be found at www.threeweirdsisters.com.

And to Talbot Mundy, with apologies for making him a CUT saint and the villains Theosophists, and with thanks for inspiration—I think he'd be amused at the homage to Ringding Gelong Lama Tsiang Samdup.

All mistakes, infelicities and errors are of course my own.

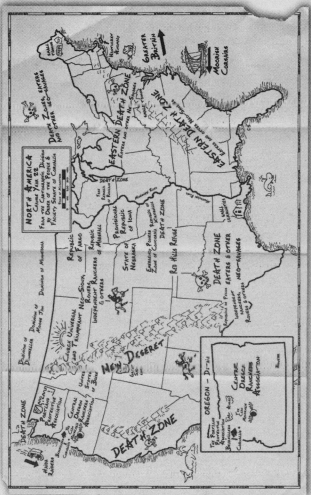

PROLOGUE

The five women fell silent as they climbed single file on the narrow woodland track, higher and higher through the long summer twilight, with the soft duff of the forest floor quiet beneath their sandals— or in one case, boot-heels. They were dressed alike in black hooded robes belted with tricolored cords. The long rowan staffs in their hands marked each as a High Priestess, and each was tipped with a symbol wrought in silver; Hecate's threefold Moon for Juniper Mackenzie and her fellow clanswomen Sumina and Melissa, Pythian Apollo's wolf for BD of the Kyklos, the snarling she-tiger of the Wild Huntress for Signe Havel, the Bearkiller regent

The air cooled, with night and with the height itself, dense with the scent of the resin the day's heat had baked out of the trees; the place they sought was three thousand feet above the valley floor. Stars appeared, glimpsed in fleeting instants amid black boughs silhouetted against the blacker sky, and the light died in the west. Eastward it tinged the snowpeaks and glaciers of the High Cascades with crimson for a last moment, like a dream of melancholy in the mind of a god, before they turned bone white beneath the stars.

At last they came out on a broad knee that jutted from the mountainside, perhaps three acres of nearly level ground. Juniper raised her staff, topped with a silver circle flanked by twin crescents, the Ever-Changing One's symbol, waxing and full and waning. A sigh went through the waiting crowd as she appeared out of the darkness; a few torches caught here a bright fall of hair or there a painted face, but mostly they were a restless mass of shadows.

Then the great drums began to beat; slowly at first, but building to a steady *boom . . . boom . . . boom . . .* like the heartbeat of some great beast. The sound echoed from the mountainsides and through the forest, and somewhere far distant a wolf howled, the lonely sound threading its way through the deep pulsing bass of the Lambegs. The *nemed* was a circle of tall oaks amid the stretch of dense turf, thick brown trunks rising to rounded dark green crowns that met a hundred feet above the ground, rustling with mystery. Within, the trees at the Quarters bore wrought-iron brackets where the lanterns would go, and a roughly chiseled stone block stood as an altar near the shallow central hearth.

Not far outside the trees a spring rose, bubbling quietly into its pool at this time of year and trickling off across the little plateau. The starry Belt of the Goddess was bright tonight; there was just enough light to show that the ground around the spring was matted with pink mountain laurel, with pale glacier lily farther out. Looming in the dimness was the figure of the Corn King, fifteen feet of man-shaped wicker frame woven shaggy with sheaves of wheat and barley.

The drums beat on, pulsing out dread, and the crowd parted for Juniper and her companions. She was a short, slight-built woman of fifty-three, with leaf-green eyes and streaks of gray in the faded fox-red mane; the hand on the silky wood of the staff had the worn long-fingered grip of a musician who'd also worked with hoe and milking pail and loom.

There was awe in the crowd's reverence; she was also High Priestess and Chief and Goddess-on-Earth, the one who had made the Clan and brought their parents through the wreck of the old world and the terror-filled birth of the new. Most of them were Changelings now—

those who'd been born since the Change, or who'd been too young then to really remember the world before.

The tall image of wheat-sheaves waited, its head wreathed in darkness. She paced forward, the hood of her robe thrown back and the crescent on her brow; she held out her right hand and a burning torch was passed to her. The strong, almost spicy smell of it went under the crackling, and the light blinded her for an instant.

A long *ahhhhhhh* went through the watchers as she raised torch and staff. The throb of Power was like wine in her veins, like pleasure so extreme that it trembled on the brink of unbearable pain, like an enormous love chiseled out of terror.

"Corn King!" she called.

"Corn King!" her four companions echoed.

"It is Your flesh that we cut with the grain and eat with the good bread. It is Your blood and seed we will sow in the Mother's earth. All hail to the King of the Ripened Grain, who dies for the Mother's children!"

"Hail the King!"

The crowd cried hail with a thousandfold voice, stronger than the drums for a moment as she touched the flame to the wheat-straw. It took with a swift crackling roar, reaching for the sky and driving back a circle of the darkness; she tossed the stump of the torch on it and picked up the tool that lay ready for her—a bronze sickle, its blade shaped like the waning moon.

As the cheer ended a man sprang out of the crowd. He was naked, save for the vermillion paint on his face and streaking his sweat-slick muscled limbs and torso; stalks of wheat were wound in his shaggy white-gold hair.

"I am Her lover, since first I wed the Maiden," he called, his voice a bugling challenge, hoarse and male and powerful like a bull elk; in his right hand was a flint knife, its pressure-flaked surface glittering in the light with an almost metallic luster. "Surely the Mother shall aid Me, as I fight for My throne!"

"I am become the Crone, and the Crone carries Harvest's Child," Juniper called, her voice as impersonal as bronze. "So must it be. So mote it be."

She crossed her wrists and turned the point of the sickle towards him; the High Priestesses raised their staffs. Another man stepped forward. He was a little older but in his full strength, slender and wiry. His hair was dark and bound with holly, red berries glistening among the spiny dark green leaves; black paint covered his face save for a rim around his eyes. The knife he held was obsidian, sharp enough to cut a dream.

"I am the King who will be," he said. "For the Wise One cleaves to the Keeper-of-Laws."

The Corn King gave a long roar and closed with him. The stone blades flashed in the light of the straw man's burning, until the tall figure collapsed in a shower of sparks. Hands grasped wrists as the men of flesh and blood swayed together, striving chest to chest. Then the Corn King staggered back, a long shallow cut across his breast. Blood runneled down from it, and dropped onto the ground. A sound halfway between a sigh and a moan came from the crowd, and the former King toppled gracefully to the dirt in a mime of death.

"*The King is dead!*" the four priestesses cried.

Women with unbound hair came forward and lifted the limp form of the Corn King, amid more who wailed grief and beat their breasts. Kilted warriors with their faces painted as if for battle surrounded the new King, circling and leaping, dancing as the razor-edged steel of their spearheads flashed in the firelight.

"*Long live the King!*" they shouted, and a ululating cheer spread through the crowd.

Pipers struck up, and bodhrans; the hoarse bellow of the long wooden *radongs* and the wild chill wailing of flutes. Behind the weeping pallbearers who carried his predecessor the new King walked towards the path that led downward to Dun Juniper. The crowd followed, singing:

"I sleep in the kernel and I dance in the rain;
I dance in the wind and in the waving grain;
And when you cut me down I care nothing for the pain;
In spring I'm the Lord of the Dance once again!"

Juniper smiled as they left and the tension ebbed; the young man who took the part of the new King was going to be *very* popular with the girls until next Beltane; it was one of the perks of the ceremonial role. Then the smile died and she shivered. The Initiates and the High Priestesses remained, and tonight was no ordinary Sabbat; not even an ordinary Lughnasadh Eve. Tonight she planned to ask a question of the Powers.

Water and salt cleansed, fire and incense purified, and chanting had sealed the Circle. Around it stood the other High Priestesses at the Quarters, for this was a greater rite; Signe in the South for her tiger-sign, grape-mistress Sumina in the West, Melissa in the North for the hearth-home, and BD in the East, for Helios of the Clear Speech. Between them the shapes of the Initiates in their dark cowled robes were lost in shadow.

Fire crackled and snapped in the shallow hearth in the center of the circle, sending sparks upward to join the starry Belt of the Goddess and the new-risen waning Moon; the clean hot-sweet smell of the burning applewood joined the strong musk from the thurible and the sap of the dew-cool forest. Red flickers underlit the shifting leaves above, turning them into rustling strangeness. The night-black woods seemed to wait, as if the forest itself held its breath.

Juniper stood before the hewn-boulder altar that bore the bowls and the Chalice, sword and athame, the Lamp of Art and Book of Shadows. She raised her arms and cried:

"Ye Guardians of the Watchtowers of the North! Oh, Lady of Earth, Gaia! Boreas, North Wind and Khione of the Snows, Guardians of the Northern Portals, you powerful God, you Goddess gentle and strong . . ."

Then the Calling. She had felt that as a oneness with all that was, or a blessing like a hand upon her head. This time it was as if she rode the storm, amid a darkness where lightning flickered and winds beat at her with clubs of hail-ice.

"We ask You for the wisdom to understand the storm

that breaks upon the world and the troubles that beset Your folk," she said softly. "Show us Your will for Your earth, and our place in it."

And then she gasped in astonishment and shock, as the Guardians at the Quarters stiffened and called out in a shivering unison like bells of crystal and brass. The earth seemed to whirl, and she wavered as nerves and muscles clenched in nausea and pain.

And she knew Sumina saw:

Squat slant-eyed amber-skinned men in furs and leather rode shaggy ponies across a plain whose bare yellow-brown vastness showed the ruins of a long-dead city on the horizon. Its tall steel buildings stood scorched by fires a generation dead, some leaning drunkenly, their windows empty as the eyes of a skull picked bare by ravens as they looked down on the horde. Black pillars showed behind the riders, where villages burned; their mounts trampled the stubble where millet had grown.

Ocher dust smoked beneath the hooves, and the breath of men and beasts showed in the chill air. They rode armed for war, curved swords at their sides and the thick horn-and-sinew bows of mounted archers in the cases at their knees; lances nodded and rippled as their column advanced. A standard went before them, of seven yaktails on a tall pole. Then they halted, where a man stood in their path. Despite the cold he wore only a long wrapped garment of yellow cloth that left one shoulder bare.

Alone and unarmed, he lifted one hand in a gesture of blessing and smiled. When he did his face showed the wrinkles of age, but the narrow black eyes were calm and shrewd . . . and Juniper knew they were smiling too, even when his face turned grave again.

One of the riders made as if to unsheathe his sword. The leader in the peaked conical helm who rode by the standard put out a hand to halt the motion.

"Don't draw your blade just yet, Toktamish," he said in a barking guttural language she did not know but somehow understood. "If the Han armies could not stop us, one old bonze can't either. Let's listen for a moment."

*   *   *

Juniper gasped again, the cool smoke-tinged air of the *nemed* filling her lungs. Her eyes blinked, as if their focus was suddenly adjusting from distances beyond what they were made to see. Less than a second had passed, though it had seemed many minutes. The hearth crackled again, and vision struck. Melissa saw—

A man lay dying, in a great four-poster bed of carved wood, each breath faint and dragging as if it would be the last; he was very old, his face pale as bleached ivory, the sparse hair on his head snow white. The room around was darkened save for a bedside lantern, but she could sense tall walls bearing paintings, and a ceiling of molded plaster; a physician in a gray nun's habit stepped back, folding her stethoscope and shaking her head.

Juniper could see men standing about—younger ones in dark cassocks, others grave with years in robes and skullcaps of crimson. Among them was a middle-aged warrior in breastplate and crested morion helmet, a tall broad-shouldered man with a battered dark brown face and strong scarred hands.

"The Holy Father will not live until dawn," the doctor said in Italian—which Juniper recognized, but had never learned. "Heroic measures could only delay the end slightly, and it would be no favor to him to regain consciousness."

The men signed themselves in the fashion of Roman Christians and bowed their heads; some of them wept silently, and one covered his face with his hands as his shoulders heaved with the quiet sobs he labored to suppress.

"He has guided us so long!" a young man whose face showed tears whispered. "Since the world was Changed!"

"God said the years of a man are three-score and ten,"another said tenderly. "Our Holy Father has lived many more than that, and those years have been a painful burden he bore willingly for us all. Let him go to the reward he has earned, the greatest of all those who have worn the

shoes of the Fisherman. The College will be summoned; everything is in readiness."

The warrior in armor removed his helmet and knelt by the bedside, gently kissing a ring on the wasted hand that lay motionless on the coverlet. Then he rose and looked at the robed men.

"And in the meantime, holy sirs, I need orders," he said . . . and though he spoke in Italian, she recognized his accent as old-fashioned American. Texan, in fact. "The tribes are stirring beyond the shotts *in South Sicily while the cities of the League argue and Queen Serafina shuts herself in Enna and delays. Decisions cannot wait, even for a great man's passing."*

Another instant, and Juniper breathed. A spark drifted upward, the same she had seen two eyeblinks before, but it was as if it crawled skyward as a glacier descended a mountainside, with a strength behind it that could grind rock to meal. BD's eyes went wide—

"I smell them!" the little wizened man who capered and danced cried shrilly as the drums throbbed out their message. "I smell them! Witchmen! Wizards!"

Beyond the fires the night lay heavy, the eyes and teeth of the crowd showing white against yellow firelight, and behind them the thatch of dome-shaped huts. They surged away as the grotesque figure capered and crawled along their ranks, looking half human in his headdress of leopard skins and cow-horns, tails dangling from his wrists and rattles on his ankles.

Only one group showed no fear; young men near-naked save for their weapons, their muscled bodies glistening with sweat in the hot darkness, ostrich plumes making their proud long-limbed height even greater. Like the rest they were of that glossy dark brown that outsiders had misnamed black, their features broad-nosed and thick-lipped. The man at their head leaned on a tall elliptical shield of mottled cowhide, a broad-bladed stabbing spear held negligently in his right hand, his pose insolently confident, as lithe and dangerous as a great dark cat.

The dancer halted before him and pointed with his beaded gourd rattle. "I smell them! Kill! Kill the wizards!"

A long shuddering sigh came from the crowd.

"Kill the wizards," the young man echoed, and his smile grew broader ...

"Please," Juniper cried into the storm of power, in a shout that was half a sob, "Please, show us our trial, here in these lands and this time."

And Signe's gaze narrowed like her totem-beast on the prowl for prey or snarling at a rival as she saw—

A young man stood looking down on a burning city from a high window. His head was shaven, and there was blood on his naked body, on belly and loins and hands; and there was something beyond humanity in his eyes. He raised his clotted hands to the crowd below, warriors in spiked steel helmets and armor of overlapping lacquered-leather plates.

"The Church is United and Triumphant indeed!" he shouted. "And I am its Prophet!"

They flourished swords and lances whose points bore gruesome trophies and chanted:

"Sethaz! Sethaz! Prophet! Prophet!"

The man's voice rose to a tearing shriek:

"I am the Scourge of God!"

"Enough," Juniper Mackenzie whispered. "Enough ..."

She staggered. A friend's arm supported her; she blinked her way back to awareness, and saw it was Judy Barstow. Her man Chuck was by her side, concern behind the elk-mask of a High Priest. BD was on one knee, leaning on her staff and wheezing in shock, and Melissa's face had gone milk-white under its ruddy tan. Other Initiates rushed to help them; only Signe stood alone, bristling and baring her teeth, hand closing on a sword hilt that wasn't there.

"Ground and center, ground and center," Judy said softly. "I'll take it from here."

Juniper struggled back towards calm, forcing each breath in and out, feeling the drumbeat pounding of her heart slow. The other woman's voice came to her in snatches:

"... *go if you must, stay if you will ... take our grateful thanks.*"

The rite made its way to its end, with the Circle opened. The Initiates filed out, and silence fell in the sacred wood. Juniper tucked the sacrificial sickle through her belt as they left the *nemed*.

Then she leaned on her staff, feeling her legs tremble, suddenly conscious of everything around about her, from the sweat-itch in her hair to the soft touch of the sandal straps on her toes. And that she was ravenous, and craved sleep almost as much ...

The others were as shock-pale as she; Sumina's merry wrinkled-pippin face clenched like a fist, BD's as fierce as her wolf. Melissa was steady, with the stolid patience of the hearth-mistress and farm-wife she'd been these two decades past but with awe and terror beneath, and Signe's valkyr beauty stood hawk-harsh, her bright blue eyes probing. She and Juniper weren't enemies now, but they weren't friends either.

"Does *that* happen often here?" she said sharply, with fear trembling on the brink of anger.

"No," Juniper said flatly. "I've had visions granted ... not often. And never *shared* like that. Not even since the Change. It was always possible, I suppose, in theory, but—"

They looked at each other and nodded, acknowledging that they had *seen*.

"But even Christians don't expect to have the sun stopped overhead *often*," Sumina said, taking a long breath.

The skin between Juniper's shoulder blades crawled, and she shuddered as her mouth went dry as milkweed silk in autumn. Yes, she loved the Lord and Lady in Their many forms ... but those forms spanned the universe of space and time that sprang from Them, and They could be as terrible as the fiery death of suns, as inexorable as Time.

A mother's kiss on her child's face came from Them, but so also the glaciers that grind continents to dust.

"I thought . . . I thought They might tell us something of the Prophet, this madman out in Montana," she said.

Signe nodded sharply. "I saw *him*. It couldn't have been anyone else." She grimaced. "And he was as nasty as . . . well, as nasty as the rumors, which is an accomplishment."

"We all did," BD said. "But more than that "

Juniper took a deep breath, another, inhaling until her lungs creaked and then slowly releasing it, and all the tension in muscle and nerve with it. Ground and center . . . strength flowed back into her body, and firmness to mind and thought. She saw the others win to calm in their different ways; walking the paths they did gave you that.

"Now, these things we saw are signs, and a wonder," she said, in the County Mayo lilt she'd learned at her mother's knee and all her Clan had imitated. "But it is not the first I have seen here, in this place."

They all glanced at the altar. Juniper had prophesied when she held her son over it at his Wiccanning; and Raven had appeared to the boy ten years later, twelve years ago now. Juniper's voice gained strength as she went on:

"I am thinking that it is Their way of telling us that the storm breaking on us is one that troubles all the world. Not in words, but—"

"Even so, that was more . . . obscure than They usually are, wasn't it?" Signe said thoughtfully.

"Not necessarily, my dear," Juniper said; Signe had a warrior's fierce directness.

BD nodded. "An oracle's voice speaks like the wind in a forest, turning and twisting like Time Herself. They don't show us more than we can bear."

"We're all mothers," Melissa said in agreement. "You know you can't speak all your mind to a child. How then could the Divine to us?"

They paused, listening to the creaks and buzzes of the summer night, letting the cool scented air flow through them, winning to steadiness once more. The lonely sobbing of the wolf's howl sounded, far and faint.

Juniper added softly: "And also we are told that unimaginable Powers are at strife in the worlds beyond the world. Our struggle is Theirs as well."

"As above, so below," Sumina murmured, one of the maxims of their faith.

"How not?" BD said. "The Powers are many; and They are One."

Juniper signed agreement; both at once were true, and you couldn't begin to understand Them until you grasped it—not just with your mind, but with heart and gut and bone.

Melissa chuckled. "And sure, we're forgetting something. You have to be careful what you ask, for They have more answers than we can swallow. We should have asked *as* mothers, not just as . . . as politicians in fancy dress."

Juniper smiled ruefully. "My Rudi's east of the mountains; with your girls Ritva and Mary, Signe, and your Edain, Melissa. We should ask about *them*."

"Sumina and I will stand as Guardians," BD said. "But . . . you don't necessarily get what you ask for; They may give you what you need, not what you want. *For if that which you seek, you find not within yourself, you will never find it without—*"

Signe smiled agreement, and completed the line: "*—for behold: I have been with you from the Beginning, and I am that which is attained at the end of desire.*"

Then she shook her shoulders; it was a getting-ready-for-a-tough-job gesture that she'd picked up from Mike Havel. Who had been her husband . . . and who had also fathered Rudi Mackenzie. It gave Juniper a moment's pang to see it.

"We should try," Signe said. "Though . . . I wish scrying were as reliable as turning on a TV in the old days."

"Well, yes, that would be convenient," Melissa Aylward said, a stout cheerfulness in her tone. "But on the other hand, there was never anything worth watching, anyway, even with a hundred channels on cable."

"There was always CNN."

"If you wanted a long story about a farmer in North Dakota who'd taught his duck to sing."

"Come," Juniper said, her momentary smile dying.

She walked from the circle of oaks to the pool that lay outside it and went down on one knee, leaning on her staff. The others did likewise. The water flowed quietly, dark and clear, reflecting only the stars and moon. Juniper raised the sickle towards the silver light in the sky with the point up, then turned it down over the water, as if pouring the contents of a cup.

"Ground and center," she said, laying down the bronze and passing her hand over the pool. "Ground and center. Be at one with each other and the world beyond."

They knelt around the still surface of the spring-fed pond. After moments that might have been hours or only minutes the focus lifted. Then each drew the wand of blessed rowan-wood from their girdles and touched the surface of the water. Signe sprinkled it with mugwort, picked at the full of the moon.

"We ask aid of You," Juniper said. "Lugh of the many skills, God whose vision dispels ignorance; Brigid, Goddess of high places and the knowledge that carries the self beyond the self. From the longing of our hearts, we ask that You gift us in this holy place with the *dara sealladh*, the sight which pierces to the hidden truth."

"Show me my child. Show me Edain," Melissa asked, and closed her eyes.

"Show me my daughters," Signe said, and did likewise. "Show me Mary and Ritva."

"I ask as Your priestess, and as a mother to the Mother," Juniper said. "Show me my son. Show me Rudi." She hesitated, and then used his Craft name: "Show me Artos."

CHAPTER ONE

High was the Mackenzie hearth
Dun Juniper, Gods-favored hall
And goodly its treasures
Song and feast, harp and verse
Rang often there and well
But far and wild were the wanderings
That Artos must endure
Hard-handed hero, well companioned—

From: *The Song of Bear and Raven*
Attributed to Fiorbhinn Mackenzie, 1st century CY

SNAKE RIVER PLAIN, BOISE/NEW DESERET BORDER
JULY 21, CY23/2021 AD

"We'd be a lot farther east if we'd gone the southern route," Edain Aylward Mackenzie grumbled quietly. "If we're going to this Nantucket place for the Sword, I'd prefer we just *go.*"

The first three fingers of his right hand moved lightly on the waxed linen string of his yew longbow as he knelt behind the boulder of coarse dark gray volcanic rock, and he spoke without turning his eyes. A bodkin-pointed shaft was ready on the rest that cut through the riser-grip, and the stocky thick-armed body was ready to bend and loose the weapon with a snapping flick.

"Yes, but then Martin Thurston would have gotten away with it, sure," Rudi Mackenzie pointed out reasonably, scanning the ground ahead with his binoculars.

"And we'd be leaving an ally of the Prophet here on our way home, and next to our own borders."

The long flatlands to the south were dark as the sun sank westward. Until a few days ago the area had been the borderlands between the United States—the United States of Boise, to everyone except its inhabitants—and New Deseret. Now it was probably the borderland between the US of Boise and the Church Universal and Triumphant, and its Prophet.

"You mean he hasn't gotten away with it, then, Chief?" Edain enquired sourly. "And we aren't doing just that?"

Ah, and it's a rare comfort you are, my friend, Rudi thought.

Not just the rock-steady readiness; the bantering grumble kept a distance between his mind and the fact that three of their friends were in the hands of an enemy who were no more likely to show mercy than they were to drift upward and migrate south like hummingbirds.

"Ah, well, and they do need fighting, to be sure." Edain's lips tightened. "I saw what they did to those refugees. They'll have to account to the Guardians about that . . . and I'm not sorry to send more of them through the Western Gate to do it."

"It was probably fated that we get mixed up with this," Rudi said. "The Powers didn't have a nice straightforward trip East for us in their minds, so."

"And they have our friends," Edain said.

Well, Rudi thought. *Odard's a friend . . . more or less. Ingolf's a comrade, and Matti is . . . well, I'm not sure, except that I care for her as much as for anyone living who's not my mother. It's not just that we're* anamchara, *either.*

He and she had sworn the oath of soul-bonding when they were ten, during the War of the Eye . . . He smiled a little at the memory of their seriousness, and their determination not to let their friendship be broken by the quarrels of their elders. Not that being young made the ritual any less binding . . .

And all of us on this trip are young, he thought, not for the first time. *Changelings, or nearly so. For good or ill, the world is passing into our hands.*

The two young Mackenzies fell silent, waiting patiently behind their low ridge of sage-grown rock. Rudi raised his head slightly and looked again through the roots of the bush ahead of him—always much safer than looking over it. At this angle there was no risk of a flash from the lenses of his field glasses.

He'd tied back his red-gold hair and wrapped a dark bandana about it, and dabbed his face with dust and soot; his gray-green eyes shone the brighter in the dusk. A few hours of sleep snatched during the sunlight hours had repaired most of the damage of days of fighting and hard riding; he'd recovered with the resilience of youth. He'd turned twenty-two just this last Yule, in fact; a broad-shouldered, narrow-hipped, long-limbed man two inches over six feet, and even stronger than he looked.

Few works of humankind showed, besides the fireless war-camp of the Prophet's men two miles away. This stretch of the Snake River plain had depended on power-driven pumps before the Change. People had fled or died when the machines failed, and the fields had gone back to sagebrush with thicker lines of scrub and the bleached skeletons of dead trees to mark the sites of homesteads. Crumbled snags of wall still here and there, and the rusted, canted remains of a great circular pivot-irrigation machine, but like most of his generation Rudi usually ignored the ruins of the pre-Change world so thoroughly that he didn't really see them, unless there was some immediate practical reason to give them thought.

The air smelled dry, of dust and sage, and hot even though the temperature was falling as quickly as the sun. The first few stars glimmered through the purple eastward. Rudi pulled a Mackenzie-style traveler's cake out of his sporran, broke it in half and handed the other part to Edain; they both munched stolidly, though the pressed mass of rolled oats and honey and nuts and bits of dried fruit tasted of nothing but a vague sweetness now. They might need the energy soon. Edain threw some of his to the big shaggy half-mastiff bitch that lay near him;

Garbh's jaws clamped down on it with a wet *clomp*, followed by smacking and slurping as she struggled to get at bits that stuck to her great yellow fangs.

Then they waited through to full dark, now and then tensing muscle against muscle to keep themselves supple without the need to get up and stretch; both young men had learned the trick of it and much else from Edain's father . . . and Aylward the Archer had been First Armsman of Clan Mackenzie for nearly two decades, and a sergeant in the Special Air Service Regiment before the Change.

There was a three-quarter moon, and the stars were very bright in the clear dry air. An owl hooted, and a jackrabbit scuttered through the ground-cover. Garbh raised her barrel-shaped head from her paws, black nose wrinkling at something she sensed but couldn't place. The same *something* brought Rudi's head up, and he put his hand on the wire-and-leather wound grip of his longsword. Edain began to draw his bow, his gray eyes darting about for a target.

"We're coming in," someone said quietly out in the dimness; a woman's voice.

Rudi relaxed, and let the sword slide back the finger-span he'd drawn, with a slight *snick* of metal on metal as the guard kissed the scabbard-mouth.

"The farmer's child breathes so loud we could have shot him in the dark," she went on, still speaking softly but not whispering—whispers carried.

Edain bristled: "*Child* yourselves," he muttered. "You're Changelings too, and not much older than I am!"

He *was* nineteen and he *was* a farmer, but also an experienced hunter of deer and elk, boar and cougar, of tigers and sometimes of men, and he'd carried away the Silver Arrow at the Lughnasadh games twice; once he'd been younger than any champion had before. His father had taught the whole Clan the art of the bow.

"You two might as well have been playing the bagpipes," another soprano added.

At least they're speaking English instead of Elvish,

Rudi thought with resignation. *When they insist on Sindarin . . . there's no better language for being insufferable in, and the Lord and Lady* know *Mary and Ritva are experts at insufferability anyway.*

The twins came in, shaggy in their war cloaks of mottled dark green canvas covered in loops stuck with bits of grass and sagebrush. Rudi had to admit they were invisible until they wanted to be seen. He was a very good scout himself; the twins were very *very* good, able to crawl to within touching distance of alert, war-wise men. If they had time enough, and sometimes it could take days.

They were also identicals, tall young women lithe as cats, their yellow hair caught up in tight fighting braids under knitted caps of dark gray wool. The faces below the hoods of the war cloaks were oval and high-cheeked and their slightly tilted eyes cornflower blue, capable of a most convincing imitation of guileless innocence.

In truth his half sisters reminded him of cats in more ways than one, including an occasional disconcerting capacity for cool wickedness. They'd also, in his opinion, spent far too much time in Aunt Astrid's little kingdom in the woods, listening to her bards recite from those books she insisted on calling *the histories*, and talking in a language invented by a long-dead Englishman. Not that they weren't great stories, but the way the Dúnedain carried on, you'd think they were as true as Táin Bó Cúailnge.

Everyone worked their way backwards until they were well below the crest of the low ridge, and then Ritva went down on one knee and smoothed a patch of dirt. There was enough starlight and moonlight to make out the diagram she drew.

"Their horses are rested now; there's good water there, if you don't mind hauling it up on a *long* rope, probably four or five saddle lariats linked together. It looks like they're going to have a quick cold dinner, give the horses the last of their feed pellets and then ride east in the darkness, to get past the Boise pickets."

Rudi nodded. The Church Universal and Triumphant

had pushed an army into the territory claimed by the United States—the one headquartered at Boise—and gotten beaten rather comprehensively. But President-General Thurston had been killed in the fight—by his own eldest son, Martin, who'd been conspiring with the CUT. He hadn't liked his father's plan to finally call elections, and to keep his own children from running for the office. Now he was lord of Boise . . . and Rudi and his friends were the only ones who knew the real story.

And in the meantime, we have a problem that isn't politics, Rudi thought. *Namely, how to get Ingolf and Matti and Odard free.*

Or it wasn't entirely politics. If you had the right—or wrong—parents, the way he and Matti had, everything you did was politics. And whoever did it, fighting was *always* about politics, whether it was this or an Assembly of the Clan shouting and waving their arms or two rams butting heads in a meadow; he'd grown up the Chief's son and absorbed that through his pores.

"Sentries?" he asked.

"Mounted," Mary said.

And I know it's you, Mary, he thought; they did that verbal back-and-forth thing to confuse people, but he could tell their voices apart. *And your faces. Well, usually.*

"So much for a bit of quiet Sentry Removal as a solution to that little problem we're havin'," Edain added. "Getting our friends out, that is."

The twins nodded soberly, not rising to the slight edge in his voice; it was too obviously true. A mounted man wasn't as good a sentry as someone on foot and hiding—much harder to miss and easier to avoid. Unfortunately they were also a lot harder to take out so quietly that nobody noticed. Killing a man silently was hard enough; doing the same to an animal as big and well constructed as a horse was much more so. Doing both together . . .

When problems that involved fighting came up, the Rangers were extremely good at sneaky, underhanded, *elegant* solutions. Astrid—the *Hiril Dúnedain,* the Lady of the Rangers—considered straight-ahead bashing *crude*. Sentry Removal was one of the Dúnedain specialties. Sometimes elegance bought you no lard to fry your spuds, though.

"Where, what pattern, and how many all up?" he asked briskly.

"They've got pairs riding in a figure-eight pattern; eight on the move at any one time. There's thirty more of them altogether, with that party that came in this afternoon, the ones who had Mathilda and Odard and his man Alex."

"About half of them are wounded," Ritva said, taking up the tale; then she grimaced slightly. "And we're not counting the six who were too badly wounded to ride fast or fight."

"Their officers killed them?" Rudi asked. *The Cutters certainly seem ruthless enough for that.*

"No, they killed the badly injured horses. The men killed themselves," Mary said flatly. "No argument about it, either. They were singing until the knives went in. Something about *bright lifestreams.*"

"And sure, Ingolf said that the Sword of the Prophet were . . . serious men," Rudi said. "Everything I've seen bears it out. And our folk?"

"Mathilda and Odard here," Ritva said, tapping her finger at the sand-map. "They're lightly bound, wrist and ankle, except when they let them up to go to the slit trench. Doesn't look like they're hurt at all, beyond some bruises; they haven't even taken their hauberks off. Odard's man Alex isn't confined at all. But Ingolf . . ." She hesitated.

"Bad?" Rudi asked, frowning.

He'd grown to like the big Easterner; he'd been a good comrade on the trail, a notable fighting man even by Rudi's exacting standards, and with a breadth of experience in many lands that the Mackenzie secretly envied. Also he'd been a captive of the Church Universal and Triumphant before, and escaped.

"They've got him in a tight triple yoke, and chains on his ankles."

Rudi hissed slightly. A triple yoke was a beam of wood

with steel circles set in it for neck and wrists; they could
be arranged so that it needed continuous effort to keep
the collar from choking you and you were never able to
take a full breath. Pendleton slavers and other people of
low morals and no scruples used them to break the spirit
of captives. They were excruciatingly uncomfortable to
start with, quickly grew into outright agony, and they
made it impossible to really sleep, while the victim could
still walk . . . if you beat them with a whip. Still, Ingolf
was a strong man in heart and body both, and he'd been
in it for less than two full days. Their plan required all
the captives to be fully mobile if it was going to work.

"Chief?" Edain said.

Rudi looked over at the younger man. Edain went
on:

"I can see why this Prophet *scabhtéara* made war on
Boise and Deseret. I can see why he conspired with
Martin Thurston. What I can't see is why he's so very
sodding eager to catch *us*"—by which they both knew
he meant Rudi—"that he's willing to endanger all his
plots and plans hereabouts to do it."

"He knows," Rudi said.

As he spoke he lifted the scabbard of his sword out
of the sling at his belt and ran it through a set of loops
on the quiver at his back, so that the long hilt ran up behind his right ear. That made drawing it just a hair more
awkward, but it cut down on the chance of a betraying
rattle; their plan *also* depended on going undetected as
long as possible.

"He knows what?" Edain said, puzzlement plain on
his square young face even in the dimness.

He's a smart one, Rudi thought.

They put on their helmets; before Rudi did he pulled
on his coif, a tight hood and collar of mail on padded
leather. Most Mackenzies didn't bother with one, thinking their brigandines of little steel plates riveted together
between layers of leather or canvas were enough. But
while Rudi was an excellent archer, the sword was his
favored weapon, and that meant coming within hand-
stroke distance.

But he's very ... practical. Gets it from his father.

"Knows what Ingolf found on Nantucket," Rudi said when they'd settled their gear, glancing eastward towards the Prophet and his armies. "And he knows what I am, and why I'm traveling there; knows it better than I do. And he'll do anything to stop me."

"How does he know all that?" one of the twins said.

"Because something ... Someone ... walks with him," Rudi said softly, as he picked up his strung bow. "I've seen it before, once at least, though not as strongly. Or possibly that Being wears him like a glove. And that One is no friend to us, or to any of humankind."

The four of them went the last thousand yards on their bellies, their bows resting across the crooks of their elbows as they crawled through the dry bunchgrass. Whoever commanded the Cutters had been wise not to start a fire—besides attracting attention, it would have killed the night vision of anyone who looked at it, and the temptation was irresistible to most people. Rudi could feel the hoofbeats of the guards approaching through the ground; he drew a deep breath, wordlessly invoked the Crow Goddess and Lugh, and rose smoothly to his feet.

Though it was dark and the kilt and plaid were fairly good camouflage, as was the dark green of their brigandines and helms, the sentries would spot them soon. And therefore ...

And I don't particularly like killing men, even bad ones. But it's ... necessary, sometimes, he thought, and let the thought flow away with his next breath.

"You take the one with the bow," he said softly to Edain.

The man was fifty yards away, riding with a shaft on the string and his reins knotted on the cantle of his saddle, controlling the beast effortlessly with thighs and balance. His head came up before Edain started to move, prompted by some warning sign, but the Mackenzie arrow was on its way before the Prophet's man could begin to bend the short thick recurve. The *snap* of the string on Edain's bracer came a tiny instant before the tooth-grating crunch of the bodkin as it smashed its way into the man's Adam's apple and out through his neck bone.

That was showing off; they were the two best archers of their generation in Clan Mackenzie, and Edain was a bit touchy about it. Rudi's own shaft went through the second man's chest, the safer center of mass, even at the price of the harder, louder *crack* as it punched into the lacquered-leather armor.

The Cutter went over the cantle of his saddle with lance and shield flying to either side. The horses reared and neighed at the scent of blood, and there were shouts from the dark camp of the Prophet's men. The twins broke to either side as hooves thundered in the dark, vanishing into a swifter version of their behind-the-lines crawl.

Good, Rudi thought, lips skinning back from his teeth, as the enemy approached with a twinkle of star-light on edged metal and a thunder of hooves he could feel through the soles of his boots. *Didn't occur to them to come on foot.*

War out here in the dry rangelands was mostly a quicksilver mounted snap-and-run, a wolfpack business. Western Oregon's country of forest and farm-field had developed different ways after the Change. The Cutters were about to learn why Mackenzie longbows were the terror of every battlefield that saw them.

But there's only two of us, remember, Rudi thought. *What I wouldn't give for a hundred, and a bow-captain shouting to let the gray geese fly!*

He pulled the hundred-and-fifteen-pound draw past the angle of his jaw Clan-fashion, and loosed at the dim shape that was a rider brandishing a shete, aiming as much by instinct as by eye. The arrow vanished in the darkness with a *whirrt* and a flicker of gray vanes as the bow surged against his left hand. The right hand snapped back over his shoulder to the quiver, twitched out another shaft, put it to the string and drew with a smooth twist that was as much gut and torso as arms against the pressure of the yew stave, nock-draw-loose, as fast as a man counting aloud one-two-three. Beside him Edain did the same.

The Cutters recoiled for a moment, shouting in confusion amidst the screams of wounded men and horses. Then their officer's voice overrode it; he was too far away to see and shoot, but Rudi and Edain both shifted aim to chance a dropping shaft at the sound. They were rewarded with a yelping curse, but the voice went on rallying his men, shouting that there couldn't be many of whoever it was and damning them for cowards. They *weren't* cowards, just jumpy and confused for an instant; they were veteran fighting men, and there were more than enough of them to overrun the two Mackenzies with numbers.

If the other part of the plan didn't work, he was going to die in the next five minutes; it would either work very well, or not at all. If it failed he couldn't even run away, not on foot.

He loosed at a flicker of movement; if the blade was *there*, then the man had to be *here*.

Not that he intended to run, anyway.

Knight-Brother Ignatius of the Order of the Shield of St. Benedict said his rosary as he waited, patient beneath the weight of his long mail hauberk and visored sallet helm, coif and vambraces and greaves and steel-backed gloves. His tall destrier snorted quietly and tossed its head with a muted clatter of peytral and chamfron and crinet, scenting the Cutters' mounts in the darkness ahead, but too well trained to bugle a challenge.

"So, so, Godfrey," the priest soothed it, thumping the leather palm of his gauntlet down on the big gelding's metal-covered neck. "Soon, soon, boy."

Frederick Thurston sat his own mount beside the warrior-cleric; a dozen Boise cavalry formed a blunt wedge on either side of them, light horse in short mailshirts, armed with saber and bow and small round shields. They'd remained loyal to the young man, believing his version of their ruler's death rather than his elder brother's. And because the travelers from the West had saved his life in that massacre, the younger son was willing to risk all for them.

Impulsive. Still, he is only eighteen, Father Ignatius thought, from the lofty height of his mid-twenties; but he had been trained to self-command in a hard school.

Yet he is one who seeks the good, I think. In somebody who may have the ruling of men and lands, that is a pearl beyond price. Wisdom can be learned—able men are common, but good ones are far rarer.

"Very soon now, my son," he said quietly.

Frederick's nod was half seen in the night. Starlight glittered on honed metal as the Boiseans drew their curved swords. They left their bows cased in the boiled-leather scabbards at their knees; shooting in a nighttime melee was an invitation to friendly fire casualties. Ignatius pulled on the strap that slung his long kite-shaped shield over his back, shifting it around until he could run his arm through the loops, and then took the long ash lance in his right hand. A long deep breath, and one last prayer. It was too dark to make out the black cross and raven on its sheet-metal cover, but he knew they were there, and what those symbols stood for.

Suddenly they could all hear horses neighing in fear, and a sudden brabble of shouting from the camp three long bowshots ahead of them, and then a scream of human pain. And the war cry of the Church Universal and Triumphant: *"Cut! Cut! Cut!"*

Ignatius filled his chest and shouted, *"Jesu-Maria!"* from the bottom of his lungs.

He swung the lance-point forward as he did, bracing his feet in the long stirrups. The curved top of the shield came up under his eyes, the blunt point at the other end reaching down to his foot in the stirrup. The light Eastern quarter horses on either side picked up speed faster than his charger, and they were carrying a lot less weight anyway. But the destrier was seventeen hands tall, and a great deal of that was leg; it caught up quickly and then gained a little with each stride. Riding at this speed over unknown ground in the dark was asking for your horse to break a leg and roll over you when it fell . . .

But I'm riding towards men who want to kill me anyway, he thought. *The Lord God has a sense of humor, eh?*

The Boiseans were shouting, *USA! USA!* as they rode. Figures loomed up out of the night, on foot and horseback, scattering or turning to fight, and the sabers slashed. The long point of the knight's lance took a mounted man in the belly; Ignatius could feel the double *crunch-crunch* up the ashwood as it speared through the front and back plates of the Cutter's armor.

Impact slammed him back against the high cantle of his war-saddle. Black under starlight, blood shot out of the Cutter's mouth in a spray that wet the cleric's shield and face. The lance broke across in a hard crack; he clubbed the stub of the shaft on a footman's head and then let it drop, sweeping out his cross-hilted sword.

"Jesu-Maria!" he yelled again. Then: "A rescue! A rescue!"

Mathilda Arminger could see the Cutter leader—not the officer in charge of the fighting men, but the one-eyed man named Kuttner—start erect and put a hand on the hilt of his shete. She tensed silently; the troopers hadn't been gratuitously cruel, but they hit the captives if they tried to speak. Beside her Odard turned his head, blinking his eyes . . . or at least the one that wasn't swollen nearly shut. He'd kept trying to talk longer than she had. Her rage had been a slow-burning fire; now it swelled up, and hunger and thirst and aches dropped away, and even the maddening consciousness of her own filthy itchiness. She was suddenly very glad the enemy hadn't bothered to take her armor, instead of being driven nearly mad by the heat and constriction.

That's arrows! she thought exultantly as she heard the distinctive *whssst*. Then: *Careful. It might be rovers or deserters or bandits.*

The Cutters knew her hostage value. Ordinary desert scum wouldn't.

Kuttner's mouth was open to shout when the noise came out of the west; horses in shocked fear, and then men.

"See to it!" he snapped.

The Cutter officer was already moving, whistling sharply for his horse. The superbly trained animal trotted over to its master; he grabbed the horn of the saddle and swung up with a skipping vault as it went by, his feet finding the stirrups. A part of her grudgingly admired the horsemanship; the man's leather-and-mail armor was lighter than a Western knight's panoply, but it was still a formidable display.

Kuttner stayed on his feet, the heavy slightly curved sword that Easterners called a shete—derived from the tool, but lengthened in blade and hilt—in his hand. His one blue eye probed the darkness. From it came the officer's bark:

"There can't be more than five or six of them! *Ai!*" That was pain, and the voice was tight when it went on: "*Get* them, you gutless sons of apostate whores! No, don't bother shooting, you idiot—you can't see them! Blades out, swing wide to either side and *charge*!"

Kuttner's head whipped to the east; there was sound from that direction too, the rumble of hooves building to a gallop, and then a mingled crash and clatter of weapons and a cry of "Jesu-Maria!" and "USA!" And then, even better: "A rescue! A rescue!"

"Kill the prisoners!" the Cutter leader barked, and ran towards the sound.

Mathilda felt ice crawl up her spine and pool like water in her gut. She'd been lying with her legs curled up; now she lashed out with both her feet. They were bound at the ankle, but she had her boots on. They just barely touched the overlapping plates of leather armor that covered the guard's legs like chaps. He hissed in anger and drew his shete, raising it for a chop. Beside him his comrade did likewise.

That was a mistake. Odard had managed to writhe around and get his feet beneath him. The young Baron of Gervais bounced forward like a jack-in-the-box, his

mailed shoulder hitting the second man in the side like
a football tackle and sending him lurching into the first.
That delayed them an instant as they staggered and
found their footing again, but they both turned to chop
at the young nobleman as he sprawled before them
with an involuntary grunt of pain as he crashed to the
ground.

That was a mistake, too. A patch of the night seemed
to rise behind them, and something flashed through the
starlight—a black hardwood dowel, linked to the one
in Ritva Havel's right hand by a short length of chain.
It whipped around one Cutter's neck with blurring
speed; the free handle slapped into her other palm, and
she wrenched her crossed wrists apart with explosive
force.

The Cutter spasmed as the huge leverage crushed his
larynx and snapped his spine like a pecan in a pair of
nutcrackers. The shete that flew out of his hand struck
Mathilda in the stomach, edge-on, hard enough to hurt
even through the titanium mail of her hauberk and the
padded gambeson beneath. She grabbed it with both
bound hands and cut the rawhide thongs around her
boots with one quick upward jerk; it was good steel, and
knife-sharp. Then she jammed the flat of the blade between her knees and slipped her wrists over to saw at
those bonds.

All that took seconds. That was time enough for the
other guard to cut backhanded at Ritva. The broad point
of the shete slashed sagebrush from her war cloak, but
she was throwing herself backwards in a full summer-
sault as the blow spent itself on air, hitting the toggle
of the cloak, and drawing her slender longsword as she
did.

"*Lacho Calad! Drego Morn!*"

The Dúnedain war cry split the night: *Flame light!
Flee night!* But half a dozen Cutters were closing in, on
horse and on foot.

Mathilda paused just long enough to slash through
Odard's bonds; he was wheezing from the awkward impact of his fall, but doggedly trying to get back on his

feet. Then she picked up one of the Cutter shields and stepped to put herself back-to-back with Ritva.

"*Haro, Portland!*" she shouted. "*Holy Mary for Portland!*"

And Mary help me, I'm as stiff as an arthritic old lady! she thought desperately.

She raised the clumsy, point-heavy shete and tried to ignore the pins and needles in her arms; this one was far too heavy for her wrists, anyway. It wobbled a little despite her best effort, and she whipped it through a figure eight to loosen her cramped arm and shoulder.

"Mary's over trying to save Ingolf's fool neck," Ritva said, and laughed.

"*Morrigú!*" Rudi shouted, and thrust his bow through the carrying loops on the bandolier that held his quiver. "At them, Mackenzies!"

All two of us, he thought. *Three if you count the dog!*

He swept out his longsword in the same motion and snatched the buckler with his left hand, making a fist on the grip inside the hollow of the little soup-plate-sized steel shield.

"I've got your back, Chief!" Edain called, and followed as he ran forward, Garbh at his heels growling like millstones.

The Cutters were all looking back over their shoulders at the sound of a second attack from who-knew-where when Rudi ran out of the night, and he thought they were probably wondering whether to shit or go blind. The crucial thing was not to let them get their balance back and their wits about them . . .

Then he was in among them, and time slowed. Vision flashed and blurred, expanding and shrinking at the same time—threats, blades and bows, and targets, joints and faces, everything else not really seen at all. It was the gift of the Crow Goddess, only to be called upon in extremity.

A jarring *thump* as he dodged in under a lance-point and cut into the inside of a man's elbow, where there was a gap between the mail on his upper arm and the leather vambrace on his forearm. The man rode on, shrieking and looking in disbelief at the spouting stump where his arm had been.

Rudi whirled away with dark drops spinning from the edge, and chopped into the hock of a horse. It screamed stunning-loud, rearing and pitching over backwards and bringing another down with it. A cloth-yard shaft went *whirrt* over his head and into a mounted archer's chest and the shaft he had meant for Rudi disappeared into the night. Another's arrow went wide as Garbh locked her fangs in the nose of the horse-archer's mount and sent it into a rearing, bucking frenzy.

Two men coming at him on foot. A thrusting lunge as he ran, and his point went under the brim of a helmet and crunched through the thin bone at the bridge of a nose and *crack* into a brainpan. His buckler stopped a full-armed cut, the force of it jarring the little shield back until the edge of the shete just touched his shoulder; then the Cutter was staggering off balance and the boss punched back into his jaw, and bone crumbling under it like candy cane in a careless grip . . .

"Ingolf! Move, man, move!"

Father Ignatius abandoned the sword jammed tight in bone and spurred his horse forward, jerking his warhammer free where it hung by its thong at his saddlebow. Godfrey's armored shoulder struck the Cutter who'd been about to chop down the dazed-looking man manacled to the yoke, but even in the dimness Ingolf's battered face looked blank and his eyes were haunted pits. The destrier reared and crow-hopped on its hind legs as the cleric slugged it to a desperate halt and wheeled it around.

Then in the midst of the melee the warrior-priest's eyes went wide. Mary Havel was fighting sword-and-shield against a short one-eyed man Ignatius recognized from descriptions, but that wasn't what made him stare.

"Lord of Hosts!" he blurted.

Rudi Mackenzie was coming through the thick of the Cutter press, killing at every second step, eyes showing

white all around pupils grown huge, teeth bared in a ululating banshee wail loud even in the clamor of battle.
A swordsman staggered back and fell, his pelvis shattered by a kick. Another reeled away with half his face
sheared off, hands scrabbling at the impossible wound.
An enemy rider struck downward with the horrified
desperation of a man finding a scorpion on his chest.
Sparks flew in a blue-and-red shower where the Mackenzie's buckler knocked the shete away, and a thrust to
the man's armpit sank six inches deep in a snap like a
frog's tongue after a dragonfly. That turned into a backhand cut ...

Even given surprise and shock the Cutters were tough
fighters; he'd seen that in the battle with the Boise army
two days ago, and they'd rallied swiftly tonight. Now
they began to give way, a first few blundering away in
panic, or lashing their horses heedless into the night,
others trying to break contact so that they could flee
without taking a blade in the back.

Ignatius knew why, and his mind stuttered. A man
could strike swiftly, or precisely, or very hard; a little
more of one meant a little less of the others, and you had
to do the best you could of all three at once. The Mackenzie was moving like moonlight on a waterfall despite
all the handicaps of darkness and unknown ground, each
blow laid like a surgeon's, each landing with the lashing
force that clove mail-links and lacquered bullhide ...
and then topped a man's head like a boiled egg. He'd
seen Rudi fight before, and had been impressed, but that
had only been a skirmish. Nothing like ...

Like a sighted man among the blind, Ignatius thought
numbly. *Like some pagan God of war.*

Then the fight was over, the survivors of the Cutter force throwing down their weapons and exploding
outward in screeching panic. All but one; the one-eyed
man landed a cut on the side of Mary Havel's helmet. A
sharp *bonk* rang, and the woman buckled at the knees.
The victor raised his shete to kill.

Cranng!

The shete blow skidded off Rudi's longsword. Strong and skilled, Kuttner cut backhanded at the bigger man's neck. The blow stopped halfway, and the longsword was through Kuttner's body just below the breastbone, two feet of blood-slick steel glistening out his back.

And he smiled, with blood running black between his teeth. And he dropped his weapon and shield and reached out with both hands; they fastened on Rudi's neck and pulled his own body forward along the yard of swordblade until the cross-guard thumped against his ribs.

"I—see—you," he rasped.

The voice had nothing to do with the bits of lung he spat out through a laughing mouth. It ground out the words like a mill that minced human bone, and it was gleeful.

"Raven—Son—of—Bear. I—see—you."

Rudi lunged backwards, releasing the hilt of his sword, striking upward with hands bunched between Kuttner's arms in a move skilled and quick and hugely strong. He might as well have struck a statue cast in bronze, and for a moment he froze in goggling surprise as a move he *knew* had to work failed totally. The blood-covered teeth grinned closer and closer, ready to gnaw off his face as the dead man giggled, and he began to scrabble desperately at the unhuman grip.

Behind Kuttner, Ingolf Vogeler moved at last, with the clumsy intensity of an exhausted ox. Staggering, his eyes showing nothing but blind determination and an even deeper hate, he drove the end of the heavy ashwood yoke across his shoulders into the back of Kuttner's head.

Thunk.

Bone crunched, and the walking corpse froze for an instant, but its grip did not loosen. Rudi hammered at wrists and elbows, struck a desperate upward blow with the heel of his hand at the angle of the other man's jaw. Kuttner's head jerked to the side, then turned back at an angle, dangling loose but still grinning. The quick savage strength of Rudi's movements turned slow, a feeble scrabbling as his face turned purple, visible even in the darkness.

But Mary Havel was already coiling up off the ground, her sword held in the two-handed grip and one foot locked around the Cutter's ankle for leverage. The sharp blade landed behind the man's knee, and cut all the way through to the kneecap. He buckled sideways and fell like a tree, taking Rudi with him.

And his hands still squeezed. Ignatius half fell out of the saddle, running forward to smash at the obscene shape; so did three or four others, and someone thumped him in the ribs with a blade that would have killed if he hadn't been in armor. He ignored it. They all flailed at the dead man until the body was cut and battered into a bloody mass of meat and bone and organs, but even then the hands kept their grip on Rudi's throat until the tendons were slit and the bones they anchored on splintered.

A panting silence fell amid the latrine-salt-and-copper odors of violent death, with the sound of someone vomiting in the background and a few cries as the Boise cavalry made sure of the enemy wounded. Ignatius looked around, and saw Edain and Mathilda Arminger kneeling on either side of Rudi's limp form. The woman tore off his padded mail coif and pressed on either side of his larynx with the palms of her hands.

"It's not crushed!" she cried, a little shrill with relief.

The Mackenzie coughed, and his eyelids fluttered open. Then he coughed again, deep and racking. Edain offered him a canteen; Ignatius didn't have time to intervene before Rudi sucked at the water, coughed and snorted it out his nose, spat aside and drank more. The cleric released a breath he hadn't realized he was holding.

Awareness returned to Rudi's blue-green eyes. "We'd best be going," he said hoarsely. "It's not a spot that seems pleasant to linger in, so."

Rudi and his companions made camp ten miles south-ward, in a place where two brick walls of a farmhouse burned out a generation ago still made a corner. That let them have a small sheltered fire that couldn't be seen at a distance; they'd sleep during the day and continue by night. They'd managed to get a fair amount of their gear out of Boise, if not the big Conestoga wagon they'd been carrying it all in. Ignatius tended a pot of stew, salt pork with dried vegetables and beans; the dark close-coupled priest was the best camp cook they had. Horses whickered in the darkness from the picket line, and their smell added to the strong scents of sage and sweat and oil and metal and burning greasewood.

Rudi finished grinding a nick out of the edge of his sword, ran a swatch of oily sheepskin over the blade, sheathed it and laid the scabbard aside wrapped in the broad belt that also held his dirk. His stomach twisted in hunger at the savory smell from the cookfire, but he winced a little as he accepted a bowl and some biscuits and took his first sip.

The swelling bruises on his throat made swallowing painful; they made *breathing* a matter of care, though thank Her of the Healing Hand that they hadn't had to insert a tube or anything of that sort. He ate cautiously, a little at a time. That was one of a symphony of pains and aches, from minor cuts to bone bruises. At that, he'd been lucky and gods-favored. The memory of those troll-strong dead hands on his throat still made an unpleasant sensation crawl over his scrotum and up his belly. It had been *seconds* away from being too late. If he hadn't decided to put on the coif before the fight . . .

Remembering Someone looking through Kuttner's eyes into his was worse yet.

"My throat's raw," he said, and hid a slight shudder. He turned to Odard instead of dwelling on the eerie otherness of what had happened:

"I didn't see your man Alex," he croaked.

I can talk. As long as I'm careful.

The young Baron's eyes usually held a cool reserve. There was no mistaking what was in them now.

And if Alex could see them, he'd not stop running until

he hit salt water, and then only so he could swim, Rudi thought.

"I didn't either, and that's why he's not dead," Odard said grimly. "And if I had him back in the castle at Gervais . . . I do believe I'd have him flogged to death. Usually having the High Justice is a bit of a bore, but there are times when it can be *very* satisfying."

Mathilda had mopped her emptied bowl with a piece of the bannock and was lying with her head on a saddle, apparently reveling in having her war harness off for the first time in three days. She was the same age as Rudi, but right now you could see how the strong bones of her face would look when she aged, and locks of her reddish brown hair clung to her forehead.

Rudi suppressed an impulse to smooth them back, then decided not to bother and did it. She smiled at him; it died away as she spoke:

"He laid Odard out with a crossbow butt and held me at the point of the bolt while he surrendered us to the Cutters."

Rudi shaped a silent whistle. "That *is* a surprise. I'd have said he was a brave man—and loyal to the House of Liu, too."

Odard's hand closed reflexively on the hilt of the sword across his lap; he was a little less than a year younger than Rudi, and several inches shorter, with a handsome high-cheeked, snub-nosed face, raven-black hair and slanted blue eyes the brighter for the natural olive-umber hue of his skin. His voice recovered a little of his usual ironic detachment as he went on:

"He is. Loyal, that is. Unfortunately he's loyal to my mother . . . the Dowager Baroness. And *she's* been in contact with the Church Universal and Triumphant. Apparently she told him . . . passwords, codes . . . to use with them if he thought he had to."

He looked away slowly. "I *told* her to stop it. I thought she'd listened. Apparently she didn't, even though I'm of age and Baron now. I'm going to have a little talk with her when we get back."

"*My* mother is going to have a little talk with her," Mathilda said. "Sovereigns before vassals, Odard."

The young nobleman looked alarmed; however furious he was with her, Lady Mary Liu *was* his mother. She'd conspired with foreigners against the Crown Princess—her man had pointed a crossbow at the Crown Princess—and they both knew that meant arraignment for high treason against the Throne.

"That . . . is for you and the Lady Regent to decide, Your Highness," he said. "I . . . I really can't say anything in her defense, only plead for mercy."

Rudi was angry enough himself, but he winced a little inwardly at the thought too. Not that Sandra Arminger, Regent of the Portland Protective Association, took any particular pleasure in inflicting pain and death. She just used it as a tool, which was considerably worse, if you were on the receiving end. Policy kept going when a sadist's pleasure in cruelty might be glutted and stop.

Then her daughter frowned. "Well . . . the way it was, they had us cornered. We would all have died, probably, if we'd fought. Alex might just have been trying to save your life. And they didn't, well, do anything to us except tie us up."

Odard shrugged expressively. "I'll still have him flogged to death if I can."

Rudi ate a biscuit to hide a slight grimace of distaste. Odard Liu wasn't the complete bastard that his father had been. Edward Liu had been—

—*what was the pre-Change word?*

What lots of Norman Arminger's original supporters had been; they'd had a term for it in the old world, not bandit or outlaw as people would say these days, but—

Ah, sure, and that's it. They said gangster *back then. Or* gangbanger.

Odard's mother had been from a Society household—a lot of people who'd been in the Society for Creative Anachronism had ended up as leaders in various places, Arminger himself among them, though only the most

ruthless had been able to stomach Matti's father. For
that matter, the PPA as a whole wasn't nearly as bad as
it had been in Norman Arminger's day, before Rudi's
blood-father killed him and died himself in a spectacular duel between their armies at the end of the War of
the Eye.

Better *doesn't necessarily mean* good, *though,* Rudi
thought. Then he said: "It's a little early to be planning
revenge, so. Unless the man presents himself within
arm's reach of you. We've more important concerns."

Mathilda sat up and focused her hazel eyes; there was
puzzlement in them now, as well as relief and affection.

"Yes, we do! What in the name of all the saints happened back there, Rudi? *You* were weird enough—"

"The Morrigú was with me," he said matter-of-factly.
"I'd have been dead about . . . seven times, else."

Matti nodded. "But what about *Kuttner*? He wasn't
just . . . just berserk, the way you got. That was . . . what
was that?"

"I'm not altogether sure," Rudi said, his voice still
hoarse.

He touched the bruises on his throat with gingerly
caution, the mark of fingers that had squeezed through
mail and padded stiffened leather and neck muscles as
strong as braided rawhide.

"But I think," he went on thoughtfully, "I truly think
that I was near as no matter throttled to death by a man
already dead himself three times over. Both parts of
which sentence are a bogglement and enough to make a
man run into the trees screaming for his mother, so."

He grinned at his own joke, you had to show willing and that went twice over when you were in charge,
but . . .

It would be funny, if only it were funny, he thought.
*Sad it is that I'm a little old to have Mother kiss my hurts
better. Though in this case, it's as a High Priestess and a
spellweaver I'd be asking it of her! And even so . . .*

Juniper Mackenzie could do many remarkable things.
Raising dead men wasn't among them, any more than
she could change lead into gold or fly by wishing it or

throw lightning bolts from her fingertips. Verbal ones, yes, but not the literal split-the-tree type.

Ignatius looked up from his task. "That was a case of demonic possession, I think," he said calmly, and handed out more filled bowls. "I've never seen anything like it myself, but the old accounts from long before the Change describe very similar things."

Rudi nodded. Allowing for the different words Christians used to describe it, he thought the soldier-monk was right.

"The Powers are many, and not all are friendly to humankind," he said, and rubbed his throat again. "As I can now painfully testify!"

Ingolf Vogeler looked up from where he sat, a blanket around his shoulders.

"I . . . I thought Kuttner was just an asshole with an eye for other people's boodlebags," he said, in his Wisconsin rasp. "When I thought he was working for the Bossman of Iowa, when Vogeler's Villains went East on that salvage mission from Des Moines. Then when he turned out to be a spy and a traitor working for the Prophet and killed my people and dragged me off to Corwin, I thought he was your common or garden-variety evil shit. And yah, there was a lot of mystical crap in Corwin, but I cut that eye out of Kuttner's head when I escaped and I thought that proved it was all just a show for the yokels."

Rudi spoke as gently as his abused larynx allowed: "After what you saw on Nantucket—the Sword—and the message you got there, I'd have been less dismissive of *mystical crap*, myself, Ingolf."

The Easterner shivered. "Yah, tell me. I was wrong. When the Cutters had me cornered, Kuttner just . . . he said a word and made a sign with his hand, and I couldn't *move*. That's how they took me alive. I couldn't move, couldn't do anything but what he said . . . It was like some sort of *spell*."

Rudi leaned over, gripping the other man by one thick-muscled shoulder and pouring strength through the contact. He could see the Easterner was bothered by the very word, although that was strange. Or maybe not; he wasn't a witch, after all, and Rudi was, even if he was no great spellcaster or loremaster like his mother. He'd seen before that those not of the Old Religion could be spooked by the commonest things sometimes.

How to hearten him? Well, the truth never hurt:

"Ingolf, my friend, you *did* move, despite the spell. You smashed in the back of his head with that yoke; and I'd be dead now, if you hadn't. At a guess, he laid an evil *geasa* on you before you escaped him last year. There are ways of doing that, for good as well as ill, and planting them deep in a man's mind with a word of power to call them out. And working harm that way leaves a man open to . . . other things; the Threefold Rule, you know."

Ingolf crooked a smile. "Yah, he got back worse than he gave me, didn't he?"

He was cored out as a cook does a pepper for stuffing, Rudi thought, and swallowed painfully.

"The command laid on you could be posthypnotic suggestion," Ignatius said with a scholar's precision; the Shield of St. Benedict were a learned order as well as a militant one. "Not necessarily magic."

Rudi grinned at him, and quoted a saying of Juniper Mackenzie: "It doesn't stop being magic because you can explain it, Father."

Ingolf's haunted dark blue eyes met his, and the Easterner touched his mouth and winced a bit before he spoke.

"You stuck a yard of sword through his brisket, and he didn't stop. Then I crushed in the back of his head, and he *still* didn't stop. Cry-yiy, that sounds an awful lot like magic to *me*."

"And I cut his leg mostly off," Mary Havel said. "That didn't stop him, either. It did make me feel better about his clouting me on the head with a sword earlier, though."

"It didn't stop him, but it *did* make him fall over," Ritva pointed out cheerfully. "Which helped everyone else cut him up and smash him and things. *Carth mag*, sis."

Which meant *useful deed* in Elvish. Neither of the twins seemed much put out; at least, they didn't show much of the dread that several of the others did. But then, they *were* witches, and Initiates; two-thirds of the Dúnedain Rangers were, after all. Even if they did call on the Lord and Lady as Manwë and Varda, which he considered an affectation, rather than using more conventional names like Lugh and Brigid.

Everyone fell silent for a moment, turning in to their own thoughts. Mary and Ritva each hugged her knees and rested her chin on them, which emphasized their mirror-image likeness. It brought out their resemblance to Rudi, too—the high cheekbones and slightly tilted almond-shaped eyes they all showed were probably from that shared blood. Mike Havel had been one-quarter Anishinabe Indian, the rest mostly Finn with a dash of Norse, all strains common in the Upper Peninsula mining country of Michigan he'd come from, long before the Change—fifty-odd years ago, now.

Their mother, Signe, probably contributed the wheat-colored hair and their eyes, which were just the shade of a morning sky; the Bear Lord had been flying her and her parents and brother and younger sister, Astrid, over the Idaho mountains not all that far from here when the machines died, and had got them down alive. And brought them to the Willamette country, and from that much had flowed . . . not least a fleeting encounter on a scouting mission that had produced one Rudi Mackenzie!

I wonder what flying like that was like, Rudi thought wistfully. He'd been up in balloons, and flown gliders and hang gliders a few times, and that was better than anything but sex. *But to be able to fly where you wanted for as long as you wanted, as fast as a bird . . .*

Frederick Thurston spoke. "I've been thinking," he said.

He was the youngest there, a year younger than Edain, still a little gangly with the last fast growth of adolescence, though at six feet he'd probably gotten all his height. His face was the color of a well-baked loaf, and his hair a short-cut black cap of tight curls; President-

General Thurston had been of that breed miscalled black before the Change.

"Sure, and that's often advisable," Rudi said. "And we've all cause to be grateful for the direction of your thoughts, so."

"I . . . I don't think I should try to fight my . . . fight Martin. Not right now."

His full-lipped mouth twisted as he spoke his elder brother's name. Rudi nodded in sympathy. *Hard, hard to be betrayed by close kin, and see your own father killed by your brother's hand.*

The commander of the little Boise cavalry detachment looked at him in alarm; Rosita Gonzalez was a dark wiry woman in her early thirties, with a sergeant's chevrons riveted to the short sleeve of her mail-shirt.

"Sir, we can't let him get away with it! He killed the *President.*"

Frederick nodded. "No, Sergeant, we can't let him get away with it . . . and bear in mind that the President was my father. Though he'd want us to think of the country first." Grimly: "Though in this case, the personal and the political go together. He has to die."

And your late President was the man you resembled, as you said that, Rudi thought. *Suddenly you didn't look young or uncertain at all. Which is interesting in itself, eh?*

The younger of the Thurston men—they had two sisters, both still girls—went on:

"But from what we've heard, he has gotten away with it *for now.* The Vice President and half the top command died at the Battle of Wendell."

"What a coincidence. Convenient for the bastard."

The usurper's brother winced; it was plain he'd loved his elder sibling.

And love doesn't die as clean as a heart-shot deer, Rudi thought.

He'd liked Martin Thurston himself, on short acquaintance and before his treachery was revealed.

A dying love kicks and thrashes, and then the carcass of it festers and it can poison the waters of your soul as surely as a dead goat in a well. Fred here is still *trying to draw what he saw down into his gut and believe it.*

But he went on doggedly: "And the others, the brigade commanders and regional governors ... they'll be his men soon enough. He's even got a fairly good excuse for restoring the State of Emergency powers, with a war on, and canceling the elections Dad ... the President ... was going to call. This wasn't something he ... did on the spur of the moment. It's long-planned. If I tried to come out in the open now, not only would there be civil war, but I'd *lose*. And that would be the end of any hope of putting things right."

Gonzalez looked at him. "What do you want to do, then, sir?" she said carefully. "Since defeat is not an option."

"Give him enough rope to hang himself. Look ... this isn't just about us, about Boise. This Prophet son of a bitch ... it's more than a warlord with a big appetite, those are a dime a dozen. I believe what Rudi says, now, and I believe Ingolf about what he saw out East on Nantucket. I want you and the others to spread the truth. Cautiously! When the time's right, I'll be back to do my part. By then, things will be ready. I'm willing to fight Martin, it's worth it, but not without a chance of beating him."

"Yes, sir," she said respectfully. "If you don't mind my saying so, that's a very ... adult way to look at it."

"I know when my birthday is, Sergeant," he said.

Her dark hard face turned to Rudi. "And you'll have this Sword you say is waiting for you on Nantucket?" she said skeptically.

"If I live, Rosita," the Mackenzie said gently. "Nothing's sure ... except that there's no hope or luck to be found turning away from a task the Powers have laid on you."

"Frankly, I never really believed Ingolf here," she went on. "No offense! I know *you* believe it, Ingolf, but ... well, a lot of stories come from the outlands. Creepy places with enchanted swords and extinct animals ..."

"There's a passenger pigeon at Dun Juniper," Rudi

said quietly. "Most of us here have seen it. *That* came from Nantucket."

"And the *Prophet* believes the story," Ingolf said. "He put Kuttner in when the Bossman hired me to go East, and Kuttner was his main secret agent in the household of Iowa's Bossman. And when I escaped from Corwin, he risked pissing off everyone on the West Coast by sending his Cutters after me. They near as damn-all *did* kill me; if Rudi and his friends hadn't been there that night ..."

Rudi touched one hand to the livid bruises that Kuttner's dead hands had left on his throat, through the mail collar and padding.

"You were there," he said. "You saw *this*."

Gonzalez swallowed and looked away. "Yeah ... Yeah, I was." She shuddered. "Hell, I saw a dead man keep fighting until we cut him to pieces. *Christ.* So maybe a magic sword isn't so loopy after all."

Ingolf nodded; he seemed to have cast off most of his chill, but he held out his big battered hands to the coals of the fire.

"It's there," he said flatly. "I saw a hell of a lot of things on Nantucket, and some of them may have been me going bugfuck, but the Sword is *there*. And the Voice, the voice that told me to go find the Son of the Bear Who Ruled and tell him about it."

Astonishingly, he grinned a little. "Didn't know what to expect ... but you're not as furry as I thought you might be, Rudi."

The Mackenzie laughed at that, then stopped himself: it hurt too much.

"What'll you do, then, Fred?" he asked the General's son. "Take to the mountains? Go West? My mother would welcome you and give you sanctuary at Dun Juniper. You might find a few Mackenzie bowmen who'd come back with you in a while as well, to be sure."

"And the Lady Regent would make you welcome in Portland," Mathilda said. Her spine straightened. "And she'd give you gold, and knights and men-at-arms to follow you. My House owes you a blood-debt now, a debt of honor."

"Or you could go to Lord Alleyne and Lady Astrid in Mithrilwood," the twins said—their voices were so close together that they had an eerie overlaid quality.

Ritva went on alone: "Aunt Astrid would *love* it. An evil usurper to put down and an exiled prince to help! It's just the sort of thing Rangers are *supposed* to do."

"Stanon," Mary said, nodding: *absolutely*, in Sindarin.

"I'll come with you, if you'll have me," Frederick said quietly, looking at Rudi. "I've got a feeling that . . . it's *real* important you get where you're going."

He smiled, and his face looked young again, despite sweat-streaked dust and new lines worn by care and grief. "And back! Don't forget that!"

"Sir!" the cavalry sergeant said. Then: "Well, I suppose it'll be interesting . . ."

Frederick Thurston shook his head, just once. "No, Sergeant. You and the troops will stay here. You'll report to your units as if you'd gotten separated at Wendell and you'll keep your heads low until you know you're safe."

He held up a hand at her protest. "And you'll spread the truth . . . carefully. When I get back, I want things to be *ready*. Major Hanks will be in charge of setting up a . . . network, I think you'd call it. I doubt Martin, the new regime, will pay any attention to an engineering officer."

Gonzalez' mouth quirked a little. "He'll probably mothball that pedal-powered blimp Major Hanks loves, sir. And that'll make him *even angrier* than he is right now!"

Rudi thought quickly, and then held out his hand; Frederick's grip was hard and strong. He shook hands all around; it had the air of a solemn rite, somehow.

"Welcome to the quest," Rudi said. "I'll be glad of your help and company, Fred."

"And we're back up to nine," Ritva said; she and her sister nodded, solemn as owls. "It's canonical."

They both looked innocent when Mathilda glared at

them, and one of them tipped Rudi a wink. He laughed himself, and rose to help Ignatius smother the fire.

"Your sisters may be wiser than they think," the priest said quietly as they worked. He went on at Rudi's raised eyebrow:

"I have been thinking of what this quest means," he said, with the scholarly precision he used for serious matters. "Have you noticed that you seem to be ... *collecting* people? Of a particular type?"

Rudi chuckled. "Sure, and I so seem to have an attraction for disinherited princes," he said.

"That is because you are a hero, I think."

Rudi frowned at him. "Well, thank you—"

The priest shook his head. "No, I'm using the word in a ... *technical* sense. I suspect, my son, that you are a hero in the sense that Sigurd or Beowulf or Roland was. Heroes accrete heroes around them—heroes, and great evils. I thought that was true only in ancient story, but apparently the archetype holds true in our lives as well."

"Ah," Rudi said softly. *Was that a goose that just walked across my grave?*

"Well, for *my* sake, I hope you're wrong, Father," he said. "I love the old stories, but sure and I'd rather listen to them than live them out."

"I too. Human beings live by their legends; but if what I suspect is true, then we are living *in* one." A wry smile. "But even Our Lord was refused when he asked that the cup pass from him."

"Something my mother said once ... that my birth-father had walked into a myth without knowing it. I hadn't expected the same to happen to me." He shivered slightly. "Does it make it better or worse that I *know*?"

"Perhaps we should have expected it," Ignatius said soberly. "We children of the Change. It took the technology of our parents from us—but that is not all. Other things are ... moving into the vacated spaces. It is as if *time* were moving backwards in some fundamental way."

"Back to the time of legends," Rudi said.

"Into the time of myths," Ignatius agreed.

"I wonder what will happen if we go too far back?" Rudi said.

Ignatius looked up at the stars. "We find God. Or God finds us."

It took Rudi minutes to cast off the mood the priest's words had laid on him.

But it's only so long a man can ponder on the deep things, he thought. *Whatever shapes the Gods have in mind for him to wear, he's also just a man.*

"Walk with me, Matti," he said. "Or rather, hobble by my side."

They walked out a little into the dark. He started to put his arm around her shoulders, and winced at the sharp stab of pain, then completed the motion.

"Sore?" she said sympathetically.

"From my face to my toes; and likely to be more so tomorrow."

Mathilda nodded. "*I'm* feeling like my own grandmother. You fought more, but I spent twenty hours tied up in a hauberk."

Rudi nodded. "I *almost* wish I had a real wound to distract me, so. But glad I am to have you back in good company, Matti, my *anamchara*; while you were gone I came to a better understanding of the great whacking hole your absence would leave in the scheme of things."

She looked up at him and smiled, but . . .

"Something troubling you?"

"It's not fair," she laughed.

"What?"

"You're *perceptive* too. Male obliviousness is supposed to be a woman's last defense."

"Ah, well, I have all those sisters, and my mother," he pointed out. "And Dad . . . Sir Nigel . . . only came along when I was ten. Gave me an insight, so it did."

Her face turned serious. "You know, when we were cornered by the Cutters, we thought we were going to die."

"By the Trickster, so did I when they cornered *me*! All ready to meet my late blood-father, so I was. And was rescued not by my own efforts but by a god from the machine . . . or at least, a machine sent by the gods."

She frowned and nodded. "Well, as they were closing in on us . . . just before Odard's man Alex laid him out with the crossbow butt . . . he said he loved me."

"Ah," Rudi said, suddenly alert. "And what did you make of that?"

Mathilda made as if to punch him in the chest, then reconsidered; it would be more painful than a playful gesture should.

"None of that question-to-a-question Socratic thing! It's irritating enough when Juniper or Father Ignatius does it! And you're no holy man."

"Well, if you're asking me if he's sincere . . . I'd have said that Odard was the great love of Odard Liu's life. But he's a man with a great sense of style, too . . ."

"Meow!" she said. "And declaring his love as a dying act would be stylish?"

Rudi smiled and shrugged.

"It couldn't have been just for advantage," Mathilda said slowly. "We were *dead*, Rudi. And that hit on the head was the real thing; he's still hurting from it. And when you rescued us . . . he threw himself under a sword to save me."

"And not even his worst enemy—the which I am not; I like him—would deny that he's a very brave man."

She glanced at him from the corners of her eyes; he could tell she thought he was being a good deal too fair. "Aren't you the *least* bit jealous? Just a *teeny* bit?"

"Sure, and I didn't mean to be insulting!"

"You are! Jealous, that is."

Steadily, Rudi went on: "I *would* be a bit jealous at the least, were I afraid you'd decided *you* were the love of Odard's life."

"But I'm not of yours," she said quietly. "Am I, Rudi?"

He turned and put a finger under her chin and kissed

her. It was gentle—with his face in its present state it couldn't be otherwise—but warm. Not the first time they'd kissed, but ...

"Woof!" she said a long moment later.

"Woof indeed," he said, clearing his throat to get the huskiness out of it. Then:

"Matti, I can't *fall* in love with you, or you with me. We've known each other too long! But the love's there, never doubt it."

"I won't be any man's lover, except my husband's," she said defiantly. "Not even yours, Rudi."

He nodded—she was as constant in her faith as he was in his, and hers put some very odd demands on her.

The problem being that it doesn't mean she dislikes my flirting with her. It just means she's guaranteed to keep saying no. Which may be fine for her, but would leave me walking in a most odd and mirth-provoking way, after a while. I do love her, but I'm not a Christian.

"And were I your handfasted man, there would be no other for me," he said soberly. "But ..."

She shook her head and sighed. "But right now, we're going to be running and hiding and fighting, not courting."

And when we get back, there will be matters of State, and of our gods, he thought.

Tears pooled in her eyes; the starlight sparkled in them, and it occurred to him that a man could drown himself there and account it a pleasant passing. He brushed them aside with his thumb.

"Shhhh, don't be sad, *anamchara*. We're alive, and together, and while those are true we won't be lonely," he said. Then, with a sly edge in his voice: "Frustrated, perhaps ..."

This time she *did* poke a finger into his ribs, and laughed, which he'd wanted. He yelped and they walked back towards the dying embers, a puddle of glowing red in the vast darkness about.

"Time to get some sleep, then," he said, and nodded to the twins; they ghosted off to take first watch.

"I'm ... going to do some letters," Mathilda said. "You

brought my writing-kit. Maybe Sergeant Gonzalez can deliver them for us, sometime."

"Now, that's a good idea," Rudi said. "But I'll do mine in the morning. We've a very long way to go . . ."

And farther still to our homecoming, he thought with a stab of longing. *And peace and rest.*

CHAPTER TWO

"Yet another of the things I learned after the Change," Juniper Mackenzie said with a rueful chuckle.

She spoke quietly and kept her face grave as the solemn young men and women of the escort fell in with bow and sword and buckler, steel caps on their heads and the moon-and-antlers sigil of the Clan blazoned on the chests of their green brigandines. It was the least she could do, since they'd been called away from field and forge and loom for this.

"My dear?" her husband, Nigel, replied.

He stood trim beside her in kilt and plaid, feathered bonnet and green jacket, ruffled shirt and silver-buckled shoes, erect as a boy despite the sixty-three years that had turned him egg-bald and washed the yellow of his mustache to white. The twisted gold torc of marriage around his neck was the twin to hers.

"When I busked at the RenFaires and Society tournaments in the old days I sang of knights and kings and princes, of battles and captivities and rescues, but never a word about how much time Arthur and Gawain and Lancelot probably spent sitting 'round a table—"

"Round or not," he said, with that slight smile that made his face look young for a moment, like a towhaired schoolboy from *Puck of Pook's Hill* bent on mischief.

"—arguing who paid what to whom and who was responsible for doing the other thing. Attending *meetings*. It's not so much being Chief I mind, or even Goddess-on-Earth, it's being a *bureaucrat*."

Sir Nigel Loring chuckled; he *had* been a leader of men before the Change—lieutenant colonel in the Blues and Royals and before that the SAS. Then one of the powers behind the throne after the Change, helping save a remnant of civilization in England before Charles the Mad had driven him into exile.

"And dealing with bumpf," he said, using a rude word for paperwork he'd taught her.

She sighed and quieted her mind as they stood for a moment in the open gateway of the fortress-village that was her home, letting the grateful heat sink into her bones and fill her tired body with an animal contentment.

"There are times I feel old indeed," she said. "Old and overworked." Then: "Well, the job doesn't grow easier for the waiting."

The day was drowsy with warmth as the sun sank towards the thin blue line of the Coast Range on the western horizon; a last few bees buzzed homeward, and a flock of Western bluebirds went over, like a chirring flutter fashioned from bits of living sky. The world was a wonder greater than any magic she'd ever made, and she had her place within it.

Ground and center. War may be coming, but it isn't here yet. My son is over the mountains among enemies, but no harm's come to him that I know. Plan for the future, yes, but live every moment as if it were forever, because it is. There is only Now. Ground and center . . .

She sighed and blinked leaf-green eyes that were a little haunted even in times of joy, for they had witnessed the death of a world.

A few weeks ago the long mountainside meadow below Dun Juniper had been crowded with the tents and bothies of her clansfolk, come for the Lughnasadh rites and the games and socializing that followed—starting with shooting the longbow and on down to prize lambs and enormous hand-reared beets and Little League softball games. Now they bore the tents of outland visitors, and their hobbled horses grazed the lush green meadows; they and their followings were too large to all guest within the dun's walls . . . and with some, it was more politic to keep them separate.

Largest was the great striped many-peaked pavilion that flew two banners. One was easy to make out; it was the crimson-on-black Lidless Eye of the Portland Protective Association, and not often seen on Mackenzie land. The other grew clearer as they approached and the wind caught at the heavy dark silk, a blue-mantled Virgin Mary standing on a depressed-looking dragon with drooping ears.

That was Sandra Arminger's personal banner, and Juniper suspected it was a joke in a subtle way; her household guards stood beneath it. Well-born young men in black armor of articulated plate and mail, graceful and arrogant as cats . . . though much better disciplined, and under the eye of a grizzled veteran who bowed and bent the knee to the Mackenzie chief and her spouse with punctilious Association courtesy. *He* had the golden spurs of knighthood on his boots.

"Lady Juniper," he said. "Sir Nigel. You are expected, and most welcome. Bors, Drogo, announce our noble guests."

Even so there was an indefinable bristling from the men-at-arms, and the same from the kilted Mackenzie armsmen behind her. A few of them touched the yellow yew staves of the longbows slung over their backs beside the quivers . . . perhaps unconsciously, perhaps not.

"Silence in the ranks," Nigel Loring said quietly, and it subsided.

Juniper looked over her shoulder. *How young they are!* she thought. *Changelings . . .*

They'd been children when the new-made Clan fought the PPA in the War of the Eye twelve years ago; few had been so much as toddlers at the Change, many not even gleams in their parents' eyes.

"Sacred is the guest upon our soil," she said softly, and saw them blush and shuffle a bit; the new world was all they'd ever known. "To even think them harm is *geasa* so long as they keep the peace. Even if we were at feud with them, the which we are not."

They touched the backs of their hands to their foreheads at that, and then managed to smile in friendly fashion at the household men of the Regent. One of those held the flap of the tent open. They went through, into the stillness of an anteroom hung in gray silk, and then into the main chamber. A ripple ran through the two-score of guests, everything from elaborate curtseys to casual waves.

She looked around, nodding. This being a formal occasion and she fifty-three, she'd decided to forego the kilt and wear a tartan arsaid, a long cloak wrapped around the waist like a skirt and then pinned at her shoulder with a broach of silver knotwork, over a shift of linsey-woolsey dyed in saffron and embroidered at the hems. Her belt was linked silver worked in running patterns, and she had a diadem with the Crescent Moon on her forehead. Even so, she felt a bit underdressed compared to some of the guests.

And this whole pavilion is so *Sandra,* Juniper thought. *She's gone camping . . . with a palace wrapped around herself, so.*

The ground was covered in softly glowing not-quite-Oriental rugs, and the walls with tapestries, both made in the workshops of Newberg and Portland; flowers and vines, lords and ladies hawking or hunting boar and tiger or dancing stately pavanes in pavilions out of dream. Lamps of fretwork in gold and silver and carved jewels hung from the peaks of the ceiling. The light folding furniture was inlaid with mother-of-pearl and rare woods. A prie-dieu and icon of the Virgin stood in one corner; Juniper made a gesture of respect to the Madonna and Child there.

"You can tell the economic pyramid up North comes to a demmed sharp point," Nigel drawled under his breath, echoing her thought.

"And that we've been married so long we're starting

to finish each other's sentences," Juniper replied. "Even the unspoken ones!"

A minstrel wearing a great hood with ridiculously long liripipes and tippets elaborately decorated with foliated dagges strummed a lute and sang softly from a corner:

> *"Her only will I sing*
> *Who, challeng'd by the Boy*
> *Or bids him wing or crowns him King*
> *In courtesy and joy."*

Serving girls in tabards and double tunics were carrying around trays of drinks and nibblements, salty cured sturgeon roe on crackers and bits of caper and smoked salmon and goose-liver paste—what Sandra insisted on calling canapés—and pyonnade, fabulously expensive because the main ingredient was candied pineapple shipped in from Hawaii or the Latin countries.

Juniper grinned as she accepted a glass of white wine from the Lady Regent's demesne estates and a little sausage on a toothpick. She'd heard that when she was being *informal* Sandra Arminger referred to this sort of thing as faculty fodder. Her gossoon of a husband, Norman, had been a medieval history professor, of all things—specializing in the Norman duchy and its offshoots—as well as a Society fighter before the Change. After March 17, 1998, he'd branched out into warlording, conquest, torture, murder and general wickedness, with the gleeful relish of a man at last living out the dreams of his heart.

Though it's true he saved many a life in that first year, if only so they'd be alive to serve him.

"Speak of the devil's widow," Juniper murmured beneath her breath.

Sandra came towards her, hands extended, the silk of her pearl-gray cotte-hardi skirts rustling, her face framed by an elaborately folded noblewoman's wimple of white satin confined by a net of diamonds and platinum. The buttons from waist to high lace collar and down the long sleeves were carved from old ivory and mother-of-pearl.

"Juniper, dear, it's wonderful to see you again," she said with a smile. "And to visit your home at long last."

For the rest she was no taller than Juniper, and her face was quite unremarkable except for the care which made her look younger than her mid-fifties . . . and the depth of thought in her brown eyes, like a shifting complex pattern at the edge of sight, never quite glimpsed.

They exchanged the air-kiss of peace; Nigel bowed over her hand.

"I like your little twelve-bedroom pup tent," Juniper said. "It takes the rough out of roughing it, sure and it does. Though a little heavier than a sleeping bag on a trip, I'd think."

Sandra chuckled. "Getting in touch with nature or back to the land always struck me as more a matter of wallowing in the dirt with the bugs. *And* the railroad runs most of the way here now."

Which was a point; horses could pull fifteen times more on rails than on the best road.

And why do I suspect Sandra would have brought the pavilion just the same even if she had to have it carried on the backs of porters?

There were two grandees with her. Juniper was glad to see she hadn't brought any of the ordinary Protectorate nobility along—the Stavarovs in particular gave her the crawls. But she could tolerate Conrad Renfrew, Count of Odell and now Lord Chancellor of the Association. He was a thickset, shaven-headed man in his fifties, with a face made hideous by old white keloid scars. His arms of sable, a snow-topped mountain argent and vert were in a heraldic shield embroidered on the breast of his T-tunic.

"I never managed to haul as much freight this way during the Protector's War," Renfrew said, grinning like something squatting on a cathedral's waterspout. "Even with an army of two thousand men to feed. The logistics were hell."

Nigel gave the man who'd commanded the Association's armies in the War of the Eye a nod of wary respect.

"We didn't expect you to besiege Sutterdown so quickly," he said.

Renfrew chuckled. "*I* didn't expect you to corncob me by looping through those damned mountains and cutting our siege lines at Mt. Angel and beating Lord Emiliano's army." A pause. "Though he *was* a complete idiot, granted. Most of those jumped-up gangbangers never did learn a war isn't an enlarged drive-by."

Juniper shivered slightly, remembering the earth shaking as the knights charged into the arrowstorm, and the sound of the horses screaming, louder and more piteous than men in their uncomprehending agony.

"Their sons, however, have learned better," Tiphaine d'Ath said. "Conrad and I have seen to that."

The woman in her thirties on Sandra's left was in what the PPA considered male dress, which was a rare thing in the Protectorate. And she was a Baroness in her own right rather than by marriage or inheritance, which was still more uncommon, her arms of sable, a delta or over a V argent self-chosen. Before the Change she'd been named Collette Rutherton, a Girl Scout and up-and-coming junior gymnast of Olympic caliber at Binnsmeade Middle School in Portland. Sandra had seen her potential.

And took the girl under an elegant, batlike wing. Better to be Sandra's girl ninja and hatchetwoman than starving or being eaten by cannibals or dying of plague in those camps around Salem, I suppose.

Together she and Conrad were the Regent's right hand, and a portion of the left.

Both sides exchanged equally courteous murmurs in a protocol that sounded ancient and was no older than the Change, cobbled together out of novels and remembered stories and playful Society anachronisms turned deadly serious. She knew Nigel found it all hilarious, despite his poker face; *his* family had come to England in the train of William the Conqueror.

Sandra clapped her hands twice. The minstrel fell silent

with a final stroke of his fingers across the strings, and
the buzz of conversation died.

"Thank you all for your company, my lords and ladies," she said. "And now, if you will forgive us . . ."

The heads-of-state and their closest advisers went
through into an inner room with a table clad in white
damask; servants set out a cold collation. Juniper took
a chair near Sandra's and waited politely while Abbot
Dmwoski of Mt. Angel spoke:

*"Bless us, O Lord, and these Thy gifts which we are
about to receive from Thy bounty, through Christ our
Lord. Amen."*

Half the people around the table joined in as he signed
himself with the Cross; Eric Larsson the Bearkiller war-
chief did, for example. His sister Signe Havel made the
sign of the Hammer over her plate as Juniper spoke:

> *"Harvest Lord who dies for the ripened grain—*
> *Corn Mother who births the fertile field—*
> *Blesséd be those who share this bounty;*
> *And blesséd the mortals who toiled with You*
> *Their hands helping Earth to bring forth life."*

"I'm Church of England, myself," Nigel Loring added
dryly, and there was a general chuckle. "All this *sincerity*
gives me hives, rather."

Dmwoski shook his finger at him. "And the Anglicans
have returned to Holy Mother Church," he said in mock
reproof.

"Taken it over, in fact, from all I've heard, Padre," the
Englishman said. "After Alleyne and John and I left, of
course."

Juniper bit into a sandwich, shaved ham and a sharp
Tillamook cheese on a crusty roll. The bread was made
from hard Eastern wheat, and fresh—almost warm—
which meant the Regent had managed to drag a portable bake-oven along with her . . .

John Brown of Seffridge Ranch and the Central Oregon
Ranchers' Association spoke first. "I suppose Juney's told
you all, her son Rudi and the, ah, Princess Mathilda—"

He sounded a little uncomfortable using the title; terminology was different over east of the Cascades, away from the influence of the PPA and the Society for Creative Anachronism. They used the old-time words there, even if *Sheriff* and *Rancher* meant pretty much the same as *Count* and *Baron* these days.

"—and the others were at my place back around the beginnin' of May. Went East with my son Bob and some hands and a big herd of remounts I was selling to the Mormons, and got into a scrap with some Rovers. Haven't heard much of them since they headed East with the Deseret folk."

Tiphaine d'Ath cleared her throat and went straight to the reports of the Battle of Wendell, flashed westward by the chain of heliograph stations in the PPA that ran from castle tower to mountain outpost down the Columbia and over the whole of the Association's territories.

"And there are rumors that one or more of the late General Thurston's sons have been intriguing with the Church Universal and Triumphant."

"Place might as well be one of our baronies," Renfrew said with a gargoyle grin at the tale of treachery and sudden death.

"And the Princess Mathilda, Rudi, Mary and Ritva Havel, Baron Odard Liu and the others were definitely there—guests of General Thurston before then, for about a week, and with him during the battle," she continued, leaning back with a nod to the Regent.

"*And* a certain knight-brother of the Order of the Shield of St. Benedict was there with my daughter," Sandra added, giving Dmwoski a slow look. "A Father Ignatius, I believe."

The head of the Order's warrior-monks spread strong battered hands a little gnarled with the beginnings of arthritis.

"My lady, he did not conspire with Princess Mathilda when she planned to . . . ah . . . abscond."

Sandra snorted. "Plausible deniability, Your Eminence? Casuistry? *Jesuitical* casuistry?"

The prelate winced; the Benedictines and their mili-

tant post-Change offshoot had never been all that fond
of the Society of Jesus. And Mt. Angel was independent,
but tiny next to the PPA . . .

Sandra raised a *that point to me* finger and went on:
"He certainly seems to have *strongly suspected* she and
Odard were going to run off and join Rudi on his . . .
his *quest*. And he *just happened* to turn up and join her
when she *absconded* from Castle Odell."

The Count of Odell looked abashed. Dmwoski replied calmly:

"Yes, and now he is with her, with sword and counsel.
Would you rather he was *not* there to help?"

"I *do* so hope his help doesn't include the last rites,"
Sandra said pleasantly. "And I would *rather* Mathilda
was safely in Castle Todenangst or in the palace in
Portland."

Her voice was calm; you needed to really know her to
hear the deadly seriousness beneath.

"It was fated, probably," Astrid said.

Faces turned towards the Dúnedain leaders. There
were four; Astrid Larsson and her husband, Alleyne,
Nigel's son by his long-dead English wife, Juniper's
own eldest daughter, Eilir, and *her* man, John Hordle—
universally known as Little John, from his massive size.
The same ship had brought the two younger English-
men and Sir Nigel himself to Oregon, back during the
War . . .

Astrid was the senior, the one who'd founded the
Rangers with her *anamchara* Eilir, when they were both
teenagers. She was as tall as Tiphaine, and as lithe and
slender-strong with a face framed in a long fall of white-
blond hair; her great turquoise eyes were rimmed and
veined with silver as well.

"Why fated?" someone asked.

"That brought the number up to nine," she said. "Nine
is the . . . canonical . . . number for a Quest."

There was a moment of silence, as everyone wondered whether she was serious or not; you could hear
the capital letters in her voice. Juniper didn't doubt it
for a moment, and wouldn't have even without that

momentary exalted look, as if she was being carried beyond the world of every day to the realm of legend and hero-tale.

I love Astrid like a daughter, and her children are a delight, but Nigel is right. She is, quite definitely, barking mad.

"And nine is a very practical number," Astrid went on. "Just enough to keep a good watch and be able to fight off a band of bandits or win a skirmish with a patrol, but not so many they stand out like an army to anyone looking."

But she's also quite functional, Juniper told herself. *Though it's a good thing she's had Eilir around all these years. And Alleyne, to be sure, and John has enough common sense for three, as well as enough bulk.*

"We know that Rudi and the others survived the battle," Juniper said. *Thank You!* she added silently, not for the first time.

Half the people around the table nodded. Dmowski looked troubled at participating in augury, even secondhand ... and Sandra a little angry.

"*Pardon* me if I don't find hints seen in a pool of water too reassuring," she said dryly.

"My lady," Tiphaine said, and then whispered in her ear.

Sandra looked grudging, then nodded. Juniper met the Grand Constable's cool gray eyes for a moment, and then the younger woman looked away. Tiphaine had been there twelve years ago when Raven came to her son in the light of common day, and Juniper thought it had shaken the cynicism she'd learned from her mentor a little. Not Sandra's of course; that would take more than the Change itself.

"And the *Prophet* certainly seems to take the whole business of the Sword seriously," the Regent said thoughtfully. "Of course, he's likely as insane as his stepfather."

"Insane but dangerous," Tiphaine said; Juniper thought her eyes flickered to Astrid for a moment.

"Which means we may be facing a coalition between

Boise and Corwin," Nigel said. "If Martin conspired with them against his father . . ."

"Boise has a damned good army," Tiphaine said. "Good infantry, and a good siege train. The Prophet has a hell of a lot of good, experienced light cavalry. Put them together . . ."

"We have a problem," Juniper said.

Almost enough of a problem to make me forget to worry about Rudi. Almost, but not quite.

"We need to start positioning ourselves," Tiphaine said. "The interior didn't suffer nearly as badly as coastal Oregon did in the Change. Say a million each in the United States of Boise, the Prophet's bailiwick, and what's left of Deseret. Even with immigration and natural increase, they outnumber us heavily."

A silence fell. Sandra struck into it:

"We must hang together, or be hung separately, as Franklin said."

"The Church Universal and Triumphant usually crucify people, but the principle's the same," Conrad added, in a voice like gravel in a bucket.

Edward Finney of Corvallis spoke for the first time, running a hand over his iron-gray hair and scratching the back of his neck; it was a gesture his father, old Luther, had used too, though he'd been taller and skinnier than his son.

"Look, I've got some pull in the Popular Assembly, well, a fair bit of pull. But I can't just tell them to do something. A lot of the farmers listen to me, but there's the Economics Faculty, the town unions . . . guilds, they're calling themselves now . . . and the Faculty Senate . . . and I'll be telling them things none of them want to hear, if we're talking about another big war."

"You can give them a bit of a push," Juniper said.

She looked over at Sandra's slight cat-smile. A white Persian jumped up on her lap, looking disgruntled from its days in a box on the way here. The Regent toyed with it and commented in a neutral voice:

"We should, as my commander-in-chief says, position ourselves. Specifically, Pendleton needs to be brought into the Meeting. Then we'll hold the Columbia as far as the old Idaho border."

"*Wait* a minute!" Finney said. "What's this *we*? You agreed not to meddle there after the War!"

"And we're certainly not going to let you take it over again and divide it up into fiefs and build those goddamned castles there," Rancher Brown said. "That isn't right, not on free American ground. Those f-f-foolish things are like nails driven into the map."

Sandra raised an ironic eyebrow. Juniper knew the thought behind it; if the interior Ranchers didn't build castles it was mainly because they couldn't afford it.

"Pendleton's a bleeding sore, a disgrace," the Association's Regent said. "It has been since right after the Change. They harbor river-pirates and they let bandits and Rover gangs fence their loot there and sell them weapons and gear. *And* they're deep in the slave trade. Pardon me: that's *compensated relocation of registered refugees.* With *accumulated welfare charges.*"

Brown shrugged, unable to contradict her. Astrid and her party nodded unwillingly; the Dúnedain did caravanguard work and bandit suppression far into the interior, and knew the truth of what Sandra had said.

Edward Finney looked unconvinced; that was a long way from Corvallis, and he wasn't one of that city-state's far-traveling merchants.

"They were unlucky," he said. "They had that civil war, right after the Change, and . . ."

"No, they weren't unlucky," Sandra said. "They were very lucky indeed; they had more food than people to eat it, when the machines stopped."

Most of the people around the table had been adults in that year of terror and famine and plague; and the others had been in their teens, old enough to remember much of it. A silence fell for an instant, as memories opened and bled.

Sandra drove the point home: "Then they threw it away fighting one another. By now they've acquired any number of bad habits."

But your arse is so sadly grimy and sooty, said the ket-

tle to the pot, Juniper thought mordantly. *Still, you have a point. The problem is, dear Sandra, that you always have at least three purposes behind any one statement.*

Aloud, the Mackenzie chieftain went on diplomatically: "They were unlucky in their lack of leadership." It was even true, if not very relevant. "Sure and it would be a good deed to clean it up . . . and Sandra has the right of it this far at least, that we can't let an invader from the East get their hands on it. The CUT *have* been active there; missionaries and such."

Nigel nodded fractionally beside her; they'd talked that over last night.

Signe Havel uncrossed her arms and leaned forward; if she and Juniper had never been friends, she'd always been a frank enemy to Sandra and the Association. Norman Arminger had killed her husband, Mike Havel; that he died first by about twenty minutes didn't reduce her personal dislike one little bit. Her voice was sharp.

"But nobody else in the Meeting countries will let the Portland Protectorate Association annex the area again. Nobody liked you snaffling off the western half of the Palouse back three years ago, Lady Sandra. It gave you too much leverage on the Yakima towns. We're *certainly* not letting you get your hands on Pendleton."

Sandra spread small, beautifully manicured fingers, silently letting everyone remember that the Palouse was in those hands. And that meant it was a buffer between the Meeting countries and the Prophet. Aloud she continued:

"But Pendleton is defenseless to anyone above the twenty-thugs-on-horseback level, and if either Boise or Corwin take it, they'll have access to the navigable Columbia. Which leads to Portland, which is our collective doorstep, not merely *my* home."

"And Corvallis isn't going to authorize the Protectorate to take the area," Finney snapped. "We host the Meeting and I don't think many would disagree with us."

"It seems we're all forgetting that there *is* such a thing as the Meeting," Juniper said.

Someone snorted. She nodded, conceding the point

but not the argument; the Meeting was much better at stopping things happening—like wars or trade tariffs between its members, or forced labor or slaving—than at actually getting everyone who attended to *do* anything positive in concert. It was rather like the old UN that way, paralyzed by mutual jealousies and suspicions, although the Dúnedain did enforce its resolutions when they could.

"I don't think there would be an objection if someone *other* than the Portland Protective Association alone were to undertake the task of putting Pendleton in order," she said.

Sandra's eyes narrowed. "We're the only ones with access and the necessary troops . . . except the CORA, and . . ."

It was Brown's turn to wince. The Central Oregon Ranchers' Association was another organization that had a *lot* of trouble getting its members to do anything but defend themselves. Sometimes against one another, over stock or water rights or sheer cussedness. Each Rancher was the law on his own land, as long as he didn't make his cowboys want to pick up and leave.

Tiphaine leaned forward to whisper in Sandra's ear again. Her murmur was very quiet, but Juniper's daughter Eilir had been deaf from birth. Lip-reading was a skill she'd learned in order to teach, like Sign.

"My Lady Regent, I don't think this is the time to play Evil Bitch Deathmatch Hardball."

Sandra shrugged. "I *do* tend to let the game of thrones become an end in itself," she said. With a little malice: "And so do you intend to have your archers leave their crofts and march two hundred miles over the mountains, Juniper dear? And to stay and rule badlands full of Rovers and Indians and Ranchers who are a *great* deal less civilized than our friends of the CORA?"

That is *a point,* Juniper thought ruefully.

Mackenzies had few full-time fighters, unlike the Protectorate. And the clansfolk had no desire at all for outland conquests; to start with, there was plenty of good land closer to home waiting for the plow.

"I was thinking we'd all send troops," she said, feeling slightly sick at what necessity made her say.

The waste of war; the blood of our best, and crops not grown, cloth not woven, land not brought back under cultivation, and what we do grow and make taken and destroyed like some ancient sacrifice while our children go without. But it is necessary. And we've had twelve years of peace, more or less. Best not to ask too much of the Powers.

Conrad snorted. "And who will run this collection of odds and sods we all contribute? The Meeting? An army run by a committee? A committee of ... how many members does the Meeting have now? Sixteen? A committee of sixteen who have to agree unanimously before they wipe their ... noses? Oh, *please*. Why not just have the troops cut their own throats? It would save time, trouble and expense."

Signe made a small grunting noise of unwilling acknowledgment, and Eric Larsson laughed aloud. They both had the little scar between the brows that was the mark of the Bearkiller A-list; that elite required its members to study military history as well as mastering sword and lance, horse and bow. Nigel's face kept the relaxed calm he used as a mask in situations like this, but his wife could feel how he radiated motionless agreement.

Juniper patted his knee under the table and went on: "And in command ... the Dúnedain Rangers. Everyone trusts them, and there aren't enough of them to get delusions of superpowerhood."

Sandra looked blank for an instant, then gave Juniper a glance of coolly irritated respect. Juniper sighed as the Regent stroked the Persian cat. It was going to be a long evening.

And Rudi ... my son, my son, where are you now?

CHAPTER THREE

The Prophet's council was made that day
When he called to him warrior and sage
"The Lady's Sword travels to the East
The Sword itself to take in hand;
Against that blade we cannot stand
And on his path he saves the weak
Who we would break."
Counsel they took, evil in shadow
Against the hero, the Witch-Queen's son—

From: *The Song of Bear and Raven*
Attributed to Fiorbhinn Mackenzie, 1st century CY

TWIN FALLS, OCCUPIED NEW DESERET

SNAKE RIVER PLAIN, IDAHO

AUGUST 20, CY23/2021 AD

"No, we should *not* kill them all, General Walker," Sethaz said, without looking away from the window.

Twin Falls had been the northern anchor of New Deseret, a rich city with many fine craftsmen, thrifty merchants, and surrounded by irrigated fields the Saints tilled with skill and ceaseless labor. Now . . . from four stories up, he could still smell the cold ash and the bodies trapped under the rubble, or hanging from crosses outside the ruined walls. Survivors were rebuilding the fortifications.

Much had been lost in the sack. That had been regrettable but necessary; both as an example, and for the sake of the troops, who'd had a long frustrating campaign until then and needed to . . .

What did they say in the old days? Sethaz thought. Then: *Ah, yes, "blow off steam."*

He had no mental picture to go with the proverb. Supposedly certain types of low-pressure steam engines still functioned after the Change—the large, heavy ones they'd called *atmospheric engines*—but such were banned in the Church Universal and Triumphant's territories. He could feel a certain cold *something* moving at the back of his mind, a lowering rage at the very thought. With practiced ease, he forbade his mind to imagine the forbidden thing.

Odd, he thought. *I don't remember what I did in the sack, either. Just . . . flashes and glimpses. Nobody else will talk about it unless I command them. That was right after the old Prophet died.*

Something had *happened* to him then. He didn't like to think about that, either. Instead he looked at his triumphant soldiers in the avenue below. A caravan of loot was shaping up; the soldiers guarding it were a mixed lot, range-country levies equipped in everything from standard CUT lacquered-leather armor to mail-shirts to vests of boiled cowhide to simple sheepskin jackets sewn with a few washers. They were all well mounted and armed, though, and they seemed cheerful.

Cheerful enough to sing from the Dictations as they mounted up and got things going with a crackle of whips and waving lariats:

> *"Keepers of the Flame!*
> *Sons of Dominion are we!*
> *From before the crux of Time—"*

"The men are in good spirits," he said calmly.

General Walker ducked his head; Sethaz could see the motion faintly reflected in the glass.

"My lord Prophet, that battalion's from Havre District—"

"The Runamuk, Rippling Waters and Sweetgrass levies? Rancher Smith commanding?"

"Yes, my lord Prophet," Walker said, blinking a little at the younger man's grasp of detail. He went on:

"And they're being released from active duty. Of course they're cheerful; they're going back to their home ranges and their herds, with a couple of girl-slaves each to screw and do the camp chores, and as much booty as their packhorses can carry. It's the ones who're stuck here I worry about."

The Prophet of the Church Universal and Triumphant was a man of medium height, sharp-featured, with a swordsman's wrists and a bowman's broad shoulders, his cropped hair and chin-beard brown and his eyes an unremarkable greenish hazel . . . until you looked deeply into them. He turned from the window and looked at him across the antique plainness of the room, which could have been pre-Change, down to the broadloom carpet and Home Depot office furniture.

The alien surroundings made Sethaz inclined to snap; he restrained himself with a practiced effort of will, pushing away the image of the soldier hanging by his ankles over a slow hot fire.

Walker was a little independent minded . . . but then, with slow communications, you didn't want a general who referred all his decisions to headquarters, either. His family had been among the first in the Bitterroot country to accept the Dictations, and they had prospered mightily.

And since the . . .

Since the old Prophet died, Sethaz thought, his mind shying away from the memory of that day. *Since my step-father's lifestream rejoined the Ascended Hierarchy.*

. . . Since then he'd been more than properly respectful. There was even a little fear in the bony face with its close-cropped head and tuft of chin-beard, worn in imitation of Sethaz' own. And a film of sweat on his forehead, but it was summer and the man wore armor and padding.

"Oh Heir of Sanat Kumara—"

The Prophet made an impatient gesture. Walker shrugged and went on more naturally:

"The damned Mormons just aren't giving up, lord Prophet. We've beaten their field armies and formally speaking we occupy everything north of Salt Lake City, but we're getting constant harassment from guerillas and the remnants of their armies lurking in the mountains and deserts. We don't dare split our troops up into small enough parcels to plant a garrison in every hamlet, we'd get eaten alive in little pieces if we did. But their civilians are the guerillas' source of food, shelter and information. Our lines of communication are longer than I like, too."

"Granted," Sethaz said. "But the population here are a potentially valuable resource, far too valuable to kill off for the sake of mere convenience. As it is the Church's dominions include too much unpeopled wilderness, without creating more here. The so-called Saints add another million to our population, which about doubles it, and more than that to our cropland and weapons production. With them, we can really get the breeding program going too, the more so as they kept such careful records. Much easier to identify subaverage mentalities, the mark of the Nephilim's soulless minions, and set them aside to reconcentrate the strain in service to True Men."

"But I'm losing troops to pinpricks every day!" Walker cried. "And lord Prophet, we can't keep our men away from their homes and ranches *forever*. We can't keep the Sword of the Prophet concentrated here forever either, they're our full-time cadre and best striking force. We must—"

He halted, flushing in alarm, and carefully keeping his hand from going to the hilt of his shete in a reflex born of sudden fear. Sethaz smiled inwardly, keeping his face grave.

"*Must* is not a word used to the Prophet of the Church Universal and Triumphant," he said softly. "I am the viceroy of the Ascended Masters and the Secret Hierarchy."

The General started to drop to his knees, then froze at the Prophet's gesture.

"You're an intelligent man, brother Walker," Sethaz said, almost genially. "You know the standard tactics for counterinsurgency work. And we do have a lot more cavalry than they do; it's why we beat them, after all. Take hostages. For that matter, the ones we've shipped East as slaves can double as hostages; make plain that their safety depends on the obedience of their relatives. Patrol vigorously, use your scouts, use our spies and collaborators and informers, chase every group of bandit rabble into the ground; and by all means, crucify any village that can be *shown* to be supporting the enemy. Except for the children. In those cases, we'll transfer them East to be raised in the Church. Many of our best and fiercest come from the Houses of Refuge."

"I thought . . . lord Prophet, we could sequester all the food supplies, and the seed corn, and dole them out in strictly rationed allotments. That would help with our own logistics, too. Administratively complex, but worth it, if you'll authorize me."

Sethaz stepped forward and slapped the older man on one armored shoulder.

"See? The Ascended Ones will speak truth to your soul, if only you open yourself to the Dictations! We have the mobility and striking power—use it, and the last of the bandit gangs will be dead, or gelded and working in the salvage teams by this time next year."

"I'll begin at once, my lord. Although altogether too many of them are escaping over the border with Boise, as well. Could we induce the new ruler there to seal the frontier?"

"Not yet. That is a delicate situation, one which needs careful nurturing. We cannot afford to fight Boise seriously. Yet."

"I doubt he is loyal to the Dictations. Even if he claims he must be discreet at first."

"He isn't. He seeks to use us, as we will use him. And when his enemies are crushed, with our men in the forefront of the battle to suffer the most losses, he thinks he will deal with us in turn." Sethaz smiled. "In fact, of course, I will deal with *him*, by the Power of the Ancient of Days."

"About the third battalion of the Sword you have on the, ah, special task, my lord. They're sorely missed in the pacification program. If I could have them back, or at least part of them—"

"No," Sethaz said flatly.

Walker shivered. So did the Prophet, in some inner core of his being. The word sounded *odd*, somehow hot and dark at once, as if it had been carved out of burning ash, like a glow of deepest black. Sethaz had not spoken so before his stepfather died. He pushed inwardly, something possible only if he was doing as . . . instructed. It was a little like arguing, but without words, and without any possibility of deception.

"They must be found," he said, in his own voice. "Found and destroyed if they cannot be taken captive. This has absolute priority. They must *not* reach the East."

He shivered again. The shining future of the Dictations stretched ahead of him, a world at peace and united on Corwin, obedient to the Ascending Hierarchy. But a shadow fell across it.

The shadow of a Bear; the beating of a Raven's wings.

"Send in the others," he said, in words that were dismissal.

Peter Graber stood respectfully aside and saluted as General Walker left the room, then marched in and went to one knee, the upright scabbard of his shete held in his left hand and his head bowed. His right fist thumped against his armor.

"Hail to the Prophet! Hail to the Youth of Sixteen Summers!"

The younger ones do it naturally, Sethaz thought. *For their elders, there will always be an awkwardness.*

Graber had an excellent record, stretching back to his childhood in the House. His appearance pleased Sethaz as well; he was a man of medium height, wiry save for the broad shoulders of a bowman, a little bandy-legged as you'd expect from one who'd spent much of his life on horseback, dark gray eyes steady. A healing scar marked his nose.

Beside him Seeker Twain prostrated himself in his dull-red robe; there was a different etiquette for the Church's spiritual hierarchy. Neither man looked at the other, though they were strangers and had been summoned to the Prophet's presence together. Instead they waited with disciplined silence while the head of the Church Universal and Triumphant paced like one of the leopards that had drifted up to contest the mountain forests with the native cougars.

"Captain Graber, what is the status of the Third Battalion of the Sword of the Prophet?"

"My lord Prophet, we are short two hundred effectives, leaving only two hundred and thirty-two men fit for duty. Another forty-eight are expected to recover sufficiently to return to frontline service in the next few months. Major Andrews lost his right hand and will be on light duties for some time. I am the senior officer at present."

"You suffered heavily at Wendell," the Prophet acknowledged. "But you fulfilled your orders, both your battalion and yourself . . . Major Graber."

Graber blinked, but his face might have been chiseled from birchwood as he ducked his head in acknowledgment of the promotion.

"Is the Third fit for duty?"

"To the death, my lord Prophet," he said promptly. "We are rested and have fresh horses; the weapons are clean and the men are ready to fight. However, we are at barely half-strength."

"Sufficient for the purpose." He turned to the desk and handed over a folder. "After Wendell, certain prisoners and bandits escaped and are at large behind our lines. They are believed to be headed East—"

He finished the briefing. "Familiarize yourself with these files. Your command will leave tomorrow morning. The file contains your written orders and a first-priority authorization to commandeer supplies and assistance as needed."

This time the pupils of Graber's eyes flared involuntarily in surprise. Sethaz nodded somberly.

"Yes, this is no ordinary band of fugitives. May the Unseen Hierarchy be with you, Major. You will be accompanied by High Seeker Twain; wait for him without."

"Hail Maitreya!"

He raised his hand in benediction as the soldier rose and left, then signaled the priest-scholar to his feet. The man stood with his arms crossed and eyes bent down, that his superior might study his face without being appraised in return.

"I am not worthy of this honor," he said neutrally.

Sethaz smiled. "No, you are not," he said. "Not yet. It is our duty to clear our lifestreams by constantly increasing our understanding of the Ascended Masters and Their plans for our world . . . and the most holy secrets of Their natures."

The other man nodded cautiously; Sethaz was repeating platitudes . . . and was also notoriously intolerant of sycophants.

"They brought the Change to humble man's sinful pride, and destroyed the wicked arts that would otherwise have destroyed *us*," Sethaz went on. "But by that Change they have . . . opened certain possibilities which were . . . dormant before it. The light of the Seven Rays now shines more clearly."

The priest's eyebrows went up. That last was *not* public doctrine.

"And the Nephilim and their soulless servants also have . . . increased possibilities open to them; but the Masters are vigilant for us. I will now demonstrate Their gifts, which long study and discipline have fitted you to bear. Meet my eyes."

Twain did.

"Is your will your own?"

"I have slain my will. The Ascended Masters play upon my lifestream as a man's hands play upon the strings of a harp."

"Are you prepared to hear the voice of the One Initiator?"

"I am."

"I—see—you."

Twain blinked, startled. Sethaz' powerful swordsman's hands flashed up to clamp his head on either side; the Prophet felt the action, but somehow as if he were observing it rather than willing his limbs to move. Their gazes locked, and there was a movement, a feeling as if the Prophet's skull were hollow, and something nested there . . . and now uncoiled to strike.

Twain gave a muffled, choking sound. His hands scrabbled at Sethaz' wrists, more and more frantically, and his feet drummed on the carpet like a man hoisted aloft by a noose around his neck. The movements gradually ceased, until the only motion the priest made was his breath . . . and then his chest rose and fell in rhythm with Sethaz. Soon their pulses thundered in unison as well. Two small trickles of blood started from the corners of his eyes, and another two from his nostrils; by the time they ran to his lips, he was grinning.

"Oh, now I understand!" he said thickly, licking the blood with relish. "Hail to the Regent Lord of This World!"

Sethaz nodded, stepping back. "Go, and serve the Masters," he said. "The Solar Logos go with you."

The High Seeker's grin was . . . disquieting somehow. Sethaz turned and looked out the window again, wondering why. The reflection prompted him.

It is because I've seen it before. In my mirror.

Then he shook his head; that made no sense, and there was much to do. He sat at his desk and took out the letter from Boise's new ruler, reading carefully once more. It was a tissue of lies, of course . . .

But from the lies a man tells, you can read the truth of his soul, he thought. His eyes went to a map, then glazed over as if he were listening to a voice only he could hear. *Yes, there's something in what he says. Pendleton does offer us an opportunity. But not quite what he thinks.*

*"From the hag and the hungry goblin
That into rags would rend ye
All the sprites that stand by the Hornéd Man
In the Book of Moons defend ye—"*

The tune had a steady thumping beat; Mackenzies used it as a marching song, though Rudi's mother had come up with the words long ago, when she was a bard before the Change. Rudi and Edain sang it—but not too loudly. A human voice wouldn't carry far in country like this, but there wasn't any point in taking unnecessary risks.

They were riding up a long open valley with a soil of something black, a coarse ashy stuff that crunched beneath the horses' hooves and raised a little dust with a strange taste, more bitter than the normal Snake River alkali. Small mountains or big hills showed here and there about them, looking as if they'd been built out of cinders—which they were. Sparse straw-colored needle-grass was scattered across the flats, and some of the hills had thick sagebrush, or even quaking aspen on the northern slopes, and some yellow-flowered rabbitbrush swayed a little in the hot wind. Nothing else moved, except a violet-green thrush that snatched a beetle stirred up by his horse's hooves; native animals hereabouts had the good sense to stay inside in the daytime, in summer.

"Ah, that was a bit of home," Edain said when they'd finished the song, and Rudi nodded. "I'll take a look at the pack-train."

His half-mastiff bitch Garbh jumped down from where she'd been sitting behind him and trotted along at his stirrup as he rode back down the line, whistling.

Edain could sing passably, which was a great deal more than his father could—Sam Aylward was longer on volume than anything else. Mackenzies generally could sing well, since it was an important part of their lives and they practiced hard, if not quite so hard as they did with the bow. Rudi had inherited a male version of his mother's talent, and she was first-rate; he sang very well indeed, and enjoyed it.

He smiled wryly. Rumor in the Clan said that the fae had clustered around his cradle to give him all the good gifts of the Lord and Lady. There was something to it, he supposed. He hadn't had trouble with his wisdom teeth and he'd gotten over his few zits quickly, too.

And all that makes my life so simple *and* satisfying, he thought sardonically. *Which is why dead men try to squeeze my throat shut. Yes, it's just one long Beltane feast followed by a roll in the clover, if you're beloved of the Powers. They give . . . or sometimes, They just delay the stiff payment They ask.*

"Interesting song," Frederick Thurston said, pushing his horse up beside Rudi.

"Heathen nonsense," Mathilda said, half joking, from his other side.

She uncorked her canvas water-bag and handed it over. Rudi drank deeply and passed it on—the water was tepid and a bit brackish, but you had to take as much as you could in desert country. His stepfather, Sir Nigel, and honorary uncle Sam Aylward had taught him that. The sun was bright and hot today, though the air was thankfully dry. Sweat was running down his flanks under his brigandine; they were all still wearing light harness, torso-protection, just in case, and it was as well to keep yourself used to the weight and discomfort. Even Father Ignatius had put off most of his panoply, though, for his horse's sake if not his own.

He's a hardy man, Rudi thought. *Though I'll never understand why Christians think it pleases their God to be uncomfortable when it* isn't *necessary.*

"Time!" Odard called.

He had a working windup watch, an heirloom. Everyone dismounted, unsaddled, let their mount roll, and began to put the tack on a remount.

Epona came over and pushed at him; she'd never

liked to see him riding another horse. The big black mare nudged again as he transferred his saddle and blanket to Macha Mongruad.

"You're middle-aged!" Rudi said to Epona, touching a finger to her velvety nose. "You need the rest. And she's your own daughter!"

He swore and lunged for Macha's bridle when her dam mooched off . . . then turned and nipped the younger mare on the haunch. A few seconds of work prevented an equine catfight, and they began leading their horses; Epona trotted off with her tail high, and her ears making a horse's equivalent of a smug smirk.

"That's a fine horse," Fred said, as they started walking.

They had a *long* way to go and even rotating the mounts and walking half the time as well it was going to wear the horses down.

"I don't think I've ever seen better movement," Fred went on, looking admiringly where Epona seemed to float along, hooves barely touching down. "But isn't she around ten, or even twelve?"

"Fifteen or sixteen," Rudi replied.

A well-treated horse with a good deal of Arab in her breeding could be worked until she was past twenty, but it was true that if he could he'd rather have left her back in the home pasture, bullying the rest of the Dun Juniper horse-herd. Warmbloods tended to break down more easily, too.

"Why did you bring her on a trip like this?"

"She'd start killing people if I left her behind that long," Rudi said.

Frederick laughed, then stopped when he saw nobody else was.

"She's vicious?" he said incredulously. "But I saw you riding her without a bit! Bareback!"

"Not vicious exactly; she just dislikes the most of humankind, the more so if I'm away for long. Which given the way she was treated as a filly isn't surprising. We've been together a long time, since *I* was about ten, and she still won't let anyone else ride her."

Mathilda rolled her eyes again. "Rudi rode her when nobody else at the Sutterdown Horse Fair could," she said. "It's part of the Wondrous Legend of Rudi Mackenzie, back home." A sigh. "It's true, too. I was there. You wouldn't have any doubt she could be vicious if you'd seen her *then*."

"Sure, and it's no miracle or magic, just that we're old souls to each other," Rudi said. At Frederick's look: "Knew each other in our past lives, so."

"You, ah—"

"Witches."

"Witches believe we're reborn?"

"Everything is," Rudi said. "How not?" He waved a hand around them. "And doesn't everything die and return; the grass, the trees, the fields? Why not us?"

Mathilda sighed again. "These are people who apologize when they cut down a tree in case it's their long-lost Great-Aunt Gertrude they're planning on repairing the barn with," she said.

"Well, now, no; it's just polite to be grateful," Rudi drawled, mock-aggrieved. "To the tree, for starters. And the fae don't like it if you're rude."

"Well," one of the twins said, "Elves go wait in the Halls of Mandos, generally speaking. But that's not really relevant since there aren't any here in Middle-earth anymore."

"And since the Straight Path is closed," the other went on. "Nowadays if you sail west, you just eventually hit yourself in the butt, coming from the east."

"I've never been very religious," Fred mused. "My family aren't, you know ... well, we're Methodists, sort of. I never really thought it was very important. I know that's sort of old-fashioned, but Mom and Dad are ... Dad was ..."

He rubbed a hand across his face, smearing sweat and dust on his chocolate-colored skin.

"But I think I'm going to have to change my mind, with all the stuff that's happened lately." A weary grin: "Though which *type* of religion should I start taking seriously?"

"There are many paths and if you walk them rightly, they all go to the same place," Rudi said.

Then he grinned himself: "To be sure, the sensible people go by the Old Religion's road. We have the best festivals, for starters! And the best music, though I grant"—he nodded to Ignatius—"that the Gregorian chant is fine stuff, but ours is merrier. And unlike Catholics we don't have to waste our time on guilt."

Ignatius simply gave an ironic lift of the eyebrows; he wasn't the sort of man to rise to a bait like that. Mathilda glanced sidelong at Rudi and smiled.

"Did he mention the way his mother magically struck a Methodist pastor dead once?"

Well, your *mother has struck a fair number of people dead, but by more conventional means,* Rudi thought. It was hot and he itched in places he couldn't scratch because they were covered by two layers of leather with steel plates riveted between, and it was a bit of an effort to stay cheerful. *Including your father's pet pope, I suspect. Not that he didn't deserve it, the creature...*

Aloud he went on: "She didn't. The Reverend Dixon just had a heart attack at a . . . a crucial moment, or so Aunt Judy tells me."

As an aside he said to Frederick: "Aunt Judy's our chief healer, a friend of my mother's from when they were girls."

Then he returned to the subject: "Matti, people *do* die now and then without someone killing them. Besides, it was before either of us was born. And he was a Baptist, not a Methodist. Or was it a Presbyterian? I've never really understood all the differences."

"*Some* sort of heretic," Mathilda said.

"Sure, you're bein' a bit narrow-minded there."

"Just orthodox," she said with a sniff.

"And isn't orthodoxy just one's own doxy, and heterodoxy another's doxy?"

Father Ignatius walked on two paces, then choked with laughter and had to be thumped on the back, tried to be stern, and laughed again. Other people joined in at intervals as the ghastliness of the Latinate pun sank in, ending with Edain and Frederick and Ingolf, who had to have it explained since their schooling hadn't included the classics.

Rudi considered making a more elaborate one about the Grand Constable Tiphaine being a very non-hetero-doxy, but decided not to—Ignatius was a bit of a damp blanket where bawdy was concerned. So was Matti, come to that, especially in a cleric's company.

His mother had made a joke once about Tiphaine hav-ing an *I won't tell, and I'll kill you if you ask* policy. Older people seemed to find that funny, for some reason.

"Ummm—" Frederick said.

He's feeling a little like the new wolf in the pack, being a stranger and all, with us knowing one another most of our lives, Rudi thought. *Or at least for a year, with Ingolf. He's lonely, too. I would be, in his place!*

The younger Thurston went on: "You know, Dad thought you guys, the Mackenzies, were, well, weird."

"We're witches. We *are* weird," Rudi said. "Or so my mother always says. Meself, I think everyone *else* is weird, but then I wasn't raised all my younger years among cowans as she was, the sorrow and the pity of it."

"What are cowans?"

Mathilda chuckled, a gurgling sound like her moth-er's laugh, but warmer somehow; it lit up her tired, dusty face like a light from within.

"Unbelievers," she said. "People with a distorted view of things. Dull, commonplace people with no magic in them who can't hear the music of the world. *Us*, in other words, as far as the witches are concerned."

Frederick gave her a glance and seemed to flush, then gathered himself.

"Ah ... Dad always said you guys in Portland were even weirder, but you and Odard seem pretty ... well, normal to me."

"You haven't seen the court in Castle Todenangst," Rudi said. "The annual High Tournament, say. It's an improvement on a battle only because the food's bet-ter and there are regular rest breaks. That's their idea of *fun*."

"It's *training*," Mathilda said a little defensively. "We use blunt swords and barriers and rebated lances. There's hardly ever more than one or two people killed. And I hadn't noticed *you* refusing to break a lance or two, Rudi."

"I have to take them down a bit, for their own good," Rudi said. "Knocking them off their horses corrects their humors, me being a mere pagan clansman and all who empties his own slop bucket. Most of the time your noble Associate can't swat a mosquito without getting a troubadour to list its noble lineage and compose an epic on the desperate battle it gave him."

And young Fred's a bit smitten with Mathilda, Rudi thought tolerantly. *Which is natural enough. She's a comely lass, my* anamchara *is, and I've always thought so, and you could warm your hands at her spirit on a cold night. Not to mention other parts, if that were her inclination, which alas it is not.*

It might cause problems, but he didn't think so; the young man seemed a sensible sort. And Mathilda had her faith's conviction of the importance of virginity right down in her bones.

A convinced virgin-until-marriage and my two half sisters, Rudi thought. *It's a merry time* I'm *going to have on this trip! Think about anything but sex, Rudi . . . think of ice and vinegar.*

He did, out of curiosity: an image slid spontaneously into his mind—one of a girl he knew named Niamh, naked, blond, lying on a bed and smiling as she raised a glass of iced vinegar and slowly licked the rim . . .

Oh, by Priapus Himself, I'm twenty-two, how am I to think of anything else? Rudi thought, tugging at the bottom edge of his arming doublet.

Then the image flashed back; this time it was Matti. That was even *more* disturbing. She wasn't conventionally beautiful, her face more strong-boned and handsome, but he could imagine how those brown eyes would light, and her breath catch as he kissed the hollow at the base of her throat and . . .

She was laughing at his joke, her head thrown back,

that laugh with a gurgling chuckle in it. He gritted his teeth. It looked like he'd have to learn to mortify the flesh, Christian or no.

"Now, if you want weird, try the Dúnedain," he said teasingly. "Living in trees and talking that fancy language—"

"I heard that!" Mary—or Ritva—called from a few yards back. "You're just jealous 'cause our traditions are *really* old! And only *some* of us live in trees."

"You do," Rudi pointed out.

"It's a *flet*. And very comfortable in all weathers, and private. *And* bearproof."

"You want to hear something really weird?" Frederick said, and waved a hand around: "This place used to be what they called a *national monument*. Dad was always going on about how we had to preserve them for the future."

Afraid he'll offend if he joins in the chaffing, Rudi thought; you had to be really familiar with people to share the game of playful insults. *But yes, he's lonely, I'd judge. And of course he's parted from all his family, his mother and his sisters.*

Rudi looked around at the arid desolation; the only reason they'd come this way was to throw off possible pursuit, and because they might as well use up fodder too bulky to carry far now that they'd abandoned the wagon.

"Well, there's something to be said for every part of Their world," he said.

The thought of harvest in the fields of home pierced his breast, and the reapers dancing in the Queen Sheaf to the squeal of pipes and rattle of bodhrans, whirling with corn poppies woven in their hair . . .

"And the forest is sacred to the Horned Lord, of course, and very comely. But *this* is the sort of place only the Mother could love, I'd say."

Rudi was a little relieved when Ingolf spoke; the big man had been nearly silent for too long now:

"Yah, I noticed that sort of thing back home—and all the way East and West, from one side of the continent to the other. You'd see these National Monument signs, and it's never anything that *could* have been good fields, or orchards or anything. Mind you, the woods can be real pretty—the maples turn colors back in Richland that I'd ride a day to see—and sometimes it's something really impressive, like this mountain carved into faces in the Sioux country, but most of these National Monuments, it's just damn ugly wilderness, rocks and stuff."

"I think they valued wilderness more, then, because there was so little of it and so much settled land," Ignatius said thoughtfully. "Strange . . ."

"We can all agree on one thing," Mathilda said decisively. "People who grew up before the Change are . . . *weird*!"

Everyone laughed agreement; Rudi nodded himself. Even his mother was strange that way sometimes, and you'd run into it like a brick wall you couldn't see.

Mary or Ritva came trotting back from a forward scout. *Ritva*, he decided as she reined in.

"Water a couple of miles northwest," she said. Her face was grim. "But there's complications."

There were about two dozen of the Mormons at the desolate little spring, refugees twice over, the first time from the Prophet's invasion of New Deseret and now from the United States of Boise. They'd picked their spot well, a declivity at the base of a tall north-facing cliff with a bit of an overhang, and with good water bubbling in a crack in the rock. It ran downhill before vanishing into the coarse black volcanic sand, and that produced a bit of greenery, which their horses needed and were busy stripping. Rudi gave the people a quick appraising glance.

They had tinder stacked and a couple of big campkettles next to it, but no fire going. About eight were women; nobody was under eighteen or older than early middle age. They all seemed to have at least one horse, but the mounts looked hard done by, and some of the people were wounded. And they all had a sword and bow or crossbow and a shield, marked with Deseret's golden bee on a blue background. A few had mail-shirts, or armor of sheet-steel plates hammered to fit and riveted onto leather jackets, both painted a greenish gray sage color.

And the place doesn't stink, Rudi thought; there was only a slight natural smell of horses, leather, and sweat and smoke soaked into woolen clothing. *Which with twenty-odd people is a good sign. They're taking care of things, tired as they are.*

Edain waved as he recognized a girl named Rebecca Nystrup—her father had bought Rancher Brown's horses for Deseret's army, back ...

Well, well. That was in May, and doesn't it seem the longest time?

Edain had been quite taken with her, for which Rudi didn't blame him, the girl being well beyond comely and near his age. He'd have been tempted in that direction himself, under other circumstances. And she'd been friendly to Edain, in a very proper way. The young Mackenzie's smile died as he took in the grimness of the little party. Rudi nodded politely to the girl but spent his attention on the rest of her land-folk.

"Colonel Donald Nystrup, 2nd Cavalry, Army of the Republic of New Deseret," their apparent leader said, a man in his thirties with light streaks in his brown beard and utter weariness in his blue eyes.

"Rudi Mackenzie," the clansman replied, swinging down from his saddle and shaking hands. "You're kin to Bishop Nystrup, I'd be saying from the looks of you. Not his son?"

"Bishop Nystrup was my uncle, and Rebecca's my cousin," he said. "But close enough."

Rudi sighed mentally as he looked at the fugitives and noted the *was.* Bishop Nystrup had been a conscientious man who did his very best for his people, in the brief time Rudi had known him. The sigh also had a little regret that the refugees were going to consume most of the food that he'd expected to feed his party through the next couple of weeks.

Threefold return, remember, he thought. *If we have to pull our belts tighter for a few days, it won't kill us.*

"It's coming on for sundown," he said. "Shall we make camp together, and perhaps make some stone soup?"

Nystrup looked puzzled for a moment—evidently the story wasn't as common among his people as it was with Mackenzies—and then his shoulders slumped very slightly as he recognized the invitation to share supplies.

"That would be a Chris—ah—kindly deed," he said. "We took what we could, but it wasn't all that much, and we lost the rest of our food in a skirmish two days ago."

Ingolf came up. "You took horses and weapons," he said, giving the group the same once-over Rudi had. "That's the essentials, you betcha. You can get food if you have to, with a bow or a shete in your hand."

Nystrup glanced at him. "I'm a soldier, but I'm not inclined to play bandit," he said, bristling a little.

Ingolf shrugged; the two men were of an age, in their late twenties, but the Easterner looked older just then.

"I was a soldier in a lot of places, straight-leg," he said; for a moment his dark blue eyes seemed lost in memory. "And I can tell you that sometimes the difference is sort of abstract. If you're planning to keep fighting the Prophet—"

"False prophet!" Rebecca said defiantly behind her cousin, and ignored his frown.

"Yah, I've got no problem with that *false* part," he said, touching his bruised face.

"You were wounded fighting the CUT?" she asked with quick sympathy.

Ingolf laughed, and she flinched a little. "You might say so. A spy from Corwin named Kuttner wormed his way into Vogeler's Villains—my outfit—got my friends all killed back East, captured me, dragged me off to Corwin, tortured me, screwed with my head, and when I escaped they chased me to Oregon; then they killed the lady I was with and damned near killed *me*, and just now they captured me and tortured me and screwed with my head *again*. You *might* say I've been fighting them. Not very effectively, but yes, I've got reason to do it with feeling."

He turned his head away and swallowed. Rudi winced slightly; he'd been feeling hard done by because he'd been dragged away from home by all this. The Easterner had lost the only home or real kin he had.

Ingolf faced Nystrup and touched his own face again; the swelling had gone down, but there was a spectacular range of colors under the dust and beard. When he spoke again his voice was altogether flat:

"Fighting the *false* prophet, especially if you're not doing it in a regular army, then you're going to have to get flexible. It's a rough game, and on both sides. You can't let people decide to just sit things out and see who wins. Better not to try at all if you're not willing to see it through to the end."

Rudi nodded soberly. Ingolf wasn't only a sworn enemy of the CUT; he'd been a wandering fighter for hire for years out East, in the fabled—and fabulously wealthy and populous—realms of the Mississippi valley, Iowa and Nebraska and Kansas. And after that he'd been boss of a salvage outfit which went deep into the old death zones, to the dead cities of the Atlantic Coast, which was just as dangerous and involved a lot of the same skills.

"Hey, *ndan bell, indo hûn*!" Mary called. Which meant *strong back, simple mind*, roughly. "Give us a hand! Not you, Rudi. The *other* strong back and simple mind. Ingolf."

"What about me?" Odard said. "I'm always ready to help a beautiful damsel or two in distress."

"If you have to ask, Odard, you'll never understand."

The young Baron raised an eyebrow, shrugged, and went with Mathilda to help hobble their horses and the four mules who'd drawn the Conestoga before they dumped it. They both knew horses well, of course; Protectorate nobles might have grooms, but they learned their way around stables from infancy. Ingolf started unloading sacks of dried beans and jerky and barley from the pack-saddles at the twin's direction. As a boil-up it wouldn't be very appetizing, but it would keep you going.

Then Ignatius got out the medicine chest, with Rudi assisting. Someone who knew what they were doing had done the bandaging—unsurprisingly, that turned out to be Rebecca—but the antiseptic ointments made from aloes and molds were useful. He'd never taken formal training beyond the first aid all Mackenzies learned in school, but Judy Barstow was both the Clan's chief healer and his mother's oldest friend and he'd been around Aunt Judy all his life. Ignatius was better than that, virtually a doctor; the Order wanted its knight-brothers to be able to turn their hands to just about anything, since they spent a lot of time on their own in places hostile, remote, or both.

"There is nobody here who won't recover, given food and rest," the priest said to the Deseret colonel when he'd finished.

"That . . . may be a problem," Nystrup said. Then he smiled: "I'd read about guerilla warfare in OCS—Officer Candidate School—and they went on about how valuable a sanctuary is to an insurgency, but it was all sort of theoretical. I'm just getting used to how much I relied on having someone to take the wounded off my hands. And yes, food's a problem too. I don't have a commissariat anymore, or local Stake storehouses."

"*We'd* have more if we'd kept the wagon," Ritva grumbled, as she measured ingredients into the cauldron.

We kept the essentials, Rudi thought. *The weapons, the medicine chest, and the cash. But no need to go into detail; best not put temptation in our Mormon friends' way.*

"If we'd kept the wagon, we'd be thirty or forty miles that way"—Rudi pointed back towards the site of the rescue—"and someone would have caught us by now."

"Yes, but it's the *principle* of the thing," his half sister said, getting out their salt-and-seasoning box. "All that lovely shopping we did in Bend, *wasted*. C'mon, Ingolf, let's give these people some help."

The Mormon women made bannock out of some of the flour, and minced a couple of desert hares as their contribution to the stone soup; the rabbits would be lean, without the fat that kept you going, but every little bit helped. Things settled down when the chores were done, and everyone sat around gnawing on hardtack while the stew seethed, chatting easily—except for Ignatius, who kept a calm, cheerful silence, and Ingolf, who brooded despite the twins' attempts to draw him out.

Rudi took another deep drink of the water; it was very clear, with a mineral undertong, and cold, which felt glorious. He'd taken the chance to strip and scrub down before the heat of the day left completely; this area was higher than it looked, and a clear night would be chilly even in August. Putting his sticky clothes back on had been a bit of a trial; he was a fastidious man, when circumstances allowed, if not quite as picky as, say, Odard.

"I'm thinking then that you aren't altogether happy in Boise territory," Rudi said to Nystrup.

"No," Nystrup said shortly, looking down at the sword he was honing.

Then, thawing: "I could tell right away that the new President, Martin Thurston, wasn't going to keep his father's . . . He was talking about splitting up the refugees, settling them a few each in Boise towns and villages, or enlisting our troops in his army—and as individuals, not in units. That meant he wasn't planning on helping us get our homes back. *And* he said he wouldn't allow any 'raiding' over the border from the refugee camps. Said it might endanger the 'peace process.' "

Rudi nodded, pursed his lips thoughtfully, and called: "Fred! The good colonel needs to talk to you. Colonel Nystrup, Captain Frederick Thurston. Yes, of *the* Thurstons."

"Damnation!" the Deseret officer blurted, when the tale of Martin Thurston's treachery had been told, amid a babble of questions from his followers.

That cut off sharply when Nystrup made a gesture. Rudi's brows rose; that bespoke real discipline and this collection of odds-and-sods wasn't a regular military unit. From what he'd heard, the Saints were an orderly folk, but it still said something about Nystrup as a man.

"But didn't the CUT try to assassinate him along with his father and younger . . . and you, Mr. Thurston?" the colonel said.

"Everyone thought so at the time," Rudi said. "I'd say the now that only the ones aimed at General Thurston were really trying to kill."

"And the one behind *me*," Frederick said.

"Perhaps," Rudi said gently. "He didn't have any real need to kill you then—you'd never have suspected. But perhaps."

And perhaps you need to think as badly of him as you can, for your own sake. I'll not hinder it.

"You think Martin Thurston's going over to the false prophet?" Nystrup said sharply. "Has already, secretly?"

"Now, there I'm less certain," Rudi said judiciously.

Odard Liu cut in; he'd been doing his share of the chores, and without any of the reluctance that Rudi half expected. Alex had done much of his master's work before the man revealed his true colors. Now the Baron wiped his hands and spoke:

"I'd say it's an alliance of mutual convenience, not an affair of the heart. Ah, some people in the Protectorate—"

Including your darling mother, Rudi thought. *Who has all the faults of Sandra Arminger and none of her redeeming qualities, sure. And who Sandra will now undoubtedly kill.*

"—have been, ummm, negotiating with the CUT too. They evidently don't demand you convert in order to intrigue with them about politics."

"Not at first," Ingolf said grimly from by the fire. "I was a prisoner in Corwin last summer. They really believe that horseshit, or at least most of them do. And they send out their missionaries everywhere they can reach."

"Does anyone in Boise know about their *President* and what he's doing?" Nystrup asked eagerly.

"That they do, naming no names," Rudi said.

"It'd probably be a real threat to health to draw Martin Thurston's attention by talking up a version of the events that isn't his," Odard said judiciously.

Frederick nodded. "But they'll be spreading the story quietly. Everyone knew Martin was . . . ambitious. Just not *how* ambitious."

"That changes things," Nystrup said; a little of the lost look faded from his eyes. "We and Boise never got along well, but *everyone* hates the CUT. If we can get people in Boise territory to help us . . . hide us, give us shelter in between raids on the CUT garrisons and supply lines, give us food and horses . . ."

"And everyone loved my father," Frederick said. "Well, nearly everyone. Nearly everyone in the United States." With bitterness. "*Dad* didn't want to be a king! With him it was everything for the country, nothing for himself."

"*Emperor* is more what Martin has in mind, probably," Odard said, tuning the lute which someone had brought along from the Conestoga. "I got those vibrations off him"—he plucked the strings—"and we talked a few times. He was *extremely* interested in the balance of power out West, in the realms of the Meeting at Corvallis. I don't think he's going to settle down to quietly rule what he has now."

"He couldn't," Frederick said. "Too risky."

They all looked at him. "Dad . . . OK, Dad ruled with a hard hand, and it was an awfully long time before he decided to hold national elections. But he *didn't* want to be king; he really wanted to restore the United States. That's one reason he waited—electing a government from just part of one State would be like an admission of failure. It really ate at him. He thought everyone would rally round once he got going and it didn't happen. A lot of our people wanted, want, to put the country back together too. Especially the army officers. If my . . if Martin is going to hold on to the Presidency, *make* it into something like being a king, or an emperor —"

He nodded to Odard.

"—then he has to make some progress on reunification."

"Conquering other realms," Mathilda said—but musingly rather than a sharp-toned correction, simply translating the young man's words into the terms the others would think in. "An emperor is a king of kings, after all. If he conquers widely, it'll make his claim to the throne solid."

"OK, if you want to call it that," Frederick said. "That's more or less what I meant. Nothing succeeds like success."

Mary and Ritva came back to sit on their haunches with their arms wrapped around their knees.

"Like Saruman and Sauron in the Histories," one of them said thoughtfully. "Both want to conquer and rule. Our side can probably use that."

"Our side?" Frederick said; not bitterly this time, but with a genuine humor in the curve of his full mouth. "All nine of us?" He glanced at the Mormon leader. "Well, with all due respect, all thirty of us?"

"You're after forgetting," Rudi said gently. "We here are not just travelers from over the mountains. What we know, we can send to our homelands—and there, our parents are people of importance, with the power to bind and loose."

"And I'm not just in charge of twenty-one fugitives," Nystrup said. "There are other Deseret units still in the field."

Kindled, he looked at Rudi. "With you to help us—"

"In passing only," Rudi said, his voice still gentle, but with an implacable determination behind it. "This isn't an affair of greedy warlords only. Those are like bindweed or couch grass; it's the work of the season to uproot them. There's more to it. The Powers are at work here, and we the song they sing."

"Soup's on!" Rebecca said.

Nystrup seemed to be glad of the interruption. He stood and faced his people, folding his arms across his chest and bowing his head with closed eyes:

"Heavenly Father, we are grateful for this food which Thou knowest we needed badly, and for the generosity of Rudi and his friends. We ask Thee to bless them and watch over them as they journey East, that they may always find sustenance provided for them, as they have so generously given to us, and we ask that Brother Rudi complete his quest safely. We also ask Thee to bless this food that it may nourish and strengthen us, in the name of Jesus Christ, amen."

The nine comrades had remained respectfully silent during the Mormon ceremony; now they took their bowls, said their own forms of grace and fell to with the healthy voracity of hard-worked youth. The stew was thick and filling, fuel more than food, the sort of thing you ate without noticing the ingredients. The refugee-guerillas devoured theirs with careful speed; one or two gobbled, but the rest swallowed every spoonful as if it were a sacrament. Rudi hadn't met many Latter-day Saints before, apart from the ones who bought Rancher Brown's horses—Mormons were thin on the ground in the Willamette country—but they seemed to be a mannerly folk; and these ones were *very* hungry.

Rudi took his bowl and a bannock and sat beside Frederick, who was prodding at his food with a spoon and looking out over the dusk-darkened plain to the north and the distant purple line of the mountains.

"All a bit of a burden, isn't it?" he said kindly.

"*Tell* me!" Frederick replied. Then, lowering his voice: "You know, I wonder if I *should* be the one to fight Martin, eventually."

"Why?" Rudi asked, surprised. There was no luck in turning aside from a fate the Powers had laid on you.

"Well . . . the whole *reason* he quarreled with Dad—turned traitor, eventually—was that he thought being Dad's son gave him some sort of special right. He wanted to be a king. I don't."

Rudi nodded. "Well, you've a point there. But think on this; if not you, who? Isn't it better you than *him*? And it isn't you who'd pay the price of a noble renunciation; it would be your people, who need someone they know to lead them."

"Urrr."

"And also, what Martin wants is to be a *tyrant*, someone who takes power by lies and force and rules for himself alone, or his own kin alone."

Although . . . he looked at Matti. *That's a precise description of your father, and* you *will rule well. Many a kingdom starts with a pirate, or a lucky soldier. Of course, he didn't have the raising of you all to himself, Matti. Nor did Sandra. My own mother's fine hand is in the making, there, too.*

He went on: "A tyrant's not the same thing as a king, sure and it isn't. A good king . . . a good king is father to the land. What his people are together, their living past and the line of their blood for ages yet to come, their land that they've fought and died for and the sweat they've shed on it every day, and the way their songs and stories and being are woven into it, all that . . . he stands for it in the flesh. And he leads them not just in war and lawmaking, but in the rites that give meaning to life, that make them a people. My folk hailed me as my mother's tanist of their own will; who am I to tell them no? Perhaps yours will hail *you*. Perhaps not. But if they do, isn't it your duty to answer their call and serve their need?"

"Yeah, I can see what . . . I'll have to think about that." A grin. "And since I'm going East with you guys, I have a long time to think about it."

Rudi chuckled. "And you're not the only one who'll be thinking. From the old stories, a vanished prince who's fated to return and make things right again may be more powerful than one who's there in the flesh. My mother always said that it's by the thoughts and dreams within their heads that men are governed, as much as by laws or even swords from without."

"Dad said something like that too. *The moral is to the physical as three is to one.*"

Rudi nodded. "Also she says that no man can harvest a field before it's ripe."

"I'd like to meet your mother. She sounds like a cool lady," Frederick said shyly.

"She is that, and a *great* lady for all that she hasn't so many airs as some, and fun too."

Mathilda came to sit by Rudi when Nystrup drew the younger Thurston aside; she had a small bunch of yellow wildflowers tucked over her right ear.

"Giving him a pep talk?" she said dryly, not whispering but leaving her voice soft; the tune Odard was playing helped cover it.

Rudi nodded; they were both the children of rulers, and knew the demands of the trade:

"It's a little worried he is, over whether it's good for him to contest with his brother for power. As his father didn't want the succession settled by blood-right, you see."

Matti leaned against his shoulder. "Well, at least he gets a choice! I'm *stuck* with it. I get to be Protector . . . and then wonder when Count Stavarov is going to launch a coup and stick a knife in my back, or the House of Jones is going to flounce off in a snit and haul up the drawbridges on their castles. Or whether the Stavarovs are going to launch a coup and"—she shuddered theatrically—"make me *marry Piotr*. You wouldn't think that even Alexi Stavarov *could* have produced a son who's more of a pig than he was, but—"

They both chuckled. "If you can call what he's got a real choice, and not just wittering," Rudi went on. "After all, Matti, *you* have a choice too. You could run off and be a sailor in Newport, or a nun in Mt. Angel. Or to the Mackenzie lands and take up a croft!" he added slyly.

She thumped his shoulder. "I can just see myself putting out milk for the house-hob . . . and leaping naked over a bonfire on Beltane!"

"There are Christians in the Clan," he said righteously. *And that latter is a rather attractive image, sure.*

"Yeah, both of them," Mathilda said in a pawky tone. "But anyway, that's not a real choice. Portland's my home, I can't run out on it . . . Things would go to hell . . . And what sort of an example would it be, shirking my duties? God called me to a task when He made me heir to the Protectorate."

"That's what I said to young Fred, more or less. Struck him with the force of a sledgehammer, so it did."

"I'm worried enough about coming on *this* trip. And there's a lot better reason for doing it than just because I don't want to sit around in a cotte-hardi listening to petitions and arguments over who gets seizin of what or whose vassal stole whose sheep."

She put an arm around his waist and leaned her face against his upper arm. Rudi looked down and batted his eyes.

"And here I was thinking it was the sweet charm of me and my beautiful eyelashes that brought you on the journey . . . *yeak!* Those bruises still hurt!"

It was getting a bit chilly; he unpinned his plaid and stretched it over their shoulders, blanket-style, and they sat in companionable silence. They'd been doing that since they were little kids . . . although the weight and warmth and fragrance of her made him a little conscious that they *weren't* children anymore.

Admittedly a bit of a gamy fragrance, but we have been on the road for weeks, and it's exceedingly female.

Odard had launched into another song; Mary and Ritva sang it, in two-part harmony:

"I hear the horse-hoof thunder in the valley below;
I'm waiting for the angels of Avalon—"

He looked up at Rudi and Mathilda as he finished, then aside to the twins with a charming smile:

"And I'd like to thank whichever of you beautiful ladies was considerate enough to bring along my lute. Perhaps it's not quite so essential as the dried beans, but I'm fond of it."

"It was her idea," Mary and Ritva said in perfect unison, each pointing at the other.

Odard's smile grew a little strained. "All right; thank you to whichever evil, teasing bitch preserved my lute. I'm fond of it."

"She's evil teasing bitch Number One," one of them said, pointing to the other. "And I'm evil teasing bitch Number Two."

"You are not! *I'm* evil teasing bitch Number Two!"

Ingolf laughed, which did Rudi's heart good to see. The big Easterner extended a hand.

"That's a pretty instrument," he said. "Could I see it for a moment?"

"It's not a guitar," Odard said in warning as he handed it over.

The man from Wisconsin touched his strong battered fingers to the strings with a tender delicacy.

"I know. My mother's sister was a luthier. Aunt Alice loved the old-timey music. She was a bit touched after the Change—she was in Racine on the day of it, showed up nearly dead at our door in Readstown six months later, never talked about how she came through—but she could make ones almost as fine as this, and play them too. Taught quite a few people."

Odard's instrument had a spruce sounding board with a carving of vines over the sound hole, and touches of mother-of-pearl and rosewood along the edges of the swelling body. It was actually his second-best lute, of course; you didn't take the finest on a trip like this. Ingolf began strumming.

"You don't have fireflies out here, do you?" he asked. "Not that I've seen, anyway."

"No," one of the twins said. "We've heard of them . . . bugs that glow?"

"Glowing bugs? Like the stars are little lights in the sky," he said, and his fingers began coaxing out a tune from the six-course instrument, plaintive and sad. "It's a pity you've never seen 'em. There's nothing prettier than fireflies on the edge of a field in a summertime night, with that sweet smell off the corn, and a little mist coming up from the river. Like stars come to earth, winking at you . . .

> *"Like the lights I shall never see again*
> *The fireflies come and sing to me*
> *Of trains and towns and friends long gone—"*

He had a deep voice, a little hoarse but true; the twins began to sing along after a while, and then some of the

Mormons joined in. Most people were happy to learn a new tune, since it was about the only way to increase your stock of music.

"Alice made that one; she surely did love the fireflies, and it was a pleasure to hear her singing while she watched them from the veranda. We kids caught some in a jar once and gave them to her, but she cried until we let them go. She was a bit touched, like I said, but good-hearted."

He passed the lute back to Odard, who gave him a considering look and played another tune. Rudi rested his chin on Mathilda's head while they listened. Yawns signaled the end of the impromptu sing-along.

"Did you bother to take a bath?" he said teasingly, sniffing loudly.

"And on *that* note!" she replied, and headed off for her bedroll.

Rudi yawned himself and stretched, looking up. The stars grew as his fire-dazzled sight adjusted, even more thickly frosted across the sky than they would be at home; the air of this high desert was thin and dry, and the Belt of the Goddess shone in red and yellow and azure blue. A little away from the fire Ingolf sat looking at the embers, rubbing his hands across his face occasionally. The relaxed pleasure that had shown while he sang was gone.

There's a man who's afraid to sleep, Rudi thought with concern. *And he isn't a man to be governed by his fears, usually. I wish I were better at mind healing, or that Mother or Aunt Judy were here!*

Father Ignatius came back from an inconspicuous tour around the outer perimeter of the camp, left hand on the hilt of his sword and the right telling his beads. He bent to speak softly to the man; Ingolf shook his head with a moment's crooked smile, and the priest went to his own sleeping place. A little way from that, something flashed in the dying light of the fire. Rudi turned his head and saw Mary snatch a gold coin out of the air; Ritva looked a little put out, and watched carefully as her twin slapped the little ten-dollar piece on the back of her left hand and uncovered it.

Rudi wouldn't have been entirely satisfied with letting that stand. Both the sisters were cat-quick, and they practiced sleight of hand for amusement and use as well, and while both were honorable neither had much in the way of scruples—you had to know them well to know how they saw the difference. Evidently Ritva felt the same way. The two young women spoke a moment more, then faced off and did scissors-paper-rock instead. Ritva lost two out of three, shrugged and rolled herself in her blankets.

I wonder what that was about, Rudi thought. He looked up; they'd take the third watch together, when *that* star was *there*. So they couldn't be settling that.

His own would start in three quarters of an hour, which was not enough time to be worth sleeping. Instead he pinned his plaid, picked up his sword and walked a little out of camp, then climbed the rock under which they'd camped. The steep crumbling surface required careful attention in starlight, particularly as he went quietly, but in a few minutes he was atop it, six or seven hundred feet above the rolling plain.

It stretched on every side, dark beneath the stars, pale where the green of sage or the bleached straw of the summer-dried grass caught a little light, the shapes of the conical hills curiously regular, and *there* a glitter on a stretch of obsidian. He controlled his breathing, deep and steady, and opened himself to the land, to the smell of dust and rock and the coolness of night.

"Well, perhaps they were wiser than I thought, the old Americans, to make this a monument," he murmured.

No light showed in the circuit of the horizon, and he could see for many miles from here. A few minutes, and an owl went by beneath the steep northern edge of the rock, a silent hunter's rush through the night that ignored him as if he was part of the landscape. Far and far a lobo howled, a sobbing sound deeper and more mournful than a song-dog. Its pack echoed the call, and Rudi nodded; he'd amused himself by counterfeiting that sound many a night when he was out in the woods and wilds, hunting or traveling, and having the fur-brothers answer him as if he were one of theirs.

What are our wars and our kingdoms to them? It makes you realize our littleness, and how everything has its own concerns, he thought. *But the Lord and Lady have given us power to mar or mend the world beyond what the four-foot brethren have. So it's for the world and all Their children that the Powers are concerned with humankind's doings, as well as for our own sake.*

He knelt and drew his sword, laying it on the sheath and sitting back on his heels, with his hands on his thighs and his vision centered on it. The forge marks in the damascened steel were like ripples in watered silk, dim and sinuous in the starlight; Mathilda had given this blade to him for his birthday when he turned eighteen and had his full height, though it had been a touch heavy for him then. The blade proper was just long enough to reach his hip bone with the point on the ground, tapering gradually from three fingers' width to a long point, and the cross-guard had been forged of a piece with it, something that took a master smith. The hilt was long enough for both single- and double-handed grips, wrapped with breyed leather cord and brass wire, and it had a plain fishtail pommel; you had to look closely to see the Triple Moon inlaid there, rose gold in silver.

Rudi Mackenzie had grasped the Sword of Art in his infant fingers, when Juniper had held him over the altar in the *nemed* at his Wiccanning. Something, Someone had spoken through her then, and she'd made prophecy. He'd been but a babe, of course, but he'd heard the words often enough since. Now he spoke them softly to himself:

> *"Sad Winter's child, in this leafless shaw—*
> *Yet be Son, and Lover, and Horned Lord!*
> *Guardian of My sacred Wood, and Law—*
> *His people's strength—and the Lady's sword!"*

A sword isn't like a spear or an ax or a knife. It's the tool that humankind make only for the slaying of our own breed, Rudi thought. *So You have chosen me for the warrior's path. And as husband to the land, father to the folk, I must walk in the guise of the God, the strong One who wards Your people. But You know my mind. I don't fear death; when it's my time to walk with You, Dread Lord, and know rest and rebirth, I am ready. I don't fear battle, though I do not delight in it. It's . . . that others depend on me and look to me that harrows my heart; my friends, my kin, those I love, those whose need I must serve. I fear to fail them.*

He'd made the usual evening devotion, but a sudden sharp need seized him; he wasn't one to be always bothering the Powers, like an importunate child tugging at his mother's kilt and whining for attention, but . . .

Rudi raised his hands above his head, palm pressed to palm:

"Bless me with your love, Lord and Lady, for I am Your child."

The hands moved to his forehead, thumbs on the center where the Third Eye rested:

"Bless my vision with the light of wisdom."

To the throat, and:

"Bless my voice, that it may speak truth."

To the heart:

"Bless my heart with perfect love, even for my foes, for each is also Your child."

To the spot below the breastbone:

"Bless my will with strength of purpose, that I may not falter on the red field of war."

To the loins:

"Bless my passions with balance, making even hate serve love."

To the root chakra, at the base of the spine:

"Bless my silent self with clarity, that I may shun error."

To the soles of the feet:

"Bless all my journey in this world, that my path be the path of honor, until my accounting to the Guardians."

Then he held his hands up, palms before his face:

"Bless my hands, that they may do Your work on this Your earth."

Finally pressed together above his head once more:

"Bless me and receive my love, Lord and Lady, for You are mine as I am Yours; you powerful God, you Goddess gentle and strong, hear your child."

Smiling to himself, he took up the sword and sheathed it, a quick flick and a hiss of steel on wood and leather greased with neatsfoot oil, and the *ting* as the guard met mount at the mouth of the scabbard. Suddenly a shooting star streaked across the dome of heaven, and he chuckled.

"Well, I can't say You don't have a sense of timing!"

Edain was waiting for him at the base of the rock. Garbh sat at his heel and grinned with the tongue-lolling happiness of a dog about to take a country walk with two of her people-pack amid thousands of interesting new scents.

"Did you see the falling star?" the younger Mackenzie said.

They headed off to the northwest, which would be their watch-station.

"I did that," Rudi said, grinning in the dark. "I did that."

"Huh?" Ingolf Vogeler said, startled out of an evil dream.

Someone was close, very close. He pretended to drop back into sleep, but his hand crept to the staghorn hilt of his bowie, beneath the folded blanket he was using as a cover for his saddlebag pillow. The rough horn slipped into his palm, and he prepared to coil up off the ground ...

"Well, I'm not here to have a knife fight!" someone whispered.

"Oh," he said; it was a woman's voice.

The face of one of the twins was close to him as she knelt, smiling. "Though I could *probably* have killed you if I wanted to."

"Oh," he said. "Well, true enough. Ah, Ritva—"

"Mary," she said. "But I sort of like you, actually, Ingolf." A smile. "That was really pretty music."

The smile was expectant; that gradually turned to a slight frown as he shoved the bowie back into its scabbard and sat up, scrubbing at his face. That was a mistake, since the bruises were still fresh enough to make him wince. His wits returned, enough to realize that she was carrying *her* bedding and dressed only in her shirt . . . though she had her scabbarded sword in one hand with the belt wound around it, like a sensible person in the circumstances.

It was late; his eyes flicked automatically to the stars, and read them as past midnight. Nobody would be up now except the lookouts.

"Uh . . ." He flogged himself to full awareness as she sat beside him and put an arm around his waist. "Umm, I sort of like you too, Mary."

I must be older than I thought, ran through his mind. *Or more depressed. A beautiful half-naked blonde is propositioning me, and I'm not actually leaping at the chance. Well, part of me is, but the rest isn't.*

Her smile returned and got broader—the part that *was* leaping was sort of obvious through the blanket. He was suddenly aware of the sunny smell of her hair, still slightly damp from bathing in the spring-water, and the way her breast brushed against his arm where she leaned against him.

"If you want me to get specific," she murmured into his ear, "you're brave and smart and you've got a good sense of humor when you're not depressed and you've got a *really* cute butt. And I've known you for months now, so that's not a snap judgment."

"Well, I was real sick for the first couple of months." Then he realized *why* he was oddly reluctant, enough that his mind was overriding the hammering of his pulse.

Saba. We'd only just met that night I rode into Sutterdown, and that was the last time I was with a woman.

The curved Cutter knife had been rising above him as

he woke beside her. He swallowed as he remembered the way she'd shrieked as the Cutter's knife went in, and the way it had looked and smelled. Far too much like the sound and smell when the hog butcher put his spiked pincers on the beast's nose in the fall ... and that lay over the memory of what had gone before.

"Look," he said slowly. "I ... last time ..."

"Ah," she said sadly, and put a hand on his arm and squeezed the thick bicep. "Saba. I'm sorry to bring it back to mind, but she'd smile at us from the Summerlands, really."

"I don't seem to be good luck for women," he said. "Not since, well, not since Corwin. My luck generally speaking sucks since then. I—" He swallowed. "I don't want to risk anyone else. I like you, Mary. I don't want to see you hurt."

"That's all right," she said sunnily. "My luck's good enough for two. *And* I'm a Ranger *ohtar*, a warrior by trade. Got to take my chances."

"Ummm—" *Christ, but I seem to be saying that a lot.* "Look, Mary ... we're friends, right? So can I ask you honestly ... you're not doing this because you're *sorry* for me, are you?"

"No, of course not!" she said. Then: "Well, not mostly. Being sad makes you more sexy; women think that way, you know."

"You do?"

"Usually. You know, the brooding thing, and it'll be a big charge to make you happy again. *If* you're interesting to start with." The grin grew broader. "And happiness is on the program."

She moved suddenly, straddling his lap. His arms went around her involuntarily, and suddenly he could hear her heart pounding as hard as his. The problem with that was that it brought back the memory of the last time *really* strongly. Mary gave a slight yelp as his hands closed on her, and then she looked down in puzzlement.

"What's wrong?" she said. "Things were fine, and then ... look, I *did* take a bath ..."

"Ummm, I'm real flattered." He was; it wasn't often

you got an outright offer like this. Of course, both times it had been witches. "As long as you really want . . ."

"Sure! I won the toss, didn't I?"

"Toss?" he said, jarring to a halt.

"Well, Ritva and I *are* identical twins. We usually want the same thing. So we tossed for you. Well, then we did paper-scissors-stone. She cheats."

Ingolf felt his jaw drop slightly. Girls back home weren't necessarily shy, or coy about telling a man their mind under the right circumstances, but . . .

"You *won* me?" he squeaked.

"It's not as if there's much of a selection." At his gape, she stroked his head and went on: "Ingolf, there's you, there's our *brother*, there's a celibate Catholic *priest*, and there's two kids. I mean, Edain? Cradle robbing."

"He's about your age," Ingolf said weakly.

"That makes him younger. And boys that age are even more dicks on legs than men *your* age. Besides, he's scared of us."

"There's Odard . . ." *And I can't believe I said that!*

"Euuu! He's been trying to get into our pants since we were sixteen! Euuu! He'd *smirk*. And it's Matti he really wants. Besides, he's too . . . smooth."

"I'm not smooth?"

"No, you're *rugged*."

"Look, Mary . . ." he said slowly. *Are these words really coming out of my mouth?* "I . . . well, I like you a lot, but I haven't, you know, thought of you that way." *Except in passing.* "Couldn't we, ummm, get to know each other better—"

That was evidently *not* the right thing to say; she reared back like an offended cat and moved away from his embrace. Half of him wanted to snatch her back . . . and he was humiliatingly aware that some of the other half was sheer fear that he *couldn't*, not after what happened in Sutterdown.

"*Eny!*" she said, and then a sputter of musical syllables he knew were Sindarin, though he hadn't learned more than the odd word. "*Men!*"

Actually, that let's-get-to-know-each-other-first is usu-

ally the girl's line, he thought, bemused, as she flounced back to where her sister lay.

Slowly a smile spread over his face as he lay back and pulled up his blankets. His body was giving a sharp protest at what he'd done, and a big part of his mind was agreeing, yearning for the sheer comfort of closeness. The rest of him . . .

Maybe she didn't just *set out to make me feel better, but for some reason I do!*

CHAPTER FOUR

Astrid Larsson, *Hiril Dúnedain,* frowned upward at the curiously graceful bulk of Castle Todenangst. The great fortress-palace of the Arminger dynasty had been built around the slopes of Grouse Butte in the first Change Years, a little east of the town of Newberg. Built by thousands glad to haul concrete on their backs and claw away earth and rock for a regular bowl of gruel from Portland's commandeered grain elevators and a taste of the whip from the overseers. In those days of the great dying it had been a good bargain.

Still a symbol of tyranny, I suppose, she thought. *Complete with dark tower. But . . .*

Now it looked as if it had been there forever, a great circuit of crenellated concrete wall and tower covered in shining white stucco, the gates like castles in themselves and the broad moat bright with water lilies in coral pink and white and purple. The high mass of the inner donjon loomed over it all where the builders had carved away the central butte and cased it in ferroconcrete, covered with pale granite salvaged from abandoned banks and rearing hundreds of feet higher than the surrounding plain of dark forest and green pasture and yellow stubble-field, vineyard and orchard and village.

Towers higher yet studded the oval wall, the greatest of all on the southern height nearest them, sheathed in black stone with glittering crystal inclusions that made it sparkle in the bright sunlight of a September dawn. Its roof was conical and tapered to a spike, but not green copper like the others. It was covered in gold leaf, and it blazed like a flame as the sun cleared the forested Parrett Mountains to the eastward, a monument to the dark and ruthless will of the man who'd reared it amid the death-agony of a world.

He's been dead twelve years. Does his spirit still linger here?

Proud banners flew from the towers, and lords and ladies in bright finery stood on the battlements to look down on the assembled armies of the Meeting. Several thousand peasants and townsmen crowded around the lowered drawbridge in their best Sunday-go-to-Church dress of jerkin and hose and cap or double tunic and wimple, ready to wave the little Lidless Eye flags they carried. A rank of soldiers stood on either side to keep them back, facing outward with their spears held horizontally.

"I have to admit, though, it's almost . . . like something out of Gondor, isn't it?" she said with grudging admiration in her silver-veined blue eyes.

That she used Sindarin kept the conversation private from outsiders. It was even more so because only she and her husband, Alleyne, and her *anamchara*, Eilir Mackenzie, and *her* man, John Hordle, stood near her. The rest of her Rangers were in a solid mass behind her two hundred strong, each standing at their horse's head, clad in light armor and spired helmets. The White Tree with its surround of seven stars and crown flew from a tall banner a proud *ohtar* held beside her own dappled Arab.

"Possibly like Minas Tirith," Alleyne said, smoothing a finger along his neat blond mustache. "Or possibly more like the offspring off a fleeting romantic encounter between Carcassonne and San Simeon. I'm certainly glad we never had to try and storm it."

Eilir nodded, and Hordle grunted agreement around

the last mouthful of a massive smoked-venison-and-pickled-onion sandwich.

"John!" Astrid hissed under her breath. "Do you always have to be *eating*? You're as bad as a hobbit!"

He swallowed and licked fingers like great sausages backed with red furze, and belched comfortably.

"Takes a bit to keep a Halfling my size going, m'lady," he said mildly, and leaned on the ball pommel of his heavy four-foot sword. "Can't roitly expect me ter live on just a bit o' lembas, now can you?"

There was some truth in that, since he was ten inches taller than her five-nine and weighed over three hundred pounds, with shoulders as broad as a sheathed sword and a face like a cured ham atop a wedge of muscle where most men kept a neck.

"Besides, it'll be all jerky and hardtack soon enough, with raisins if we're lucky. Maggoty dead horse if we're not."

She nodded. The allied army was drawn up on the great open fields that sloped down from Todenangst's south gate towards the forest of oak and fir along the Willamette River; they served as green pasture for the castle's horses in peacetime, and now they blossomed with orderly rows of tents and pavilions. The smells of any war-camp—woodsmoke, scorched frying pan, slit trenches inadequately shoveled in after use, horses, leather and metal and sweat—mingled with the mild sweetness of the crushed grass.

The Rangers had the center station since she'd be in command. To her right were the thousand Mackenzie archers that Juniper had brought, beneath the banner of the antlers and Crescent Moon; beyond them were the two hundred and fifty Bearkiller A-listers with their black bear's head on crimson, all full-armored and equipped with lance and horseman's bow; flanking them were a hundred knight-brothers of the Order of the Shield of St. Benedict from Mt. Angel, with the cross-and-raven emblazoned on their shields.

To her left was the Corvallis contingent, standing with

their burnished armor and equally shiny field catapults, and the orange-and-brown flag of that rich city-state, with the letters PFSC above for the *People and Faculty Senate of Corvallis.* The flag bore the image of Benny the Beaver, a rodentine head scowling ferociously and baring chisel teeth. Her brother-in-law Mike Havel had called it *dorky beyond words* to use the university's football flag as a battle emblem, and she had to agree, but at least today they didn't have those cheerleaders in short skirts leaping and cavorting and making pyramids in front of the troops. She'd always *hated* that, particularly on serious occasions.

The Portland Protective Association's contingent was on the far left. Several hundred were armored lancers on destriers, knights and men-at-arms riding great steeds that themselves wore armor on head and neck and chest. A thousand were footmen, half with spear and shield, the rest crossbowmen. The Association's men stood a little apart from the others—all of whom had fought the Protectorate during the War of the Eye twelve years ago.

Or at least their parents and elder siblings did. That's going to be awkward, she thought. *Far too many of us have the memory of friends or kin killed by those men under the Lidless Eye banner. And vice versa, I suppose.*

There was a stir in the crowd of commoners. Heralds in bright tabards and plumed hats marched in a double rank through the open gates of Castle Todenangst, formed lines on either side of the roadway and raised their long flare-mouthed silver trumpets. From behind them came the white glitter of polished armor and the glow of embroidered silk and vestments, and the flutter of heraldic banners. The trumpets screamed in high sweet unison, and then a great voice cried out as the echoes died among the walls and towers:

"Our sovereign liege-lady, Sandra Arminger, Regent of the Portland Protective Association for Crown Princess Mathilda Arminger! Lord Conrad Renfrew, Count of Odell and Chancellor of the Realm! The lady Tiphaine d'Ath, Grand Constable of the Association! His Grace,

Abbot-Bishop Dmowski of Mt. Angel and Head of the Commonwealth of the Queen of Angels! Lady Juniper, the Mackenzie of Clan Mackenzie!—"

"The glory of the Elder Days, and the hosts of Beleriand," Astrid murmured softly, as the Protectorate commoners uncovered and bowed, or sank into deep curtsies before their rulers and those of the allied realms of the Meeting.

"Yet not so many, nor so fair," Alleyne replied in the same quiet voice. "And they're coming to us, and not vice versa."

"And not enjoying it at all, some of them," Astrid said happily. "It hasn't been a nice day for Tiphaine, at all, I imagine."

Even here in the midst of the castle, in the arming chamber of the Grand Constable's quarters, you could hear the low grumbling surf-roar of voices from the walls and the field to the south. It was time to go; she had to meet Sandra and Conrad and do the ceremonial necessities. Tiphaine d'Ath wasn't looking forward to it, but that had been true of a lot of the work she'd done for Sandra since the Change. You couldn't complain about the pay or benefits, and it was usually interesting.

"And they say *I'm* obsessed with fashion!" Delia de Stafford said.

"We've all got to look pretty to keep up the Association's credit in front of the foreigners," Tiphaine said, then looked down as the last buckle snapped home.

"Very neat, Lioncel," the Grand Constable said to her page, who was also Delia's eldest son. "But you musn't touch the plates with your bare palms; just the fingers. They smudge a lot more easily than the old chain mail did."

The harness was her parade armor, the same design as her field kit and just as practical in terms of stopping sharp or pointy or heavy things wielded with ill intent, but a good deal more showy, since the plates were made of chrome steel and burnished—*white armor*, the term was.

The page blushed painfully as only an eleven-year-old

boy could do, and buffed away the marks with a chamois. He stood back after a moment; his younger brother Diomede knelt and wiped down her greaves and the steel cover of her riding boots. Unconsciously Lioncel's hands clenched in admiration as he stared at the slender form of steel and black leather he'd helped arm, her pale eyes nearly the color of the burnished metal.

That all showed to better advantage because of the tailor's-style three-valve wall mirror. The rest of the room was mostly bare and lined with sheets of salvaged marble and shelves bearing spare parts, polish and tools. Empty armor racks like skeletal mannequins showed where her field kit had been packed up. The room had a rich clean odor halfway between metallic and that of a saddler's shop.

Maintaining a chevalier's armor was something pages worked on, under the supervision of squires, as part of the noble career path. The two boys walked around her with anxious eyes and ready cloths, to see if anything needed touching up, from gorget to the golden rowel spurs of knighthood.

"Now make your devoir to your lady mother. And then go and tell my lords the commanders that I'll be along shortly," she said, picking up her gauntlets. "Lioncel, take the helmet for me. Diomede, my sword belt."

They did, glowing with pride and pacing side by side, making a pretty picture in their dark liveries and brimless caps, one black-haired and the other almost as white-blond as Tiphaine herself.

Nice kids, she thought. *Even if they are males.*

Tiphaine had never had the slightest impulse to reproduce, even via turkey baster; Delia *was* enthusiastic about children, though, enough to use that venerable pre-Change technology. And the proforma marriage to de Stafford had served to ennoble her as well as to make her offspring respectable.

"*I'll* do this part," she said.

She stood, a little awkwardly in her seventh month and the maternity version of the long-skirted cottehardi; the pregnancy had fleshed her delicate brunette prettiness out a bit, too. Tiphaine bowed her head for the flat, round black hat with its roll about the brim, and then stood as Delia arranged it on the Grand Constable's straight blond hair, twitching the broad tail to fall down past a steel-clad shoulder. A small livery badge at the front bore the d'Ath arms, quartered with Sandra Arminger's.

"And this," Delia said.

She unwound a long silk scarf from her headdress—a tall pointy thing with a passing resemblance to a brimless version of a witch's hat—

Which is ironic, Tiphaine thought.

—and looped it around the Grand Constable's neck, tucking the ends beneath the mail collar. Tiphaine fell to one knee for an instant, took her hand and kissed it; their goodbyes had to be private.

And since I ended up in this Paleo-Catholic feudal wet dream of Norman's, that's the way it's going to stay, dammit . . .

"Come back safe," Delia said, fighting to smile.

"With my lady-love's favor to hearten me, how can I fail?" she said whimsically.

Her hand touched the silk. For a single moment, as their eyes met, the neo-chivalry didn't seem silly at all.

"And if you start dallying with any pretty cowgirls, it'll *choke* you," Delia said, smiling through eyes shining with tears. "I've enchanted it . . . and I'm a witch, you know."

They both smiled; Delia actually *was* a witch, albeit closeted in that respect as well. While the Old Religion wasn't illegal in the Protectorate anymore, it wasn't anything you advertised if you were a member of the nobility, either.

"Never, my sweet," Tiphaine replied over her shoulder as she turned to go. "I don't like the smell of the rancid butter they use as face cream out East."

Signe Havel noticed that Chuck Barstow, First Armsman of the Clan Mackenzie, was humming under his breath as they walked towards the banner of the Dúnedain Rangers—protocol said the commanders of all the allied contingents should be there for this. Technically she should have been riding out from the castle with the other heads of state, but *damned* if she'd spend even one night beneath the same roof as the widow and partner-in-crime of her husband's killer.

And since Mike killed Norman Arminger too, I don't think Sandra Arminger feels very hospitable where I'm concerned, either. Though she'd hide it faultlessly.

Then Chuck began to sing, very softly indeed beneath the crowd-noise, his eyes on the splendors of Castle Todenangst and the feudal state of the party riding out through the gates amid caracoling horses and the snap of lance-pennants:

"Em Eye Cee, Kay Eee Wy, Em Oh You Ess Eee . . ."

He was a lean sinewy man in his early fifties, with thinning sandy hair and long muscular legs showing beneath his kilt, and he'd been around thirty when the Change struck. It took Eric Larsson and his sister a bit longer to recognize the tune; the Bearkiller leaders had been only eighteen then, forty now. Eric coughed into a fist like an oak maul encased in a steel gauntlet to conceal his initial bellow of laughter, the plates of his composite armor rattling, and Signe shot them both a scandalized look.

Well, yes, it does *all have a touch of Disney, but this isn't the moment!*

And that castle wasn't a fantasy for children made of plaster and lath; the walls were very real mass-concrete many yards thick, and the towers held murder machines and flame throwers and lots of completely serious soldiers with spears and swords meant for use, not show. If you had the men-at-arms, you got to decide what constituted reality.

Eric grinned, a piratical expression with his Vandyke beard and yellow locks flowing to his armored shoulders. A golden hoop earring glittered in his right ear.

"Says the man in a kilt and a feathered bonnet," he

said to the Mackenzie Armsman. "Not to mention a golden torc."

Chuck snorted. "Hey, the torc's just our equivalent of a wedding ring, nowadays. And I was doing this stuff"— his fingers tapped the hilt of his sword—"when I was eighteen."

"Geezer! So was I, but by then it was real life, not fantasy," Eric said cheerfully.

"Says the man whose younger sister thinks she's the great-granddaughter of Aragorn son of Arathorn and Arwen Undomiel," Chuck shot back.

"It's not quite *that* bad; she just thinks she's their *remote* descendant," Signe said. "Anyway, we Larssons *do* come from a very ancient line of sand and gravel magnates in the eastern part of Middle-earth."

"I thought your folks made their money off wheat and timber here in Oregon," Chuck said. "Back about a hundred years pre-Change."

"Yeah, but before then we farmed sand and broke our plows on rocks in Småland for Freya-knows-how-many *thousands* of years."

Eric inclined the ostrich-feather plumes of his dress helmet towards the Dúnedain banner for an instant.

"Chuck, did I ever tell you the one I made up for Astrid, back before the Change?"

He whispered; they were getting closer, even with the general hubbub.

"No, Eric, I don't think you did. But feel free."

As softly, Eric went on:

> *"Ho, Tom Bombadil!*
> *Tom Bumboydildo!"*

"*Shut* up," Signe said, suppressing an unwilling smile. "Besides, you need to dance and click your heels with that simpering look and the daisy stuck up your nose, for the full effect."

The Bearkiller banner was borne by Bill Larsson, Eric's eldest son; he was nearly as tall as his father, with hair of brown curls and a skin the color of lightly toasted wheat bread and just this year the brand of an A-lister between his brows. He exchanged a look with Mike Havel Jr.; the fourteen-year-old rolled his eyes slightly despite the tight discipline of the Outfit his father had founded. They were both obviously wondering *what* the hell their elders were talking about. Chuck's foster son Oak carried the Clan's moon-and-antlers flag; he was thirty-one, and about as bewildered.

Changelings, Signe Havel thought, with fond exasperation.

And a stab of pain. Even that slight tilt to Mike's head and the habit of raising a single eyebrow was so like his father . . .

They fell in beside Astrid and the others. *And she's being the Noble, Stern, Wise, Grave, Kindly Leader,* Signe thought as she took in her younger sister's pose. *Well, she* can *carry it off with style. A bull-goose loony she may be, but she's still a Larsson.*

Astrid exchanged a single regal nod as Sandra Arminger approached; they were both sovereigns. Cardinal-Archbishop Maxwell raised his crosier and signed the air in blessing; Juniper Mackenzie did the same with her staff topped with the Triple Moon—she was in a formal arsaid today, and jeweled belt and headband with the sign of the Crescent Moon on her brow. The others made brief greeting, but this was a military occasion, strictly speaking.

Then Tiphaine went down on both knees before her sovereign. She drew her longsword, kissed the cross the hilt made, and then raised the blade on the palms of her gloved hands.

"My liege, my sword is yours, and all my faith and obedience, under God."

Sandra took it—a little awkwardly, since she was petite and had never been a warrior of any sort. She turned to Astrid and extended the blade.

"My Grand Constable's sword I tender to you, Lady Astrid of the Dúnedain Rangers, in token of your command of this army."

She had a high voice, but trained to carry by a generation of public events. Tiphaine rose and then went down on one knee facing Astrid—the lesser salute to a ruler not her own, and done with liquid grace despite the sixty pounds of armor. Astrid's eyes met hers for a moment; then the Ranger leader swung the sword with casual expertise in a shimmering arc that ended with it presented to Tiphaine hilt-first.

The Grand Constable took the blade and sheathed it without glancing down. "Lady Astrid, at my ruler's order I tender you my obedience and faith so long as this alliance shall last; so help me God."

She extended her hands, palm pressed to palm, and Astrid took them between her own:

"Grand Constable d'Ath, so long as this alliance shall last, I acknowledge you as second-in-command of this army, and in my absence or if I should fall, its commander. So witness the Lord Manwë and the Lady Varda, and the One Who is above all."

Signe's eyes went a little wider. That *hadn't* been on the agenda! Sandra's expression mirrored her own, under a control that couldn't be called *iron* because it was far too supple.

Now, that was *a smart political move, little sister,* Signe thought grudgingly. *And you did it despite the fact that you hate Tiphaine as much as I do Sandra . . . and unlike Sandra, Tiphaine hates you right back. She's not nearly as emotionless as you'd think, underneath that* Icy Elegant Killer Dyke *facade.*

The Association contingent raised a cheer, hammering their weapons on their shields and shouting out, "Lady d'Ath! Lady d'Ath!" The sound grew as the news spread to those out of earshot; the harsh male chorus echoed back from the walls of the castle, and frightened skeins of wildfowl into flight from the Willamette behind them, rising like black beaded strings into the cloudless sky.

It sounded a lot like *Lady Death*, which was Tiphaine's nickname in Portland's domains.

The cheer gradually swept down the ranks, since it

wouldn't do to leave the Protectorate troops on their own. Each group joined in its own fashion—you could tell the banshee shrieks of the Mackenzies as soon as they came in, or the Bearkiller growl of *Ooo-rah*. And the warrior Benedictines of the Order of the Shield sang a few stanzas of a military hymn instead of just yelling:

"Kyrie Eleison, down the road we all must follow—"

The other leaders made their variations on the same speech as Sandra, and the commanders of the forces they'd contributed did homage to Astrid; Eric was grave as he went to one knee and put his hands between hers—Signe had been half afraid that he'd absently call their younger sibling *sis* or *peanut*. As the affair wound up Sandra looked aside.

"Isn't that your son, Lady Signe? He's the living image of his father these days."

"Yes," Signe said brusquely. "He is."

And I have him and his four sisters, Signe thought, and knew Sandra was thinking it as well. *While your precious singleton Mathilda is off East of the mountains in the Goddess-knows-what peril. I don't wish* Rudi *any ill . . . not anymore, and I love Ritva and Mary even if they're difficult and prickly. But* your *daughter, on the other hand, is all you've got . . .*

"A handsome lad, but then, his father was the most beautiful man I'd ever seen, in an extremely masculine way. In fact young Mike looks a great deal like Rudi. With less red in the hair, of course," Sandra went on politely.

Ouch, Signe thought.

It was true, too; Mike had been Rudi's blood-father. That brief encounter with Juniper Mackenzie had been before they were married, but . . .

Don't try to get into a meaner-than-thou contrast with the Spider of the Silver Tower, she reminded herself.

"He'll be going East with your brother?" Sandra went on.

"Yes," Signe said. "He's a military apprentice now, and among the best of his year."

And this isn't a time when a ruler can keep himself safe, she thought. *I don't wish Rudi ill, but my son will have his own heritage. And to do that, he has to have experience and to gain it in front of the other warriors.*

"Ah, yes, that Spartan-style thing you Bearkillers have," Sandra said smoothly, looking at her out of the corners of her brown eyes. "I pray that every mother's child shall return safely."

It isn't a time like that, Signe thought, controlling her glare. *But, oh, how I wish it was!*

> *"Hey, hey, laddie-o*
> *Paint your face and string your bow!"*

Juniper Mackenzie waved as she passed by the campfire where they were roaring out the old marching song to a skirl of pipes and a hammer of drums. The air in the Mackenzie encampment beneath Castle Todenangst was thick with the smell of woodsmoke and grilling food and the incidental odors that even a cleanly folk couldn't avoid, as the sun fell westward behind the towers in a blaze of black and golden clouds above the Coast Range. It had been a warm afternoon, perfect for the speeches and rites; she and Judy Barstow were still in their robes of ceremony as High Priestesses and carrying their staffs.

"This is how it starts," she said sadly.

"Hopefully, it will be over soon, at least this first phase," her handfasted man, Nigel, said beside her. "Though I hesitate to say *Home before Christmas* . . . or Yule. That prediction hasn't got a happy history."

"Wars are always easier to start than end," Juniper agreed, and sighed. "Sure, and you can start them yourself, but the other side must agree for the dance to stop. And their outcomes are never certain. If it weren't for all that, and the waste and pain and grief and sorrow and general wicked black ugliness, it's a splendid and glorious thing war would be."

"Hey, hey, lassie-o
Plant the stake and face the foe!
What use the lance and the golden rowel
As their faces turn white at the Clan's wolf-howl?"

She winced slightly; that was a song from the War of the Eye, and not too tactful now considering the time, place and circumstance. Though there were Protectorate folk mingling among the Mackenzies. One dark young squire was even dancing to the beat of the war-chant—the golden bells on his shoes twinkling in the air as he did what the old world would have called a breakdance and clansfolk no older clapped and cheered him on.

"They're all so *young*," she said despairingly.

"You asked for volunteers," Chuck Barstow said with infuriating reasonableness, and his wife Judy nodded. "So you get the young ones who don't have kids and crofts depending on them."

"They weren't *born* yet when the Change came."

"Or near as no matter. Even Oak"—his foster son—"doesn't remember the old world much, and he was . . . what, nine, when we found that school bus on the way here?" A shrug. "It's all easier for the Changelings."

Judy Barstow silently reached over and put a hand on her shoulder; Juniper covered it with her own for an instant, grateful for her oldest friend's presence.

Only a scattering of the warriors were old enough to have fought in the War of the Eye, mostly the bow-captains, and they were quieter. The two couples passed another fire where the youngsters were kneeling in pairs, touching up the savage patterns swirling across their faces and bodies and limbs in soot black and leaf green, henna crimson and saffron gold.

"*That's* a bit early," Chuck said dryly. "They're going to run out of war-paint before there's any fighting, if they keep *that* up every day."

One tall girl among them suddenly sprang up and snatched a sword free, whirling naked into a battle dance around the fire with the sharp steel flashing. Her painted face contorted as she leapt and lunged, her eyes blank and exalted as they stared beyond the Veil, graceful and deadly as the cougar whose catamount shriek she gave. Her blade-mates joined her, screaming out the calls of their totem beasts, their bare feet stamping the measure as they invited those spirits to take possession on the road to battle.

Juniper shivered slightly, watching the snarling faces and the steel that flashed bloodred in the light of the dying sun.

"Oh Powers of Earth and Sky, what is it that you've brought back, to run wild once more upon the ridge of the world?" she said softly. "You know, I don't understand the younger generation. I love them, but even Rudi . . . we were never as strange to *our* parents."

"I don't *think* so," Judy said dryly; her old friend had always had that gift of bringing her back to earth. "But they and we didn't have the Change between us. You'd have to skip back quite a few more generations to get that, eh? Go far enough back, and we'd be the odd ones, not the Changelings."

"They . . . they *accept* things in a way we didn't," Juniper said.

Her companions all nodded.

"They speak English, but they don't speak our language. When they say 'time' or 'death' or 'rebirth,' it means something different from the way we used the words," Judy said.

Death . . . how many of these happy youngsters will lie stark and dead in a month's time, all their fierceness and beauty gone too soon? Juniper thought. *And rebirth, yes, but death comes first, and we are right to fear it, for it is dreadful to pass through the dark gate, even if you know what waits beyond.*

They walked beyond the fires and the encampment, into the woods that lay along the river, parkland kept as a pleasaunce for the castle-dwellers of noble rank, a pretty amendment of nature. Far eastward the tiny perfect white cone of Mt. Hood caught the dying sun for an instant, flushing pink and then fading away as the first stars appeared.

A few birds sang, and the river ran slow beneath the willows, glimpsed through the big oaks of the old parkland, some tangled with green English ivy. They came to a clearing where green grass was starred with red paintbrush, green-sweet beneath the cooler forest smell; a bank of poison oak had been turned fire-red by last week's early frost. A doe and two fawns were grazing there, half a hundred yards away; the mother raised her head sharply, then bent again as she saw no movement. There was an added stillness as the humans withdrew their presence, a trick they all knew well.

Judy nudged Juniper softly and leaned close to say quietly:

"Left," she whispered, and Chuck and Nigel froze as well, with the smooth alertness of warriors and hunters.

Juniper turned her head in that direction and almost started in surprise. Not far along the forest edge was Chuck and Judy's son Oak, and his wife, Devorgill, and their children, who'd come along to see him off. One was a baby at the breast, and there was his daughter Lutra and his son Laere. Oak was looking at his parents and grinning. As far as looks went he might have been Chuck's blood-child, a big rangy-muscular man a little past thirty, with long tawny mustaches that dropped past his shaven chin and a shaggy shoulder-length mane bleached by the harvest suns that had tanned his body to the color of his name-wood.

That showed because he and Devorgill were wearing only their kilts and sandals and a little body paint—his was a badger's head on his chest—while the children went naked and barefoot, as young Mackenzies often did in warm weather. They had a basket on the ancient but well-maintained rustic picnic table and the remains of a meal set out on it, a chance to take one last supper together without the bustle of the camp or the strained formalities of the castle. The adults' longbows and quivers and sword belts leaned against an alder behind them, and a long-headed battle spear, though it would be a mad bandit indeed who dared to come *here*. Still, habits learned in the years of the great dying stuck hard and got passed down.

Juniper nodded back. The children's gaze stayed fixed on the spotted coats of the June-born fawns, who peered about at the world big-eyed. She could hear the low whisper of Laere's five-year-old voice as he asked:

"Are you going to hunt them, Dad? There are an awful lot of people here the now, they must need an awful lot of food too."

"No, boyo, that I will not, and for two reasons," Oak said.

Devorgill moved, laying a gentle finger on Lutra's mouth as the girl started to burst forth with the answer before her younger brother. Oak went on, in the same low voice:

"When's it lawful to hunt, my little Laere?"

The boy was his father in miniature and minus twenty-odd years; his hair was a mop of white tow and his eyes brilliant blue in his freckled, summer-darkened face as he frowned in thought.

"For food ... an' ... an' when they try to eat our gardens?"

His mother spoke: "That's true; but you must also never hunt a doe in fawn, or any deer less than a year old. That brings a curse, unless you're starving and make a special rite. The Mother's hand is over them."

Young Lutra nodded, making the dark brown hair that fell in a thong-bound horsetail to the small of her back bounce. She spoke quietly:

"And this is a place that's never hunted, like a *nemed*, so they're not man-wary and it's *geasa* to kill here, sure and it is."

Laere stuck his tongue out at her, and she replied in kind, being all of five years older herself.

"But we can go and visit them in peace today," Oak said, smiling down at them with a warm delight on his rugged face. "The wind's from them to us. Come, and let's see if you can walk *very quietly*. Step when I do, and be as careful as mice!"

He took each by the hand, winking at his wife—and at Juniper and Sir Nigel and his own parents.

Father, son and daughter walked out into the dappled, darkening shade of the clearing, still lit by a few beams of the setting sun slanting like orange fire through the tall trees. Both children walked softly, but no more so than their woods-wise father's hundred-and-eighty pounds of bone and hard muscle. He kept the deer in focus but without meeting their eyes when their heads turned, avoiding a predator's fixed gaze. Each step flowed like slow water, and whenever their heads came up and scanned he stopped smoothly without the least betraying jerk, as natural as grass swaying in the wind. The children followed his movements intently.

The doe walked a little away from the fawns, her tail quivering, her reddish brown coat fading to darkness as the light failed. Closer . . .

Lutra dropped her father's hand and reached out. A fawn sniffed her fingers, began to dodge, then stopped as she gently ran her hand down its neck. It tilted its head and looked at her oddly as if wondering what she was. Laere tried to do the same with the other, but he moved a little too sharply. It shied, and a stick crackled beneath its hooves; the doe brought her head up and made a sharp bleating sound.

Juniper chuckled a little then as the deer bounded away, in arcs that made them seem like weightless shadows that vanished under the trees. The two children stood waving and calling farewells for a moment, then came back to their blankets.

"That's her saying—*Great Goddess, foolish child, it's a* human!" Juniper said, and the others laughed as her singer's voice made it sound very like the doe's bleat. "*They'll eat you! Will you be friends with a* wolf *next*?"

"Grandma!" Laere said, and charged past Juniper to hug Judy around the waist and be lifted up on her hip and given a smacking kiss.

"Merry met," Juniper said to Devorgill and her children and her man.

That was a little formal for people who lived in Dun Juniper year-round, but Oak *was* off to war tomorrow. It would have been inconceivable for the son of the Clan's Chief Armsman not to march with the warband, and Oak was bow-captain for Dun Juniper's own contingent.

"Merry met, Lady Juniper," they replied.

Lutra had hair as seal brown as her mother's and eyes the dark green of fir needles; she made a solemn reverence, bowing her head with hands pressed together and thumbs beneath her chin. That was a little *too* formal for the occasion, but the girl was obviously feeling very adult and knowledgeable today.

"Dad says I can go hunting with him next year," Laere said proudly, trotting back to stand by the man.

"To help with the camp chores," Oak said firmly; his hand ruffled the boy's head in a rough caress. "With your sister. Neither of you is old enough to hunt yet, not for years, not until you can make a kill quick and sure."

Lutra nodded. "You know the song of the law, Laere," she said.

Laere looked like he'd rather stick his tongue out at his sister once more for playing at old-and-wise *again*, or possibly pull her hair this time, but had too much in the way of manners to do so in front of the two awesome old women with their staffs. Juniper smiled at him and sang softly, just a snatch of it:

> *"Let the death be clean as life's release*
> *So we show our honor to the beast*
> *For your own death you will understand*
> *When you hold life's blood within your hand—"*

The boy smiled back and continued in a pure treble:

> *"Though we draw the bow an' we w-w . . . uh . . ."*

His father and mother came in to help him as he wobbled:

"—and we wield the blade
We respect the Law the Gods have made;
For we know not when the shadows fall,
And the Huntsman comes to claim us all."

"And the shadows *have* fallen, and now we'd best go back to the camp, before it gets too dark and you two take a chill," Devorgill said, burping her youngest and wiping up the results with a cloth. "Merry part till later, mother Judy, Lady Juniper."

They walked off. As they passed, Juniper could hear Laere talking to his father:

"I wish I *was* old enough to go with you and Grand-dad to the war! I'd take a *hundred* heads, like the Hound did when Maeve invaded Ulster! Chop-chop-chop!"

His sister's outraged tones faded through the forest: "*Laere!* You bloodthirsty little brute of a boy! That's just in the stories! It's *geasa* now!"

Juniper looked up, and saw the first stars hovering over the snowpeaks of the Cascades.

"And we must go back to the castle, and smile and look brave at the feast," she said. "What a fraud I feel!"

Nigel faced her as she turned. "My dear," he said, putting a hand beneath her chin and kissing her. "You are without doubt the bravest of us all."

"He *is*?" BD said, her weathered, wrinkled face blank for an instant. "*Murdoch* is a spy for Lady Sandra?"

Astrid Larsson leaned back in the chair and nodded—not smugly, she hoped. The little chamber was *very* private, with only one narrow slit window high up on the curving outer wall; Castle Todenangst was full of places like that, nooks and crannies you could get to without anyone being the wiser and leave unnoticed.

Unless someone's watching from a secret passage, of course. I think Sandra did a lot of the detail work on the plans for this castle.

The light was good, gas-lamps with incandescent mantles, unaccustomed brilliance for an hour this late and reflecting off wainscoting of blond oak. There was a table of fine polished mahogany, a few chairs, a rug, and a bottle of wine and glasses by a bowl of raisins and walnuts and hazelnuts. Despite the charming little fireplace with its tiled surround of hummingbirds and meadowlarks it was a bit oppressive after a life spent mostly in the wilds or on the open roads, or at most in Stardell Hall with its loose scatter of homes through forest.

She could feel the uncounted tons of steel and concrete above, almost *smell* them under the odors of wine and burning fir-wood. And imagine the dungeons below, and the great foundations where the Fortress of Death-Anguish gripped the soil of the land.

But there are advantages, she thought. *Privacy seems easier to come by amid many people. Odd.*

She sipped at her glass of wine and watched the older woman think.

"He's good, then," BD said. "I've dealt with Murdoch and Sons every time I swung out that far East, and I'd never suspected he was her man in Pendleton."

BD was from the Kyklos, a scatter of independent villages around Silverton, not far north of the main Dúnedain holding in Mithrilwood. Besides being a High Priestess of the Old Religion she ran the Plodding Pony service, which delivered high-value freight over much of Oregon, and which had employed Rangers as escorts almost as long as there had been Rangers in this Age of the world. That sort of business led to the collection of information as naturally as breathing. It also made you a shrewd judge of character.

Astrid went on: "Murdoch has been working for Sandra since before the War of the Eye. She planted him in Pendleton when we made the Protectorate withdraw from the area, after her husband was killed. And he's got . . . connections there. Sort of an underground."

BD looked down at the map and her eyebrows shot up. "*I'll* say! But how are you going to use them?"

Astrid shrugged. "I'm not altogether sure," she said. "But I'm a little uneasy about just marching up to Pendleton's walls and telling them to surrender so we can guard them against Boise and the CUT whether they like it or not. We can't even *prove* that either power is planning to move on them."

"You don't think you can beat the Pendleton Round-Up?"

"I don't *want* to beat them in a stand-up battle and I certainly don't want to burn down the city or lay the countryside waste. We Rangers generally don't go in for mass head butting. It's . . . crude. And Pendleton's just badly governed, not *evil* like the CUT and its Dark . . . Prophet. Every man we kill will be one who isn't on our side later, in the real war, when Rudi returns with the Sword. We ought to be able to make *something* of an asset like this Murdoch and his . . . connections."

She leaned forward. "You've been there in person. Tell me about the Pendleton Bossman, Carl Peters. The things that don't get into written reports."

CHAPTER FIVE

Cold falls the night where nothing sounds
Save weeping and the grief of the weak
Hot his heart and ready his hand
He and his companions sworn and trusty
Blade and bow ready for avenging of wrongs
Though wiser it were to think of the Sword
That waited where the Lady had bidden—

From: *The Song of Bear and Raven*
Attributed to Fiorbhinn Mackenzie, 1st century CY

Caravan, Rudi Mackenzie thought. *They're putting together a big one, for a place that size. Or a big one's passing through. Not about to leave just now, though.*

They were a lot farther north and closer to the edge of the mountains now; the stark foothills of the Pioneers were just ahead on the other side of Silver Creek, mostly summer-bleached grass up steep slopes, with shallow valleys leading northward. A little higher he could see groves of quaking aspen—and, alarmingly, some of them were beginning to turn, a hint of gold where none should shine. They had to get over the Rockies, and *soon*, if they weren't to risk being hit by bad snowstorms in the passes. The ones they could use, at least; the lower ones would be strongly garrisoned by the Prophet's men, or even fortified.

Maybe we should *have headed south through Nevada and tried the mountains there!*

The creek was about a mile away, flowing from west to east and flanked by a narrow band of fields watered through irrigation channels. Most of them were dun yellow reaped grain with dust smoking off the stubble at this time of year, but the alfalfa was so deep a green that it seemed to hum, and there were fields of potatoes and apple orchards as well. Split-rail fences marked off the cultivated land, an island in a huge rolling wilderness of lava beds and gritty sagebrush-dotted soil southward, mountains to the north.

The settlement wasn't large, no bigger than a Mackenzie dun, room for twenty or thirty families if they didn't mind living tight. It had a well-kept fifteen-foot rammed-earth wall on a fieldstone base, topped with a sloping roof of timber and sheet metal, with one square tower beside a gate. Barns and sheds, corrals and vegetable gardens lay outside, but nothing higher than a man's knee rose within bowshot of the wall. The gate was open, and there were animals and people and wagons milling around before it, and herds of horses under the eye of mounted cowboys moving across pasture and stubble to the north and west.

"Get me Nystrup," he said softly, lowering his binoculars and tapping them thoughtfully on the red-gold stubble on his chin. "I don't like this. There's something wrong."

Ritva nodded. "Not enough people working. Too many horses. And where are their herds? And there should be more smoke from inside the town, too—more cookfires and a couple of smithies."

She ghosted away. A sage grouse walked past Rudi a few minutes later, pecking at a grasshopper, and overhead two hummingbirds fought a dive-and-buzz duel like ill-tempered flying jewelry before flitting off towards the river. Some sort of black-and-white insects were a haze over the creek, almost like slow-motion snow; when he brought the glasses back up he could see the silver forms of trout leaping for them now and then.

The banks of the stream were green with willows and dense with reeds, and blue herons stalked through them with their beaks cocked. Ducks swam on the waters as well, cinnamon teal and mallards.

It would have been a remarkably pleasant-looking place after weeks of short rations and fear, but . . .

Nystrup slid into place beside him. "It's one of our settlements," he said without preliminaries. "About two hundred and fifty people, and it was the center for some outlying ranches; the last big thing to happen here was moving a bunch of people up from Pocatello right after the Change, part of our resettlement program. I don't know how it's fared just recently."

A warm breeze stirred across the land, raising dust devils. It fluttered out a flag from the pole atop the gate tower; a many-rayed sunburst, gold on crimson. The banner of the Church Universal and Triumphant. Below it was a smaller triangular flag, with three triangles outlined in white on blue—some Rancher's brand mark, the personal sigil of whoever commanded the CUT's forces here.

"Well, that answers the question as to how they've fared," Rudi said. "Not well. Ritva, keep watch."

His half sister settled in behind a clump of gray-green rabbitbrush, a tall shaggy plant that had clumps of yellow flowers and smelled like a sweaty saddle. She went still beneath her war cloak; even at only a few feet, and knowing where she was, Rudi found her hard to see.

He eeled backwards on his belly until they were well out of sight before standing. Nystrup turned and made an arm signal; by the time they were back at their cold camp most of the Mormon guerillas were there too, leaving only the minimum perimeter of lookouts.

Rudi glanced at Ingolf. The Easterner shook his head. "I passed a lot farther south than this, when I came west. Around Bear Lake."

"We can swing around them," Mary said. "Move south, then back north to cut the road again."

Rudi shook his head in turn. "We're out of food and we haven't been able to hunt much," he said. "I don't know how they've been able to press us so hard . . . but they have. We've spent more time covering our tracks than running, and we've been running farther north than east."

Silence fell; they were *hungry*, in the way you could only get when you combined not enough food with working hard. Several of the wounded Mormons had died; the hale members of their band weren't weakened much . . . yet.

But we don't have much time before we are, Rudi thought unhappily. *And the horses are losing condition. I wouldn't like to have to rely on them if we had a running fight, or the enemy were in sight and we had to break contact. We need to get them good grazing and rest.*

They might have been able to make more progress if they'd kept all the food they'd had and cut the Mormons loose immediately. On the other hand, that would probably have been bad luck as well as wrong . . . if there was a difference.

Ingolf rubbed his jaw thoughtfully, the cropped beard scritching under his callused fingers. The sight made Rudi's face itch slightly and he consciously stopped himself from imitating the gesture; he hadn't been able to shave for the past week, and the silky stubble was annoying. Plus the hairs came in white along the thin scar on his jaw, making him look ridiculously older than his real not-quite-twenty-three.

"You know, we haven't seen any sheep or cattle or horses around here. But the range has obviously been grazed. Until lately, at least," Ingolf said.

"There's stock in the corrals," Rudi said. "And a *lot* of horses. Hundred, hundred and thirty."

"That would mean fifty or sixty Cutter levies," Ingolf replied. "The Cutter soldiers are mainly Ranchers, or even Rovers"—which meant nomad, more or less—"not full-time fighters like the Sword of the, umm, *false* prophet. They get hives if they don't have at least one remount for every fighting man. It makes them feel pinned down."

Nystrup sighed. "We were always being surprised

by how fast they could move, and how many men they could throw at us," he acknowledged. "It hurt us, and more than once."

"The Church calls them up to fight when they're needed," Ingolf said. "A ranch isn't like a farm—the old people and kids and women can keep it going pretty well for quite a while, at a pinch. Cowboys can make most of their own war gear, too, and their ordinary work is damned good training to fight."

"Besides the horses there were six or seven hundred sheep, maybe half that number of cattle," Rudi went on.

"Not as much as there should be," Nystrup replied. "I've never been here myself, but from the reports and the taxes they paid and the way it looks, this is good land."

Ingolf made a gesture of agreement. "I'd say what's likely happened is that a couple of ranches' or Rover bands' worth of levies hit the place just recently, on their way home. Some of them have already left with part of the stock. The ones there now plan to loot it bare before they leave—they're shorter on craft-workers than you Saints are and they're always short of tools and so forth likewise. I'd say they're about halfway through the process here in . . . Peekaboo?"

"Yes," Nystrup said grimly. "We counted on that, their being backwards, too much during the war, and on their absurd superstitions about gears and machinery." He looked at Ingolf shrewdly. "You have an idea?"

"Sort of. We have to know what's going on in there, and if we can get some supplies and fresh horses for your people, Captain. It would take a pitched battle to fight for them, and we're not in shape for a stand-up fight, and they outnumber us. But if we send in some people who can pass for . . . oh, I don't know, merchants from one of the Plains towns come West to buy up plunder, that sort of thing. There are a few places like that in the Sioux country, tributary to the tribes. Then we could *buy* what we need. Last I heard, the CUT and the Sioux had made peace."

"We don't have much contact with the Sioux," Nystrup said. "The CUT was always between us and them. Most of the Indians in New Deseret are ... were ... friendly and part of our Church. I don't think any of my people could fool the Cutters."

"Well, I've had a *lot* of contact with the Lakota tribes," Ingolf said, with a lopsided smile. "Mostly not too friendly, as in, contact with their arrows and shetes and tomahawks. That was my first war, when our Bossman in Richland sent men to help the Republic of Marshall fight 'em. And later when I was working for some traders in the Nebraska country, I rode guard on a caravan they sent out West, to Newcastle, and I got caught there for the winter. There was this girl ... anyway, I can't pass for a Sioux, but I think I could buffalo outsiders who'd never seen the place into supposing I came from that town."

Rudi felt a broad smile growing. "Sure, and that *is* an idea. You think it's possible?"

"Like I said, most of the Cutter levies are just cowboys, or a few are farmers or townsmen," Ingolf said. "Yeah, they believe in that crazy religion—or say they do, if they're smart, anywhere Corwin controls—and they're suspicious of outsiders, but they're just ... men, otherwise. I saw a fair number the first time I was a prisoner of theirs; they let me out a bit once I'd convinced them I'd swallowed their line of bullshit."

"Well, if we were to try it, certainly you'd have to be one of our spies," Rudi said musingly. He looked around. "Their leader, in fact. I'd be another ..."

Ingolf spoke again: "Three or four men would be the maximum. No less, though. Corwin makes a big noise about how safe their territory is for traders, but nobody travels with a lot of cash all by himself. And there should be a woman—a Mormon woman."

Rudi blinked. "Why?"

"Camo-cover, Rudi. We'd be refugee-traders as well as buying loot in general."

"Slaves, the Cutters call them, don't they? It seems a bit too honest for them."

"Refugees is the word out East, and some places allow that sort of thing; everyone's always short of working hands. Say four men and ten, twelve horses—we'd have the horses to carry stuff. We'd be pretty popular, too; coin's a lot easier to transport, and they'd want to change some of what they've taken into hard cash."

"We don't have any of the CUT's minting," Rudi mused. "Or any from farther East. Boise currency might do at a pinch, but not the Association's or Corvallis."

"The Sioux don't coin, but they do use gold and silver. A bar of gold's a bar of gold. And at the least we could buy up some folks and get them out to their kin, and enough supplies."

Rudi winced a little; he hated the thought of playing slaver even as a deception, but it was a legitimate ruse of war.

"I'll go if they need a woman," Rebecca Nystrup said.

Her cousin opened his mouth, then closed it again. It *was* good protective coloration. Rudi sympathized with him as he visibly suppressed the desire to say that she'd do no such thing—he could scarcely order one of the other women to do it, when his own kin had asked for the nasty, dangerous job.

"I volunteer!" Fred Thurston said.

"Sorry, Fred," Ingolf said. "You'd stand out too much."

Frederick looked at him blankly for an instant, then struck the palm of his hand against his forehead. "Right. Damn, I hadn't thought of that. We haven't gotten far enough away from Boise for people to just take me for myself."

Black folk were even thinner on the ground here in the interior of the Northwest than they were on the Pacific Coast—Mrs. Thurston was Anglo, but her husband's African strain was plain in her son, too plain for him to pass for Hispano or Indian.

And since his father had been ruler of Boise ever since he brought order out of plague and chaos in the first Change Year, the association of *young black man* and *Prince of Boise*—specifically, *fugitive prince with a massive price on his head*—would be all too likely, even for Cutter levies from beyond the Rockies. Their leaders at least would have some familiarity with local politics.

Rudi ran the rest of his band through his mind. They couldn't take any of their own women; Cutter females were close-kept, even more so than in the Protectorate back home. Which left . . .

"Edain . . . and Odard, I think," Rudi said. "Would Edain's accent pass? Or mine, for that matter?"

"Sure," Ingolf said. "You get all sorts of funny ways of talking in little pockets and backwater settlements, nobody can keep track of them all. These Montanans all sound like hicks with head colds to me anyway. You'll have to leave the skirts"—he grinned at Edain's bristle—"pardon me, the kilts, behind. Odard's OK too—you could pass for part-Injun, my lord Baron. Most of the folks who call themselves Sioux look pretty much like white-eyes these days, mostly because they *are* white-eyes, but the important families are likely to have the old blood."

Odard Liu nodded; his father had been half-Chinese, and it showed in his coarse crow-black hair, high cheek-bones and the fold at the corners of his blue eyes. Father Ignatius had similar looks save for black eyes, courtesy of a grandmother from Vietnam, but his tonsure wasn't the only thing that made him too unmistakably a Christian cleric.

"Happy to volunteer," the Association noble said dryly. "Even ex-post-facto."

Mathilda snorted. "You volunteered for everything when you joined up, Odard."

He gave her a charming smile, and a courtly sweeping bow that went oddly with his grimy wool and leather outfit and shapeless floppy-brimmed canvas hat. Somehow it evoked the image of the impeccable court fashion he delighted in at home.

"That is most true, Your Highness. My sword is ever at my lady's service."

Ingolf made a passable imitation of the bow himself

as she blushed and cleared her throat. He spoke briskly: "You can be the Injun prince, if you want, Odard. It'd be likely we'd have a chief's son along, if the local tribe where we came from were putting up part of the money."

"No time like the present," Rudi said, looking up; six hours to sunset. "We'll have to have a set of signals—"

"Stop right there, strangers!"

The words were backed up by half-a-dozen stiff horn and sinew horseman's bows drawn to the ear. Ingolf let his balance shift back a bit, and Boy halted between one pace and the next; his favorite mount had a lot of quarter horse in his bloodline, and would pass anywhere in the plains-and-mountain country. Rudi managed that as well, and Edain, which Ingolf had worried about—the younger clansman's horsemanship had improved over the past couple of months, enough to pass for a city-man from Newcastle. Odard had mastered the cow-country style too, and it was different from the long-stirrup Portland seat. At least he'd been brought up on horseback, which was something you couldn't counterfeit.

One thing that wouldn't pass was a Sioux who couldn't ride, he knew.

Everyone in their party raised open hands in the peace gesture; except for Rebecca Nystrup, of course, but hers were handcuffed, with the chain looped through a ring on her saddlebow. The Cutters eased off on their draws, which was reassuring—it was all too easy to let a bowstring roll off your fingertips if you held it too long. An arrow in the face killed you just as dead whether it was intentional or not.

The leader of the patrol was in his thirties and looked much older, with a plainsman's wrinkles and a nose that had been damaged by frostbite once, leaving part of a nostril missing. The others could have been his brothers, cousins, or even his son if you counted one in his midteens. Most of them wore simple boiled-leather breastplates with the Church Universal and Triumphant's sunburst on it over thin sheepskin jackets, though the leader had a mail-shirt instead, and their metal-strapped leather helmets were at their saddlebows, traded for broad-brimmed hats in the hot sun.

All of them had knives, tomahawks and heavy-bladed shetes at their waists, quivers full of arrows over their backs, and round hide shields and lariats hung from their saddles. And a powerful aroma, the harsh rank musk-sweat of men who lived on meat and milk and hadn't had occasion to wash themselves or their clothes lately, added to horse and leather and iron greased with tallow and the odor of lank straggly hair of various shades. Several had minor wounds that looked fresh but not immediate. Their equipment was well made and beautifully cared for, though, and their horses glowed with health and careful tending.

Ingolf held up his hands and smiled. "We're peaceful traders, men of the Dictations," he said.

Peaceful but too tough to rob conveniently, was conveyed by his looks and gear, and that of the men behind him. Swapping around among the nine comrades and the Mormon guerillas had given them suitable equipment, suitably varied. Even Garbh helped with the picture, her massive shaggy barrel-shaped head held low and showing her teeth just slightly at the strangers after Edain called her sharply to heel.

"You're of the Faith?" the leader said, his eyes probing. Over his shoulder: "Jack, Terry, backtrack 'em a couple of miles. Keep your eyes open and check there aren't any more. There's all sorts of buzzards circlin' around hereabouts."

Two of the Cutters reined around and galloped eastward down the remains of US 20, riding on the old graveled shoulders of the road to spare their horses' hooves from the cracked, frost-heaved asphalt that was breaking up in pale chunks. Ingolf went on:

"No, we're not of your Church, but we have permission to travel in the Church's lands by the Prophet's treaty with the *Oceti Sakowin.* We're out of Newcastle, which is an ally of the Seven Council Fires."

Ally meant *pays the Sioux off so they don't raid,*

of course, but a man from there would use the polite phrasing. Ingolf nodded towards Odard, who managed to look haughty enough for a modern-day Sioux chieftain—something that came naturally to him—and stared over the Cutters' heads. People who didn't know Indians well tended to think they were impassive; in the Richlander's experience, they were as cheerful and chatty as most folk, unless they thought the occasion called for solemnity.

Which this does. But don't overdo it, Odard.

Ingolf went on:

"This is the worthy *itancan*"—which meant *chief*, roughly—"*Wahuk'eza Washte*, Good Lance."

Odard had insisted on that one when Ingolf ran him through a list of Sioux names, although the suggestions from the rest had started with *Two Dogs Fucking* from the twins and gone downhill from there.

"He's here to, ah, watch over his people's interests in this trading venture."

Odard lifted a hand with the palm out, made a surly grunting sound, and said the Lakota equivalent of *Hello, how do you do?*, as he'd been carefully coached:

"*Háu kola! Doe ksh kay ya oun hey?*"

To Ingolf's horror, the Cutter leader raised his hand in a similar gesture and replied:

"*Háu kola! Wakantanka kici un.*"

Which meant *Hello, and may the Great Spirit bless you*, and just about exhausted Ingolf's knowledge of the language as well unless you counted swear words and phrases you learned on campaign, like *Reach for the sky!*, *Where are the warriors?* and *Give me your money/horse/weapons/food*.

Sweat broke out on his forehead, prickling through the coating of dust; this wasn't *fair*. Most of the people who *rode* with the tribes and called themselves Sioux didn't actually speak it, apart from a few words they threw into the more usual English to sound authentic— the same reason they tended to go in for leather and beads and feathers even more than the tribesmen with more of the old blood. To run into a non-Indian who actually *knew* the language when their own pretend-Indian didn't would be . . .

Just like the rest of my luck since I first met Kuttner. Like meeting Saba and having her die the same night.

He hid a shudder; priests had told him—including ones he respected—that there was no such thing as fate, that there was only a man's choices and the will of God. But there were times when he thought he *was* cursed, and not only him, but anyone he cared for. Rudi's hand made the smallest of gestures towards the hilt of his borrowed shete. But if it came to a fight, they'd almost certainly die. Ingolf forced himself not to gasp with relief when the Cutter chieftain smiled and went on:

"The Prophet says we're to treat all you of the Seven Council Fires as brothers, now that we're at peace with the Lakota tribes. May you come to the truth of the Dictations! I'm Jed Smith, Rancher of Rippling Waters in Havre District, and these're my kin and my riders."

Upper Missouri River, Ingolf thought. *Damn, that's pretty close to the frontier between the CUT and the Lakota. Just our luck. A long way north of Newcastle, though, thank the saints!*

Then Jed went on casually: "You'd be kin of the mayor down in Newcastle?"

"Larry McAllister?" Ingolf said, feeling the beads of sweat start up again.

Thank God I actually stayed there and not so long ago!

Aloud he went on, equally relaxed: "No, but my father's a good friend of his—he sponsored us when Dad moved in from Casper, right after the Change."

Good friend and *sponsored* meant someone who got protection in return for favors and political backing . . . which in Newcastle involved showing up with your shield and shete from time to time.

What did Father Ignatius say . . . right, client *and* patron.

Jed Smith nodded, satisfied. Ingolf made the introductions under their assumed names. The Montanan went on:

"What're you trading for? Doesn't look like you have much to trade with, unless it's the crowbait remuda you got there or—"

He indicated Rebecca with a jerk of his head, though he'd politely kept his eyes from her face; the girl was in ordinary overalls, but had a CUT-style kerchief hiding most of her fair hair. Ingolf smiled back and indicated her with a salesman's sweep of his hand:

"No, we're buying and we're paying in bullion. Anything you brave soldiers of the Church might have picked up. Cutlery, cloth, wine—"

"No chance of that here! The misbelievers don't drink it, or even beer or whiskey or applejack. I haven't tasted wine but once myself—traded West from Iowa."

Ingolf nodded. "But mostly we're buying refugees, like this girl here. Skilled workers, if we can get them. *Slaves*, you say, don't you, instead of *refugee*?"

Jed nodded. "That's the word in the Dictations."

Just then Jack and Terry rode back up. "Same horses for miles back," one of them said, pointing behind him with his bow. "We checked on the hoof marks. Nobody joinin' or leavin'."

The other scout spoke to Ingolf:

"But they had good stock and tools here. They make stuff you wouldn't believe was new instead of salvage. And plenty of right pretty gals, too, even if they're sulky. We kilt all the grown men, o' course."

Ingolf sighed as if he'd been expecting that and regretted it. Even if his regret wasn't for the reasons his audience assumed, he *had* expected it. Ranchers didn't need masses of field labor, and a man you couldn't trust to ride the range alone and armed was useless as a cowboy. Women did most of the processing work on a ranch, though—tanning, leatherworking, weaving, milking, whatever—and they were easier to keep. If nothing else their children pinned them down, and by Cutter custom the children were free if they took the Church Universal and Triumphant's faith when they came of age.

"Shut up, Jack, y'damned pup," Jed said crossly; at a guess, he was afraid his subordinate would lower prices by prattling about how much they'd gained. "You run your mouth too much."

In friendly wise he went on: "That's a nice one you picked up there, Mr. Vogeler. Lively in the bedroll? She's quite a looker, yes indeed. How much did you pay for her? Get her from someone heading home?"

"That's right. Don't know what she's like in the sack," Ingolf said casually. "Yeah, she's easy on the eyes, but she's also a good weaver, cloth and rugs both, and a cheese-maker, which is what I was looking for. Refugee ass . . . *slave*, you folks say . . . is cheap and looks don't last, but good cheddar cheese or cloth always fetches a price. We paid forty-five dollars for her, cash money—weighed out silver, that's easier than coin for big purchases."

He could see the Rancher mentally adding half again to that. Odard spoke up, making a sweeping gesture at the same time:

"She will go to the tipis of my people. I have spoken. Ugh."

Jesus, don't play it too heavy, Ingolf thought, but the Cutter leader nodded. *OK, a lot of Sioux do talk like that. 'Cause they think people expect it, I suppose.*

"As you please, Chief," Smith said. "The Dictations say a man may do as he wants with his own within the law, right? C'mon, then, you Newcastle men, and you, Chief Good Lance. Plenty of room for lodgings and I hope you'll do fine business here."

He grinned; combined with the mutilated nose and the straggly beard, it looked fairly alarming as he went on:

"*We* surely did!"

Picabo had been a little farming and tourist hamlet before the Change. The Mormons had walled it in, and added more buildings—settlements within a defensive perimeter were always as crowded as people could bear, to keep the length of rampart that had to be held as short as possible. Most of the buildings were homes, thick whitewashed adobe on the first story, white-painted frame covered in clapboards above, with steep-pitched shingle roofs.

Rudi noticed that they'd also added the sort of touches Mackenzies would, if more tidy and less flamboyant— window boxes and plantings of flowers, trees and bushes along the streets, a small playground with slides and swings, buildings that would have been their church and school. The village had piped water from a tank on salvaged metal legs with a whirring wind-pump atop it, but irrigation channels also tinkled pleasantly in stone-lined ditches on either side of the streets, to water the fruit and blossoms and herbs. None of the white farmhouses or workshops had burned down . . .

"Nothing got torched when you took it?" Rudi asked one of the Cutters.

The man riding next to the Mackenzie chieftain was about his own age or a few years younger; it was hard to tell exactly, with the weathering of their harsh climate making them all look older to eyes reared in the gentle Willamette country. Not many of the Cutters were over thirty, and half were in their teens. This one had shaggy black hair, a wispy young beard, green eyes and a missing front tooth; he cackled laughter at the question.

Jack, Rudi thought, remembering his name.

"Nope, we didn't fire a single lit-up arrow," the young plainsman said boastfully.

Even a modest wall with a fighting platform behind it could give defenders a big advantage. Picabo's had a roofed hoarding as well. If you didn't have a modern siege train, the quickest and easiest way to storm a defended town was to shoot fire arrows over the wall into the roofs and then rush the defenses while folk turned aside to fight the fire, as they must. And there was no sign of any siege equipment more sophisticated than a lariat or improvised ladder among this band of CUT levies.

"That must have taken some doing," Rudi prompted. *And you like to talk, Jack,* he added coldly to himself.

Jack laughed and slapped his thigh; a couple of his

friends chuckled too, although a few of the older men rolled their eyes at his chatter.

"It was dead easy, friend!"

"How did you get over the wall, then?" Rudi went on.

A caravan guard was the next thing to a soldier, and the question was natural.

"That's Uncle Jed for you," Jack laughed gleefully. "Said we could get ashes and dead bones at home without the bother of fightin' for 'em, 'cause all we had to do there was ride on down to Billings and look at the ruins. So we druv a bunch of these Mormons we'd caught a bit south of here right up to the gate ahead of us, making like they was coming here for sanctuary."

Jed had been listening. He looked over his shoulder now with a slight feral smile:

"They really *had* been coming here for sanctuary. Which made it more convincing, you know what I mean?"

Rudi nodded soberly. He didn't like Jed Smith, but the man was no fool, unlike his nephew. The younger man went on:

"We had our men mixed in among 'em in the same clothes and their blades hid."

"They opened the gate without making sure?" Rudi said, a little surprised they'd fallen for the old trick.

"The rest of us hung back a little, whoopin' and shooting arrows and makin' like we was chasing them. We'd kept their kids so they'd play along, and they all yelled out to hurry up so's they could get inside before we caught 'em. By the time the ones inside this Peekaboo place knew the score, the gate was already open and we had a wagon full of rocks halfway through. With the wheels ready to be knocked off, so they couldn't drag it away, and then they couldn't shoot us without hittin' their own folks."

"That was clever work." Rudi looked around, counting households and multiplying, then subtracting because Mormon women rarely bore arms. "But there would have been hard fighting still. They should have had . . . what, sixty or seventy men under arms? You've a deal less than that, I see."

Jed Smith looked back at them, silently at first this time; his brows were up, and there was a wary respect in them. Rudi swore inwardly. The last thing you wanted an enemy to do was respect your wits. The older man spoke after a moment's considering stare:

"Maybe there was sixty or seventy fighting men here before the war, that would fit with how many women and kids. But I've lost more men from Rippling Waters Ranch in the past three-four years than I like, and we *won*. I figured it had to be a lot worse for them, and I was right. And they were surprised, and we had more men then—two other bunches were with us. It weren't no fair fight, which is the way I like it, youngster."

"I kilt three of their fighting men myself," the one called Jack said.

"In your dreams, maybe, Jack," another of the Cutters said. "Unless every arrow you shot off was guided by the Masters, personal-like, and since one nearly hit *me* in the butt cheek I sorta doubt that."

"Well, I kilt one for *sure,* Lin, which is more than you can say." To Rudi: "Uncle Jed says they thought all our troops were still down south along the Snake."

"And you took no losses?"

"Naw. Well, they killed Kennie. He got a spear in the gizzard while we were rushing the gate, he was an old guy, nearly forty, slooooow, and he never did learn to keep his shield up under his eyes, them geezers are like that."

"Watch your mouth, pup," Jed said. "I ain't going to see thirty again neither, and I can still whip you any day of the week and twice on Sundays."

"Sorry, Uncle Jed. And Dave, my second cousin Dave Throsson, not Big Dave Johnson who got killed at Wendell, he took an arrow in the leg, but we fixed him up good and poured whiskey in it so's it hasn't gone bad so far, and Tom Skinner got his ribs stove something terrible when he got pushed out of a window by this gal he was chasing—Lord—"

Jed Smith looked over at him with a cold eye. Jack cleared his throat and corrected himself:

"—by the Ascended Masters, didn't we all laugh when he fell straight down with his stiff dick waggin' out! That's all *our* ranch lost, apart from some cuts and little shit like that. We got hurt a lot worse at Twin Falls, and we had a right bad day at Wendell; *that* was a real fight, let me tell you!"

"You took the village with only one dead?" Rudi asked.

"One from our ranch, like I said. Those stupid bastards from the Runamuk and Sweet Grass outfits lost six, maybe seven, and plenty more hurt bad, but *they* couldn't pour piss out of a boot with directions written on the heel anyways. It was their fault a bunch of the enemy got away, out over the north wall, too—*their* fault and no one else's, the greedy sons of bitches, running on in before they were called. They're gone now. Uncle Jed sent them on along with their share, and good riddance."

"And the plunder was good?"

"Plunder?"

"Taking their things."

"Ah, the salvaging, you mean! *I'll* say it was good! The misbelievers were richer than rich, I tell you. And this time we got it all to our own selves, on account of we took this way home just so's we'd hit some places the main army didn't get to yet. Uncle Jed thought of that. I know the Sword of the Prophet do the hardest fighting, saw that my own self at Wendell, but it's enough to anger a man bad the way they get the best pick of—"

Jed Smith threw a look over his shoulder again, and Jack went on hastily:

"Anyway I got ten bolts of that good tough linen cloth the misbelievers make, saddlemaker's tools, twenty bucks in coin, some rings and pretties and blankets and sheets and dresses and cookware things for Jenny—she's my intended—two young gals who'll take the work off Ma now that she's getting the rheumatism so bad, a good oil lamp with a glass chimney, a bunch of other stuff, and I fucked until I couldn't raise a stand no more."

"You can believe that last part at least, mister, not that it would take much with *him*," another young Cutter said, and he and Jack exchanged mock punches before the talkative young ranch-hand went on:

"Plus I got six good horses earlier, and some more coin back in Twin Falls, but we sent that all East with the first folks from our district released from service. Like the Prophet says, the unbelievers are spoil for the Brotherhood of Light-bringers. Priest says *spoil* used to mean good stuff, not meat that's gone off."

Rudi made himself smile and nod. Picabo stank of spoiled meat in truth now—of death, like rancid sweet oil smeared into your nose and mouth. The Eastern levies who'd taken it hadn't bothered to clean up the bodies except to roll them out of the way, probably because they were planning on leaving soon, and flies were thick. They were thick on the eight men crucified upside down to the inner side of the adobe wall with railroad spikes, too. Fortunately they all seemed to be dead now, but it hadn't been quick, even for the ones who'd had small hot fires lit beneath their heads.

At a guess, Uncle Jed wanted to ask those some questions.

"Those ones tried to sneak back for their hoors and brats," Jack said with a wave. "But Uncle Jed knew they would, and we were ready for them. The Black Void drank 'em down!"

The young man went on in a less boastful voice: "You folks got much silver?"

"Plenty, for the right goods," Ingolf said over his shoulder.

"That's fine, fine. I sure would like to turn some of the stuff I got into silver. Then I can trade it for livestock back to home a lot easier than riding through blizzards to line camps and swapping around all winter. My Jenny's father won't let us get married until I have at least twenty-five heifers in the Rippling Waters pool besides a good remuda—"

"Jack, like I told you, stop flapping your lips. The horse-flies will get in there and buzz around in your empty head. Here's the house I'm using," Jed Smith broke in. "You Newcastle men can have the one next door. Some of our folks was using it and cleaned it up before they left and I'll send some of the gals in. You can start your barterin' in the morning, and then we'll leave. We close up tight at night here."

"What's that one?" Rudi said, pointing with his chin at a building with boards nailed over the windows to make an improvised prison.

A few of the Cutters were lolling about on the steps, one whittling at a stick with a foot-long fighting knife, another sitting propped against the wall with his floppy hat pulled over his eyes and his strung bow across his lap. Rudi thought he was asleep until he saw an eye following the horses. A Mormon woman carried a yoke with two buckets of milk up the front steps as the mounted men passed, and others followed behind with aprons full of loaves of bread or covered pots of cooked food wrapped in towels against their heat. They turned their heads aside to avoid meeting the eyes of the Cutter patrol, some of whom called out greetings of their choice.

"Oh, that's where we're keeping the brats," Jed Smith said. "They're part of the Prophet's portion of the spoil."

"Brats?" Ingolf inquired.

"Their kids, the ones too young to be worth anything, under about six. We've got orders to look after 'em careful, for the Houses of Refuge. A lot of them can be raised in the Faith, you see. Or if they're soulless, they can go to the breeding pens."

"Yeah, some of 'em will end up in Corwin," Jack put in. "Not just working—they get to be priests or in the Sword of the Prophet. That don't seem—"

"Jack, *what did I say* about flapping your lips?" Jed barked. "Don't your ears work or are you a natural-born damned fool like the minions of the Accursed?"

He whirled his pony around with a shift of balance and thighs, and slapped the younger Cutter across the face with his leather hat, hard enough to sting. The younger man yelped and then fell silent, face red.

"See you folks in the morning," Jed went on. "May the Masters keep the Nephilim from your dreams."

"Uff da," Ingolf swore in a tired voice, running a hand over his head and kneading at the back of his neck. "I'd forgotten how much I don't like this kind of shit. And how much I *really* don't like the Cutters."

Smith's *cleaned up* had been a relative term; no bodies left to rot, or human excrement in corners, basically. Little things like the fan of black congealed droplets that arched across one wall of the kitchen where they'd been left by the backswing of a blade didn't count. A team of village women with mops and brushes had come in to give it a going-over, working in silence like machines in the old stories. When they left, the comrades sat around the kitchen table, beneath a bright lamp; sunset came early inside a close-packed walled town.

The women had left food, too, and Rebecca Nystrup had started a fire in the ingeniously designed tile stove with its iron top.

"Your people have some evil foes," Edain said awkwardly, patting her on the shoulder.

She nodded silently and began making dinner— slicing ham and cracking eggs into a couple of big frying pans where melted butter browned, and chopping potatoes and onions for hash. Edain moved automatically to help her as the good smell of cooking mingled with the stinks.

"No!" Ingolf said with quiet emphasis, the tone contrasting with his relaxed, casual posture and expression.

Rudi looked at him curiously. The man from Richland was sitting at the head of the table, where he could see out the window into the little walled garden that fronted the house, and through the open door as well. Nobody was close enough to overhear them . . . but they were visible from outside too. It would be suspicious if they closed up before the night grew cool.

"It'll look damned funny if you're helping the bought woman with the chores, kid," Ingolf said flatly. "Not only that she's supposed to be a slave, but Cutters don't hold with men doing women's work at the best of times. Plus, generally speaking, sweet helpful types just plain don't take up the business we're supposed to be in."

Edain sat and moodily pulled apart one of the loaves, buttering it and biting into the warm fresh bread. Rebecca looked over her shoulder and said:

"But thanks for the thought," and he nodded, blushing.

Rudi tore a loaf as well. The bread was well made, with an egg-glaze crust that crackled when he ripped it. The butter was sweet and fresh too, although they had to keep a piece of cloth across it to deter the flies. It was the flies and the smell and the thought of where the flies had been that made him hesitate, and evidently the same occurred to Edain just as he was swallowing, for the younger clansman turned a little green under his ruddy tan.

You didn't grow up squeamish about stinks or bugs in a Mackenzie farming dun, but this . . .

"Ground and center," Rudi said quietly, making himself eat.

Food was life, human toil and the sacrificial blood of the Powers, so it was sacrilege to waste it; and he was going to need his strength, and he'd done without a good deal for the past week. Odard murmured a prayer before he took some of the bread himself, which surprised Rudi. He'd always thought that the young nobleman was only conventionally religious because it was expected of him. He'd confessed to Father Ignatius a couple of times on the trip, but once he'd had to go back a day later before the priest would agree to communicate him, and he'd come away from that one with his ears turning pink.

Sure, and a man's inward self is like the woods on a moonless night, Rudi thought. *Even your own self. Especially your own. It always surprises you, sometimes with a noise, sometimes with a jab in the eye.*

Ingolf spoke to Edain; his voice was rough, but Rudi thought he detected a certain sympathy in it:

"There are going to be worse things to see and smell before we reach the East Coast, kid," he said. "You've got to get case-hardened pretty quick."

"I've seen fights before and men killed, sure and I have!" Edain snapped. "And worse things ... like that Haida raid we were caught in, up near Tillamook on the ocean, Chief, and what they did to that poor woman and her bairn. But this is ... very bad."

Rudi replied: "It's worse because here the raiders won, Edain. The which they didn't at Tillamook, and you can claim some of the credit for that."

Edain looked heartened. Rebecca set the plates of food before them and then sat at the foot of the table herself. Rudi found he was hungry enough to enjoy it after all, and a deep drink of cool milk rich with cream. The day's heat was fading, though the thick adobe walls of the farmhouse's first story radiated a little of it back.

"This is ... squalid," Odard observed. "And did you *smell* those animals? I'm no rose myself, not after the way we've been traveling, but ..."

Ingolf gave a short dry laugh. "Oh, I know why they're a mite rancid," he said. "They're from the Hi-Line."

At their glances he went on: "I've talked to men who've been through there. You can travel fifty, sixty miles at a time and not see a single tree. The only way to heat water or cook is over dried cowflops. And the winters are almighty cold. You get out of the habit of taking baths, or taking off your clothes at all mighty fast, out there."

Odard nodded. "I do hope we don't run into anything worse."

The Easterner made a sound, but this time it wasn't a laugh of any sort. Rudi looked at Ingolf, but the Easterner's eyes were blank, as if all his attention was focused within.

"Worse?" he said softly, coming back to them. "Oh, yeah. I've seen as bad as this, during the Sioux War. That was a hard bitter fight, and a lot of ... questionable ... things got done. By us and them both."

His hands closed and opened unconsciously, and he swallowed as if the food had turned sour in his mouth before he went on.

"East of the Mississippi, that's a whole different

thing. It's like God pulled out the plug at the bottom of the world, and everything human drained out. And then something . . . else . . . came trickling in, and messed things up, twisted them. I don't mean just the Change. I swore I wouldn't go back to the deadlands again, not even for a fortune . . . and now I'm headed back all the way to Nantucket because of a vision and a dream. Go figure."

Edain paused a minute, swallowing, then doggedly cut another piece of ham, dipped it in the mustard pot, chewed and swallowed. Everyone was silent for several moments. That was the way they were headed, into the death zones, where the hordes fleeing from the stricken cities had overlapped and eaten the earth bare, and then each other. Not everyone had died, not quite, but their descendants weren't really human anymore. The stories were gruesome even at a distance; enough rumors had trickled back from the borders of California. From what Ingolf said the mega-necropolis on the Atlantic Coast was just as bad, and he'd seen it firsthand.

"That's as may be," Edain said stoutly; dangers rarely daunted him when they arrived, and never beforehand. "You said these Cutters were just men. Well, that they may be, but they're roit bad ones an' no mistake."

Rudi mopped his plate and poured himself more milk from the jug. Halfway through, he wondered if the women who'd milked the cows had spat in the bucket, but finished anyway. They'd have reason.

"They are men. Men who've been encouraged to give guest-room to the worst parts of themselves," he said thoughtfully.

Edain made a protective sign. "They're blaspheming the Goddess, that's what they're doing," he said. "I just hope we aren't caught in Her anger."

He held his hands up before his face. "Use these my hands to avenge Your likeness, Dark Mother, Morrigú Goddess of the Crows, Red Hag of Battles. So I invoke You."

Rudi nodded soberly and joined in the gesture and the prayer. "So mote it be!"

We fight, we of humankind, he thought. *Man against man for pride and power, tribe against tribe for the land that feeds us and our families ... That's the nature of things, the way They made us, neither good nor bad in itself. To fight is the work of the season, just as wolves fight one another for lordship of a pack, or a whole pack battles another for hunting range in a bad year to keep themselves and their cubs from hunger.*

But taking women by force wasn't war. Nor just a crime, either, not even a serious one like murder in hot blood. As Edain had said, it was a profanation of the holy Mysteries, the divine union of Lord and Lady, Spear and Cauldron, that made all creation.

Mackenzies buried a rapist at a crossroads, with a spear thrust in the soil above; and they buried him living when they could, as a sacrifice to turn aside the anger of the Earth Powers.

These Cutters have overstepped the bounds They have laid on us, and must pay for it.

The vengeance of the Lady could be slow; it was also very thorough.

Thorough to the point of being indiscriminate, sometimes, Rudy thought grimly, feeling the hairs along his spine crawl a little. *It would be well to make ourselves that vengeance, before it falls from somewhere else like an avalanche on all and sundry.*

"Hard times make for hard men," Odard said. "Things were bad everywhere right after the Change, from what the oldsters say, and you had to be bad yourself sometimes to survive. I imagine Montana was the same, even if they weren't as crowded. My mother doesn't talk about those times much, but some of the older men-at-arms who served my father do. From what our, ah, hosts have let fall, there hasn't been much order or peace out there since then, except what the CUT imposed at the sword's edge."

Rudi nodded; that was true enough that he could be polite. His own mother had had to drive away strangers and foragers, lest the Clan-in-the-making and its neighbors be eaten bare before the first harvest. And to keep out the plagues which had killed as many as raw famine did. Away from habitation you still found the skulls lying in the brush by the overgrown roads, or bones huddled in heaps in the ruins. Sometimes they'd been scorched and cracked for the marrow.

But what Odard said was true only to a point. There was doing what you had to do to ward off death or worse, and there was treating disaster as opportunity.

"You know Chuck Barstow?" he said to the Association nobleman.

Odard nodded. "I've met him. First Armsman for you Mackenzies now, after Sam Aylward retired."

Rudi nodded himself. "He was a Society fighter before the Change. On the day, he lifted two big wagons and their teams from a . . . living-history exhibit, whatever that was . . . in Eugene on his way to Dun Juniper with the Singing Moon coven. And he loaded the wagons with food and tools and seeds he . . . picked up . . . along the way, and drove along cattle and pigs and sheep they acquired likewise, with worthless money or just by lifting them. This was before people had a chance to eat everything, you see, or even to realize what was happening, the most of them."

"There you are then," Odard said. "All our parents did that sort of thing. If you have to—"

"And he ran into a load of lost schoolchildren along the way, and picked *them* up too, and adopted three of them himself," Rudi finished, interrupting him. "Oak— he used to be named Dan—has three sons and daughters of his own now."

"Oh," Odard said, and cut himself a wedge from the cheese.

Rudi didn't say any more; Eddie Liu, the first Baron Gervais, hadn't been *that* sort of man, and everyone knew it.

In your father's day, Odard . . . Matti's father's day . . . your lot were just as bad as these Cutters, for all the fancy titles. Eddie Liu and Norman Arminger among the worst of them; not just hard men, but rotten bad. If they'd won the War of the Eye, you'd be worse than you are yourself, my friend, and even so there are things about you I don't much like.

And at least Arminger's had been a mortal evil, while the CUT seemed to corrupt everything it touched.

And . . . he remembered the dead man laughing.

"The times *were* very hard indeed," Rudi went on aloud, controlling a slight shiver at that recollection. "But hard isn't the same thing as bad. It depended on the leaders and what sort of things were in their souls, and what paths they led their folk down. My mother says a tribe is like a man; it becomes more itself as it gets older, and as what it does writes on the heart. Things were . . . loose, for a while after the Change. They could be turned this way or that. Now they're getting set again, for good and ill."

Ingolf shook himself and loaded his plate, doggedly plowing through eggs and ham and fried potatoes. When he glanced up at Rudi, the haunted look was gone for now and a tough shrewdness back in charge.

"I gather we're not just going to buy some supplies, and ransom some people, and ride quietly away, Rudi?"

"No, that we are not," Rudi said forcefully. "Not if we *can* do more. I won't command us to certain death—but I will take a risk."

"*I'm* the one who was raised on tales of knights-errant," Odard said dryly. "We have the Princess to think about, Rudi . . . and your precious Sword. We have a long way to go. We can't right every wrong we find, not when we're outnumbered fifty to four. We're fugitives, not an army with banners and trumpets. I don't mind a fight, but . . ."

Rudi nodded; that was true. And he didn't doubt Odard's courage. It had been shown often enough that there was no need for him to go out of his way to prove it.

"I'm not going to try to right every wrong," he said. "But when the Powers shove one under my nose, and it smelling no better than a goat turd on a hot day, then it becomes my business."

"Yes!" Edain said, his eyes bright.

Rebecca's blazed. "*Thank* you," she whispered. "Thank you both."

"You're welcome," Rudi said.

"Well, then we need more information," Ingolf said practically. "More than we can get cooped up here. And that Jed Smith may have acted real friendly, but he's no fool like his nephew Jack. He'll let us see just as much as he thinks is needful for him, and not a bit more."

"No, he's a dangerous man," Rudi acknowledged. "He'll keep a close eye on us."

"Not on all of us," Rebecca said.

A sharp scream came from the middle distance, and then sobs and the sound of men laughing. She shivered, but went on:

"My people here will know all we need."

CHAPTER SIX

Avenger the Archer high-hearted
Deadly the skill of the bowman's hand
Stronger still is fate hard woven
Than any shaft nocked by mortal man—

From: *The Song of Bear and Raven*
Attributed to Fiorbhinn Mackenzie, 1st century CY

Peter Graber, newly promoted Major in the third battalion of the Sword of the Prophet, was a believing man. He recited from the Dictations nightly, or the Book of Dzhur, and had since he was a child in the House of Refuge. He treasured the occasions when he could feel that chanting bring him into contact with the Beyond, a joy as great as holding his firstborn son in his arms, and greater than any his wives could furnish. The Ascended Masters would welcome his lifestream in time, and eternal glory would be his.

He believed that so deeply that danger to his life aroused only an animal wariness, not the fear some men felt. And his combat record had been excellent as he rose from trooper to squadron commander; against the Powder River Ranchers, the Sioux, the Drumhellers, and then in the great battles of the Deseret War and most recently at Wendell against the US of Boise.

But I still don't like this Seeker, even if he comes from

the Prophet's right hand. There's something ... wrong ... about him.

Right now High Seeker Twain was just an unexceptional-looking man of about thirty-five, wiry and tough, with a dull red robe over his traveling clothes, huddled on his horse with a blank expression on his face as beads of sweat ran down through the dust. He rode well enough to keep up, but not to the standard of the Prophet's elite guard regiment, or even as well as the average cowboy. Graber would have placed him for a townsman, if he hadn't been so uncomplaining of hardship ... but then, the Seekers had their own code.

Fifty of the Sword were spread out to either side, in a single rank to make it easier to spot any turning in the trail they followed. The dull russet brown of their lacquered leather armor faded against the volcanic soil in the distance, with an occasional eye-hurting blink as the lance-heads above them caught the harsh noonday sun. The men rode in disciplined silence except for an occasional order from an under-officer, the spiked helmets rising and falling with the walk-trot-canter-trot-walk pace.

The noise came from the slow steady pounding of hooves, the clatter of the hard metal-edged scutes of their war harness, creak of saddle-leather, the dull clank of a shete scabbard against a stirrup iron or the rattle of arrows in a quiver.

Unavoidably they raised a plume of dust, in this stretch where even sagebrush was sparse; they rode into a wind out of the east, so the dust fell behind them rather than hanging about to get in nose and eyes, but it would be visible for some distance. The remuda, the remount-herd, was behind them, and its cloud was larger. Most of the Snake River country wasn't so different from the plains of Eastern Montana or the Powder River ranges, though a bit drier. This particular eerie stretch of cinders and conical hills was strange, though, and he distrusted it.

"High Seeker," he said respectfully.

You told us to come this way, and now my battalion is scattered over a front a hundred miles wide. Now tell us how to get out of it! I'm going to lose horses soon, if we don't get to forage and water. May the Nephilim eat your soul in the Black Void if I'll lose good men without an explanation!

"High Seeker?" he repeated.

The man's pupils were shrunken to pinpoints, and his jaw worked as if he chewed a bitter truth. Graber shrugged with a slight clatter of gear and swung up a clenched fist. The unit halted within three paces, horses as well trained as the men. Dust smoked backwards; he could hear a slight hissing sound as the heavier particles fell out. Everyone dismounted; you stayed out of the saddle whenever you could, if you wanted your horse to last.

"We'll wait for the Scout," he called. "Loosen girths but keep the tack on."

All his men could follow a trail; they were trained horse soldiers, and hunters besides, and many came from ranching families. The Scout wasn't of the Sword; his tribe were called the Morrowlander Troop, and they lived deep in the forests and grasslands south of Corwin, what the old world had called Yellowstone. Rumor said that they'd fallen from the sky right after the Change.

Graber didn't believe that; but they *were* almost inhumanly skillful trackers. They served the Church by sending their best for work like this, and paying a tribute in hides and furs. In fact, his superiors had said something about their *ancestors* being Scouts . . . some weird woodland cult of the olden times.

Graber considered taking a stick of jerky or a hardtack biscuit out of his saddlebag; he was hungry. Then he decided not to, as an example to the men of rising above material things. Instead he took off his helmet, unsnapped and peeled out the lining, then poured in a measured quantity of water. His horse drank eagerly, chasing the last drops around the bare metal with its lips. The rest of the unit followed suit.

Only then did he drink from his canteen himself, a precisely measured amount. No need to check on the others; the under-officers would see to water discipline.

And we are *the Sword of the Prophet,* he thought proudly, as he finished exactly the amount that the lowliest trooper would have. *In the Sword there is no Rancher or cowboy or refugee, only servants of the Messenger of the Ascended Masters . . . Dammit, how did he* do *that!*

Somehow the Morrowlander Scout got within a few hundred yards before he was spotted. His horse was shaggy but sound; the Scout ran along beside it at an effortless distance-devouring lope with one hand on the simple pad saddle he used, using the beast to set his pace.

He was a tall lean man, dressed in moccasins and fringed leather leggings dyed in mottled colors and a brownish green tunic over a shirt starred with circular badges sewn with bows and tents and other curious designs. A kerchief went around his neck, the ends held through a leather ring. Plaits of red hair held with leather thongs and stuck with eagle feathers bumped on his shoulders beneath a bandana, and he was lightly armed, with knife and tomahawk and bow. Three parallel scars gashed his cheeks on either side of a snub nose.

"Scout," Graber said politely.

"Prophet's man," the Morrowlander said, equally expressionless, saluting by putting three fingers to his brow with the other folded under his thumb.

Then he held out his hand. Graber tugged thoughtfully at his brown chin-beard; the grimy paw held a horse-apple, and one that was fairly fresh.

"How long ago?" he said.

"Two days. Wind scrubs out the hooves in this place, but they went this way. Water about half a day's ride north, a little east—spring beneath a big hill. The nine rested there, and met some more."

"More?"

The Morrowlander grinned, showing strong yellow teeth. "Here."

He opened his other hand like a conjuror, with a twinkle in his blue eyes. In it was half a glass ornament, a golden bee.

"Mormons," Graber said thoughtfully, and whistled sharply in a signal to summon the under-officers.

His three subordinates gathered around him; there should have been four noncoms and a lieutenant, but casualties had been heavy at Wendell. All of them squatted and leaned on their sheathed shetes as they watched the Scout sketch in the dirt.

"How many?" one asked.

"Twenty, twenty-five of the Deseret men," the Scout said. "They came in from *here*"—his finger traced a route—"but they don't have many remounts, and their horses walk tired. And the nine we chase came in like *this*, met them there at the spring. The nine have plenty good horses"—he opened and closed his hands, showing the number—"some very big, never seen any tracks like that before. Big but not slow. They buried their ashes, and their own shit, but not the horses'! All rode off together, the nine and the Deseret men, making east and north."

"Two days ago?"

"Two days. Traveling slow-a-bit, walking, riding, walking. Half our pace. Be careful. They have *good* lookout, and they watch their backtrail. Their scout almost spotted me, I think. Had to wait half a day hidden up, buried myself in the dirt."

Another grin. "He didn't see me, though! I like to meet their scout, someday."

He tapped at his tomahawk to show how he'd like to meet the unknown man. Graber grunted and pulled at his beard again. That the nine were traveling at a long-distance pace argued that they didn't know someone was right on their trail—they were trying to conserve their horses for a long haul. He wished he could do the same. A ridden horse couldn't equal a fit man for long-distance endurance, though you could do better than foot-speed with a string of remounts.

Provided there's grazing, he reminded himself. *Which there isn't, here.*

"Northeast is old Highway 20," he said, drawing a line at the base of the wavy marks the Scout had used to represent the mountains. "They may be trying to cross the Tetons. Or work north through the mountains and *then* across; there are old tracks there."

"Bringing twenty-five Mormons into Church territory, sir?" one of the under-officers asked. "Pretty much like holding up a sign that says: *Hurrah, we're here, now kill us!*"

"A lot of it's Church territory that's pretty thin on people, just around there," Graber said thoughtfully. "And they may not be taking the Mormons . . . but we'd better catch them before then. General Walker will be pleased if we finish off some bandits at the same time."

Suddenly the Seeker spoke. "Give me two of your arrows, Major Graber."

Graber blinked in surprise; at the statement, and at its sheer disconnectedness. He obeyed automatically, reaching up over his right shoulder and twitching out two of the long ashwood shafts. As it happened they were both armor-piercing bodkins with narrow heads like a blacksmith's metal-punch.

The Seeker took them and studied them for an instant, then slowly licked each head. Graber controlled a grimace of distaste; there was something *dirty* about the gesture. He took them back reluctantly, and only because you never had enough—there were thirty-six shafts in a regulation quiver, and you could shoot them all off in a couple of minutes skirmishing.

"By the Ascended Masters," someone muttered.

It had been said softly, but the Seeker smiled; Graber wished that he hadn't.

"By the Masters indeed," he said, and the smile grew broader. "Oh, we have learned much, and we shall learn so much more of Them!"

"Do you have anything to say?" Graber asked neutrally. *Technically I'm in command, but . . .*

The Seeker nodded, his eyes growing distant again.

"There," he said. His arm stretched out, the hand like a blade, pointing precisely northeast. "There. The Son of the Bear . . . the Son of the Raven . . . where the weak are strong and the vanquished slay."

Graber felt sweat prickle out on his face, more than sun and armor would explain. He looked at the Scout, and the lanky man shrugged and pointed more nearly straight north.

"Mount," he said harshly. "We'll go for the spring and then track them from there. Until we reach it, water only for the horses."

His under-officers sighed and shifted slightly with relief; the big canteens on the pack-saddles were nearly empty. The reserve on the men's belts wouldn't last long.

"We'll push the pace now, and stop just long enough to water at the spring and fill our canteens. Change off with the remounts every hour, but no rest stops until dark."

As he swung back into the saddle he racked his brain for what lay ahead. A string of small Mormon settlements at the foot of the mountains; General Walker had said they were to be mopped up at leisure, as troops became available. And one pass over the Rockies eastward, so obscure they hadn't bothered to garrison it. Would any of the levies be heading there on their way home? Possibly not . . .

These misbelievers will not defile the homeland of the Dictations, he thought; the Prophet had given him this mission *personally,* and that was honor beyond price . . . and responsibility heavier than a mountain. *By the beard of the Prophet, I swear it!*

PICABO, EASTERN IDAHO
SEPTEMBER 12, CHANGE YEAR 23/2021 AD

Edain Aylward Mackenzie heard Rebecca squeal in shocked alarm, and then a cry of rage and a smack like wet laundry hitting a rock. He whirled, his hand snapping to the hilt of his unfamiliar shete.

They were in the Covenstead at the center of the town . . . no, the Saints called it a Meeting House. The center was a big hall lit by clerestory windows around the edge where the bright light of dawn showed. One half was full of pews, the second—oddly—equipped with basketball hoops and a recessed stage, and there had been big folding partitions that could close off one from the other. It smelled of wax and paint and lamp-oil and careful cleaning, or at least those had been the predominant odors until recently.

One of the Cutters was rubbing at his fuzzy cheek. It was Jack, and his face looked as if it had been well and truly slapped. There were a dozen or so there, working on their gear or muscling bundles of loot out to the wagons. Some of them were grinning and haw-hawing—he'd noticed that young Jack didn't get much respect, despite being their leader's nephew. Others looked angry. Jack himself certainly did. Rebecca backed towards the Mackenzie, her cheeks flaming and visibly forcing herself not to rub where she'd been goosed.

Edain elbowed by her; the sooner they were distracted from the Mormon girl, a woman of the vanquished enemy, the better. The men of Rudi's band—Ingolf's—were supposed to be from a friendly or at least neutral realm, protected by treaty. He pushed forward and thrust his face into Jack's.

"Now, why would you be thinking you could get away with that, boyo?" he asked quietly. "The girl's not yours."

Though maybe you can *get away with it, if it comes to a fight with these shetes*, some part of him thought.

Not afraid, but considering as he would the weight of a billhook and the look of a hedge.

If they don't all just mob me. But I'm thinking the curse of the Goddess is falling on you the now, and me Her instrument.

He was a passable fair-to-middling swordsman ... with the gladius-style shortsword and small buckler that most Mackenzies used when things got too close for the bow. He'd never had more than a little cursory practice with the weapon the Easterners had developed from the machete.

Of course, there's no reason for you *to know that*, he

thought, and stared at the blue-eyed Montanan, his own gray eyes as flat and cold as his father's.

Not many men cared to face Samkin Aylward in that mood. Garbh was beside him, growling slightly and eyeing the Cutter in a way that was quite obviously focused on where to bite first. Jack split his attention between the two threats and took a step back.

"Mister, you'd better collar your she-dogs—both of them," he said, his own hand on the hilt of his weapon. "We of the Church Universal and Triumphant don't take back-talk even from our own free women, much less slave bitches."

Someone spoke sotto voce behind him: "Yeah, that's why Jenny chased you round the bunkhouse with that frying pan last Messenger Day and you were hollering about how sorry you were."

His voice rose to a falsetto squeak: *"Oh, please, darlin', don't hit me no more. I promise I'll be good!"*

"You shut the fuck up, Lin!" Jack snarled, truly furious now.

He drew the long curved sword at his hip and pointed it at his comrade, then swung around to face Edain once more. The broad point-heavy slashing blade was quivering a little from the tightness of his grip as he spat out:

"Look, mister, you owe me for what your she-bitch there did. You can pay in coin, or lend her to me long enough to teach her manners, or I'll take it out of your hide!"

With an effort at self-control: "I'll even pay you for her time, though you rightly should pay *me* for properly breaking her in."

"Is it that you're after calling me a pimp the now, boyo, or just a coward?" Edain said flatly; he could feel the sweat trickling down his flanks, but nothing showed on his face. "Well, every man chooses his end, they say. If it's the day you want to die, just say so. For if I draw *my* blade, I'll cut your throat where you lie begging."

Jack's face twitched slightly; there was another haw-haw from behind him. He'd backed himself into a place where he had to fight or lose credit, and Edain had just upped the stakes to life and death.

First time I've ever done that, he thought. *In cold blood.*

"Hey, fellahs, no need to get all bloody about the bitch," one of the Cutters said. "It ain't worth it. There's plenty more of them. They don't grow shut."

"Maybe Jack wanted this 'un because the others hit him with a frying pan," another added, which got more laughter. "Hell, you know, I'm getting tired of 'em all. I'll be glad to get back home and see a woman who's glad to see *me*."

"There's one as is, Artie? News to me," one of his comrades said, and they laughed again.

They were all a little more casual than Edain would have expected, and less inclined to take their comrade's part. Mackenzies rarely fought one another beyond a behind-the-barn punch-up now and then. It was against the law, for starters, and if someone was hurt badly a priestess might curse you or your dun outlaw you. The PPA allowed duels, but under an elaborate formal code and only between Associates.

These are wild men, he realized. *Guts and skill at arms are everything to them. And they're away from whatever law they have at home, and used to killing from this war they've been having. That works for me now. If I win, that is . . .*

A thought struck him. It was a risk . . . but less of one than meeting the other man with cold steel. Mostly less for Rebecca; if he lost a fight, she'd be in the Cutter's hands.

"Or we could try a bit of a game, if you're man enough for it," he said.

"Ah, dang it to the Black Void," one of the spectators said. "I was lookin' forward to a fight. All this lying around eating and sleeping soft and screwing's got me feelin' bloody."

"Game?" Jack said suspiciously.

"We'll shoot for her," he said. "Bow against bow."

The Cutter visibly restrained himself from speaking. He looked at the longbow across Edain's back, and his eyes narrowed in thought. Archery was a skill that had spread far and fast after the Change—most rural areas had had at least a few hobbyist bow-hunters who suddenly found their pastime deadly serious business. Bowyers had been rarer and more precious than gold. Edain's father had been a hunter and student of the English longbow from his childhood—it was an old family tradition of the Aylwards—and Western Oregon was full of good yew, which grew like a weed in the understory of the great mountain forests.

But these Easterners were horsemen, raised in the saddle in an empty land. Bows meant to be used from horseback were the only kind they knew, short powerful recurves modeled on pre-Change hunting styles but far heavier on the draw. Those complex constructions of laminated sinew and wood and horn needed months to make and were the single most expensive things most cowboys would own.

To Jack the Mackenzie weapon probably looked like a simple bent stick, the sort of awkward makeshift primitives without real bowyer's knowledge would improvise. His uncle wouldn't have made that mistake, but . . .

Jack isn't the sharpest shaft in his family's quiver, I'm thinking.

"Well, if you're that anxious to lose the bitch, I'll take you on," Jack said, confirming Edain's estimate. "Rounders or rovers or at the bull's-eye?"

Then he grinned slyly. "I'll even sell her back to you for forty-five dollars . . . later."

Edain nodded, but the audience groaned. "Ah, hell, it's not even worth gettin' up to go watch you two shoot," one said.

"Did anyone ask you to come along, Lin?" Jack said. "*I* didn't hear it. Sitting on your ass sucking on a jug's more your style."

The lanky brown-haired one named Lin snapped his fingers. "*I* know!"

"You don't know much," Jack said.

"I know an old story," Lin said enthusiastically, " 'bout

a cowboy that got in Dutch with this Bossman, so the Bossman made him shoot an apple—"

The Cutters cheered and clapped when he'd finished; evidently they thought that a lot more entertaining than a simple shooting match; they were making bets as if it was a settled thing before the story was fully told. Rebecca sucked in her breath sharply. Aylward the Archer's son felt his skin go pale, and clammy with cold sweat.

He wouldn't have expected one of these grass-country men to have heard of William Tell.

"I don't know how long we've got," Ritva murmured.

Or is it Mary?

Rudi couldn't tell while he stood looking down southward on the little town of Picabo. He was half a mile north of the town wall, and several hundred feet up on the scrub-covered slopes of the hill. From this distance it still looked the pleasant place it must have been once.

For one thing, you can't smell it, he thought grimly.

Here there was nothing but the clean warm wind, and the scents of rock and dirt and sage. His half sister was behind him, and close enough that they could talk, but she was invisible beneath the lip of a ravine. To any casual observer in the town—and he'd noticed that at least one Cutter was always in view wherever he went—he was simply looking out over the valley of Silver Creek and the long plains beyond.

"It's not a place I'd linger of my own will," he said.

"Bad?" she said.

"No, it's a merry place, like an inn where you'd be glad to get your feet up and have an ale and a song in good company. Well, if you don't mind rape, plunder, murder and the stink of rot and the flies crawling over your face and your food. Tell me more."

"We're not *sure*, but . . ." the young woman said. "We backtracked and watched our trail, and . . . it's possible there was someone there, scouting around our campsites."

"Possible?" he said; he'd hoped they'd broken contact with the Cutters in the lava country.

"If there was, they were really, really good at not being noticed. More of . . . a feeling . . . than anything definite. We didn't want to take more than a few hours to check."

Rudi's eyebrows went up. He wouldn't care to try playing dodge-the-scout with Mary and Ritva working as a team. They'd had very careful training from experts all their lives, natural talent, and for their age a lot of experience in varied types of country. Aunt Astrid kept her Rangers busy.

"There was only one, though, *if* there was one. He *could* have been a wandering hunter being cautious, but I didn't like it. Meanwhile, Ritva—"

Ah, so it is Mary. Someday I'll be able to tell the difference without looking close.

"—found where the other people who cut their way out of this Picabo place were. Hiding half a day's travel north of here; they had a hideaway in the hills, with a deep tube well and some caves, and supplies. There are about thirty; all men, say twenty fit to fight—the rest are badly wounded."

"Ah, that explains something," Rudi said, doing a little mental arithmetic.

Explains the men with the fires under their heads. But presumably they didn't talk . . . probably Jed Smith didn't know the right questions to ask. Brave of them to attack, but foolish . . . Still, in their place . . .

"The Cutters are pulling out of here tomorrow," he said.

"Hit them at dawn?" Mary said.

"No, they'll be expecting something then, or at least sort of expecting and taking precautions. Their leader, Jed Smith, is too shrewd by half. Here's what we'll do—"

He finished and she repeated the salient points back to him. Then she cleared her throat.

"How's Ingolf?" she asked casually.

Aha, Rudi thought, but carefully kept the smile out of his voice and off his face.

"Better," he said. "It helps him to have work to do—

and he's been doing a good job of it. I couldn't have carried it off in a thousand years, not without a lot of experience I haven't had."

"Well, you'll be twenty-three in December, Rudi. You'll have a chance to accumulate it."

He nodded, and thought: *If I'm not laying stark for my totem bird to eat my eyeballs fairly soon.*

"I'd better get back," he said. "It wouldn't look good for Ingolf's assistant to be absent through all the bargaining."

"Manwë and Varda watch over you, Rudi," she said soberly.

"And the Lady hold you in Her wings, and the Lord ward you with His spear, my sister," he replied softly.

Then she was gone; there wasn't a noise, just a feeling of emptiness, and perhaps the staccato *chuck-chuck-chuck* calling of an oriole was a little louder. Rudi rose smoothly, his sword scabbard in his left hand, and half slid down the slope; there was a click of rock and sliding earth—*he* wasn't trying to be quiet. Epona greeted him at the bottom with a snort, throwing up her head from where she'd been grazing, and then trotting over. He caught at the saddlebow and vaulted up as she passed, giving her a friendly slap on the neck as his feet found the stirrups. They needed no conscious signals; she turned her head towards the village gate and floated into a canter, taking a rail fence with a bunching of the great muscles between his thighs, and landing with a deceptive thistledown softness.

She pulled in her pace as they approached the gate. Rudi wrinkled his nose, and Epona snorted through hers; she knew what that smell meant. There was enough of a breeze to make it more tolerable than inside the wall, though. The Cutters had the captives they were ready to sell there, together with bundles of other loot, and the women's tools and goods of their making—cloth mainly, but also some handicrafts. Ingolf had been running them through their paces, questioning them sharply on their skills.

"Lifestreams of the Masters and the hearts of the

Men of Camelot, but that's a purty horse!" the Rancher said as the Mackenzie cantered up.

"Not just her looks, either," he went on, and listed her points. "You or your kin have any of her get?"

"Back home in Newcastle," Rudi said, inclining his head respectfully. "A stallion at stud, and a colt."

The good manners were acting, of course, but Rudi felt an unpleasant moment of empathy with the man; he had to, when someone appreciated Epona so knowledgeably.

Which gives me the crawls, the man being so detestable otherwise, he thought. *Yet what man is all of one piece? He may be a loving husband and kind to animals and concerned for his folk.*

"I wouldn't use her as a riding horse, not on a long dangerous trip or for war," Jed said, shaking his head. "Waste of a good broodmare, you ask me."

"We've a good stud, back home in Newcastle," Rudi said with a shrug.

The Mackenzies were passing as Ingolf's young cousins—Ingolf and Rudi were about the same height and build, and all of them not so different in coloring or cast of features that they couldn't be close kin. Supposedly they dealt for a family business, farms, smithies and weaving workshops, and livestock—which latter made them respectable enough for a Rancher to deal with as near equals.

"I'll say you do! If only you could bring some up our way, I'd give seven, eight hundred for a stallion colt out of her, if the sire was anything."

The Cutters were all passionate horsemen and horse breeders; Jed would have been content to talk over Epona for longer yet, and drop some heavy hints about buying her, though there wasn't the slightest doubt he knew she was well past mark of mouth. Ingolf cleared his throat.

"Don't mean to hurry you, Rancher, but . . ."

Jed sighed. "Yeah, we got to get goin'. All right, you want them to strip down?" He jerked a thumb at the captives. "It's not as if they were respectable."

"I'm not buying them for their looks," Ingolf said, shrugging. "It's their work I'm interested in."

Jed slapped him on the shoulder. "You're more sensible than most men your age," he said; he was perhaps a decade older than Ingolf's twenty-eight.

Which means he was fourteen or fifteen when the Change came, Rudi thought suddenly. *I wonder what sort of lad he was. And what might he have been, if the old world had not died in an instant.*

"Most of my boys, they get a sniff of a woman and they can't think of anything but putting her flat on her back," he went on, with a male laugh. "Or bent over a saddle, according to taste."

Ingolf shrugged again. "Silver's harder to come by. And gold doesn't take sick and die on the road, or run off and get et by wolves or tigers, or get the galloping miseries and kill itself. Silver and gold you can trust."

"Oh, things can get confusing for a while when someone finds a big cache of bullion in one of the dead cities," Jed Smith said.

Ingolf grinned; the old time's coins were worthless, except as raw materials for arrowheads, but the new currencies hadn't settled down yet either.

"How often does that happen these days?" he said. "The ones near where people live have been picked over, and the others . . . friend, you do *not* want to go there."

"Yeah, I've heard," Jed said. "So, what do you say to forty-five dollars a head for these twenty-five? And the older children thrown in with 'em."

"I say you're kidding me and it's not funny," Ingolf replied. "I say you're a thief. I say you'd get half that much in a wet dream. I say get serious or don't waste my time."

Jed scowled at him. "They'd fetch that back to home."

"You're not home," Ingolf pointed out. "You've got over a hundred women and their kids to get back to your ranches over the mountains, all the way to the Upper Missouri. They'll have to walk, and it's getting late in the season. What happens if you run into blizzards in the high country?"

Jed reflexively cocked an eye at the heavens; they were mostly blue, with a few towering clouds like mountains of whipped cream in the sky. Anyone who made their living from the earth and feared the weather's fickleness would recognize the glance. So would a soldier.

"Should make it before the passes snow up, if we push 'em," Jed said.

He absently popped the lash of the riding quirt thonged to his wrist. Ingolf shrugged.

"That'll wear on them. And you're not planning on keeping them all yourselves, are you?"

"Oh, Black Void, no. They'd be nearly as many all up as the free women on Rippling Waters then. That'd be trouble, 'specially at first, give 'em too much chance to dream up something bad together. We'll swap at least half for livestock. Our range on Rippling Waters can carry a lot more than we've got, good grass goin' to waste."

Ingolf looked at him in surprise; a cowherd could double every three years. Jed caught the glance and explained:

"We've had a couple of bad winters, and lost some to lobo-wolves and tigers, more of the damn things every season. There've been too many prime hands away fightin' to ride guard proper *or* to cut enough field hay. A healthy woman who knows weaving and cheesemaking or leather work will fetch ten good breeding an' milking heifers or twenty steers, easy. That's why I let the Runamuk and Sweet Grass boys take most of the stock from here; easier to get one gal home than twenty cow-beasts."

Ingolf smiled like a wolf. "That may have been true before your war with Deseret ended, but now the prices you get for everything you took will go down, sure as sure, with so much loot chasing the livestock. And the women will eat every day, and some of them will die and leave you with nothing for your trouble. Selling some to me now means you don't have to try and move them in a glutted market . . . and the bullion you get you can carry on one packhorse and lend out at interest until prices for livestock drop again."

Jed grunted, pulling at his beard and looking as if he'd tasted something sour. Ingolf had explained his bargaining strategy to Rudi, and it was based on the Cutters' wants, just as a real trader's would be. In the end, cattle and sheep and horses were the only wealth that was really real to the plainsmen . . .

"Well, hell, Mr. Vogeler, you're makin' me feel guilty at unloading any of 'em on you," Jed said dryly. "Mebbe I should pay *you* to take 'em off my hands."

Ingolf shrugged. "Newcastle's a city. There are plenty of workshops there, and farms around it, and police and a town wall to keep order. We make a lot of stuff for the Sioux and for trade—they buy our buffalo-hide shields and our bows as far east as Nebraska—and we can make more if we get more hands. Hell, if you could sell us men, we could use them in the coal mines and the lamp-oil works."

"Which means you can afford to pay more than my neighbors for the gals."

"But they're not worth as much to *you*, which is what matters in a bargain. If I push on to Twin Falls, I'll get what I need even cheaper; I can buy from the Church's officials, or your army quartermasters. *And* you're not selling me the best you have here and you know it. Come on, Mr. Smith, make it worth my while to turn back now and save an extra two weeks' travel."

"You'll get a lot more than forty-five dollars each when you get home," Smith pointed out.

"On the ones who live; some won't," Ingolf said with an air of patience. "Plus there's the tax to the *Oceti Sakowin*, and the cost of transport, food, depreciation on working stock and those wagons I want to buy from you, and my men's wages . . . I'll give you fifteen each for all twenty-five and that's generous. They're none of them as good quality as the one we've already bought. And I should get a bulk purchase discount—"

Rudi had been avoiding looking at the women who

waited, mostly in stolid silence beside the little bundles of food and spare clothes that would go with them, many with children clutching at their skirts. A few of the women wept, but the children were too frightened, and most of their mothers looked like they'd used up a lifetime's tears. They all glanced back at Picabo, though, as a party of young Cutters came through the gate, whooping and shoving one another in rough horseplay. Edain and Rebecca were in their midst, and they both looked as though a wagon had just run over their puppy.

No, Edain does, Rudi thought. *Rebecca looks more like a queen surrounded by oafs, and walks like it. She's a fine brave girl . . . no, a fine woman, and no mistake . . . but perhaps not the best person to impersonate a slave.*

Jed and Ingolf turned from their leisurely bargaining. They listened to the story—told in bits and pieces by excited youngsters—and the older Cutter's scowl would have done credit to a summertime thunderhead.

"You damned pup!" he said after a moment, and snatched his hat off. He looked as if he'd like to hit Jack with it again, too. "What're you thinking of, playing grab-ass with someone else's property? And these folks are guests in our camp, under the Prophet's protection, too! You're a disgrace to the Rippling Water brand!"

"It was a little forward of her ass he grabbed," Lin put in, and then subsided at a look.

Behind him Odard looked at Ingolf and Rudi, his eyebrows fractionally raised. The man from Wisconsin shook his head very slightly, and Rudi flicked his eyes in agreement. If the "Sioux Chief" intervened, there was no telling how things might go—probably back to a duel to the death between the two young men.

For once Jack wasn't backing down from his uncle's anger; he certainly looked determined enough. He flushed at the Rancher's insult, but stood straight and went on doggedly:

"Uncle Jed, she *hit* me. In front of everybody! And he didn't do anything but try to face me down! Am I supposed to let a slave gal hit me like that, or a stranger walk on me?"

Jed spat disgustedly just before the pointed toes of Jack's tooled-leather boots and then waved him aside. He lowered his voice as he spoke to Ingolf:

"Mr. Vogeler, I'm sorrier than I can say about this. I can't make the pup apologize . . . not even if they were still fixing to fight serious. As it is, though . . . well, if the arrow hits your bought gal, I'll give you two of ours in recompense, and you can pick which. And *Jack's* going to pay for it, you can bet on that!"

Rudi walked over to Edain. "What happened?" he said quietly. "Beyond the obvious."

"Father Wolf be my witness, Chief, I just challenged the filthy *scabhtéara* to a shooting match!" Edain whispered frantically. "I figured I'd be sure to beat him at that, but it would be even odds with cold steel. It was *those* sodding bastards who had the idea about the apple!"

The brown-haired Cutter named Lin cleared his throat as his comrades and others of the Rippling Waters men gathered around, letting their preparations drop.

"Hear the terms of this shoot!" he said, trying to be formal. "Eddie here can shoot three arrows. If he misses the apple and the gal with all three, then our own Jack gets the gal, or Eddie pays him forty-five dollars cash money. If he hits the gal, then he and his bear the loss 'cause he isn't as good a shot as he claimed. If he hits the apple, then Jack has to pay *him* forty-five dollars fine for groping his bought gal and being a natural-born stupid dumb fuck as we all know he is."

"Fuck *you*, Lin!"

"Not while there's sheep on Rippling Waters, Jack," Lin said cheerfully. "They smell better'n you, too. Let the fun begin!"

"No help for it, then." Rudi studied the younger Mackenzie's face. "Ground and center. No, I *mean* it, clansman! Breathe in—breathe out. Slow and steady."

Edain obeyed, and a little of the gray tightness left his face as he controlled lungs and heart.

"I don't know if I can do it," he said, and held up his hand.

There was a slight quiver to it.

"You *can*," Rudi said. "You're the laddie who won the Silver Arrow younger than any before you, and then beat me for it the next year!"

Edain's grimace showed his teeth. "That was just a target!"

"And *this* is just a target," Rudi said, and forced all sympathy out of his voice; if he couldn't banish fear, he'd have to make Edain use it. "And that's what you're going to do, because you must. Invoke Them ... and then get out there and let the gray goose fly, clansman!"

The young Cutters had hustled Rebecca over to the town wall. She stood with her arms crossed, staring straight ahead with a faint smile on her face as they placed the apple on her head; it was a large one, bright red, and still unwithered. Rudi looked aside and noticed Jed Smith looking at Edain ... with a considering expression in his eyes.

"That young nephew of yours is a mite soft," he said quietly to Ingolf. "Getting all bothered about a bought gal, as if she were kin or his sweetheart."

The man from Wisconsin shrugged. "Young guys are like that around women," he said. "Especially young, pretty women."

"You should've let him screw the bitch silly and get over it," the Rancher said.

"Well, Good Lance decided he fancied her, you see. I'll still get her sale price, but otherwise ..." Ingolf shrugged. "I'm not going to piss off a Sioux clan who're good friends now to let my own nephew blow off some steam and get the girl out of his head."

"Ah," Jed said, glancing over at Odard. "Good thing he's not too mad about this."

"He may be. Hard to tell, with Injuns. But they're sticklers for taking up a challenge, you know—at least, the Sioux are."

"Right. Well, I'd have lent you boys some of ours ... let's hope your Eddie can pull off that shot. I swear, even if Jack *is* my sister's son, the little bastard is such a pain in the ass, I almost wish it was him there with the apple on his head!"

Edain strode out to the mark Jack drew in the scrubby grass with a boot heel. It was fifty yards to the wall where Rebecca waited, far enough that her face was mostly a blur and the apple only a red dot. He looked expressionlessly at her, at the movement of the grass in the light irregular wind. Then he stripped off his leather jacket, tossed it to the ground, and laid bow, quiver and sword belt on it. Jed made a grunting sound and watched more closely as the young clansman flexed his arms and rotated them slowly to stretch sinew and tendon, working his fingers as well. Cords in his forearms stood out sharply, moving beneath the taut white skin. Edain was only average in height, but he looked strong even in that company, and he had quite a few scars for a man so young.

Then he picked his leather-and-steel bracer, adjusting the straps to fit his bare forearm, took up the bow and strung it Mackenzie-style—bottom end over the left instep and right thigh over the riser, pushing down with his body weight as his right hand slipped the cord into the notch in the elk-antler nock. When that was done he picked the agreed three shafts from his quiver, all with hunting broadheads that had started their lives as stainless-steel spoons. The triangular heads were honed to razor sharpness, and they glittered in the strong sunshine as he rolled each arrow over his thumbnail to test its straightness.

He's using broadheads because he hopes they won't break the skull bone even if he misses, Rudi thought sympathetically. *Not a hope, my friend. At that range and with a draw that heavy . . .*

"That's a good bow," Jed said slowly. "Strange-looking, but it's made by someone who knows what he's doing."

"We've got first-rate bowyers in Newcastle," Ingolf said. "Have since the Change."

"But I've seen Newcastle bows, and they're our style, pretty much—we buy some from you, traded hand to hand. I've never seen one quite like that 'un."

"We got the idea from farther east," Ingolf said easily. "Just these last couple of years. Too long for easy horseback work, but some of the younger men have taken them up."

"What's that wood? It doesn't look like bois d'arc."

"Yew. Grows in the canyons," Ingolf lied with easy fluency.

Jed Smith could almost certainly read, unlike many of his younger cowboys. But he probably didn't have occasion to do so very often, and he certainly couldn't go look up the natural vegetation around Newcastle, Wyoming.

Ingolf went on: "They're good for hunting on foot in the Black Hills up north of town, or shooting from the town walls. Don't have to cure in a hotbox, or be lacquered against the wet. And they're cheap, a tenth or a quarter the cost of a saddlebow, so you're not out of pocket so much if you damage one."

Smith grunted again, rubbing at his jaw. "Might be worth the trouble, then, for townsmen," he said with kindly scorn for men who lived behind walls and worked on foot.

That turned to an instinctive duck and snatch at the hilt of his shete as Edain drew, turned on his heel away from the town wall, and loosed. Jack *did* throw himself flat; Edain had wheeled to face him, and there was nothing wrong with his reflexes. He lay on his back with his fighting knife naked in his hand, gaping upward at the trajectory of the arrow Edain had shot nearly straight up. There was a murmur of amazement from the watching cowboys as something fell back—two things, the arrow and the mallard duck it had transfixed.

The bird thumped into the dusty earth not more than arm's length from Jack's gape. Two of his friends dodged neatly as the arrow plunged into the dirt with a *shunk!* The young Mackenzie strolled over, pulled the shaft out of the dirt, then leaned over the Cutter.

"Are you not going to thank me, then, Jack-me-lad?" he inquired mildly, reaching out with the end of his longbow to nudge the limp blue-green shape of the bird. "You've the makings of a fine roast-duck dinner there, and the flight feathers will do for fletching when you've plucked it. And I'll ask no more of you if you decide to call this quits. Save yourself forty-five dollars, friend . . . and enjoy your duck."

Rudi found himself smiling involuntarily. Jed Smith snorted a laugh, and the young Cutter's friends roared until they staggered around wiping at their eyes and slapping one another on the back; a few fell helpless and drummed their heels on the ground. Several urged their comrade to accept the terms, between sputters and whoops. Skill with the bow was the thing they admired most in all the world, after horsemanship and raw courage.

Jack came back to his feet with a shoulder roll. The Cutters all looked a little awkward to Rudi's eyes when they were afoot, though they were as graceful as panthers in the saddle. That didn't mean the young man wasn't strong and quick, and Rudi judged that he'd be good with a blade. He didn't draw, quite . . .

"You got two more shafts, or the split-tail is mine," he said with quiet venom, all garrulousness washed out of him by the hate that made his face go white around the nostrils. "Now shoot. I'm of a mind to see how many ways I can fuck that bitch and *you* can keep your forty-five dollars."

Edain shrugged; Rudi thought he alone could see the flash of despair in the archer's eyes, but anger was deeper. He turned and smoothed the fletching of the arrow against his lips, blowing softly on the feathers and setting the shaft on the string. Then he stood stock still while he took one long breath, drew past the angle of his jaw and loosed in a single continuous movement.

The arrow flashed out, seeming to drift as it gained distance. There was less than a second before it struck . . . and Rebecca Nystrup pitched forward on her face, limp as a sack.

Silence fell for a long moment. "Well," Jed Smith said. "Want me to finish her off for you?"

CHAPTER SEVEN

B D fanned herself with one dangling end of the loose sun-turban she wore over an inconspicuous steel cap. A quarter mile ahead of her eastbound wagon train on Highway 84 was a baulk of timber studded with blades, mounted on old truck axles with modern spoke wheels. And besides the ten men behind it on foot with pikes and crossbows, a round dozen or more armed cowboys waited to either side.

It all looked tiny in this huge landscape, beneath a sky blue from horizon to horizon; the weather was clear and dry, typical for fall hereabouts. And just on the comfortable side of warm, also standard, but the wind was from the east and it held the slightest hint of autumn beneath the acrid scent of dust. But no view with that much edged metal in it was particularly friendly.

"Tía Loba?" the head of her guards said, as some of the cowboys cantered forward and flanked them to either side, just within bowshot.

"Keep calm, Chucho," she said. "We'll just walk on up to them and have a talk."

The slow creak and clatter and bounce of wagon travel went on, and the figures around the barricade grew from dolls to men.

"Whoa!" she said, pulling on the reins, just as they barked out: *"Halt!"*

Dobben and Maggie were well trained, once they

woke from their patient ambling daze; the big half-Suffolk lead pair came to a stop inside six paces, the rear pair had to halt perforce, and she pulled and locked the brake lever. The four other carts behind them came to a halt as well, and the six guards reined in beside them.

They were just far enough away that the Easterners would have to come to her if they wanted to talk without shouting, which was what she'd wanted. Silence replaced the clop of shod hooves on the freeway's broken asphalt, silence and the long hiss of the wind through the rolling fields on either side. You couldn't see Pendleton proper from here—it was down in the river valley about six miles farther east—but you could just make out the rounded heights of the Blue Mountains on the horizon.

"And this used to be a tourist spot," she muttered to herself.

BD looked around casually, wiping her forehead on the tail of her turban and checking for more armed men. Northward was a reaped wheat field with some of the shocks of grain still standing in yellow tripods, but elsewhere the rolling swales around had long since gone back to arid wilderness. Pale bleached-brown bunch-grass studded with the olive green of sagebrush rippled in waves; a flock with a mounted shepherd and his dogs and guard llamas drifted south of the road, moving slowly through the middle distance. Farther off some pronghorns danced, and a pair of buzzards swept in and perched on the tilted shape of an old telephone pole not far away. It moved slightly under their weight.

I hope *that's not an omen*, she thought. *And of course, this was the Oregon Trail before it was Interstate 84. Not all that different from the way it looked when some of my ancestors came through in ox-carts.*

Footmen and mounted archers alike scowled at her party, and there were *two* flags flying from a post by the road. One was the expected blazon of the local Rancher—the Circle D in black on light green. The other was the white-on-red cowboy and bucking bronco of the Associated Communities of the Pendleton Emergency Area.

What everyone else calls the Pendleton Round-Up, BD

thought. *Or, alternatively, "those Pendleton sheep rapers." But they usually don't bother with the flag. Pythian Apollo witness I am getting too old for this.*

She was just short of sixty now, and getting a bit gnarled. People said she was tough as an old root, but . . .

Yeah, tough as an old root, and stiffer. People age faster these days, she thought. *I spent the past generation heaving loads and hauling on reins, not behind a keyboard. It's time to sit by the fire and tell the grandchildren stories.*

Then, smiling to herself: *Who am I kidding? The Powers gave me my marching orders back at Dun Juniper last Lughnasadh, and Apollon confirmed it.*

Her guards closed up around the lead wagon; they and the wranglers were her own people from the Kyklos, mostly unofficial nephews—or in one case, a niece-by-courtesy. They favored Japanese-style armor, another legacy of hobbyists-turned-deadly-serious right after the Change. The outfit included flared helmets and armor of metal lozenges laced together, and they carried naginatas, five-foot shafts topped with curved swordblades. Quivers and asymmetric longbows rode across their backs, and katana and wazikashi at their belts.

They were also bristling a little at the show of force. Young men . . .

"Whoa, *everybody*," BD said loudly, carefully not touching the naginata that rode in a scabbard behind her, or an assortment of concealed weapons on her own person. "Let's be sensible here; it's good for business."

She climbed down from the seat and rubbed at the small of her back, looking deliberately as nonthreatening as possible; she was in shapeless linsey-woolsey pants, belted tunic and boots, practical traveling garb. An expert could probably catch the mail-vest beneath, but that was just a reasonable precaution traveling in lands without much law. Peering at the cowboys, she saw a face she knew, and got out her glasses to confirm it.

"Hey, Rancher Jenson!" she called; Sandy Jenson was an old customer. "What is this? *Another* shakedown? If you people don't stop this shit, nobody will come this way at all, and then where'll you be?"

The Rancher walked his horse over, followed by some of his retainers. They were certainly loaded for bear; Jenson's long reddish beard splayed down on a mail-shirt of the short type that cow-country fighters wore if they could afford it, and the men behind him fairly bristled with weapons and bits and pieces of armor. One had an arrow on the string of his recurve and they were all scowling.

Twenty cowboys, she thought. *Hmmm. That's a quarter of the riders Jenson can bring to a fight. Enough to cut into the Circle D's usual routine. It must be fairly serious. Plus those other guys look like Pendleton City militia.*

"This isn't a transit fee, BD," Jenson said, using the local terminology for *shakedown.* "The Bossman says he's heard you Westerners may be getting ready to invade. We've been called up to guard against spies and infiltrators."

"Hey, Sandy, you know me," BD said. "I've done business with you and I did business with your father."

She jerked a thumb over her shoulder at the pony drawn on the canvas tilts of her wagons, scuffing along amid puffs of dust.

"The Plodding Pony Service is neutral. I carry stuff, I buy, I sell. Everybody benefits. And I'm not exactly hiding or sneaking around here. Also I'm old enough to be your mother. Do I *look* like Jane Bond?"

That went past him; he'd been about nine when the Change happened.

"Do I *look* like a spy?" she amplified.

"You're from the Willamette. Your bunch—"

"—the Kyklos."

"—yeah, the Kyklos, you're part of the Corvallis Meeting," he said, but his frown relaxed a bit.

Unexpectedly, one of Jenson's cowboys spoke, a gangling youngster with a scatter of spots.

"She's an abomination, a woman doing a man's part," he said. "And flaunting herself shamelessly in man's garb. The Ascended Masters say—"

Jenson turned in the saddle and extended a finger into the skinny youngster's face.

"George, it's a free country and you can take up that half-baked stuff if you want, but if you feel like preaching, you do it on your own time, understand? And *not* on my land. *I'm* the Rancher here on the Circle D, and I happen to be a Presbyterian, which I'll thank you to remember."

"All right."

"*What* did you say, boy?" he barked, raising his quirt. "Let me hear that again."

"Yes, sir, Rancher Jenson, sir," he added sullenly.

"That's better. Now apologize to the lady."

The young man stared at the horizon. After an instant he ground out: "Sorry, ma'am."

Jenson nodded. "You get on to Pendleton and see about those horseshoes I ordered. *Git.*"

He turned back to BD, ignoring one of the older hands cuffing the young man on the back of the head and muttering a curse.

"Sorry, BD. We've had some odd preachers coming through past couple of years. George there never did learn to look in a horse's mouth before he bought it."

"Hell, Sandy, if he can get excited about my flauntingly shameless old legs, and in these saggy-assed pants at that, either the boy's not getting enough or I'm *really* flattered."

The Rancher relaxed with a grin, and several of his men laughed; George flushed under his tan and hunched in the saddle, turning his mount and flicking the end of his long reins to either side. The quarter horse took off in a spurt of gravel.

"Did *you* hear anything about an invasion, BD?" his employer said.

"Not offhand, but I've been on the road for weeks; I'm out of Bend this time. It doesn't sound very sensible to me, though. Nobody's bothered you all this time, why start now? And usually the Meeting can't agree on the right time of day for dinner, much less invading hither and yon. What would be the point? To steal your oh-so-rare and valuable wheat?"

Actually, I got off the railway in the Dalles only three

days ago, she thought. *Special express pedalcars. And for once the Meeting* did *agree on something, and without talking about it forever plus three days, either.*

None of that showed on her face; a trader and a Priestess both had to learn self-control.

Jenson took off his helmet, which had a llama-hair crest, and scratched at his scalp.

"Nothing personal, but from what I remember and what Dad said, you people left us to rot back when, with everyone against his neighbor and gangs of refugees from the cities and whatnot," he said.

"Hard times all over, the first year or two," BD said shortly.

And a hell of a lot harder for me than you, Sandy, she added behind a calm face.

At 6:15 P.M. Pacific Time, March 17, 1998, BD had been driving southbound on I-5 in Portland, a mile and a half north of the Terwilliger exit, and she'd been pushing forty. Jenson had been a child, and a child on a ranch with more cows than people, far enough from the cities that they had enough food to take others in, rather than fighting over scraps or shivering with cholera as they lay dying in a ditch.

More than half the human race had died in the year after the Change; in North America it had been closer to nine-tenths. But *this* area probably had more people now than it had then—certainly it did outside the city of Pendleton proper.

Jenson went on: "Then that son-of-a-bitch Arminger comes and tells us he's going to *pacify* the place, which meant handing the ranches out to his cronies here and his gangbanger thugs from Portland. I *do* remember that. Then you make his troops leave and we had *another* round of fighting. Thank God that Bossman Carl finally got things under control."

BD restrained herself from arguing with the spin he put on the past twenty-two years of local affairs; getting into a political dispute was never good business . . . particularly if you *were* spying. Though Bossman Carl Peters wasn't as bad as he might have been—for one thing, *nobody* could exert enough control here to be a real tyrant.

"Look, Sandy, can I do business here or not? I've got my expenses to meet, you know. If I have to turn around and go home, the sooner I find out the better. And I'd appreciate a letter from you telling me to go home, so I can claim act-of-the-Gods and not have to pay nondelivery penalties to the shipper."

Jenson looked harassed. "Hell, BD, *I* know you . . . but you are from Meeting territory and . . . well, you've got armed guards with you."

"Well, by the Gods, I should hope I do!" she said, letting a little temper show. "You know as well as I do how many Rovers and road people and just plain old-fashioned bandit scum are running around between here and the Cascades. I travel with this many guards in CORA territory, too, when I've got valuable cargo—and I don't do bulk freight."

At his bristle, she went on: "Come round and look at my load and then tell me if I'm hostile to Pendleton, Sandy. Yeah, and those pikemen are from the Bossman's townee militia, aren't they? Have one of them over too."

He dismounted—a bit of a concession, since interior ranchers and their followers generally saddled up even if they were just going from their front doors to the outhouse. The townsman in the steel-strapped leather breastplate and kettle helmet came over as well; his round dark face was frankly hostile, and his little black mustache twitched.

Both their faces changed when she pulled out a claw hammer and opened the first of the flat crates that made up half her cargo. The lid came up with a screech of nails, and . . .

"Jesus!" the Rancher said, taking up one of the swords and giving a few expert cuts that made the cloven air whine. "Now, that's the real goods!"

"Yeah, I'm delivering them to Murdoch and Sons, on consignment from Bend," she said. "See the Isherman stamp on the boxes?"

The *WSIS*—for Weapons Shop of Isherman and Sons—was branded into the cheap pine boards.

She waved an envelope. "All the paperwork's in order. Now, if I was a spy for someone trying to attack you, would I bring weapons in that your Bossman can buy?" she said reasonably.

I might, just to disarm—snork, snork—your suspicions, she thought. *And there aren't enough in these wagons to make much difference to an actual war. It's not as if I'm hauling in a battery of field artillery, after all. You guys are short of that stuff.*

"And the barrels have mail-shirts, by the way," she went on. "Good light stainless steel with riveted links, none better, in the usual assortment of sizes. Plus helmets . . . it's all in the invoices."

Even the militia officer was impressed; Pendleton had never developed the sort of semi-mechanized arms shops that were common farther west, where water power was easier to come by. Mail-shirts were expensive everywhere, but more so here.

"The Bossman *will* be interested," the militiaman said. He extended a hand. "Captain da Costa, Carlos da Costa."

"Beatriz Dorothea," she said. "But everyone calls me BD."

BD shook with a firm squeeze and met his eyes squarely—also tricks of the trade. She'd heard of him, if not met him before; his family had a tannery and saddle-and-harness-making workshop. She told him:

"Tell Bossman Carl to talk to Murdoch; I'm just hauling this stuff for a fee plus commission."

Then she hesitated, as if making a painful calculation. "If you need some yourself, Sandy, I suppose . . ."

The Rancher looked tempted; a landholder out here always had to be ready to skirmish with his neighbors and outfitting his cowboys well was important in keeping them loyal. Under the militia officer's eye he shook his head.

"No, thanks. I can afford what we need, and we make

most of our own gear on the ranch anyhow. But you're doing us all a good turn, BD, and I appreciate it. Want to stay the night at the ranch house and have a steak dinner, and huevos rancheros and a shower before you head in tomorrow?"

He looked hopeful. Without any prying eyes but his own sworn men he might well "accept" a gift she could write off as a cost of doing business. BD caught his eyes and let hers slide a little towards the militiaman; that would be excuse enough. And . . .

Well, Sandy's not exactly a guest-friend, she thought. *That was a sacred bond. But I have eaten his bread and salt beneath his roof. I'd rather not do it again when I'm here with . . . well, sort of hostile intent. It's for their own good, really . . . but that won't help Sandy or any of his people who get in the way of an Associate's lance or a Mackenzie arrow or a Bearkiller backsword.*

"I think I should head straight in, with this cargo," she said. "But I'd appreciate it if I could send the wagons and teams right out again and keep them on the Circle D for a little while. Prices at Pendleton livery stables inside the wall are atrocious."

"Fine, and stay as long as you want coming out," Jenson said generously.

"I'll get a permit!" Captain da Costa said. "You're right, Doña Dorothea, a load this important should go *right* into town! Just you wait there and I'll fetch the paperwork—"

The last was said over his shoulder as he walked back towards the barricade.

"Who's he?" Jenson asked idly, sighing regretfully.

He jerked his head at the man sitting beside the driver of the second wagon, a great hulking hunched figure with a shock of shiny-black hair.

"Oh, that's my cousin Hugh," BD said. "He's simple, but there's no harm in him, and he's certainly useful to have around when there's heavy lifting to be done. Those boxes weigh a fair bit."

At the *Hugh* the big man gave a vacant grin and wiped

his nose on the back of his hand; there was a thread of drool slowly making its way down from the corner of his thick-lipped mouth.

"Here, Hugh!" BD said in an admonishing voice.

She handed him a handkerchief and he made a stammering cluck and used it, clumsily.

Captain da Costa returned with his form; behind him his men pushed in careful grunting unison, and the barricade rumbled aside.

"Just show this at the gate, Doña."

"And the Bossman is putting on a 'do' tomorrow night," Jenson said. "All the Ranchers and town bigwigs ... Hey, why don't you come? Murdoch will be there, too."

Da Costa nodded vigorously again. "You're a public benefactor, Doña," he said. "I'm sure Bossman Carl would be *delighted* to see you."

"I'll be there," BD said. *But he may not be delighted about it at all.*

Seven miles was more than an hour's travel at preserve-the-horses wagon speeds. That gave her enough time to take in the surroundings thoroughly without making it obvious.

"Oh, my, oh, my," BD murmured, as they passed the ruins of the old State Hospital and swung south. "Ares is on hand."

There were tented camps outside Pendleton; most of them were sited so they weren't in view from I-84, but she could catch glimpses of them. Most of them were the casual affairs a Rancher and his retainers would make when they were away from home, remarkable only because there were so many. But it was getting on for sundown. Campfires showed there in the rising ground south of town, adding to the smoke-and-outhouse scent of the town in general; and some of them were suspiciously regular, laid out in neat rows, or in one case a complex system of interlocking triangles.

Pity I can't use my binoculars, she thought. *But that would be a big I AM A SPY sign.*

She laughed a little sadly as they turned north on an overpass still labeled *Exit 209* in faded, peeling paint, where the old John Day highway had approached town. Around them was the usual messy sadness of ruined suburbs that surrounded most still-inhabited towns; burnt-out houses or buildings torn down for their materials, truck gardens and livery stables and smelly tanyards and plain weed-grown wreck with bits of charred wood or rusty rebar poking up through it.

"*Tía Loba?*" her nephew-guardsman asked.

"Chucho, that underpass over there used to dump cars onto Frazier, because Emigrant was one-way."

His dark young face looked puzzled, and he pushed up the brim of his helmet to scratch with gloved fingers.

"You could enchant a road so that it only went one way in the old days?" he asked. "You are pulling the leg of me, *Tía*. Flying I believe, the pictures that moved I believe, but not *that*."

"Changelings!" she muttered with a shrug.

"Oh-ho," the man who was *not* BD's simple cousin Hugh said.

Traffic had thickened as they approached the gate, and slowed. Now the reasons were obvious. Chucho dropped back tactfully; he knew that "Hugh" was not as he seemed, and had carefully avoided learning any more.

Pendleton had been divided by the Umatilla River before the Change. Afterwards it had shrunk, in fighting and chaos and as people dispersed to the surrounding farms and ranches, but there had been no total collapse. Now it had four or five thousand people, in a rectangle on the south side of the river perhaps two-thirds of a mile long and a third wide. The inhabitants had built a wall with towers, out of concrete and rubble and rock around a core of salvaged girders; so much was unremarkable, although the construction was more recent and cruder than many, with rust-pitted iron showing on the surface.

What the pseudo-Hugh was looking at was a cluster of men examining the gate and its heavy valves of metal-sheathed timber.

BD had never seen the gear they wore, but she'd heard of it, and seen sketches by agents and far-traveling merchants. Armor of steel hoops and bands to protect the torso and shoulders, fastened with a complex set of brass latches; high boots; rounded helmets with neck-flares and hinged cheek-pieces and short cap-bill pieces over the eyes. All of them carried broad short stabbing swords, worn high on the right side of their belts . . . except for the man with a transverse crest on his helmet, who had his on his left hip. He also bore a swagger-stick or truncheon of twisted vinestock, tapping the end into his left palm. Closer and BD could see that he had a red kerchief tucked into the neck of his armor.

Boise regulars, she thought. *United States Army, as far as they're concerned. Sixth Regiment, from the shoulder-flashes.*

There was plenty of time to watch the commander with the vinestock pace about examining the gate and the two square flanking towers, since the usual evening crush of wagons and carts was trying to get through—and moving more slowly than usual, as the guards checked them with extra care. The strangers in the odd armor weren't shy about getting in people's way, either.

"Christ, civvies!" their officer said. "It's thick and it's solid, and that's all you can say for it. You could bring a covered ram right up to the gate!"

"Fubarred," his companion with the sergeant's chevrons on the short mail-sleeve said. "Looks like they based the design on an illustration from a book of faerie tales my mother used to read to me, Captain."

The officer reached out, a slight smile on his hard clean-shaven face, and playfully rapped the swagger-stick on the man's helmet. The steel went *bonk* under the tough wood of the vinestock.

"That's *Centurion*, Sergeant. The rank structure's been modernized."

"Yessir, Centurion. Glad President Martin got around to it, sir. It's a wonder we . . . or someone . . . didn't take 'em over before this if this is their *capital*. Lewiston has a lot better defenses and *it* wouldn't be a pimple on Boise's ass."

"Considerations of high policy, soldier—and stick to business. It'll be a lot better with a couple of eighteen-pounders and some heavy darters up top, on turntables and with steel shields. We'll put the lifting triangle right there and—"

The line inched forward. The gate-keepers were militiamen, ordinary shopkeepers and craftsmen taking the duty in turn with their homemade armor over normal working clothes. One of the Bossman's personal guard was there too, besides the usual clerk to collect the customs ducs—yet another local term for *shakedown*. He was a big young man in a hammered-steel breastplate and helmet with ostrich plumes, above tight red-dyed pants and elaborately tooled thigh-boots turned down to the knee; she guessed that someone *had* been looking through an illustrated book when they designed the outfit.

Or possibly the cover of a bodice-ripper, she thought wryly. *Or maybe that book of faerie tales. If he had pointed ears and whiskers, he'd be a dead ringer for Puss in Boots.*

A small mustache of the type Pendleton men favored was fiery red as well, naturally so judging from his milk-white-and-sunburn complexion. He took the letter and read it through slowly, moving his lips, then went and examined the opened box in the wagon.

"All *right*!" he said. "Fan-fucking-*tastic*. Go right on through, ma'am! I'll report this to the Bossman's House. No, you fool," he went on to the clerk. "Weapons imports are duty free for the duration of the emergency."

The Boise centurion looked up from a sketchbook. "Weapons?" he said.

Strolling over he looked into the crate and took one of the swords out. It was a straight longsword in a plain sheath of black leather over wooden battens, with aluminum at chape and lip; he drew the thirty-inch blade and looked down the edge, then hefted it to test the balance.

"Not bad. This is well-made equipment, for its type."

"Yeah, it is," the Bossman's guard said.

He didn't bother to keep the hard note out of his voice. There was a badge on his shoulder that had three intertwined capital R's, but despite the appearance it wasn't a Rancher's brand . . . exactly. That stood for Registered Refugee Regiment. Technically the man was a Registered Refugee, roughly equivalent to a slave in Pendleton, except that the men of the Regiment belonged to Bossman Carl Peters. Who had either come up with the idea on his own or gotten it out of some book on Middle Eastern history; its members had privileges ordinary freemen could only envy, and were correspondingly unpopular with townsmen and Ranchers both.

They were fanatically loyal to their benefactor and the two hundred of them were a major reason the current incumbent had managed to survive and hold on to power far longer than any previous overlord here.

The young man went on: "And they're for the Bossman. *Our* Bossman, His Honor Carl Peters. Any problem with that, straight-leg?"

"None at all, Lieutenant, none at all," the centurion said; he didn't seem at all put out by the unflattering term for a regular. "Our leaders are all in alliance to serve America, right?"

Which would have been more tactful if he hadn't used the tone a man would humoring a boy. BD left them talking with strained politeness as they went through into Pendleton proper. It was darker inside the walls; the streets were straight and fairly wide—especially Emigrant, down which they traveled—and the potholes had been repaired with packed gravel or remelted asphalt. But the town had been built up, two- or three-story structures of adobe or salvaged brick and wood frame standing cheek by jowl with others that had been kept unaltered for a century or more to preserve Pendleton's Old-West atmosphere before the Change. And . . .

"Hugh" was up walking beside her wagon now; his six foot seven was tall enough that they could talk quietly even with her sitting on the driver's seat and him hunched over and lurching. You tended to forget how tall he was until he came close, because he was even broader in proportion, built like an old-time high-rise, square from shoulders to hips.

"Lot of men in town," he said, in a voice with a soft drawling burr.

There were; young men, mostly. Many of them were ordinary cowboys from the ranches of Northeastern Oregon, but some were in uniforms of mottled sage-and-gray cloth, or coarse blue-green. Every second building seemed to house a saloon or eating-house or some combination on its ground floor, or to have been converted to such; the air was thick with the smell of frying onions and grilling meat, and sweat and horse manure and piss and beer and the sour tang of vomit, loud with raucous guitars and pianos and voices singing or shouting. And *every* building had the Pendleton flag flying, which was unusual.

As the sun dipped below the walls behind them the dark grew thick; Pendleton didn't run to streetlights, even lamps at crossroads like Sutterdown's, much less the sophisticated methane gaslights of Corvallis or Portland. The yellow glow from windows made it possible to steer the wagons without running over anyone ... if you were careful of figures collapsed half off the sidewalks.

They came to their destination, a compound taking up half a block, with a discreet MURDOCH AND SONS, IMPORTERS over the main gate and a blank twelve-foot wall all around the perimeter, not quite a fortification, but a real deterrent in the sort of factional squabble the city had had before the current Bossman took over.

The building just before it had a large sign reading WORKING GIRLS' HOTEL, and it was in the ornate stone and terra-cotta style of long ago, a century or more before the Change. Some of the girls were leaning out of the upper windows wearing very little, and shouting invitations that sounded more than usually tired and frazzled. Just as the Plodding Pony wagons passed, a figure catapulted out through the swinging doors and sprawled in the dirt of the street with a thud. He'd come with a boot in the buttocks, and lay for a second sobbing with rage and frustration and the raw whiskey that made his movements vague and tentative.

"Whoa!" BD shouted.

Her not-cousin grabbed at the team's bridles. Together they kept three tons of Conestoga and sixteen hooves from rolling over the prostrate figure.

The man tried to get up again; it was Rancher Jenson's cowboy George. He lay for a moment with horse dung in the fuzzy sheepskin of his chaps, and then rolled aside to dodge the saddle, saddlebags, bedroll, quiver and cased recurve bow that were tossed after him. He clumsily scooped the arrows back into the quiver and used the saddle to push himself partially erect.

"I want my money back!" he screamed from one knee, fumbling at his belt for his shete. "And my horse!"

A thick-set woman in a sequined dress came to the doors and leaned out. A massively built man loomed behind her, a classic whorehouse bully in a tight crimson shirt and expensive blue jeans, belt with a silver-and-turquoise buckle and tooled boots with fretted steel toe caps, his eyes flatly impassive and an iron rod in one fist. He pointed with it, and the cowboy let the hilt of his blade go. It was the woman who spoke, in a harsh raw voice:

"Kid, at your age if you can't get it going after twenty minutes with the Buffalo Heifer, you need a doctor, not a whore."

There were grins and laughter up and down the street as she went on:

"And you didn't have enough money to pay for what you gambled anyway. Be thankful we didn't keep the rest of your gear for kickin' up a fuss. Next time leave the sheep alone for a while before you come into town, rube."

The young cowboy staggered on past, the saddle flung over one shoulder. BD caught his gaze for an instant; it was sick with an unfocused rage that must be eating at his soul like acid, and she winced slightly in unwilling sympathy.

And some of the strangers were looking around them entirely too alertly for soldiers whooping it up before action. The crawling sensation between her shoulder blades didn't go away until they'd swung the wagon train into Murdoch's courtyard.

"Welcome, BD!" Murdoch said.

He was a middle-aged balding man, heavyset in a way rare nowadays, with thick brown muttonchop whiskers whose luxuriant curls compensated for his bald spot. He also wore what Pendleton currently regarded as a respectable businessman's evening dress—a good imitation of pre-Change copper-riveted Levi's tucked into tooled boots with pointed toes, fancy belt with ceremonial bowie knife, ruffled white shirt, floppy string tie, a cutaway tailcoat in good brown homespun, and a waistcoat embroidered in gold thread, with a watch and chain as well. The formal felt Stetson with its band of silver conchos was in his hands, and he looked as if he was *not* crushing it with an effort of will.

"Good to see you, BD, good to see you," he burbled. "Let's get the cargo into place!"

Grooms had led the teams away. Workers appeared and began unloading the wagons, and a steward led the Plodding Pony employees to a bunkhouse. BD stopped her chief guard with a hand on the arm.

"*Tiu?*" he said.

"Don't get settled in, Chucho," she said quietly. "Just water and feed the horses, load some oats, then hitch up. Tell the gate guards and the people at the barricade out on 84 that you're heading for the Circle D, but don't turn off at Jenson's place. Keep going west; push the horses as hard as you can without killing them."

He nodded, unsurprised. They were working for the Kyklos and the Meeting, and they were getting paid for it . . . but the family business could do without losing its capital assets, too.

And I like Dobben and Maggie, she thought. *I've traveled a lot of miles staring at those equine rumps.*

"Hugh" helped with the crates, slobbering and grunting but heaving two at a time up onto his broad stooped shoulders. When the last of them was stacked, Murdoch made a production of giving his day laborers their pay, with a little extra for the ones who worked for him regularly.

"You boys get on home to your families," he said. "And Sim, tell the house staff they can go home early. With my wife and the boys off visiting relatives, I can shift for myself tonight."

One of them grinned at him, a youngish man. "*I'm* goin' next door, patrón," he said.

"It's your money now that I've given it to you, Stan," Murdoch said. "Remember, tomorrow's a holiday—time off for the Bossman's speech. See y'all at the House!"

They left, swinging the big entry doors of the warehouse closed. Murdoch's smile ran away from his face as they did, and he checked the lock on the smaller entry door beside it, moving confidently in the darkness, as a man did when he was intimately familiar with a place.

"This is bad tradecraft, letting two agents know each other's identities," he said in a voice that was much colder and had less of the twanging local accent when he turned to face them. "All these years we've been doing business and I didn't know you worked for the Lady Regent until I got that message—"

"*With*, not *for*, Ben," BD said patiently. "I'm a perfectly genuine businesswoman. I just do . . . things on the side sometimes."

And pull yourself together, Ben. It's hard enough to control my own nerves without having to deal with other people's.

"And maintaining your cover isn't going to be important soon," she went on. "Or do you *want* to be here when the trebuchets start throwing thousand-pound rocks and bundles of incendiaries over the wall? Even Sandra can't make sure a siege engine doesn't drop a boulder or a jug of napalm on your head."

He was silent for a moment, fiddling with an expensive incandescent-mantle lantern; then it lit with a hiss, and a circle of yellow-white light drove the dense blackness back.

"No," he said quietly. "That's why I got my family out on the train to Walla Walla last week. But I've . . . been here and *in* this character for a long time. Since the War of the Eye. I keep slipping mentally and thinking I *am* my cover. And . . . I've got friends here. My wife was born here, and so were my children. I don't want to see Pendleton wrecked 'in order to save it.' "

"Going native?"

A sigh. "No, not really. It's not *such* a bad place . . ."

"If you don't end up sold to the woolen mills, or the Working Girls' Hotel, or worse," BD said. "Besides, hopefully we can make things a lot easier on the ordinary people. I'm not a great fan of the PPA, but even they don't do that sort of thing."

Anymore, she tactfully left unvoiced, and went on aloud:

"That's what *this* mission is all about, at least as far as I'm concerned. Plus the strategic stuff about keeping the Prophet and Boise at bay."

Murdoch nodded. Then he started as the big man beside BD straightened, took the soft pieces of rubber out of his cheeks, spat on the concrete floor, and pulled a pillow from under his coat. Suddenly he seemed much bigger . . . and not simple at all. And when he took off his gloves, the auburn fuzz on the backs of the great spade-shaped paws was a horrible mismatch for the raven thatch on his head.

Murdoch's eyes bulged. "You're—"

"John Hordle, at your service," he said, in the rich accent of rural Hampshire, still strong after a generation here in the Western lands.

"You're *Little John* Hordle! The one who killed Big Mac!"

"The very same. That disguise works a treat, even if you 'ave to drool an' slobber a bit. A bit undignified, innit? Still, it's worth it. Not so easy to hide, when you're my size."

Murdoch nodded. "Come on, then."

"You know," the big man said as they walked towards the office that was partitioned off from the floor of the two-story warehouse, "back when I was a nipper in 'ampshire growing up around the Pied Merlin—me dad's family's pub—I always fancied the Wild West. Clint Eastwood an' all them old shows on the telly. Shame to have me romantic notions ruined, innit?"

He jerked a thumb over his shoulder at the doors and the courtyard, and the street beyond:

"Or maybe it was different before the Change, the first time?"

"Not much," BD said. "Except they had guns so it was louder, and there wasn't a city wall, so it might have been less crowded. There were forty saloons and sixteen bordellos here back when it was a real cow-town with about two thousand people."

"It's the mobilization," Murdoch said defensively. "The town's bursting at the seams right now—it's worse than the Whoop-Up. And you saw the foreigners?"

"Yes. The Boise men I recognized, but . . ."

"CUT," Murdoch said grimly. "Not just the wandering preachers—we've been getting them for years—but soldiers and officials out of Corwin."

"When?" Hordle said.

"A few of them two weeks ago, then the rest just the past three days; and it's not just troops, there are high officers of both them and the Boiseans quartered at the Bossman's House. The Cutters are acting in concert with the Boise people. Carl Peters invited them in, but . . ."

"But the bugger has forgotten the saying about the camel's nose. Quick work on the villains' part, though," John Hordle said. "And we're not before time, eh?"

Murdoch put the lantern down on a desk for a moment, and then stepped to the rear wall of the office where a picture hung.

"I could let you down with the winch," he said. "But that section's closed off from the rest on the inside. *This* part doesn't officially exist—"

The picture was a Remington print set in an ornate frame—*Coronado's March,* all desert and dust and lances and armored *Conquistadores.* BD glanced at it, then suddenly realized . . .

You know, down in the Southwest, something precisely *like that might be happening right now and that could be a* photograph *of it.*

She shivered slightly and set the thought aside. If you'd lived through the past couple of decades, you got used to things like that; you also got used to pushing them away when they hit you again.

There was a *click* as the merchant-spy's fingers explored the frame of the print, and then a section of wall the size of a small door swung open. He led them into the staircase beyond; the temperature fell as they descended through dirt held back by boards and then into a broad tunnel of coarse light-textured volcanic rock like hard dense pumice.

The lantern left a moving bubble of light in darkness Stygian enough to make the nighttime streets seem like noonday, showing ancient posters and even dust-choked storefront windows. There was a cold smell of abandonment and mouse droppings, like an old house where nobody had lived for a while.

"Welcome to Underground Pendleton," Murdoch said, a little nervous as he went on: "Dug by the Chinese."

"Chinese?" Hordle said.

"There were a lot of Chinese workers here once," Murdoch said; he seemed to have a perverse pride in local history, even the more questionable bits. "They dug tunnels so they could get from one part of town to another. It's easy, the rock's soft and cuts like cheese."

"Why not use the streets?"

"Because the local Anglo-Saxons had a habit of shooting them on sight for no particular reason besides a dislike of Chinamen," Murdoch said.

"I've 'eard of the *underground economy*, but this is ridiculous," Hordle said. "Roit useful for what we've in mind, though. You said there was tunnels, but this is a bloody maze, mate."

"Then they used part of it for illegal businesses, and then for tourists before the Change," Murdoch went on. "It's all shut up now, too dark and stuffy to be useful. Officially I just have some storage chambers down here . . .

but your people have been going over the plans and . . . ah, here we are!"

He came to a stout door and knocked three times quickly and three times slowly before opening it, letting out light and warmer air and a pleasant smell of burning pinewood. The chamber was brightly lit, by lamps and by a small hearth built into—or dug out of—one wall; Hordle blew out his lips in an expression of relief at the score of figures seated within around a long plank table, with the remains of a meal scattered about.

The burble of Sindarin conversation died away as the door opened, though several waved to BD as to an old friend. BD understood the Elven-tongue well enough, since she'd been hiring Dúnedain Rangers for caravan security for years, and it was the language they usually spoke among themselves. She'd been working with them as long as they'd existed, in fact, though to listen to some of them you'd think their grandparents had stepped off the boat from Numenor, having quietly skipped the Fourth Age somehow.

Sometimes she shuddered to think what the generation born in steads like Stardell Hall in Mithrilwood would be like, raised by crazed Changelings with their heads full of stories they *believed*.

And they make me *feel old*, she thought.

Hordle and Alleyne Loring were the eldest of them all at forty. Astrid Larsson and Eilir Mackenzie were thirty-six; and they'd been the *founders* of the Dúnedain. The rest of the party were in their late teens or their twenties. All of them were in Dúnedain working gear—black leather and wool, mostly, and soft-soled elf-boots, but with the tree-stars-and-crown blazon on their chests done in dark gray, rather than silver-white. One of the nearest was a striking woman in her thirties with bowl-cut hair that was naturally the color that dye had given Hordle's own brown curls, and leaf-green eyes the same color as her mother, Juniper's.

Hello, luv, Hordle Signed to the black-haired woman; she looked up with a smile from a litter of maps.

And aloud, since the three bright lanterns hung from

the rocky ceiling and the firelight gave ample light for
Eilir's lip-reading skills:

"Well, dear, I'm 'ome."

No, you're in a cave under an enemy city full of thousands of people who'd like to kill us all, Eilir replied;
she was still smiling, but there was a bit of a bite in the
gestured speech. *Our* children *are back home in Stardell
wondering where the hell we are and when we'll be
back.*

Hordle winced.

"No problem with the weapons, John?" Alleyne Loring said, mercifully changing the subject.

He spoke English for Murdoch's sake, in an accent as
British as Hordle's, but of the manor-and-public-school
variety, and smoothed his close-trimmed yellow mustache with a finger.

"Dead easy." A deep chuckle. "No better way to
smuggle weapons than in wagonloads of ... *weapons*!
No problem getting our lot in?"

"You're the last, old chap. They've tightened up their
security, but they're still not stopping harmless unarmed
wanderers in ones and twos."

"You'd better get the gear unloaded and get ready,"
Murdoch warned. "I don't think the Bossman will send
his people over for his weapons tonight, but I'm not
absolutely sure he won't ... and there are more men in
town than you expected."

"Cutters. And Boise regulars," John Hordle said, repeating the details that Sandra Arminger's spy had given
him. "Seems the Bossman got an attack of the nerves
and decided 'e needed some friends."

"Tsk," Alleyne Loring said. "He forgot the origins of
England."

Murdoch and BD looked at him, and there was a grim
smile on his handsome fine-boned face as he went on:

"The first English in England—two outlaw chiefs
from Jutland named Hengist and Horsa and their merry,
hairy band of pirate cutthroats—"

"Sound like lads after me own heart," Hordle observed.

"—were invited in by a chief of the Britons named Vortigern. The Romans had withdrawn, and Vortigern had a problem with the Picts kicking up their heels. He decided that the obvious thing to do was hire some Saxons to fight the Picts for him rather than go to the dreadful bore and bother of doing it himself."

"What happened then?" Murdoch asked.

The smile turned wolfish; for a moment it was easy to imagine Alleyne in a bearskin tunic, leaping out of a Dark Age war-boat with a *seax* in his fist.

"Shortly thereafter the Jutes and their Saxon and Anglian relatives had England, and the Britons had ... Wales. Despite all King Arthur could do. And Vortigern made that mistake despite a late-Roman definition of rapacity: *He could teach piracy to a Saxon.*"

A tall woman who'd been sitting with her legs crossed and her hands resting on her thighs opened her eyes and swung her legs down from their lotus position. Her head came up, crowned with white-blond hair in a tight-woven fighting braid, and she met Murdoch's eyes. The Association spy shivered a little in that pale gaze, the hyacinth-blue pupils rimmed and shot with silver threads. She stared silently for a few seconds, and the man who Pendleton knew as an importer squirmed.

BD sympathized; people meeting the *Hiril Dúnedain* for the first few times often had that reaction. She'd known the girl ... woman ... since she was fourteen, and still felt that way sometimes herself.

"We aren't expected at the Bossman's feast," Astrid Larsson said. "But I do think we'll drop in anyway."

Alleyne smiled. "*Crashing* the party, rather like thirteen dwarves coming by unexpectedly for tea."

"But even less welcome and more troublesome," his wife said. "And if there are emissaries from our ultimate enemies there ... so much the better. We'll spend tomorrow going over the details, but with luck and a little effort we can skip the war and go straight to the victory, which is always the best part anyway."

Hordle rapped his knuckles on the wooden table.

Murdoch muttered and retreated, banging the door behind him.

Alleyne made a *tsk* sound and dropped back into the Elven-tongue. "You shouldn't spook him, my love, just because he works for Sandra Arminger. He's on our side now. The whole Portland Protective Association is. And he's been quite cooperative."

"We're fighting the same enemy at the moment, *bar melindo*," she said. "That isn't exactly the same thing as being friends, darling."

A dozen of the Rangers filed past and trotted up the stairs to fetch the gear. BD stepped aside as they left and nodded to the four leaders, then stepped over to look at the documents on the table. One was the blueprints of the Bossman's house. The other was a map that showed Pendleton, the modern town, in considerable detail. Across it—underneath it—lay a network of dotted red lines . . .

"Well, that's imaginative at least," she said, as the details of the plan leapt out at her. "It's going to be tricky, though. Particularly the 'getting away alive' part."

And I'm glad I sent my *people out of town!*

Eilir nodded and replied in Sign: *Don't worry. Murdoch has really done a very creditable job with these tunnels since the end of the war. The last war, I should say.*

"Just like Sandra Arminger to have a *literal* mole here, burrowing away for the past twelve years," Astrid said dryly, and they chuckled. "She isn't called the Spider for nothing."

A clatter of footsteps, and the Dúnedain returned with boxes and crates and barrels carried on their shoulders, or slung between them by the rope handles. A little brisk hammering opened them, and men and women crowded around.

"Ah!" John Hordle said, seizing his four-foot bastard longsword and running his hand along the double-lobed grip. "Felt naked without this, I did. A big bloke's not worth buggery without 'is bastard."

Which sentence sounds absolutely indescribable said

in Sindarin with a Hampshire yokel burr, BD thought with a mental groan.

Meditatively, glancing at Astrid, Hordle went on: "Aren't we supposed to be generals? Sitting around map tables looking important, while the younger generation do the work? This is too 'ands-on for my taste, now I'm past forty and a dad and sensible."

Astrid smiled and spread her long-fingered hands. "Are there any among our people better suited to lead this endeavor, my brother?"

"No, I suppose not," Hordle grumbled, shrugging into a mail-coat covered in dark green leather and cinching it with a broad belt.

BD stretched her own back with a silent groan. Her mail-vest was light, but she'd worn real armor now and then, and detested every minute of it. Hordle was probably so accustomed to it that he didn't even notice. It was like the sword; he didn't feel natural without it.

"But I thought we came here to fight a battle?" he went on plaintively, turning his head slightly so that he could wink at Eilir unobserved; she giggled silently. "There's a murdering great army out there west of town, thousands of them sitting on their arses with nothing better to do than eat and scratch themselves, and here *we* are doing *their* work."

"The best battle is the one you win without fighting," Astrid said serenely.

Hordle rolled his eyes and spoke to Alleyne Loring. "I *hate* it when she gets all profound like that!" Then to Astrid: "And you put *Tiphaine d'Ath* in to look after the troops."

Astrid's smile was slightly cruel now. "That was her punishment. Do you imagine there's anywhere in the world she'd rather be than *here,* right now, John? And when the bards make their song, they'll sing of *us*, while Tiphaine gets three lines saying she looked after the troops well enough while we were gone."

The smile grew broader, and unexpectedly she giggled like a schoolgirl. "She'll be snarling about that when she's ninety."

"Let's hope the song doesn't say she gallantly avenged our 'eroic deaths instead," he replied.

"I intend to die heroically of extreme old age and general debility, in bed, with my great-grandchildren gathered around weeping," Alleyne said crisply. "BD, you should have something to eat and get some sleep. It's going to be a busy day tomorrow."

BD did, with John Hordle pitching in beside her; there was cold roast beef and pungent kielbasa and fried chicken, bread and butter and hot pickles, tortillas and beans, tomatoes and radishes, with sharp cheese and apple tarts to follow. She'd been too worried to be hungry up until that point, despite the eight hours since lunch; suddenly she was ravenous, and constructed several sandwiches as massive as her dentures could handle. Anyone who didn't think wrangling wagons all day was hard physical labor had never done it. Hordle ate enormously but neatly as he joined in the planning session.

When BD finished she tapped the small keg by the door for a mug of the beer. So did John Hordle, but apparently it didn't make *him* feel sleepy; of course, he was a generation younger, in superb condition, and had a hundred and sixty extra pounds of mass to sop it up. There was bedding down in the other end of the chamber; she wrapped herself in blankets and sheepskins, and felt herself fading swiftly. As she did she overheard Astrid:

"Besides, it is not by force of arms alone that we will prevail in this war. We keep the enemy's attention on us and that helps Fr . . . ah, Rudi and the others."

"Inspiration's one thing. Plagiarism is something else again," Alleyne said in a severe tone, and the four laughed.

BD sighed and prayed: *Oh, Apollo, guard your priestess! Artemis of the Hunt, let me not be the prey! And look out for Rudi and the others too. They're going to need it.*

CHAPTER EIGHT

Curse and ill-wishing have no power
Save that the heart lets them in
Hard the lesson learned by the undefeated
That strength and right may end in ill—

From: *The Song of Bear and Raven*
Attributed to Fiorbhinn Mackenzie, 1st century CY

Rancher Jed Smith yawned and turned over in his bedroll, conscious of the growing light in the east and the frosty air on his face.

That was a good dream, he thought sleepily. *It's good luck to dream of home.*

He'd been there, out where the horizon went on forever. Where the grama and wheatgrass brushed against your stirrups and ran in rippling waves beneath the biggest sky in the world, cloud shadows racing the wind across prairie green with spring and thick with blue lupine and white pennycress and golden gromwell, so beautiful it made the breath catch in your throat . . . and the air was fresh enough to hit like a shot of whiskey. Riding his own range and his herds had been around him, red-coated, white-faced cattle up to their hocks in the good grazing, sheep fat with the grass of a year with no drought, a promise that all his folk on Rippling Waters would be full-fed and warm come the blizzard season.

Dry mild wind on his face, a good horse beneath him, his sons Ted and Andy and Mark riding by his side, grown to tall men and talking horses and hunting, grass and cattle. The land at peace again, not even a feud on his borders. Then somehow he was at the head of his table, forking steaks from the serving platter onto plates, while Katy spooned out beans and Lorrie came in with a basket of biscuits in each hand and the kids were young again as they bowed their heads for the grace from the Book of Dzur ...

He yawned again and shook the last of it off; it wasn't quite dawn, and he *could* go back to sleep for another half hour. One of the perks of being the Rancher was that you didn't have to stand a guard-watch yourself, but he always got up and did the rounds himself at least once a night, in enemy territory. And at unpredictable intervals.

Dad taught me that. But he forgot, that once.

And he and Gramps and that whole party had been left stripped and butchered by a gang of road people who crept past a sleeping sentry. Jed had been only twenty then, but he'd held the Rippling Waters spread together and led them into the embrace of the Dictations.

It was pleasantly warm inside the glazed leather sleeping bag; it was made of sheepskins with the fleece turned in, and the girl who shared it with him now was as good as a campfire. She'd been much less sullen last night, and the thought and the feel of her and the scent tempted him to have another go while he had the chance—women generally didn't like it in the morning, and a sensible man didn't push his wives that way too often. It wouldn't be the same even with the bought gals they kept, when they got back to Rippling Waters.

Whatever the priests said *should* be, a man's wives *did* object if he diddled the slave girls openly in his own house, in the morning or otherwise. And Church law might say a man could correct his wives with a quirt if they scolded or back talked, but a man who tried that too often was asking for trouble with them and maybe with their kin, and it didn't make for a happy home life either. The only worse thing than having your women quarreling was having them gang up on you.

He was a man who liked tranquillity and smiles under his own roof-tree, not sulks. Everyone on the ranch had to pull together for things to go well—though an occasional quick one behind a haystack did no harm.

And I'm not nineteen no more, he thought. *C'mon, Jed, get up, take a leak, lead the morning prayers, get some breakfast and chicory inside you and git this outfit on the road. Those Newcastle men'll be splittin' off today; good riddance. Long way to home, so up an' at 'em! Sooner we're back, the sooner we can start getting the place back running smooth.*

The decision saved his life. He pushed the woman aside and was yawning and stretching rather than helpless on his back when she turned, snatched his bowie knife and drove it at his throat.

He'd grown to manhood in the years after the Change when chaos and death went stalking through the Hi-Line country, and survived them. There was nothing wrong with his reflexes, even in the strait confines of a sleeping bag. The blade slithered along his forearm in a shallow cut as he blocked it, turned his hip to take the attempt to knee him in the crotch on his hip bone, and smashed his forehead down into her face. That hurt him, but nose and cheek bones crunched under the blow and she screamed in shock and agony. The bowie dropped from her hand. He snatched the hilt; the cutting edge was turned in and he stabbed downward twice with all the strength in his lean corded arm and shoulder. The scream cut off in a gurgling, choking sound.

There were more screams as he pushed himself clear of the twitching body and climbed to his feet. And a shout he recognized all too well from the past few years:

"Come, ye Saints!"

Though he wasn't used to hearing it in high-pitched female voices. The dim light showed a heaving, thrashing confusion in the rocky flat where they'd camped; he dropped the bowie and snatched out his shete just in time to cut down another woman running at him with a wood-chopping ax already wet with blood.

"Rippling Waters men! Here, here, *here*!" he shouted in the rally call. "Back to back!"

He quickly stamped his feet into his boots, which were the only part of his clothes he had taken off to sleep, and caught up his shield. A man came running, limping with blood on his knee but with his shield and shete. Another, and another . . . and his horse came trotting as well, and then a clump of men. He jerked his cow-horn trumpet loose from the pile of gear on the ground as they formed up around him and blew a long dunting blast, *huuu-hhhhrrr-uuuu!*

"Here, here, *here*!"

The light was waxing, and he could see half a dozen little fights going on, and men sprawled bloody and still in their bedrolls, one going down under half a dozen shrieking women armed with knives and a camp kettle and snatched-up rocks. How had they planned it? But that didn't matter now; if they could just live through the first couple of minutes, strength and weapons would beat down any amount of desperation. A woman could knife a sleeping man, but that was about all she could do.

"Here, here, *here*! Kill those bitches!"

Then the trader Ingolf came loping; his shete was wet too. More of his party was behind him. They'd be useful, but they were running away from a mob of women—

Then the hatchets and knives in their hands registered, and the blood dripping from the steel. The women weren't chasing the Newcastle men; they were *following* them into battle. Rage warred with disgust.

That gal of theirs, Rebecca. She went around among the others before the shoot . . . They must have used her as their go-between for this!

"Hey, Rancher Smith," Ingolf called. "Why don't you kill *me*? I'm more your size!"

Steel slammed into steel, shedding a tail of sparks, banged on shields. His sworn men and kin closed in on either side of him and threw the outlanders back.

"Bastard!" Smith wheezed. His arm dripped blood, and one of his men took an instant to tie it up. "Lying bastard! *Cut! Cut!*"

Rudi Mackenzie leaned aside and thrust past Edain's back, feeling bone pop and crunch as the point went through the body and into the dry gritty soil. The Cutter named Jack tried to scream once as the blade nailed him to the ground, writhing around the steel and coughing out a single gout of dark blood that steamed in the cold dawn air.

"I had him!" Edain said—almost snarled.

From the red-purple blotches on the dead Cutter's throat he was right. And Garbh's fangs had already cut his hamstring; the right leg sticking out beneath his dirty shirt looked as if it had been chewed to rags, which was a pretty accurate description.

"We don't have time to settle scores," Rudi panted.

A rally shout sounded, and the dunting of a war-horn, and someone screamed out: *Cut! Cut! Cut!* A good many other people were simply screaming.

"Come *on*. We've a fight to win."

Edain came, snatching up his bow. Odard was finishing a man already wounded by the woman who sprawled beside him dying slowly with a crushed larynx; he whipped the shete around his head in a Portland-style flourish blow, and the sharp edge drove halfway through the Cutter's neck.

"Haro! Face Gervais, face death!"

Odard surprised the Mackenzie by dropping to his knees for an instant and pressing the heels of both hands against the woman's throat.

"All I could do," he panted, loping on beside him. "If the tissues don't swell shut . . . and damn this peasant's overgrown weeding tool! I want a proper longsword, and a knight's shield!"

The three young men came up with Ingolf; the big Easterner was just pulling his shete out of a man's back, bracing his foot on the body to get the broad point free of the bone.

"The sentries?" he said.

"Dead," Rudi replied succinctly.

"Let's go pay a call on Rancher Smith," Ingolf said quietly. "Kill them ourselves, or wait? I'd *like* to kill them, but . . ."

"Let's see how things lie," Rudi said. "Nystrup should be here soon, but it's better to overrun them ourselves, if they're still rocked far enough back on their heels. We can't let them get their feet under them."

They ran on, past wagons and horses wandering loose or rearing and tearing at their picket ropes, past blankets and tumbled cookware and bodies lying still, or crawling or writhing or clutching themselves and calling for their mothers—high-plains cowboys and Mormon women both. The smell of blood and filth mixed with brewing chicory and scorched bacon that had fallen into the embers.

Some of the wounded just shrieked with pain greater than they had ever imagined, and those were of both sides too. The Mormon women still standing fell in with them, running or hobbling at their heels, holding weapons snatched from their captors. Rudi was disappointed when he saw the Cutters' forming shield-wall; there were thirty men still on their feet, though many of them were wounded. They all had their shetes and shields, and many had managed to snatch up bits and pieces of their war-harness as they ran to the sound of the horn and the rally-call. His own folk had all been able to put on their gear, mostly leather with pieces of steel riveted to it, but Ingolf had his mail-shirt.

A good many of the women were naked and barefoot, and none had more than a shift and drawers.

"Here, here, *here*!" the Cutter leader called. "Kill those bitches!"

"Hey, Rancher Smith!" Ingolf cried; there was a note of playful ferocity in his voice, release from the role he'd had to act. "Why don't you kill *me*? I'm more your size."

Rudi saw Smith's face change, twisting into something inhuman. Then he and Ingolf were at handstrokes, their blades lashing out in the hacking Eastern shete-style. An arrow flashed past the Mackenzie chieftain's shoulder, and lanky brown-haired Lin toppled backwards limp as a rope, with a gray-fletched Mackenzie arrow in his eye.

"Now be eating that, and a sodding apple too, *a phiosa chaca bréan*!" Edain shouted. Then in angry frustration: "Get out of my *way*!"

The mass of women ignored that; ignored anything. They threw themselves on the Cutters' points in a shrieking mass, sheerly mad—at home he'd have said the Dark Goddess had them, from the fixed glaring eyes and the froth on some lips. Rudi engaged a Cutter himself, bringing his round shield up in a looping curve to stop the downward stroke of the shete without blocking his own vision. The weapon banged on the hard leather; he threw it sideways with a twitch of his long arm, but another came at him from the side and he had to block that . . .

Even Lugh can't fight two, he knew angrily; not in a straight-up fight between lines. *There aren't enough of us!*

Then three women threw themselves on the man ahead of him, so quickly that he nearly put his back out halting his own strike; one grabbed at the Cutter's shield, the second hung on his sword arm despite a chop that sliced open her leg to the bone, and the third leapt up and wound her legs around his waist and stabbed him in the face, over and over again with a long-tined roasting fork held in both hands, her arms pumping like a water-driven machine in a foundry. She stopped only when a tomahawk whirred across the width of the Cutter formation and sank into her skull with a *chock* that was horribly like an axman landing a cut on a tree.

Rudi's shete and shield moved as fast as he could turn and wheel and strike, a blur of motion, but the other two women died in the next three seconds; one quickly with a shete thrust to the gut, the other thrashing and gobbling with half her face cut away. Then an arrow struck his own shield with a hard whirr-*thuck* and a blow like a sledgehammer, the sharp point showing on the inside of the curve of bullhide and sheet metal and wooden frame. He blocked, struck, blocked, skipped backwards two steps to give himself room to look to either side.

"Cover!" he snapped.

He retreated again and crouched behind an over-turned wagon. Edain was beside him.

That's as well, Rudi thought, wincing at what he saw. *This isn't war. It's ... sure, and I don't know what it is, except that it's ugly.*

The mass of women had struck the Cutter shields with a reckless fury that made them more effective than he'd dreamed; half a dozen of the plainsmen were down, dead or badly hurt. But for the most part they hit the wall of shields edged with sharp swinging metal and *splashed*, the way a man might if he'd been shot out of a catapult at a castle's ferroconcrete ramparts. They had few proper weapons, no shields or helmets or armor, and none of the Cutters' hard-gained fighting skills; and while they were strong from churn and loom and hoe, the enemy were stronger still by far.

Rebecca had said the women were all willing to die rather than be led away captive; and they were. It would be good if they accomplished something by it. Trying to fight with them would do nothing but see Rudi and all his companions dead at their sides.

"Cut, cut, *cut*!" the war cry rang out.

Then the rush was over, and the recurve bows of the plainsmen began to snap.

Moments now, Rudi thought, judging the distance to their horses. *Nothing more we can do unless Nystrup comes. What's keeping the man?*

He pursed his lips and whistled for Epona. Another arrow slammed into the wagon beside his ear and he ducked backwards. The sun was up now, over the peaks eastward, and casting long shadows down the road. A knot of horsemen came over the rise, dust and gravel and bits of broken asphalt paving flying up from the hooves of galloping horses, and Rudi let out his breath in a *whuff* of relief. They were supposed to have been here a little earlier, but things like that happened in fights, and there'd been no way to coordinate more than to say *at dawn*.

Then he saw that the Deseret guerillas and his own companions were shooting backwards from the saddles, and arrows flickered towards them. They had most of Rancher Smith's remount herd running ahead of them, though, running wild-eyed and with their heads down.

What—

There wasn't time to give way to bewilderment. Epona was there, drawing ahead of the other horses with every step, moving with a grace that was beautiful even then. Rudi leapt with all the power of his long legs, three bounding paces and a snatch at the saddle-horn. It slapped into his hand, and he clamped down with a blaze of determination, pouring will up his arm and into fingers and wrist. Two-thirds of a ton of horse tore by, and his grip turned the momentum that threatened to rip his arm out at the socket into a vault that landed him in the saddle and his feet in the stirrups seconds later.

That was good, because they'd almost run into Rancher Smith and his men. Epona reared, crow-hopping on her hind legs; Rudi leaned forward until his face was in the black silky-coarse hair of her mane. Her forefeet milled like steel-edged clubs. A shield cracked under them, and the arm under it, and another man catapulted backwards as a shod hoof crushed his face. Rudi caught himself as his legs clamped down on his mount's barrel. The Cutters' rank was broken, more by the rush of riderless horses than by the mounted men and women behind and among them; the Easterners were too surprised to fight and too brave to run.

One of them shook himself out of his daze and ran in at Rudi's side; it was Rancher Smith, moving with lizard-quick skill to slash at Epona's hamstring. With most horses it would have worked. The big black mare had already set herself, her head around and judging the range. She kicked out with her left hind, powerful and accurate and blurring-fast. Smith would have died then if he hadn't turned his rush into a frenzied leap backwards, dropped his shete and tucked his shield into his gut as he realized what was happening.

The hoof punched into it with a *crack* like mountain ash breaking in the coldest part of winter, and the plainsman flew backwards, his feet off the ground for six feet or more. Then he rolled across the rough ground, shrieking as it battered his broken forearm amid the warped and shattered remnant of the shield's frame. The *thump* when he struck a wagon's wheels was enough to stop the sound.

Rudi ignored him; a man Epona kicked wasn't going to be a problem anytime soon, even if he was lucky enough to live. The mare spun beneath him, agile as a cow pony despite her size; sparks shot as her hooves scored rock.

There were men coming behind Nystrup's Deseret guerillas and Rudi's own companions. Men in the lacquered-leather armor and spiked helmets of the Sword of the Prophet, a score or more of them, their ranks disordered with the hard pursuit that had left them clumped in ones and twos and little bands. A swift glance told him their horses were spent, laboring, their necks and forequarters thick-streaked with lines of yellow-white foam, but the riders were ready with bow and lance.

"Too many!" he called. "Run!" Then: *"Edain!"*

The younger Mackenzie was shooting at the oncoming troopers of the Sword; one went down, another, another. But there were too many for any single archer to stop, even an Aylward; a Cutter was coming, his horse's gallop a wheezing shamble, but faster than a man could run and with his lance leveled. From the look of Edain's set face, gone milk-white and staring, he didn't intend to stop killing until he died. The Dark Mother had him, and the Devouring Shadow was a dangerous thing to evoke.

Epona moved, responding as if she were part of him. His desperate sword stroke knocked the lance out of the line that would have brought it into Edain's chest. But that meant it struck *his*, and Rudi wheezed in astonished agony as the blade scored across his flank and slammed him back against the cantle of the saddle. Armor snapped, and something within him. Half a second later the horses struck shoulder-to-shoulder, and the Cutter's lighter gelding went back on its haunches and then over backwards with a bugling scream of terror; the Cutter's scream was cut off as the weight landed square across him.

Edain shot again, and again. He reacted only to struggle blindly when Rudi threw his shete aside, snatched him by the back of his jacket and tossed him with a grunt of back-crackling effort across his pony's saddle. White fire washed across Rudi's eyes at the effort, and injured muscle tore.

"*Go!*" he shouted, and Epona nipped at the gelding's haunch.

It shot eastward with a squeal, and Rudi turned again. More Cutters were coming at him, more of the Sword of the Prophet—and they were close enough that he'd only be lanced or shot in the back if he ran. The first went by him at the gallop; he ducked in the saddle so that the lance went over nearly close enough to part his hair, then rose and smashed the hammer edge of his fist down on the man's neck. Something cracked, but the Mackenzie froze and grabbed at his side; it was as if he were coming apart, and only the strength of his arms kept everything inside from tumbling out.

A whirring *thock*, and a hammerblow that forced a grunt out of him and a feeling of intense cold. He stared for an instant at the arrowshaft in his right shoulder, punched through leather and mail and planted deep in bone. The arm wouldn't obey him, and Epona turned and bounded eastward on her own.

Whirr-*thock*. Another impact, in his back this time. Blackness.

"No," Jed Smith said, looking up from his back at the officer of the Sword standing over him.

"What did you say?" Major Graber barked.

Jed Smith hissed between his teeth and stiffened into quivering silence as one of his men set the bone that had snapped under the torque from the arm loop of his broken shield. Then he gasped as the splints were bound with coils of bandage. It was a simple greenstick fracture and ought to heal in a month or so . . .

"I said, *no*," he rasped tightly. "What part of that don't you understand, Major?" Then, to his own man: "Whiskey!"

The cowboy who'd set the arm handed him a flask. He drank, letting the cold fire burn down his gullet. It took away a little of the pain, and more of the heart sickness.

"I'm on the Prophet's business!" Graber said incredulously. "And I need those horses."

"And I've been fighting for the Prophet, the old Prophet, since before you got your first hard-on!" Smith snarled. "And I need them horses worse than you do."

He jerked his head at the chaos of the camp. "I lost more men this morning than I did in the whole Deseret War, and half my horses. I'm not giving you the rest, not when I have to get wounded men back to Rippling Waters . . . and these kids, somehow, *and* our plunder, what's left of it."

"We'll leave you our mounts," Graber said. "They're better stock than yours and there are more scattered back for ten miles."

"They *were* good stock," Smith said, taking another swallow of the raw grain liquor.

As if to make his point, one that had been standing with its head down slowly collapsed, going to its knees and then to its side in a clatter of gear. The trooper of the Sword knelt beside it, stroking its muzzle as it rolled its eyes in blind supplication.

"Now they're foundered and half of them are like to die and most of the others will be wind-broke until they *do* die. I'm not leaving my men stranded here with nothing but this dog fodder to ride and the passes due to close soon and that's that."

Graber's face was slick with sweat and the mud it had made of the dust on his face. He still glanced around at his men, and Smith knew exactly what he was thinking. There were at least twenty-five of the Rippling Waters men still fit to fight, and they were grouped around their Rancher and glowering at the regulars out of Corwin—whose arrogance nobody liked. Half the Sword troopers were scattered back along the way, walking and carrying the tack from their foundered mounts.

Graber thought he might—would—win any fight, but that would leave his command utterly wrecked and easy prey for any band of Mormon guerillas, or half a dozen other threats. And Corwin would be very reluctant to punish a powerful Rancher with a distinguished record of early support for the Church.

The Major of the Prophet's household troops slowly flushed, until his face was brick red, then stared at Smith with his lips moving—verses from the Dictations.

"*The wise . . . man . . . is . . . known . . . he . . . commands . . . his . . . passions*—"

The blood of rage slowly ebbed, and he spoke calmly:

"Four horses, then. Four fresh horses."

Smith pushed away the throbbing hot-and-cold sensation of his arm, and the growl of the whiskey in his empty belly. Corwin would *not* be happy if he denied all help . . . and he didn't want to, either. The Dictations and Book of Dzhur said a man had an obligation to repay, for good and ill. The false merchants who'd said that they came from Newcastle had built up quite a balance.

"Fine, Major. Pick 'em yourself," he said. "We're going home. Consider them a gift in the service of the Church."

Graber nodded curtly and turned, pointing his finger to one horse after another. His men ran to prepare them in silent obedience, and the officer said:

"Scout! High Seeker!"

A tall lanky man with his hair in braids ambled over; he looked tired, the way a horse did after pulling a hay cutter for a day, but strong as seasoned wood anyway. The Seeker . . . Smith blinked. *He* didn't look tired, or fresh, or like anything, somehow.

"It'll be days before we can move," Graber said. "I may have to find fresh horses, *somewhere*. Follow them. Mark the track. *Don't* lose them."

"I haven't yet," the Scout said.

The man in the robe the color of dried blood shrugged and nodded, smiling.

"Shit, *shit*!" Ingolf Vogeler said. "We *can't* stop, not here. It's bare as a politician's lie!"

Mathilda looked at him wide-eyed. "He ... those arrows have to come out. He's *badly* hurt. But—"

Father Ignatius nodded without turning as his fingers worked. Ingolf looked around; the Mormons were getting ready to leave, turning north into the mountains or southward to the Snake River sagelands. Edain Mackenzie sat by Rudi, elbows on knees and face buried in his hands, his dog pressed against him and whining softly as she stared up into his face.

Epona was a little distance off, giving soft snorts of equine distress. He'd thought for a moment he'd have to kill the mare before she'd let them pull Rudi off her back.

"I'm sorry," Nystrup said, at his own horse's head. "You've done well by us, but I have to get my people out of here. We'll scatter, and that will draw some of them away."

"Not if their scouts are as good as I'm afraid," Ingolf said, beating his right fist into his left palm. *"Shit!"*

Nystrup winced. "Goodbye ... and we'll pray for him. For you all."

Ingolf took a deep breath as the guerilla leader mounted and legged his horse southward; the others were looking at him anxiously, and you had to show willing. Nothing broke men's morale faster than the leader showing the flibbertigibbets.

The problem is that if this had happened during the Sioux War and he was one of my troopers, I'd give Rudi the mercy stroke and we'd run like hell to save the rest of the outfit, he thought. *Not exactly an option here!*

"Father Ignatius?" he said.

The cleric finished his examination. "I don't know how much damage the arrow in the shoulder did, but moving him will make it worse. The one in the small of the back is a more immediate danger. The point turned when it broke the mail-links. It is lodged at a slant and it is far too close to the liver and to several large blood vessels; motion may work it inward. And four ribs were broken, and there's soft-tissue damage. But if I operate now, he cannot be moved at all for some time or there will *certainly* be fatal bleeding."

"He'll *certainly* die if we stay here until the Cutters arrive," Mathilda said; her face was drawn, but her mouth was firm and her brown eyes level. "Their guardsmen, the . . ."

"Sword of the Prophet," Odard said neutrally; he was watching Rudi with an unreadable expression in his narrow blue eyes.

"The Sword of the Prophet, they'll be slow, from the state their horses were in. But the other one, this Rancher Smith *could* come after us quickly."

"If he wants to," Ingolf said. "He doesn't know we've split up. If he did want to chase us, he'd be here already. But *someone* will come after us, and sometime from the next fifteen minutes to the next couple of days."

"We could move a little north and find a place to hole up, *then* tend Rudi," Odard said. "I don't like to risk moving him more than absolutely necessary."

Mathilda nodded anxiously, and clasped his hand where he rested it for a moment on her shoulder.

Ingolf looked around, drawing on the maps in his head. They were several days out of Picabo—call it a bit over a hundred miles eastward as the crow flew. The mountains had been closing in from the north for a while, but there was still open country to the east north of Idaho Falls. It would be crawling with Cutter patrols . . . but probably with Mormon guerillas, too, and if they could—

"No, we're going to head east, fast," he said. "This is too close, too easy to saturate with men once they get organized. We've got to break contact. The only part of Wyoming the CUT doesn't really control is thataway. And the mountains start well west of the old state line. We'll have to chance it. When we get to the mountains, we can tend to Rudi."

They all looked at him, then at the wounded man, and most of them looked westward as well.

"Cross-country," Mary—or Ritva . . .

No, that's . . .

"Right, Mary."

Her troubled face gave a brief flash of pleasure as he used the right name.

"You and your sister are going to have to cover our backtrail."

CHAPTER NINE

"And I thought *our* political speeches were dull,"
BD said quietly.

"*Shhhh!*" Murdoch said.

They'd gone on for hours, in the great oval amphitheatre where the yearly Round-Up was held. At least they were over, and the VIPs and their families had shifted into the Bossman's house with the coming of sunset. She could hear the fiesta for the commons going on outside, a surf-roar of music and voices in the distance.

The Bossman's residence was a compound rather than a single building, out at the northwestern corner of town at the edge of the river and surrounded by its own strong wall. Within were barracks and storehouses and workshops, as well as the patios and gardens around the actual house, a rambling two-story structure with a red-tile roof and arches upholding balconies with wrought-iron grills. Strong yellow light spilled through the tall windows of the house, and torches on the pillars and walls round about lit the brilliantly clad couples, the servants in their white jackets and bow ties, and the *charro* costumes of the mariachi bands who moved about.

Long tables were set out buffet-style, with chefs in white hats waiting to carve the roasts and hams; whole yearling steers and pigs and lamb roasted over firepits behind them, the attendants slathering them with fiery sauce wielding their long-handled brushes like the forks of devils in the Christian hell. The rich scent of roasting meat drifted on the air, and the little spurts of blue smoke rose in the lantern light.

Interesting assortment of costumes and uniforms, BD thought, accepting a glass of wine.

She wasn't wearing a peplos tonight; no point in hanging out a notice. Instead she'd opted for a long denim skirt embroidered with geometric patterns around the hem, jacket, belt with silver-and-turquoise conchos and tooled-leather boots . . . what a Rancher's wife or mother would probably wear here. The owners of the big herding spreads were the most numerous element, many of them getting a little boisterous as they talked about what they'd do to any invaders of the sacred soil of Pendleton; those that weren't feuding with one another, of course.

When the hour came, her job would be to stick close to Bossman Peters. He was a big man, broad-shouldered and with the beginning of a paunch straining at the buttons of his embroidered waistcoat. His dark brown hair was thinning on top, and his bushy muttonchop whiskers were going gray, but his laugh boomed hearty, and the little eyes were shrewd.

Estrellita Peters was beside her husband, in an indigo dress with a belt of sequins, and ivory-and-turquoise combs in her high-piled raven hair. She was seven or eight years younger than her husband's mid-forties, slight and dark with a face like a ferret, albeit a pretty and extremely cunning one. Rumor said that she was rather more than half the political brains of the family business. Two sons in their teens followed dutifully behind their parents, one rather heavyset in a way that only the families of the rich could be nowadays, the other lean and quick.

Not time to get close to them, BD noted, swallowing past a dry throat and covertly drying her palms on her skirt. *Just keep an eye on them. And in the meantime, look for anything unusual.*

The foreigners were gathered together in two clumps,

on the tiled veranda near the broad iron-strapped wooden doors of the house proper. BD sidled closer.

One group was in blue, or long robes of a dark reddish brown color. *The Church Universal and Triumphant,* she thought.

They all wore neat little chin-beards; the soldiers in blue-green had their hair cropped close, the robed priests—Seekers, she'd heard they were called—were shaven-pated. The priests were glaring at any number of things; some of the guests were smoking tobacco, which their faith forbade, and there were women with uncovered hair, or some wearing pants, and mechanical clocks. All of them maintained a disciplined quietness, except their leader.

Could it be him, *here?* BD wondered. *He's around thirty, that's the right age . . . medium height, brown beard, hazel eyes . . . Trouble is, that's a description of Everyman just as much as it is of the Prophet Sethaz!*

He was certainly more sociable than the others, smiling and chatting easily with a succession of Pendleton VIPs. Some of the Ranchers avoided him—the Mormon ones, in particular, who were a fair scattering of the total. And the smaller minority who'd taken up the Old Religion as it drifted eastward were even more frankly hostile.

And that's Jenson's cowboy . . . George, she thought, puzzled.

The young man was in one of the dull-red robes, his head newly shaven. Their eyes met just for an instant, and BD shivered. The rage she'd seen was still there, but it was transfigured, focused like light from the edge of a knife, a gaze as blank and pitiless as the sun.

The other clutch of outlanders were even more exotic. BD's lips quirked; they were exotic because they were so like things she'd seen in *her* youth. The green uniforms with the service ribbons, the berets, the polished black shoes, the archaic shirts with collar and tie, even the neat *high and tight* haircuts. The only thing different from the old Army of the United States was the swords at their belts; shortswords, or cavalry sabers for a few. Young men, mostly from their mid-twenties to their thirties, and notably hard-faced even by modern standards, with impassive rock-jawed features and wary, watchful eyes.

Their commander turned, the four stars of a general on his shoulders. BD's eyes went wide in shock, and she turned naturally to place the wineglass on a tray.

Martin Thurston himself! she thought; self-promoted since his father's excessively convenient death. *Oh, Astrid, I think you've let yourself in for more than you thought!*

"My Lady Grand Constable, there's a deserter," her squire Armand Georges said. "She's asking to see the commander, and she has documents."

"She?"

"It's a woman, my lady. A cavalry sergeant; Boisean army."

Tiphaine d'Ath's brows went up; that was rare in the interior . . . and of course in the Association territories. And the Meeting had sent this army here because they were afraid the US of Boise and the Prophet *might* be intervening; apparently they hadn't been worrying without cause.

"I'll see her here."

She flipped the empty porridge bowl back to the scullion, yawned and finished coffee brewed snarling-strong to wash down the taste of the bland mush and dried fruit and the scorched bacon that had gone with it.

At least coffee always smells *good brewing*, she thought. *Even when it tastes like soap-boiler's lye.*

She was feeling a bit frowsty this morning, with wisps of her pale hair still escaping from the night's braid. The black arming doublet she wore—like a jacket made up of vertical tubes of padding—and the leather pants tucked into her boots both had the faint locker-room smell that never came out once they'd been worn under armor, with metal-and-oil from the patches of chain mail under the armpits that covered the weak points in a suit of plate. The leather laces that dangled from strategic spots to tie down the pieces of war-harness always made her feel like an undone boot at this stage, but there was no point in putting on sixty pounds of steel just to look spiffy. Not yet. It tired you fast enough when you had to wear it.

That freedom and the coffee were about the only mark of rank, that and a private privy. You didn't take pages or hordes of servants or a pavilion on campaign— at least, *she* didn't, not even when they were operating along a railway—and her tent was barely big enough to serve as a map-room when her bedroll was tied up.

The war-camp of the allied army was just waking, a growing brabble across the rolling plateau as light cleared the far-distant line of the Blue Mountains beyond Pendleton. The high cloud there caught the dawn in streaks of ruddy crimson that faded to pink froth at their edges. Fires smoked as embers were poked up and stoked with greasewood and fence-posts and brush. Faint and far to the south she could hear the Mackenzies making their greeting to the Sun:

> "*. . . my soul follows Hawk on the ghost of the wind*
> *I find my voice and speak truth;*
> *All-Father, wise Lord*
> *All-Mother, gentle and strong . . .*"

Her mouth quirked. Some of her own troops were praying too—*Queen of Angels, alleluia*—more of them were just scratching and stretching and getting in line by the cookfires, or turning in and trying to sleep if they'd been on the last night-watch. A few were singing, a new song—

> "*He spoke to me of the sunrise lands*
> *And a shrine of secret power*
> *Where the sacred Sword of the Lady stands*
> *And awaits the appointed hour;*
> *The hero's right, Artos his name . . .*"

The quirk grew to a small cold smile. That was Lady Juniper's work, if she'd ever heard it. It didn't do to forget that the Chief of the Mackenzies had been a bard—a busker, they'd said in those days—back before the Change. For that matter, half the troubadours in the Association's territory trained down South, for all that it prompted rumors you were a witch. And that story about Rudi's secret name, Artos, had been circulating since the Protector's War. Sandra knew with the top part of her mind how powerful song-born tales could be, but Tiphaine thought the Lady Regent had trouble believing it down below the neck.

Her squire made a signal. "Rodard has the deserter, my lady. Here are the documents she carried."

Armand was a tall young black-haired blue-eyed man in his early twenties, ready for knighting and hoping for it during this campaign. He and his younger brother Rodard were also the nephews of Katrina Georges, who'd been Tiphaine's companion from the time the Change caught their Girl Scout troop in the woods until she was killed in the War of the Eye . . . by Astrid Larsson. It gave Tiphaine a little twinge to look at their boldly handsome faces, though the resemblance wasn't as strong nowadays.

He was already in half armor, breastplate and mail-sleeves and vambraces on the forearms; his brother wore the older-style knee-length mail hauberk. She took the packet of sealed papers and turned back into the tent, and looked at the T-shaped stand that carried her war gear and shield.

This will be my last war, I think, at least for leading from the front, she thought with cold calculation; she'd lost just a hair of her best speed, and it would get worse. *Now, let's see if I can go out with a bang.*

The folding table had been set out, and canvas stools. She sat on one and waited; by reflex her fingers itched to open the report on the table, which was the one about reconditioning the railway to here from the Dalles. Keeping four thousand troops fed and supplied out here in the cow-country wasn't easy, and the Protectorate had agreed to take on the logistics as part of its share. But paperwork would eat every minute of your time if you got too obsessed with detail work, and questioning a valuable prisoner was also important.

She liked to keep her hand on the pulse of intelligence; possibly because she'd been as much a spy as anything in the first years of her work for Lady Sandra.

Not to mention a wet-work specialist, she thought wryly, and touched one of her knives—not the obvious one on her sword belt.

Rodard had his sword out as he showed the prisoner in; his brother stood outside the tent flap to make sure nobody got within earshot without permission, even if they had the rank to muscle through the perimeter of spearmen. With the east-facing flap back there was good light and she was sitting to an angle to it so she'd be in shadow.

Always an advantage, to see without being seen.

The deserter had a square dark olive Hispano face and black eyes and coarse straight bobbed hair so dark there were iridescent highlights; around five foot six or seven, Tiphaine thought, and in her late twenties or early thirties—hard to be sure when someone spent their days outdoors in this dry interior climate. Lean, wiry and tough-looking, probably quick and very dangerous with a sword . . . Which was no surprise; in their line of work a woman had to be extremely good to compensate for the thicker bones and extra muscle men carried. She wore breeches and boots that had the indefinable look of uniform, dyed mottled sage green, and a waist-length mail-shirt with chevrons on the short sleeve: light-cavalry outfit. The belt held laced frog-mounts for a saber and dagger, and there was a slightly shiny patch in the mail on her right shoulder where the baldric for a quiver would rest.

She came to attention and started to salute, looked down at her bound hands, and shrugged.

"Ma'am, I'm Sergeant Rosita Gonzalez—"

"That's *my lady d'Ath*," the squire whose sword hovered near her back said.

"Gently, Rodard, gently," Tiphaine said, her voice empty of all emotion, like water running over smooth rocks. "She came to us."

"I'm looking for Grand Constable d'Ath," the prisoner said. "I've got messages from, ah, Princess Mathilda and—"

Tiphaine didn't sit bolt upright. Rodard didn't raise the sword or swear; he and his brother had been trained in her household for more than a decade, as pages and squires. Instead the Grand Constable untied the bundle of letters and looked at the seal on the first. It wasn't the usual shapeless blob of tallow, but a crimson disk from a stack of premade blanks, the type the Chancellor's office used. And the seal-ring was one she recognized, the Lidless Eye crossed by the baton of cadency.

"Seals can be duplicated, Sergeant," she said softly. "Or taken from prisoners."

The other woman looked at her warily; not afraid, exactly, but obviously conscious of the sword behind her, and of the pale gaze on her. A poet had once described Tiphaine d'Ath's eyes as the color of berg-ice floating down the Inland Passage on a sunless winter's day.

"The Princess said you'd say that. So she gave me a message that only you two would know, and nobody would think to ask her."

Torture out of her, Tiphaine thought, and was slightly surprised at the surge of anger she felt. *Well, I did help bring the girl up from her cradle . . .*

She nodded, and the prisoner approached. Rodard rested the needle point of his longsword over her kidneys, and Tiphaine leaned forward to hear the whisper:

"She said that you met Delia at the party, when she was serving at your feast when you took seizin"—the woman from Idaho mispronounced the feudal term—"of Ath, and Delia asked if you wanted to look at the embroidery on something."

Tiphaine's eyes narrowed a little, as close to a smile as she would get here-and-now. Mathilda had been there at that first feast at Castle d'Ath; it had been just after she rescued the girl from the Mackenzies, and was ennobled for it and given the fief. For that matter, Rudi Mackenzie had been there too, since she'd captured him in the same raid, and Sandra had wanted to get him out of Todenangst and from under Norman's eye. She hadn't thought Mathilda had known ... but Delia had always gotten on well with the Princess, and had a perverse sense of humor.

"Right, you're from the Princess, Sergeant," she said. "What were the circumstances?"

The noncom gave her a brief précis; the noblewoman's eyebrows went up.

Lady Sandra is going to have kittens, she thought. *Matti prisoner of the Cutters ... and Odard's man working for, or with them. Which means Odard's* mother *still is ... Hope the headsman sharpened his ax after the last one. Or it might be the rack and pincers ...*

"But there's more," Gonzalez said. "President Thurston ... Martin Thurston is here. Four battalions of regular infantry and one regiment of cavalry—that's how I got here—and a lot of field artillery. And the Prophet Sethaz, he's got about the same of *his* goons, all cavalry. About a third of them the Sword, the household troops, the rest of them ranchlander levies, but they look like they know what they're doing. They got a lot of experience in the Deseret War."

Now, that changes the equation completely, Tiphaine thought. *Our preemptive strike just got preempted.*

"And there was something going on at the Bossman's house last night," Gonzalez said. "Fighting, and then a fire. Then we were ordered out to beat the bushes all around the town, with the priority on anyone trying to break west. Meanwhile it looked like the whole force was getting ready to move in your direction. As soon as those Pendleton *tontas* got their thumbs out."

Ah, Tiphaine thought. *Astrid's little black op didn't go as planned. But it didn't go* entirely *pear-shaped either, not if they're looking for fugitives rather than putting the heads on spears outside the gate.*

"I can make it back if you let me go *right now*," Gonzalez said. "My squad are all in on it and they'll cover for me. Any longer and I've got to stay."

"Rodard, release her and give her back her weapons and her horse. Then get to Rancher Brown and tell him I need two hundred of his men, or as many more as he can get here within half an hour, ready for a running fight. Armand, send for Sir Ivo and Sir Ruffin, and then arm me. And call for couriers!"

She dipped her precious steel-nibbed pen into the ink bottle, and wrote:

To the Regent: I have confirmed the authenticity of the enclosed.

Then she threw that in a preaddressed courier bag and handed it to the first of the messengers, a slender whipcord man in leathers.

"Get this to the forward railway station for forwarding to Portland, maximum priority," she said, and was writing again before he'd left the tent.

By the time Sir Ivo arrived she'd sent six messages out, several clerks were writing out more, and the camp noise was beginning to swell as getting-up turned into frantic-scramble.

Ivo pulled up before the open flap and swung out of the saddle; he was wearing an old-style hauberk and conical helmet, and the loose mail and padding made him look even more troll-like than usual. Ruffin was on his heels, with his mail coif still hanging down behind and his squires scurrying behind *him* with visored sallet helmet and shield and lance. Ivo pushed his helm back by the nasal bar and looked at her as she stood to let the squire fasten the more elaborate modern gear on her, bending and twisting a little occasionally to make sure the adjustments were correct.

"This to First Armsman Barstow, over with the Mackenzies," Tiphaine went on to one of the clerks, who beckoned to a courier. "Ruffin, you're in charge here until I get back."

"Back?" he said.

"Something needs doing, and I don't have time to brief you. Ivo, get me two *conroi* of the Household men-at-arms." Those were at full strength; that was a hundred lances. "Full kit, *now*."

He left at the run. She went on: "Ruffin, the enemy's strength is much higher than we expected—Boise regulars and the Prophet's men are here, about two thousand of each."

He grunted as if someone had hit him in the stomach; that turned even odds into something like two-to-one against the allied force.

"We're going to have to fight to break contact, rock them back on their heels, then use the cavalry to hold them off while the infantry retreat. Get the heavy stuff moving out *now*. If it can't be on the rails or roads in an hour, burn it."

The last of the armor went on, the metal sabatons that strapped over her boots to protect her feet. She stepped over to the table and sketched with her finger on the map. "Put the Mackenzies here, and—"

Ruffin was nodding soberly as she concluded: "I should be back in about an hour. If I'm not, get this army out. Concentrate our troops at the Dalles, but alert the border forts as well."

"I'll handle it, my liege," he said; the heliograph network would flash it all over the Association by the end of the day, and the news would be in Corvallis by midnight. "God go with you."

"Or luck," she said, with a cruel smile as she thought of her immediate errand.

Astrid Larsson had killed Katrina Georges, back in the War. Tiphaine's own oaths meant that she had to do her very best to rescue the *Hiril Dúnedain* and her husband and soul-sister and brother-in-law . . .

Which will be sulfuric acid on her soul, if only I can pull it off.

Armand handed her the sword belt; she ran it around her hips twice and buckled it, tucking the double tongue through, and then pulled on her steel gauntlets. The coif confined her braided hair, and she settled the sallet helm with its expensive lining of old sponges on her head and worked the visor. Daylight vanished save for the long horizontal bar of the vision slit, then returned as she flicked the curved steel upward again.

A groom led her destrier Salafin up, and she swung

into the high war-saddle. Armand handed her the shield and she slung it diagonally over her back like a guitar in the old days, the rounded point down to her right. By then the CORA light horse were ready, and the block of tall lances and steel-clad riders and barded horses that marked the Portlander men-at-arms, with their arms blazoned on their shields.

"My lords, chevaliers, and esquires of the Association!" she called.

She reined in ahead and turned the war-horse to face them as she drew her sword; the barding clattered as the big black gelding tossed its head and mouthed the bit. "Our souls belong to God, our bodies and our lives to our liege-lady—"

"A cheer for the Princess Mathilda!" someone called from the ranks of the knights.

"Haro!" rang out from a hundred throats.

Tiphaine blinked, as horses caracoled and lances were tossed in the air in a blaze of pennants. She'd had Sandra Arminger in mind. Sandra was respected, and feared. The Grand Constable was feared, and respected. Evidently Mathilda was . . .

Loved? she thought, as she thrust her blade skyward. *Well, she's their generation. I suppose a lot of hopes are riding on her.*

"—and our swords belong to Portland! You have given your oaths; now you shall fulfill them, and I at your head."

Oddly enough, Chateau generals were obsolete now that real chateaux had made a comeback. She chopped the longsword forward.

"Haro! Holy Mary for Portland!"

The destrier stepped out beneath her, and the light horse from the CORA fanned out eastward. Beside her Rodard held the banner of the Lidless Eye, and the black-and-crimson of it fluttered in a cool breeze from the distant Pacific. The winter rains were coming . . .

I wonder what the hell happened with our pseudo-elf's plan? Tiphaine thought, beneath the running assessment of terrain and distances playing out against the map in her head. *Usually she's pretty good, or at least she has the luck you expect for small children and lunatics.*

"Here," Astrid Larsson said.

She didn't need to take the radium-dial watch out of the leather-covered steel case at her belt; even in the deep darkness of the tunnels, her time-sense was good. This was just short of midnight, time enough for the Bossman's party to really get going above, and for everyone to punish the wet bar hard. Pendleton men drank deep at a fiesta, by all accounts.

They had a single lamp lit. She saw Eilir put her hands against the concrete blocks of the wall ahead of them and close her eyes.

I can feel the music and the dancing from above, she signed. *Sounds like quite a do!*

Good, Astrid replied. *Get the line of retreat ready for us,* anamchara*!*

Eilir sped off down the tunnel with her four helpers and their burdens. Astrid put her left hand on the hilt of her longsword and tapped the silver fishtail pommel against the blocks: *tap*, and then *tap-tap-tap*.

A wait, while she listened to the blood beating in her ears. The air was cool and dry here, and dusty, but there was a faint living smell that the rest of the tunnels hadn't had, more like a storeroom. There was even a slight scent of spilled wine soaked into flooring. Behind her there was a slight clink and rattle as the others of the Ranger assault party did their final equipment check. Astrid took a deep breath and touched her weapons and gear; beside her Alleyne did the same and gave her a thumbs-up.

And then not far away: *tap-tap . . . tap-tap . . . tap.*

"We could use a few dwarves," he said whimsically, and brought his heater-shaped shield round onto his arm.

"We'll be above ground fairly soon," she replied. "Lantern out, Húrin!"

Utter darkness fell, like having your eyes painted

over, as the lantern's flame died and the mantle faded to a dim red glow and went out.

Alleyne's cool voice sounded: "John, you do the honors."

She could feel the air move as the big man turned and groped for the steel lever that stood upright in a niche. The lever was fastened with a pin; there was a slight *chink* as he pulled that free to dangle—that little chain to keep it from getting lost on the floor was *so* typical of a plan with Sandra Arminger behind it—and heaved. There was a moment while the inertia resisted the huge muscles she knew bunched in his tight black sleeve, and then the wall ahead of them began to swing up.

Once it started the movement was smooth and sure, as counterweighted levers swung the steel plate and the camouflaging blocks up out of the way. Sound came through the four-foot gap in the wall, faint and far, a hint of music and a loud burr of voices and feet.

The cellar beyond was dimly lit by occasional night lanterns, but it looked bright to dark-adapted eyes; the secret door opened between two huge wine-vats, looming above them and resting on double X-shaped cradles. A figure waited, in the bowtie of the Bossman's servants. He gave back a step at the sight of John Hordle's bulk uncoiling from the low entranceway to his full towering height, the long handle of his greatsword standing up over his right shoulder.

"Quickly!" the spy said then, licking his lips. "The way's clear up to the kitchens."

"Good," Astrid said. "You should go now."

The man nodded jerkily and scurried away. They gave him a few seconds lead, and then followed. The cellars here were sections of tunnel, joined by narrower linking passages; they went by rows of barrels of various sizes for wine and beer and brandy and whiskey, flour and salt pork and salt beef, shelving with potted meats and vegetables and jams and jellies, sacks of onions and potatoes and bins of dried peppers and beans, vats of pickled eggs and sauerkraut, racks of hams and flitches of bacon in wrappers of waxed canvas . . . all the varied supplies a great household needed.

It reminded her a little of the storage sheds at Stardell in Mithrilwood, down to the deep rich mélange of smells and the arrogant air of a patrolling cat, before the moggy took one horrified look at the strangers and fled with its ears back in a flying leap to the top of a stack of boxes full of apples. There it arched its back and hissed and spat with a sharp *tsk!* sound, its eyes glowing green in the faint gleam of a lantern.

"Peace between us, sister!" she laughed. And a sudden thought: "Every second pair, take some of that lamp-fuel."

They shouldered large jugs of it, ten-gallon models of pre-Change metal full of pure alcohol. The map was printed on her brain. And *there* were the metal stairs that led up. She went first in a soft-footed rush.

"Húrin, Melendil," Alleyne said, his sword indicating two.

The pair halted just below the top of the stairs, ready to deal with anyone who came by. Astrid led the rest up a corridor that led past a fuel-store with billets of firewood and sacks of dusty-smelling charcoal.

"Morwen, you and Aratan wait here," she said softly. "Soak down this stack and keep fire ready, but hidden."

The two of them took the metal jugs and began pouring the spirit over the combustibles. She led the rest into the flagged hallway beyond and took a deep breath. The smells of cooking food were strong from the doors ahead, from frying onions to baking pastries with their buttery richness; this was the kitchens, where the made dishes would be prepared while the whole carcasses roasted outside. She and Alleyne looked at each other, nodded slightly, and pushed through, each turning to one side with shield up and blade poised.

The light was painfully bright, from lanterns set all around the great rectangular room and hanging from the groined arches of the high ceiling. One wall was lined with cast-iron and tile-and-brick stoves and ovens and grills; the central island and the counters all around were lined with cooks and scullions hard at work, chopping and rolling and setting out arrangements on bright silver platters. The sounds of knives and tenderizing hammers and rolling pins dropped away as flushed, sweating faces turned towards the dark-clad warriors who rushed through the doors.

A small party of Rangers sprinted to the other exit that gave on the main house, tall metal portals with oval glass windows set in them. A man pushed a trolley of empty serving plates through it, then froze with the doors swinging behind him as a sword point pricked him behind the ear. The rest of the Dúnedain fanned out to either side of her, arrows on the strings of their drawn bows, the vicious triangular heads motionless.

"Hear me! We have no quarrel with you," Astrid said. "Only with your master."

Her clear soprano filled a sudden silence broken only by the flicker of flames and the sputter of fat dripping on embers. She knew their eyes were all on her sword, the blue light of the lanterns breaking off the honed edge.

And the most of these people will be thralls, not willing servants.

Just then a burly cook cocked back his hand with the cleaver in it. John Hordle had his sword in his right hand, but the left shot out and clamped on the man's fat bull-neck. Fingers like wrought-iron bars drove in, and the man purpled and then went limp. His head hit the brown tile of the floor with an unpleasant *thock*.

"But we will kill if we must," she added.

Two dozen pairs of eyes followed the point of her sword as if hypnotized. She pointed to another set of doors, these of oak. That led to the day-pantry where supplies were stored for immediate use. It had only the one entrance, and it was windowless, with walls of thick adobe.

"In there. All of you; take that one on the floor, he's not dead—"

She shot a glance at Little John Hordle that said he'd *better* not be dead.

"And be *quiet* about it."

They obeyed in a clumsy scramble; despite her demand for quiet, there were crashes as crockery cascaded to the floor and silverware chimed. In a minute they were all tightly packed among the barrels and crates and jars and crocks; she could see some of them crawling up on the emptied shelves. One of her Dúnedain shoved the door closed, dropped a wedge and heel-kicked it to seat it tightly. The portal wasn't particularly strong, and the kitchen workers should be able to hammer it down in time, especially since the hinges were on their side. That wouldn't be soon enough to hinder her plan. Everyone waited, their eyes on her ...

Except for one who was flicking slices of glazed roast pork loin into his mouth from a plate where they were arranged and chewing with relish.

"*John!*" she hissed, enraged. "Not *now*! Great deeds await us!"

"Not bad, roit tasty touch of apple in the glaze, but a bit 'ot. They put chilies in *every* bloody thing out here."

The sudden wave of fury vanished, and left her balanced and sure. She smiled at him, and turned to her folk. Alleyne poised beside her, shield up and eyes grim.

"*Now,*" she said.

BD forced herself not to take another glass of wine. She didn't usually try to drown anxiety, but her throat was dry and tight, far too tight to try any of the little nibblements going around.

God, these cowboys can pack it away, she thought, watching men who'd downed racks of lamb-ribs and heaped plates of roast beef with all the fixings taking fruit tarts and pastries of pine nuts and honey and cream from the silver salvers.

Not to mention the way they can drink. *I'm impressed, and I was in Barony Chehalis for a Stavarov wedding!*

Instead she chose a glass of cold herbal tea—not many of *those* had been taken. She supposed they were kept for the Mormons among the Bossman's followers. Her eyes kept going back to the clock, willing the hands to slow down. The room got more crowded, as the night outside grew colder and more people moved into the heated interior of the house; if anything it was uncomfortably warm here, with fifty or sixty people in the big ballroom besides the great wrought-silver chandelier above with its spendthrift weight of wax candles, and the lamps in their wall-sconces.

Then the doors to the kitchens burst open, and her throat squeezed shut at the shock, even when she'd been expecting it.

"Lacho Calad! Drego Morn!" rang out, and a stunning bull-bellow of: *"Every one of you buggers freeze and nobody'll get 'urt!"*

The three Dúnedain leaders made a beeline for the Bossman and his family, a half dozen more at their heels; they didn't use their swords to kill, but battering shields and the flats of the blades scattered men and women out of their way in a chorus of screams and groans. More Rangers pushed the musicians off their dais and covered the ballroom with drawn bows.

A third party ran to the outside doors and slammed them closed, shooting the bar home in the wrought-steel brackets that looked merely decorative until you realized that they were as thick as a man's wrist. The Bossman's house wasn't exactly a fortress, but those doors were made of heavy oak beam and plank, strapped with iron as useful as it was ornamental, and the hinges were on the inside. The windows were small, high in the exterior walls, and barred by steel grillwork. The Rangers had stout padlocks and chains to fasten the bar in place; nobody was going to open that door soon without sledges and bolt cutters.

The screams and babbling rose to a crescendo; most of the men present were drunk, a fair percentage of the women were too, and nobody had time to think or adjust to the sudden shocking violence. The guards around the perimeter of the room *were* sober, and they were armored and armed with shetes and glaives, but the Bossman was in the center of the room and they weren't, and it took them crucial seconds to switch their mental settings from *ceremonial guard* to *muscle squad*.

There were metal bangles at BD's studded belt. She pulled one of them free, and her wrist did a quick snap-flick-and-roll; that put the blade of the balisong butterfly knife out and the handle that had concealed it in her hand. Two steps took her to Estrellita Peters' side; she threw one arm around the smaller woman to pinion both of hers, and set the knife blade to her throat.

"*Don't* do anything foolish," she snarled.

Suddenly anyone looking would know why she'd been called *La Loba* in one of Mexico City's tougher schools forty years ago.

The Bossman's wife jerked very slightly, and a trickle of blood ran down the smooth olive skin of her throat; the scent of the rose-essence perfume she wore was strong this close. Her eyes rolled down towards the knife hand with a reflex like a startled horse, but there was absolutely nothing wrong with *her* wits, and she froze into immobility.

Her sons noticed almost immediately; their hands went to the silver-hilted daggers they wore, but the elder one, the one with the swordsman's build, stopped and shot out his right hand to his brother's wrist instead.

"Be still, Jorge! She might hurt Mama!"

Carl Peters himself took a little longer to wrench himself out of the initial bewilderment. His hand went to the well-worn hilt of his shete, but then stopped again for an instant as he saw the glitter of the little knife at his wife's throat.

"Kill her, *querido*!" Estrellita gasped. "She won't dare hurt me!"

"Try it and she bleeds out," BD rasped, the skin between her shoulder blades itching; she made the knife dimple the skin again. "Better her than a thousand boys dead and a city burning."

In the seconds he needed to decide to draw his sword anyway Astrid and the others were there, and they made a shield wall around the ruler's family and two points were at his throat.

"Rangers!" Peters blurted, taking in the tree-and-stars blazons on their leather-covered mail-shirts. "God, what are you bastards doing here?"

"Nobody expects the Elvish Inquisition," Hordle said good-naturedly ... but his sword was four feet long, and he was holding it as effortlessly as if it were a yardstick.

"We're not going to harm you, my lord," Alleyne Loring said smoothly; the cultured tones conveyed sincerity ... and the rock-steady point of the longsword did as well. "Your memory as a martyr would be a formidable threat. We just need to take you away for a bit of quiet negotiation."

As he spoke several of the Rangers grabbed the Peters family and trussed their wrists behind their backs. BD stepped back with a wheeze of relief ... which turned to a yelp of agony as Estrellita Peters brought her narrow heel down on the instep of her foot, hard, the instant the steel wasn't touching the skin over her jugular.

"Toma! Cabrona!" she snarled.

The whole sword-edged circle of captors and captives began to move smoothly back towards the exit to the kitchens; the guests were mostly unarmed, and goggling with surprise anyway.

We're going to do it! BD thought as she hobbled along. *The Kindly Ones be praised.*

Then she made a propitiatory gesture with the fingers of her right hand to avoid the jealousy of the Fates. The Registered Refugee Regiment guardsmen had forced themselves through the crowd; there were a dozen of them clumped together in a bristle of glaives. BD saw horror warring with anger on their faces, but Peters had himself well in hand by now. Someone was beating on the door from the outside, and then it began to boom as someone quick-thinking organized a battering ram out of a stone bench. A few more of the guardsmen began beating at the chains with their glaives as the Dúnedain there retreated to join the others.

Peters is going to tell them to stop. Apollo, but I'm glad of that! Those points look way too sharp.

The Bossman gave the Dúnedain a wry look and raised his voice. "Well, boys—" he began to say to his men.

"Kill," Sethaz said.

BD gave an involuntary moan; the single word was not loud, but it seemed to vibrate in the little bones of her inner ear, running out along veins and nerves like a dry hot wind that made every sinew in her body creak. A guardsman leveled his glaive and lunged. Alleyne smashed the heavy blade of the weapon upward with his shield, but the other man turned it and caught the rim with the hook on the reverse, dragging it down so his mates could stab across it. Spears poised amid obscene curses; Peters shook his head in startled futility. Alleyne killed the man who held his shield with a single snapping lunge to the throat, withdrawing the longsword with a cruel professional twist.

The crowd had stood gaping as the black-clad Rangers swarmed in. Now they roared as the guardsman twisted, blood spraying ten paces from his slashed-open neck. Roared and surged forward; the first fell to the sweep of John Hordle's sword, three men spinning away, a hand flying loose, another slashed open across the chest, the last screaming through a split jaw. The four-foot blade looped up and poised, but the snarls of the ones beyond were bestially unafraid, teeth red with the spattered blood. The salt-iron stink of it mingled with the food and spilled drink until her stomach clenched and nearly climbed up her throat.

"Back to the doors!" Astrid called, in a voice like a trumpet. "Quickly!"

The Dúnedain bows began to snap; the archers were backing up themselves, shooting as fast as they could draw shafts from their quivers and loose. A guardsman went down with an arrow through his face; there was a *tunk!* as another punched through a breastplate. The glaive clattered on the floor as its wielder went down on all fours, coughing out blood and bits of lung. The green-uniformed Boise men had closed in around their President in a flicker of blades; then he shouldered his way through with his saber out and led them to the attack, a reckless white smile splitting his brown face.

BD ducked behind one of the Rangers. The man fell an instant later when Thurston's curved sword bit through the mail beneath his jerkin, cutting the great muscle of the shoulder and breaking the bone with a greenstick *snap* that made her feel as if someone had run a copper pick along all the surfaces of her teeth painfully hard. Alleyne Loring stepped into the gap, and they were at each other in a rage of steel.

BD fell as well, then set her teeth and reached out to grab the fallen man and drag him backwards. Pain shot through her back; Estrellita Peters had kicked her just above the base of the spine and leapt over her, and her sons followed her, lost in the not-so-miniature riot.

Turnabout's fair play, BD thought, and set herself to crawl and pull the wounded man again.

That gave her a view through a momentary gap. The red robes and blue uniforms of the Church Universal and Triumphant had closed around *their* leader too, though they hadn't been allowed weapons. She could see him behind them; he was standing with arms raised and spread wide, on wide-planted feet, and his mouth was stretched in what might be a smile—it bared his teeth, at least, and there was a joy in it that made her want to close her eyes and beat her face against the hard tile of the floor in an effort to scrub the memory out of her head.

His eyes were an ordinary brown, but she could see *something* surfacing there, like a dead body floating up towards the surface . . . an absence, an un-meaning . . .

His hands swept closed on the head of the cowboy she'd heard called George. As they did the young man's expression became a mirror of that on the face of the Cutter prophet leering over his shoulder.

"Kill," Sethaz said again, and it was no louder than an ordinary speaking voice, but it seemed to echo back and forth within her skull.

The young man grinned, moving in jerks, like a man whose limbs were attached to strings. But these strings wove him through the complex obstacles of battle like a weaver's shuttle through the loom.

"Look out!" BD shouted, trying to move away on the blood-slippery tile and pull the man with her.

The sound was lost in the uproar, but a Dúnedain arrow struck the young man in the shoulder. The arrow sank deeply; it was a powerful bow, and close. His lean body recoiled with the impact, flexing loosely; then he reached up and pulled the arrow out and threw it away, advancing with that same fixed grin. John Hordle stepped forward. The great blade of his sword spun up and around and down in a hissing loop, lost in the guttural roar that split his face beneath the thatch of bristling dyed hair.

George moved aside, just enough, and the greatsword sliced empty air and smashed into tile with a crackle and a shower of sparks as it pierced to the lime-rich concrete beneath. His fist lashed out and caught Hordle beneath the short ribs, and the big man's breath came out in an agonized *huff!*

Then he was past, and Astrid came at him in a lunge, fluid and smooth and so fast she seemed to *stretch* rather than move, with the round shield she carried hugged impeccably against her.

The young man's hands slapped together, and the blade of the longsword was imprisoned between them. Astrid Larsson froze, her silver-veined eyes going wide, and the hands jerked forward, punching the hilt of her sword out of her hands and into her forehead.

The *thock* resounded even through the white noise of riot. The sword clattered on the tile floor near BD's nose, the shimmering water-patterned steel flexing as it jumped and whined and fell back again. One of George's hands flashed out and caught Astrid by the throat as she began to crumple. The other clamped down on the top of the woman's head, ready to twist ... and BD recognized the gesture. She'd killed hundreds of chickens that way herself, these past twenty years and more, and before then in Mexico when she was a girl.

The balisong was in her hand again. She reared up

on one elbow and sliced at the back of the young man's knee. The finger-length blade was honed to a wire edge; it slid through denim and flesh and with only a little *tick* of extra effort when it cut the tendon. George howled, a sound of bestial frustration rather than pain, and lurched before his other leg could adjust to carry his weight. Hordle was turning even as he did, and the blade spun—horizontally this time, from left to right across the other man's shoulders. The head came free, and fell beside her.

BD looked into the dead man's eyes. And they looked back at her; his mouth was still grinning as she saw consciousness flow *back* into them, a single instant of utter horror before the blackness.

I'm going to faint dead away, for the first time in my life, she thought with a curious detachment, and did.

"No," Sethaz said. "Do not waste more men down that tunnel. Send them to scour the land outside the walls instead. We'll have a battle to fight tomorrow anyway."

Thurston of Boise gave him an odd look, a single nod, and then turned to stride away, issuing orders to the men around him even as he did.

Estrellita Peters stood before him, flanked by guardsmen and with her hand resting on the shoulder of her eldest son. Behind them servants were clearing away the ruins of the Bossman's feast. She swallowed and met the Prophet's gaze for a moment before she shifted her eyes to look over his head. Her voice was still calm as she spoke:

"The thanks of my family and Pendleton to you, my lord Prophet. My husband has been abducted by these vicious bandits, but at least you saved me and my sons from captivity. In the future, you and yours may carry weapons here as you please."

Sethaz smiled, a wryly charming expression. "For the present, Doña Peters, we'll be wielding our weapons outside the walls, against your enemies."

She nodded. Her son spoke, eagerness on his seventeen-year-old face.

"Your man was so brave, and so quick and strong! He defeated the head of the Rangers, and knocked down *John Hordle*! The truth you teach must have much in it, if you can inspire men so!"

The Bossman's wife gave her son a warning squeeze, and he cleared his throat and extended his hand. Sethaz took it in both of his, a firm shake:

"Thank you for rescuing me and my mother."

"Your mother did a good deal to rescue herself," Sethaz said, looking into the dark young eyes. "We will speak more of such matters later, Mr. Peters."

And a whisper, felt along the edges of his mind: **I—see—you.**

CHAPTER TEN

As fire forges steel
So pain brings wisdom forth;
Not lightly won, but with blood
All the God suffers is known
By His chosen ones—

From: *The Song of Bear and Raven*
Attributed to Fiorbhinn Mackenzie, 1st century CY

I bind your eyes, your nose, your ears, brother deer, Ritva Havel thought, turning her will into a dart. *By the Hunter and the Huntress, come to meet your fate!*

Then she withdrew her mind, becoming one with the musty scent of damp decaying leaves and wet earth and pine sap from the twigs that studded the loops set on her war cloak, the feel of water soaking through the knee of her pants from the damp earth where she knelt, with the gray light through the misty rain. The mule deer was a second-year buck, his rack of antlers still a modest affair. He was plump with autumn though, his ruddy-brown coat glossy, working his way down from the heights where the snow season had already started.

Here it was just cold, the drizzle slanting down through open forest of tall slender lodgepole pine and short, squat limbers, knocking more of the faded old-gold foliage of the quaking aspens and narrow-leaf cottonwoods to flutter down and make the earth beneath slippery with wet duff. The brush ahead of her and to either side was viburnum, scarlet in this season; the withered red berries were still dense on the spindly stems, and the deer was working its way along the edge of the tongue of woodland, nibbling at the fruit while its tall ears swiveled like a jackrabbit's and the black-tipped white tail quivered over the snowy patch on its rump. Mountain bluebirds called as they flitted from branch to branch, feeding on the same bounty.

Closer, and she could hear the slight mushy *tock* as the deer's hooves cleared the ground. Her own breath scarcely moved the gauze mask, but her stomach abruptly cramped—they'd been *hungry*, and Rudi needed better food if he was to heal. Fifty yards, forty, thirty . . . you looked at the spot where you wanted the arrow to go . . . twenty . . .

I am the bow and the arrow, the hunter and the prey . . .

The bow came up as she drew to the ear in a single smooth motion, and the cloak fell away from her arms. A slight creaking came from it as her arms and shoulders and gut levered against the force of the recurve's stave, stretching the sinew on the back, compressing the laminated horn on the belly and bending the slice of yew between them. The string lifted from the final curve at the tips, the bow bent into a deep C, and the arrow slid back through the cutout in the riser. The deer began its stiff-legged leap even as the string rolled off her fingertips.

Snap. The string lashed the hard leather bracer on her forearm, and there was a quarter second's blurring streak through the air. *Thunk.*

That was the distinctive wet sound of a broadhead striking flesh. The quick-release toggle of the war cloak snapped under her fist and she cleared the viburnum in a single raking stride, ready to chase or shoot again. Starlings rose in a chittering flock from the trees around her as she moved, hundreds wheeling in perfect unison and coasting downward to new perches. She reached for a new arrow; an injured animal had to be run down and given the mercy stroke or a hunter would lose all luck, and you couldn't always count on a quick kill. This time the deer took three staggering steps and collapsed, its limbs kicking for a moment; then it stretched out its neck and went limp.

"Good!" Ritva said, wiping off her bow and sliding it into the case against the wet.

She stopped and gathered up her cloak, slid her sword through the buckled frog on her belt and slipped her buckler onto the spring-loaded clip on the sheath. The deer's eyes were blank by the time she arrived, beaded with drops of the rain that pooled like tears. Her arrow had sunk to the fletching behind the ribs on the left side, angling sharply forward and either striking the heart or severing the big veins next to it as the razor-sharp triangular head punched in. The death had been very quick; a single moment of surprise and pain, and then the dark.

"I'm sorry, brother," she murmured, glad of that.

She bent and passed a hand over the deer's eyes, and then her own; touched a finger to the blood and then to her forehead.

"Thank you for your gift of life. Speak well of me to the Guardians. Go now and play beneath the forever trees on the mountainsides of the Undying Land, where no evil comes, until you are reborn."

To the forest: "Thank you, Horned Lord, Master of the Beasts! Bring this my brother's spirit home to Her who is Mother-of-All. Witness that I take from Your bounty in need, not wantonness, knowing that for me also the Hour of the Hunter shall come, soon or late. Earth must be fed."

Then she bent and caught the deer above the hocks, heaving backwards and pumping her legs to keep it moving, and wheezing a little too; the carcass weighed as much as she did, and she wasn't a small woman. You needed a tree to gralloch a deer properly. Hanging it up by the hind legs made it drain thoroughly and it also made it easier to gut and quarter.

Also she wanted to get out of the open meadow; they

hadn't seen any sign of pursuit for a while, but these alien mountains weren't the friendly confines of Mithrilwood, or even the further Cascades, where you could kindle a little fire and eat the liver fresh as was ancient hunter's right. Spit ran into her mouth at the thought; there was nothing like liver or kidneys right out of the beast, grilled on a hot twig fire with no relish but a little salt.

"If you *could* get a fire going in this misery," she muttered to herself.

A trickle of skin-rippling cold rain ran down inside her collar. The rest of her clothes were just damp, but they'd be wet soon if this went on. You got used to that if you spent a lot of time outdoors, but that didn't make it any fun. And it leached the heat out of your body, which meant you had to eat more.

Then her head came up beneath the shadow of the lodgepole she'd selected, and she frowned as she blew on her fingers to keep them supple; you *didn't* want your grip to slip when you were using a skinning knife.

What's the matter? she thought. *Is it the weather?*

The low clouds hid the peaks eastward, and even the glacier-polished granite upper slopes of this broad valley. And yes, it smelled like it was going to get a lot colder; maybe snow, maybe heavy snow. They were well above five thousand feet here, and it could be dangerous, even though she wasn't all that far from camp. But it wasn't that which made the skin between her shoulder blades itch.

As if absently, she whistled softly as she cut a branch for a spacer, trimmed it to points on both sides, ran those between hock and tendon, tied a rope to it and hoisted it up. There was no reply from Mary . . .

Uh-oh. Something is wrong!

Her senses flared out, but the rain was stronger now, a white curtain of noise, blurring sight and drowning scent. Four trees big enough to hide a man stood close by.

It was the smell that warned her, even in the damp; a sudden shift in the wind brought the scent of woodsmoke soaked into fur and leather, and the distinctive taint of wool cloth full of old dried sweat wet again with the rain. She'd just started her whirl and lunge when arms long and cable strong clamped around her from behind. The man whipped her sideways, and her wrist struck the tree trunk painfully. The knife skittered off, pinwheeling into the mass of dead leaves and fallen needles.

Ritva hunched her shoulders and threw her weight downward, but the arms gripped harder and lifted her off the ground—the man was strong as a bear, and tall as one too, and knew what he was doing. A half-dozen thin red braids wound with eagle feathers and bits of turquoise on the ends swirled around her face as they struggled. She whipped her heel backwards, and heard a grunt as the boot connected with a knee.

"Keep still, woman!" a voice grunted in her ear, harshly accented and smelling of stale breath and un-scrubbed teeth. "I win badges for wrestling!"

Ritva *did* keep still for an instant—and then whipped her right foot back up over her own shoulder as she felt him adjust his grip. You had to be *very* limber to do that, but it took him a little by surprise. The toe of the boot didn't crack into his face; he'd pulled his head aside. But it did graze along his jaw, and that made the arms slacken a bit. Not enough to wrench free; they were so bear tight she was having trouble breathing, but enough so that she could get her left hand down along her sword sheath.

No point in trying to draw it, she thought. *But . . .*

Her fingers closed on the grip of her buckler. She stripped it out of the clip, swayed her hips to one side, and did her best to smash the hard, hard edge into her unknown assailant's groin. Again he was too fast, but the edge hit his hip bone instead, and even without much leverage the thump was enough to paralyze him with pain for an instant. In that instant she stamped down on the instep of one foot, and felt something yield. She was wearing laced boots, and he apparently had some sort of soft moccasin on instead.

A grunt of pain and bad breath by her face, and she wrenched herself free. The motion turned into a whirling circle-in-place, but as she turned her hand snapped down on the hilt of her sword and swept it out. The steel swung in a blurring arch of silver in the gray rain as she turned, but the man suddenly wasn't there; he'd flung himself back and pivoted in the air above the waist-high swing of the longsword, then backflipped again, hands down and then snapping upright. His tomahawk and long knife flicked into his hands.

"Ieston esgerad gweth lín!" she snarled in baffled fury that tasted like vinegar at the back of her mouth. "And then I'll stuff them down your throat!"

Nobody had a right to be that fast, except her and her sister. Well, perhaps Aunt Astrid, and Rudi, and by reputation Grand Constable d'Ath. And nobody whatsoever had any right to be able to sneak up on her that way. Nobody had, not for years.

The man grinned at her and circled; she turned on her heel, keeping the sword and the buckler up. He was tall, as tall as Rudi; lanky rather than leopard-graceful, but the crushing power of those long arms was a dreadful memory. He'd known what he was doing, too; if he hadn't been trying to subdue rather than kill she'd be dead or crippled or at least unconscious already.

Just a trace of a limp. And he doesn't look like there's any armor there, she thought.

He was wearing fringed leggings of mottled buckskin and a long woolen shirt covered in rondels of cloth sewn with images—a bow, a canoe, a horse, more—and a bearskin tunic over that. If he had a backpack or supplies, he'd cached them elsewhere.

"You are not like the women of the Prophet's men," he said.

The fighting-ax and bowie made precise, lazy circles to draw her eyes; she kept them on his, instead, and let the focus blur a little so that peripheral vision would be sharper. The white plumes of their breath puffed out into the chilly falling drizzle, slowing as they controlled the impulse to pant.

"They are sheep," he went on. "You are a she-wolf, like our Scout women, worthy of badges of merit of your own; I have followed you many days, and seen your skill. I will take you back to the Morrowlander camps northward, and you will bear strong cubs. The Prophet can go find comfort with his wooly ewes."

"*Alae, nago nin, hwest yrch!*" she said. "*Oh, bite me, orc-breath!*"

She was used to male admiration, but this was ridiculous. To herself she added: *He didn't notice that there were two of us? Where* is *Mary?*

"And—" the man began.

He attacked as his lips began to move, sweeping the hammer of his tomahawk towards her temple and flipping the bowie into a reverse grip so that the foot-long blade lay along his forearm, ready to block a cut.

Clung-tung!

Steel rang on steel as she swept the buckler around and up to knock the tomahawk aside. The impact nearly tore the little steel shield from her hand, and did send a jag of pain through her wrist and forearm, making her grit her teeth and work the fingers against the wooden grip to get the numbness out. The sheer strength was shocking, but Ritva was used to male warriors who were stronger than she was; men her height often had twenty pounds more muscle on their arms and shoulders. She wasn't used to fighting men that *fast*. She had to duck, because the deflection barely sent it over her head.

Ouch! she thought, and lunged, her right foot throwing up a ruck of forest duff as she extended.

The Scout was used to fighting with men who used shetes, point-heavy slashing blades with the balance thrown well forward of the hilt. He leapt backwards and landed with a grimace of surprise. A spreading red spot showed where she'd touched him, on the front of his wool shirt just above the solar plexus. She could see his eyes widen a little as he took in her sword and what it implied, thirty inches of double-edged steel starting at two thumbs' width and tapering to a murderous fang.

The shete hit hard, but once a blow was parried or missed its weight pinned the wielder's arm for an instant, and there was enough time for an agile man to get inside with shorter weapons. The Western longsword in Ritva's hand moved like light on sparkling water; it could drive at him like a spear, and cut anywhere along either side as quick as the flick of a beetle's wings.

Now he would fight to kill, for survival's sake.

"Lacho Calad!" she shrieked, and attacked. *"Drego Morn!"*

"Akela!" he shouted back, grinning.

Ting! The sword skidded off the blade of the bowie, and she jerked her torso back just enough that the tip of the knife scored the green leather over her mail-vest. *Tack*, and the return cut at the side of his leg was caught by the tough rawhide-bound ashwood shaft of the tomahawk; he tried to twist the sword out of her hand by turning the notched blade of the hand-ax against it. She leapt backwards, launching a frantic stop-thrust as her foot came down on a root . . .

In the end it came down to who slipped first. He skipped aside from a rush as she came in foot and hand behind the point of her sword, and the narrow head of the tomahawk came down on her left shoulder. It didn't cut through the light mail, or break the bone beneath—not quite. She gave a hiss as cold fire washed through that side of her body and the buckler slipped out of her fingers. Pivot, *lunge*—

Wet leaves skidded out from beneath one of the Scout's moccasins. He still fell backwards, but the point drove into his shoulder until it scored bone; she could feel the ugly jarring sensation up the blade and through the hilt. The fine steel bent and then came free again as she recovered. He threw the tomahawk, and won a few seconds when the top punched her ribs and she grunted with the impact. Then she lunged again, and the point sank four inches into his thigh.

That was enough. She recovered and retreated, right foot shuffling back to left and left moving back in turn, her mouth open as she brought her breathing back under control. Suddenly she was stiff and her legs wobbled, and she leaned forward a little to take the air in; her sight dimmed for an instant as the diamond clarity of life or death passed. Her enemy had a hand clamped to the leg wound, but blood welled around it, and the shoulder was bleeding too, and that arm was useless for now.

I'm not getting near him, he's too dangerous, she thought; her own left arm was still weak, and the shoulder was starting to really hurt where the ax had smashed flesh against bone. *I'll wait until he bleeds out some more and weakens, then finish him.*

The man saw it in her eyes, and nodded respect. Ritva raised her sword in salute.

"You fought well," she said, and in English. "Speak no ill of me to the Guardians; I'll make it quick."

He grinned, showing his strong yellow teeth; the face beneath the braids was turning a little gray.

"You let me live, I tell you about your sister," he said. "I give my word—honor of a Scout—I will not fight you or your people again. I go to place deep in woods, heal up."

Painfully, he brought three fingers to his brow in some sort of ritual gesture. She looked into the pain-glazed eyes and nodded.

"You're the one who's been dogging our tracks?" she said.

"You're good tracker, but I'm better!" he said, proudly boastful even then. "A Scout of thirty badges! I track you for the Prophet's men, with a priest."

"A priest?" she said.

"War-priest out of Corwin. High Seeker, they say." He spat aside. "Warlock, evil. We split up this morning when you two do—capture one, make her talk, he says. We know you all stop, make camp, hunt for food."

"Are the Cutters behind us?"

"Many days. Lost their horses, had to find more, not too many and not too good, pushed 'em too hard. Not used to nursing bad horses. We leave sign for them to follow. Go to your sister. Go *now.*"

Ritva gave one crisp nod, toed the bowie knife over to where the man lay—he could cut bandages with that, enough to staunch the bleeding so he could get to wherever his gear was stowed—and ran.

*   *   *

Closer, she slowed, ghosting from tree to tree. If Mary was still up the tree watching, she'd ...

Then she heard the scream. It came from the right place, and she slowed still further. Her left arm was still weak, too weak to use her bow.

Move swiftly, but don't dart; it draws the eye.

The rain had tapered off to a falling mist, but that cut visibility, too. A snort from a horse as it caught her familiar scent; their dappled Arabs were tied up to a line strung between two trees, but there was a third there—a strong nondescript brown beast, looking worn down as if by long hard riding. She ghosted closer ...

Mary screamed again; she was up against the hundred-foot pine she'd been using as a blind, and a man in a robe the color of dried blood was holding her by the throat. Holding her off the ground, and squeezing, and her face was a mass of blood. The Dúnedain longsword lay on the ground nearby, and a shete; they were both red, the sticky liquid turning thin and dripping away as rain washed the steel.

"Look ... at ... me," the man—the priest—in the robe said. "I—see—you."

His other arm ended short of a hand, and it had a rawhide tourniquet bound around it; even then Ritva found a fractional instant to be astonished. An injury like that would leave a man flat on his back with shock for days, at a minimum! And the hand was lying not far off.

"Look ... at ... me," he said again. "Tell ... me ..."

The words sounded *dark*. Not just deep or gravelly; as if they had more weight than words could bear, as if they were *suffused* somehow, like a man's face when he strained at a heavy load, like a weight that dimpled the surface of the world as a heavy footstep would a sheet of taut canvas. Suddenly the cold wet sapped at Ritva's strength with a feeling of dreary hopelessness. A wrongness that only flight could cure, enough space between her and this thing that she wouldn't have to *think* about it anymore. She couldn't walk towards *that*.

Instead she ran to him. "Try looking at *me*!" she screamed, gathering her will.

The sword flashed down as he turned and released her sister; he batted at the gray-silver streak with his injured arm, but the blade raked across his chest. The wound wasn't instantly deadly, but she could see the skin split and blood well out . . . and then stop.

And he smiled. He smiled at her.

"I—see—you," he said.

Lord of Blades, be with me! she thought desperately; and the fear blew out of her. *Maiden of the sword, aid me!*

She set both hands on the hilt of her longsword as he came towards her.

He's like the guy Rudi fought. He doesn't feel pain, her mind thought dispassionately. *Or shock. And so he won't faint or go wobbly. Maybe he won't die right away if I stick him through the heart. No point in thrusting. And if he can get that hand on me, I'm dead. Damn slippery wet ground! But he's got to reach for me first.*

He did, moving in a jerky series of motions, as if he were being operated by a puppeteer, and not a very skilled one. But the grab nearly caught her arm; he was *fast*.

Ritva whirled away, and she cut. The tip of his thumb caught against the point of her sword. The man looked down at it, flexing the rest of the hand, then bringing it to his mouth to bite off the mangled bit and swallow it. Then he grinned at her as red ran down his lips, mixing with the rainwater.

"Clever," he said. "You—are—too—clever. All—of—you."

"Thiach uanui a naneth lín le hamma," she spat, and began a lunge. *"You're ugly and your momma dresses you funny."*

It was a feint, and the man betrayed himself with a snatch at her sword wrist, ignoring the glittering menace of the point. She cut backhanded . . .

It became like a fight in a nightmare; cut and back, cut and back, against a figure that would not *fall*, no matter what she did, that stumbled after her even when she landed a drawing slash on the belly. Once three fingers closed on her left wrist, and the shocking strength in them made the bones creak. She leapt up and drove both her feet against the man's chest and heard bone snap as she tore free and rolled away in three full back summersaults. He was *there*, raising a foot to stamp the life out of her; she cut at his leg, kicked again and again to pull herself free.

He tried to crawl after her even then, but the leg was hanging by a thread. His body stiffened, and he made a sudden sound—a croaking scream, and life came back into the flat stare, as if the man had been poured back into himself and was suddenly alone in his skull once more, naked before the pain of what had been done to his body. Then he went limp.

Ritva put the point of her sword into the soil, kneeling and holding on to the quillions, breath whooping in and out as she struggled not to vomit or give way. Her vision narrowed in to a dim tunnel that was muddy colored at the edges. When she could stand she went to Mary and knelt beside her. Her twin was lying curled around herself, hands across her face, making small sounds through her clenched teeth.

"Let me see it," Ritva said, pulling at her hands. "Let me see it!"

"I killed him. Then he hit me," she mumbled, and let her twin pull the hands away.

The face turned up to the rain was her own . . . or it had been. Now there was a slash running down from just above the nose to the left cheek, and the clear matter of the eye was mixed with the blood.

"I'll get the kit," Ritva said, swallowing.

They had some morphine left, though not much. She tried to stand and nearly collapsed herself as she put her weight on her left arm.

The bloodied hands caught at her. "I killed him. Then he hit me."

*   *   *

A dog barked, a *wooorugh* of greeting and of alarm at the scents of pain and injury. Ritva forced her eyes open, and saw Garbh dancing before her horse, fur bristling.

"Mother of God, what happened to Mary?" Ingolf's rough voice asked.

The sound took a minute to penetrate the fog of cold and exhaustion that wrapped Ritva's mind more thickly than the building snowstorm did the forest around. The Richlander caught at the bridle of her horse; Ritva swayed in the saddle, automatically tightening her grip on her sister who rode before her. The other twin's face was a mass of bandages—that helped keep her warm, too, along with the cocoon of blankets she'd rigged, and Ritva's own body heat, though she was shaking with a chill that seemed to go straight to her gut and spine and into her head.

Their campsite was hidden in a hollow, a set of dome-shaped shelters of tight-woven pine branches; the snow was starting to catch on them, turning them into white curves, and flakes hissed as they were blown sideways under the hood of the same construction that covered their fire. More slanted down out of darkness, like ribbons of white between the tall slim mountain pines. Everyone else came boiling up; some asking questions, Edain grimly silent and moving like a windup toy in the old stories. He silently unslung the quartered deer from the led horse and took it over to the hearth and set to his share of the other chores.

Ingolf lifted Mary out of her arms. Odard and Fred and Mathilda caught Ritva as she started to topple, tended to the horses, half carried her over to the largest shelter and through the low door of blankets and branches. It was warm within—warmer, at least—with rocks heated in the fire and changed as they began to cool. Father Ignatius began to unwrap the bandages around Mary's head; someone helped Ritva pull off her wet gloves and thrust a mug of hot broth into her hands, and she managed to wrap her fingers around it before it spilled. The liquid almost scorched her mouth, but she could feel every drop of it as it made its way down her gullet and into her nearly empty stomach. She'd eaten the deer's liver, raw, but nothing else in the . . .

"How long?" she asked, through chattering teeth.

Another mug of the broth came, and she was suddenly aware of the salty aroma of the boiled-down jerky and minced squirrel. She forced herself to sip, and help as others got her wet clothes off and herself into her sleeping bag; more of the hot rocks went into that as well, wrapped in her spare clothes. Her mind began to function again as her core temperature rose, enough to be conscious of how weary she was, and even of how the light of the lantern slung from the apex of the shelter jerked and twisted on the anxious faces around her. The pine scent was overwhelmingly strong, like a cool cloth on a fevered brow.

"You've been gone a day past when we expected," Ingolf said. "What the hell happened?"

She described it in short words, ending with: "They're not going to follow us anymore. But the warlock and the lunatic with the badges left a blazed trail to where Mary and I met them. That's only twelve, fourteen miles east. How's Rudi?"

The others remained silent, silent as the blanket-bundled form who lay on his stomach not far away. Father Ignatius said from where he worked:

"He's no worse . . . well, perhaps not much worse. The antibiotic cream is containing the infection, but the wound in his back in particular doesn't want to heal . . . of course, the conditions haven't been very good for convalescence."

His breath sucked in as he undid the last of the bandages. Everyone looked; Frederick Thurston winced and looked away almost immediately, but he was the youngest of them.

"I'll have to remove the remains of the eye, cleanse and stitch. The wound is already angry . . . I wouldn't have expected that, so soon and in cold weather."

Ritva blinked. "I cleaned it and packed it with the powder!"

Ignatius nodded, hands busy. Mary stirred, and gave a stifled shriek as she came aware again, then subsided into a tense shivering quiet.

"Can you hear me?" the warrior-priest said, as he swabbed her face.

Ingolf was on her other side. The cornflower-blue eye swiveled from the cleric to him, then to the rest of them, and to Ritva, and she sighed. Her hand came up, and the Easterner took it.

"I . . . can hear you. It's seeing you that's a problem! How come there's two of you when I've got only one eye left?" Mary said, and bared her teeth in what might have been a smile.

Ignatius nodded sober approval, took the vial of morphine from the kit, frowned a little as he saw the level, and then began filling a hypodermic. Ritva remembered bargaining for the precious painkiller in Bend, with Mary as the other half of her . . .

"I can't use too much of this," he said, as someone came in with a kettle of boiling water and poured it into a shallow basin; the shelter was already set up as a sick-room for Rudi. "I'm afraid there will be some pain."

"Alae, *duh*," Mary said.

Ritva flogged herself into wakefulness while the work went on; her sister's other hand was in hers, and the bones of Ritva's creaked under the pressure of her grip. Ingolf sat at the other. When it was over, he helped wipe away the sweat of agony.

"Feels . . . like nice . . . stitching," Mary said, timing the words to her breath to control it. "We never were . . . good at embroidery."

"I've used some of the numbing oil," Ignatius said. "You should sleep now, my daughter."

"Thanks," she whispered. Then her eyelid fluttered. "Guess . . . I can live with . . . one eye."

"No," Ritva said. "You'll have three, sis."

"Five," Ingolf said.

He waited until her breathing grew regular, then tucked the hands inside the sleeping bag.

"How soon can she be moved?" he asked the priest.

"Ideally . . . not for weeks," Ignatius said, and then shrugged wryly as he tossed the last of the soiled cloths into a bowl. "But moving her will be much less risk than moving Rudi."

Ingolf's battered face closed in like a fist. "We have to. Move 'em both. Twelve miles isn't enough, even with the storm to cover our tracks."

Unexpectedly, Frederick spoke: "I've seen reports on these mountains. From now on, the storms can come one after another for weeks. We could get stuck here. But there are caves farther up this valley. Dad used them for, uh, scouts, back when we were having problems with New Deseret."

Ingolf nodded. "We need to get farther away . . . a cave would be right. We'll rig two horse-travois."

Ritva let her mind drift away. *I don't have anything I have to do right now*, she thought. It was enough to make her smile, as the dark flowed up around her like comfort.

WESTERN WYOMING, GRAND TETON MOUNTAINS
OCTOBER 15, CY 23/2021 AD

Rudi Mackenzie dreamed.

In the dream he rose from his sickbed, looking down for a moment at the thin, wasted form. Edain watched by his side; now and then he poked at the low fire that burned with a canted wall of piled rocks behind it to absorb and throw back the heat. The others were dim shapes in the depth of the cave; Epona looked up and whickered at him, and Garbh bristled a bit and whined until Edain absently stroked her head.

He turned from them and walked out through the gap in the pine branches that blocked the entrance, knocking a little snow down on his bonnet. He was whole, and free of pain; looking down he saw that he was dressed in his kilt and jacket and plaid, knee-hose and shoes. His senses were keen, but the blizzard outside was only bracing; he could hear the wind whistle in the Ponderosa pines, and feel the sting of driven snow on his face, smell the dry, mealy smell of it as branches tossed in the thick woods above and below.

But I'm not really cold, *somehow,* he thought, smiling to hear the moan and creak of the wind's passage.

He walked down the path. An overhung ridge of rock topped with three twisted trees made the trail kink, creating a sheltered nook in the storm. A man stood there, leaning one shoulder against the rock. A brisk fire burned at his feet, throwing smoke up to where the wind caught it above the ridge and tattered it into the blowing whiteness. To one side a tall spear leaned against the cliffside, broader-headed than most horseman's weapons; he thought there were signs graven in the steel. A horse stood some distance off, unsaddled but with several blankets thrown over it and its head down. It was a big beast, but hard to see; the wolflike dog that raised its head as he approached seemed massive as well. Saddle and bedroll and gear lay beside the fire, and a pot steamed over it.

The man was tall too, taller than Rudi but lean. As the Mackenzie came closer he saw that the stranger was old; at least, his shoulder-length hair and cropped beard were iron gray. His dress was that of the Eastern plains and mountains, neckerchief and broad-brimmed hat, sheepskin coat and long thick chaps of the same, homespun pants and fleece-lined leather boots, poncho of crudely woven wool longer at the rear than the front. Closer still, and Rudi could see that the lids of his left eye closed on emptiness; the other was the color of mountain glaciers, and as cold.

"You're welcome to share my fire," the man said, making a gesture towards the pot.

His voice rolled deep, cutting through the muted wind-howl. Rudi nodded, swallowing a prickling sensation as he bent and poured himself a cup—thus making himself a guest. Not everyone felt that to be as sacred as Mackenzies did, but most folk would think three times before falling on someone they'd invited to share their food. The liquid was chicory—what most in the far interior called *coffee*—hot and strong and bitter, but this somehow also tasted of honey and flowers and a little of hot tar.

The dog growled at him a little, one great paw across a meaty elk thigh bone . . .

No, Rudi thought suddenly. *It's a wolf, not a dog.*

The gray man nudged the beast, ruffling its ears as he bent to pour himself a cup from the battered pot of enameled metal.

"Quiet, greedyguts," he said. He glanced up; a raven sat on a branch that jutted over the rock, cocking a thoughtful eye at the wolf's meal, and another sat beside it with head beneath wing. "And you two remember what happened the last time, and think twice."

Then he leaned back against the rock again, blowing on his chicory and waiting, relaxed as the wolf at his feet.

"I'm called Rudi Mackenzie," the young clansman said slowly, as he straightened and met the other's eye; strength flowed into him with the hot drink, easing a weakness he hadn't sensed until that moment. "But I'm thinking the now that I know your name . . . lord."

The older man's features were jut-boned, bold of chin and nose, scored by age but still strong, as were the long-fingered hands that gripped his own cup.

"Call me Wanderer," he said. He smiled a little. "And I know your father."

"Sir Nigel?" Rudi asked.

"Him too. But I was thinking of your blood-father. You might say he bought a ticket to the table I set out; him and many of his kin, from out of deep time."

Rudi finished the cup and set it aside; the last of his discomfort seemed to vanish with it. He raised his head and met the Other's gaze.

The eye speared him. For a moment he seemed to be looking *beyond* it, as if the pupil were a window; to a place where everything that was, was smaller than that span across the eye. Then a flash, a searing that was more than light or heat, while being itself flexed and shattered and re-formed in a wild tangle of energies; then a wilderness of empty dark where stars lit, like campfires blossoming . . . and then guttering out as they fled apart, until there was another darkness, one where the stuff of his body itself decayed into nothingness. And in that nothingness, a light that *looked* at him.

Rudi blinked and swallowed, daunted but not glancing aside. The deep voice went on:

"Shall I show you your fate, boy? Shall I tell you if you die untimely or live long?"

"No, my lord Wanderer," Rudi said softly. "My mother is a weaver, and I know that every thread has its place and is part of the whole. All men die. None die untimely, and no man may live a day longer than he lives. So if you've come to lead me away, I am ready."

He dared a smile. "Though I've heard you send your daughters for *that* job."

And there's a good deal I'd rather do first . . . he thought.

Suddenly an image came to him, painfully bright; a room with a bed, and Matti's face exhausted and triumphant as she looked up to him from the red crumpled-looking infant cradled in the crook of her arm, and a shadow of his own exultant joy.

The Wanderer laughed, and though it was a soft chuckle there was an overtone to it like the crackle of lights over the mountains in winter. There was approval there, but by something greater than men or their hopes and sorrows.

"Good! Though you won't be meeting Göndul, as your father did. You've pledged yourself to another, and I'm not inclined to quarrel with Her."

Rudi's mouth quirked. "It seems you've something else in mind then, my lord the Wanderer," he said.

The figure nodded. "But unasked, I will tell you this: you won't die in the straw of sickness, nor of an arrow in the back, even a cursed one. Though you will not live to feel your shoulders bend with age, or see your hair grow gray."

"How, then?"

"You will die by the blade, sword in hand. The King's

death, the given sacrifice that goes consenting with open eyes, dying that his folk may live."

"As my father did, whose blood renewed the land. Thank you, then, lord Wanderer. Though I've seldom called on You by name."

The Wanderer flicked away the grounds in his tin cup and tossed it to the damp earth beside the fire. "No?" he said. "But your mother has called on Me, in her grove, when you lay wounded and near to death. And you have as well. Come."

He put his hand on Rudi's shoulder. They took three steps to the edge of the trail to look downward, and his poncho flared in the wind, seeming longer now. A dead leaf flickered out of it as it masked Rudi's face for a moment, and then he sucked in his breath.

I know that path! he thought.

It was nightfall on the roadway that ran westward from the waterfall and mill to the gates of Dun Juniper, where the schoolchildren practiced an hour or two shooting at the mark most evenings. The trees beyond and below were Douglas fir, taller and thicker and closer-set than the pine forests of the Tetons, each dark green branch heavy with its load of snow. It was a softer fall than the blizzard about him, of flakes larger and wetter . . . the snow of a winter in the western foothills of the Cascades, one that would lay a few days at most, not grip the land like cold iron until the end of May.

Close at hand a column of kilted children were walking through the gathering dark, cased bows and capped quivers over their shoulders, with a few adult warriors among them—one had a lamp slung on a spear over her shoulder, a globe of yellow light in the fog white of the snow.

"That's Aoife Barstow," he said slowly. "She and her lover died fighting for me when the Protector's men came, only a little later . . . I offer at their graves every year."

The children started singing. He recognized one clear high ten-year-old's voice. It was his own.

> *"Upon his shoulder, ravens*
> *His face like stone, engraven*
> *Astride an eight-hoofed stygian beast*
> *He gathers the fruit of the gallows trees!*
> *Driving legions to victory*
> *The Bringer of War walks tonight!"*

"By the name you invoked, by the blood she spilled, by the offering made beneath the tree where she died," the man said softly. "By these you called, and I answer at the appointed time."

"She . . . named others than you, lord Wanderer. As have I, full often."

Images passed before his eyes; he couldn't be sure if they were shapes formed in the swirling snow, or his own imaginings, or as real as the blood he could feel beating in his throat . . . because that too might be illusion. A tall charioteer's shape edged and crowned with fire, tossing up a spear that was a streak of gold across the sky and kissing it as he rode laughing to battle as to a bridal feast; a woman vast and sooty and bent, wielding a scythe that reaped men; a raven whose wings beat out the life and death of worlds. His hand went to the scar between his brows, where a real raven's beak had touched him in the sacred wood.

"When I hung nine days from the Tree, I became a god of death," the one-eyed figure said. "When I grasped the runes of wisdom I learned many names."

He looked up. One of the great black birds moved in the skeletal branches above them. It cocked its head and gave a harsh cry and launched itself away, gliding down the slope on broad-stretched wings.

"And Raven and I are old friends."

They turned back to the fire. *If this isn't the final journey, then I must be dreaming*, Rudi thought, as they crouched by the red flickering warmth, across from each other, sitting easily on their hams.

The gray-haired man reached into a pocket, brought out tobacco and papers, rolled himself a cigarette single-handed, then lit it with an ember he picked out with a twig. He handed it across the fire; the Mackenzie took it, and inhaled the smoke—he'd done the same before, visiting with the Three Tribes. For a flickering instant as he inhaled the harsh bite across his tongue the shape on the other side of the flames had a prick-eared, long-muzzled face, and two braids of hair beside it beneath the hat.

"Are you truly that One men named the Wanderer?" Rudi asked boldly.

He could feel his fear, but it was slightly distant, like the cold of the wind. And well might a man be afraid, to meet Him on a lonely mountainside. He *was* a god of death; the lord of poetry and craft who'd given the runes to men and established kingship, but also bringer of the red madness of battle, of everything that lifted humankind beyond themselves. His favorites got victory, but they died young, and often by treachery.

A puff of smoke. "What would your mother say?"

She'd answer a question with a question, some distant part of Rudi thought wryly. *And if I complain, say that you can only truly learn the truth you find yourself.* Aloud:

"That the forms the God wears . . . or the Goddess . . . are many. And that they are true, not mere seemings or masks, but that they're not . . . not *complete.* As are the little gods and the spirits of the land, or the Fathers and Mothers of the animal kind. They speak to us as we need them, if we'll but listen. For how can a man tell all his mind to a child, or a god to a man?"

The other nodded. The great wolf raised its head and looked at him, then put its massive muzzle on its paws again.

"A wise woman, Lady Juniper, a very wise woman . . . and not least in knowing that what she knows isn't everything that is."

"You'll be talking to me in riddles and hints, then, I suppose, lord Wanderer?"

The eye pierced him. For a moment he felt transparent as glass, as if he could suddenly see his entire life—not in memory, but through an infinity of Rudis—stretching back like a great serpent to the moment of his birth . . . and his conception . . . and before. As if all time and possibility were an eternal Now.

"Look, then," the Wanderer said. "If you can bear it."

For a moment the mountain about him stood stark and bare, only here and there a charred root exposed by the gullies cut by long-gone monsoon floods. Heat lay on it like a blanket, through air gray and clear and *thick* with the tears of boiling oceans. Then it changed and was green once more . . . but *different*, somehow; there was a wrongness to the way the trees were placed, a regularity that held patterns as complex as those you saw in a kaleidoscope, layer within layer. A rabbit hopped by . . .

. . . and silvery tendrils looped around it, thinner than the finest wire. The beast gave one long squeal and then froze as they plunged beneath its skin. Then it seemed to blur, as if it were dissolving, until nothing was left but a damp patch on the ground. Involuntarily Rudi looked down at his own feet. The Mother's earth was beneath him, and he expected to feed it with his body and bones someday . . .

But not like that! he thought.

"Those were evil fates, lord Wanderer," he said. "And true ones, I'm thinking."

"Evil for more than men," came the reply. "Now, tell me, Son of the Bear. What would you do with a little child you saw running with a sharp knife?"

Rudi's mouth quirked. "Take it from her, lord Wanderer. Swat her backside so that she'd remember, if she were too young for words."

"And a child who took a lighter and burned down your mother's Hall and all its treasures, so that many were hurt?"

"The same, perhaps with a bit of a harder swat. And call in the heart-healers to find the source of her hurt, and I'd see that she was watched more carefully, and better taught."

Walker nodded. "You wouldn't kill her? Even if you thought she might do the same again, and all within would die?"

Rudi made a sign. "Lord and Lady bless, no!" he said in revulsion, and then wondered if he'd spoken too quickly. "What a thought! If it was necessary, we . . . I . . . would keep her guarded always."

"Some men . . . and some women . . . would have that thought. Some would act on it, and kill the child."

The single eye looked out into a world that was once again pines glimpsed through snow.

"And some would have joy in the thought; or inwardly thank the chance that gave them the argument that it was necessary."

"Lord Wanderer, I don't understand."

"You don't need to. Just remember this: the world"—somehow Rudi knew he meant more than merely Earth—"is shaped by mind. And the world in turn shapes the stuff of mind. And now a question for you: what is the symbol of Time itself?"

"An arrow?" Rudi asked.

The tall figure laughed. "A hero's answer, if I ever heard one! And I'm something of a connoisseur of heroes. That's natural enough. You're at the age for it, for war and wild faring. So . . . watch."

He turned and took up the great spear, its head graven with the same symbols that glowed on the brooch of his blue-lined gray cloak. Then his arm went back, paused, whipped forward with the unstoppable certainty of a catapult. The spear disappeared into the snow in a blurred streak.

"Was that a straight cast?" Wanderer asked.

"Very straight, lord; and I wouldn't like to be in its way."

They paused, in a silence broken only by the whistle of the wind. The single gray eye watched him, a chill amusement in it. Something warned Rudi, perhaps a whistle of cloven air that wasn't part of the storm's music; he turned and jumped backwards with a yell, nearly stepping on the wolf's tail. The spear flashed past, smashing a sapling to splinters as it came, and then there was a deep hard *smack* as the Wanderer caught it. His long arm swayed back with the impact, and then he grounded the weapon and leaned on it, the head glinting above his head as the dark wind blew flecks of ice past into the night.

"That *was* a straight cast," Wanderer said. "But the line only seems straight because you can't see its full course. Draw it long *enough* and it meets itself, like Jörmungandr."

"I don't understand!" Rudi said again, baffled.

"You don't need to ... yet," the gray one said. "No man can harvest a field till it is ripe, but the seed must be planted. The heroes offer to me for luck and victory. But the Kings ... they ask for wisdom, if they have any to begin with."

"I'd be glad of that," Rudi said; he felt like arguing, but ... *that wouldn't be wise at all.*

"Would you? Then know this. Fact becomes history; history becomes legend; legend becomes myth. Myth turns again to the beginning and creates itself. The figure for time isn't an arrow; that is illusion, just as the straight line is. Time is a serpent."

Rudi blinked. He noticed the bracelet around one thick wrist, where the coat rode up; it was in the form of a snake, wrought of gold so finely that the scales were a manifold shiver that seemed to spin away in infinite sets.

Wanderer stepped closer. "Your friends are waiting for you, Artos, son of Bear and Raven," the tall gray-haired figure said. "Go!"

He clapped a hand to Rudi's back. The touch was white fire, and the Mackenzie stiffened as if existence shattered about him.

"I've got it!" he heard a voice say.

Gods and holy men, never a straight answer, he thought as he bit back a groan.

The white fire still ran in his veins; it narrowed down to a patch on his lower back, and he could hear the voice again. It was Father Ignatius.

"Holy Mary and every saint and God the Father, Son and Holy Spirit be thanked. *That* was why!"

Shuddering, Rudi felt the sting as something swabbed at the wound, and a hand dropped a pus-stained bandage into a bucket. He could smell the sweetish odor of it, oily and with a hint of something like vinegar. Then real fire bathed it.

"I'm sorry, Rudi, but it's necessary," the priest's voice soothed.

A hand took his; he knew it was Mathilda's, and tried to remember not to crush her fingers. Then he realized he couldn't, not even if he tried; her hand was carefully gentle on his. His whole body felt like the limp blood-and-matter soaked rag, hot and weak and stiff at the same time, with localized throbbing aches in his shoulder and back. He could speak, but he simply did not wish it. Even lifting his eyelids was too much effort.

"There was a fragment of the arrowhead still in the wound," Ignatius said as he worked. "But this time the probe found it as I was debriding the dead tissue. Praise to the Lord in His infinite mercy! And Praise Him that Rudi was delirious through it. It's far too close to the Great Sciatic."

"Will he heal now?" Mathilda said anxiously.

"That is with God. But there's a better chance."

Another voice: Odard's. "He needs proper food and warmth and a real bed," the Baron said. "So does Mary. My lady, let me take a little food and try to find a settlement. Ingolf, you said—"

"—that they're not all Cutters in this part of the country, south of Yellowstone, yes," the big Easterner said. "But the operative word is *not all.* And my information's a year out of date—a year ago, Deseret was holding out, too."

"I'm willing to chance it," Odard said.

"Are you willing to not talk, if they do take you?" Ingolf said.

"I . . . think so," Odard said.

"Thank you, my old friend," Mathilda said softly.

Then a complex whistle came from outside; Ignatius' hands finished fastening the band across Rudi's back, and he heard the soft *wheep* of a sword leaving a scabbard, and the little rustle of an arrow twitched out of a quiver.

"*Gîl síla erin lû e-govaded vín!*" Ritva's voice, and then in English: "I've found friends!"

Then in a strong ranch-country twang: "*Gate gate pāragate pārasamgate bodhi svāhā, y'all!*"

"We've got to move you, Chief," Edain Aylward Mackenzie said gently.

The blue-green eyes opened, more like jewels than ever in the shockingly wasted face, and Rudi smiled at him.

"Good . . . glad to be . . . going somewhere," he said.

Edain swallowed. "It's going to hurt."

"Means I'm not dead yet!" Rudi said.

He looks different, Edain thought. *Better. But still sort of . . . like glass.*

"Glad to have you back with us, Chief," he said.

The strangers had a stretcher with long poles on the cave floor now, next to the injured man; it could be rigged as a horse litter, and it was padded with sheepskins. Together they eased him onto it; the thin face convulsed a little as they set him down.

"Sorry, Chief!" Edain said.

"Glad . . . to have you . . . there, boyo," Rudi said.

"I don't know why," he said suddenly, as if a boil had burst inside him. "I got you wounded! And—"

Rudi opened his eyes again; he looked tired, but more *there*. "Bullshit," he said crisply.

"What?" Edain rocked backwards, as if slapped on the cheek.

"You were going to say you couldn't save Rebecca. But you did save her, in the fight with the Rovers, remember?"

Edain shook his head. "And killed her later!"

"So you couldn't save her always. You're not going to live forever, boyo. You've saved my life more than once—but I'm not going to live forever either! Someday I'll die whatever you do, or *I* do. It's not just going on that makes life. That's fear talking; or the fear of losing

someone. I've ... wrestled Thanatos knee to knee, this
last while, and I know. It's when you beat fear every day,
that's when you're immortal. And I want you with me."

He reached out and caught Edain's wrist. "You're
my friend ... you're my comrade of the sword and my
brother. My brother doesn't run out on me!"

Edain gulped, and took a deep breath. "Right, Chief.
It's just ..."

"Grief's hard."

"That it is." He straightened his shoulders. "So's the
work halfway through harvest, but *that* never stopped
me."

CHAPTER ELEVEN

"They're holding out there!" Sir Ivo said. "St. Michael must be looking out for them!"

"You're right," Tiphaine said.

She resisted a temptation to sip at her canteen, despite the dry dust blowing across the land. What you had to go through to pee in one of these steel suits . . .

Ivo crossed himself, and she reflected that sometimes it was a bit lonely, being one of the last agnostics.

"God grant that they're still alive when we get there," she said with pious hypocrisy.

Even my girlfriend's a believer, she thought. *Just a different set of beliefs.*

She raised her binoculars again, adjusting her visor as it went *tick* against the leather-covered metal of the field glasses. The thin chamois on the palms and fingers of her gauntlets let her adjust the screw easily enough. The action was nearly two miles west of the Pendleton city wall, on a hill about twelve hundred feet high. It was bare and not too steep, and several hundred of the enemy cavalry were swirling around it like bees around sugar, surging up the slope to shoot with their recurves and then back again in the quicksilver Eastern style.

The binoculars brought it suddenly, startlingly close; there were about a dozen Dúnedain on their feet, hiding behind rocks and ridges, and as many wounded. A party of the Pendleton horsemen surged up to their position with shetes in hand, and then a giant figure rose beneath the hooves. A long blade glittered as it hacked through both a pony's forelegs to cast the rider screaming down at the man's feet, where he died an instant later. The rest of the Easterners rode away, shooting behind them as they retreated . . .

This is so *tempting,* she thought. *What a song the bards would make of Astrid's Last Stand . . . that overgrown peasant Hordle with a circle of his foes at his feet and a broken sword in his hand . . . blood-stained banners, faces to the foe, eternal glory . . . no, no, I promised Sandra.*

Her knights were out of sight from the enemy's position behind a ridge. In the little dry valley ahead waited two hundred of the CORA cowboys under Bob Brown of Seffridge Ranch. Their commander was looking back at her; she raised a gauntlet and chopped it forward with her hand extended like a blade. The cowboys had their bows out and arrows ready on the string; they started their mounts forward. The agile quarter horses managed to build speed even as they climbed the little rise ahead of them, and she could see the sudden alarm on the other side as the solid block of horses and men came over the crest.

"Yip-yip-yip-yip-yip—"

The alarm call rang out as the Easterners started to draw together to meet the CORA attack, turning westward and away from the beleaguered little party on the hill. Cow-horn trumpets blatted as the two loose swarms headed towards one another, and the Western Ranchers' shout went up:

"Cora! Coraaa!" interspersed with raw catamount shrieks.

"And about now," she murmured, and in that instant the foremost in either band rose in the stirrups and shot.

The arrowheads twinkled in the midmorning sun as they plunged downward. That was how they liked to fight out here in the cow-country, only coming in to close quarters when an enemy had been savaged by arrow-fire. Normally for heavy horse to try and strike them was like trying to beat water with a sledgehammer. Water whose spatters turned into viciously dangerous stinging wasps as it flew away.

But ah, if you can trick them into bunching up to receive a charge, she thought, with a slight cold smile, as she returned her binoculars to their padded steel case. *Then it's more like using a sledgehammer on a bowl of eggs.*

She turned in the saddle. "Now, my iron-heads, I'm going to do you a favor," she said, looking at the eager young faces, shadowed by raised visors or bisected by the nasal-bars of the older helms. "Now I give you a chance to die with honor!"

They cheered, shaking their lances in the air. *And they actually think I am doing them a favor,* she thought. *It's true what they said in the old days. Testosterone rots the brain, not to mention listening to the bards when you're young.*

She held out her own right hand, and Armand thrust the lance into it. Tiphaine rested the butt of the twelve-foot weapon on the ring welded to her stirrup-iron, shrugged her shield around and brought it up. The banner of the Lidless Eye came up beside her, and the destriers began to walk. They'd keep the pace slow until just before arrow range . . .

BD looked up from the wounded as she heard the high harsh singing of the Portlander oliphants, the long curled silver trumpets holding the sustained scream that meant *charge.* It was faint with distance, but the sound was as startling as it would have been to hear a chorus of girls singing a festival hymn to the Lady of the Blossom-time. She'd grown so used to the thought that she would die here amongst angry strangers and the smell of wounds that it took a moment for what her ears heard to filter through to her mind.

Out of the corner of her eye she saw Eilir's eyes move. Her head was a mass of bandages, seeping red where an ear had been sliced; there was another wound on one thigh, a shete-cut.

"The Portlanders are here," BD said, and then repeated it in basic Sign in case she was too dazed to read lips.

Eilir sighed and closed her eyes. Not far away from her, Astrid roused a little and turned and tried to vomit. It was only a dry retching, and when she sank back her face was gray. One of the wounded with a splinted leg dragged himself over and helped her drink. Abstractly, BD sympathized—the pain would be savage, and a concussion like the one she'd gotten from her own sword hilt *would* keep her immobilized for weeks, and *might* cripple—but it was Astrid's plan that had gotten them into this mess. BD didn't want her dead, but she had to admit there would have been some justice in her getting hit so hard the brains spurted out of her ears.

It would have been worth it to avoid a battle, she thought. *But it looks like we're going to have the battle anyway.*

Part of it was taking place right below. The Easterners had better things to do than lob arrows at the little cluster of Rangers atop the hill, and she risked rising from behind a ridge of rock and clay to watch.

Most of the horsemen were fighting the CORA men, at close quarters and handstrokes now that their quivers were empty. Dust hid most of the action, but the sun glinted off the edges of sabers and shetes and axes. Eddies in the earth-mist showed men who hacked and died; she saw a doll-tiny figure topple to earth and go beneath the hooves, anonymous in ranch-country leather and wool, and another dragged from the saddle by a flung lasso.

The sound of their curses and war-shouts came up the slope that was also littered with bodies of men and horses, some still thrashing or trying to crawl away, others motionless. Overhead turkey vultures waited, sweeping in broad circles with their black-and-gray wings outstretched. Ravens skittered lower on the wind. One went over close enough for her to see the clever black eye it cocked at the ground, judging its time.

They're always *on the winning side,* she thought.

Then the Association's trumpets screamed again; much louder this time, and closer. From here she could see what the men lost in dust and rage below couldn't, the line of a hundred lances catching the morning sun as they came over the low rise to the westward. The pennants were snapping with the speed of their passage, and the big horses had had time enough to build momentum.

The CORA men withdrew if they could, most of them turning north and south in clumps and ones and twos, their mission done. The wind from the west blew the dust away, just in time for the Pendleton Ranchers' men to see what was coming at them. Some tried to turn their agile cow ponies and run; some charged forward, or shot the last arrows cunningly hoarded against extremity. Shafts hammered into shields, or rang off the sloping surfaces of helmets and the steel lames of the barding that covered the horses' necks and shoulders.

But the Portlander knights were at the full gallop, their tall mounts faster over the short distance remaining, their enemies' ponies tired and confused. The long lances dipped in a shining ripple; the hammer of four hundred hooves pounded the earth like war-drums, like thunder; even here she could feel the vibration in the bones of earth, and divots of the hard dry soil flew skyward. Plumed helmets bent forward as the men-at-arms braced themselves in the high-cantled saddles, shields up under the visors to present nothing but shapes of wood and bullhide and steel to their enemies.

Even in that noise, the deep-voiced shouts of *Haro!* were loud.

Then they *struck*.

There was no crash; instead a series of heavy hard *thud* sounds as lance-heads slammed into flesh with a ton-weight of armored horse and armored man behind them. Men were lifted out of the saddle, rising in the air like obscene kebabs until their weight cracked the tough ashwood of the lance-shafts. The destriers bowled the lighter Eastern horses over by main force as they struck breast to breast; she saw one pony pitch over backwards and land full on its screaming rider. Then the knights were through the loose mass of their enemies, throwing aside broken lances. The swords came out, bright and long, or men snatched up the war-hammers slung to the saddlebows, and the knights went raging among their lightly armored foes like steel-clad tigers.

BD sank back down, wincing a little. *No need to watch.* She'd grown used to what edged metal did to the god-like human form, but there was no point in looking at it if you didn't have to.

Hooves thudded up the slope, and Alleyne Loring and John Hordle stood to raise their blades in salute as Tiphaine d'Ath reined in. The Grand Constable had the stumps of three arrows in her shield, and another in the high cantle of her saddle; her sword glistened with a coat of liquid red so fresh it had not even begun to clot, and more spattered up her arm and across the articulated lames of her breastplate.

She used the edge of her shield to push up the visor, and her face showed framed in the mail coif, red and running with sweat as she drew in air through a wide-open mouth. Fighting in armor was brutal labor at best, worse than hauling a plow like an ox.

"We'd best get going," she said, timing the words to her breath. "They'll be here in strength soon; it's going to be a busy day. I've got ambulances."

The light well-sprung vehicles were bouncing up the slope behind her, two tall spoked wheels for each, and a pair of fast horses to draw them.

"We've got the Bossman," Hordle said, jerking his thumb at a man who lay bound hand and foot. "Wasn't 'alf a nuisance, dragging him through the tunnels."

"Then we got something out of this," Tiphaine said.

"Not as much as we thought," Alleyne said. "Thurston and the Prophet are *both* in Pendleton. And Estrellita Peters, too, for them to use as a puppet."

Alleyne turned and helped his wife to her feet. She blinked, squinted, and then raised one hand in acknowledgment.

"I commend the army to your care, Lady d'Ath," she said.

There was a lump the size of a robin's egg on her forehead just above her nose, and she squinted and blinked at the tall steel-clad figure.

"To both of you," she added owlishly, then swallowed and forced clarity on herself with a visible effort. "I've seen the new Dark Lord. This time he's the genuine article."

I'm a gardener, Chuck Barstow Mackenzie thought.

That had been his first love, growing things, though the Barstow family had already been two generations off the farm when he'd been born. One of his first memories was helping his father plant a Japanese cherry tree in the backyard, his small hands pressing the peat moss and potting soil down around the little sapling, and he'd checked it daily and laughed with delight at the first blossoms.

He'd been working in the city Parks Department in Eugene when the Change happened, and thirty years old.

How the hell did I end up a general? the First Armsman of Clan Mackenzie thought. *OK, so I was in the Society . . .*

"Halt!" he called, and his signaler—his younger son Rowan—unslung the cow-horn trumpet and sounded it: *huuuuu-hu-hu!*

The column braked to a stop, the dust of their trailbikes falling ahead of them. He was on horseback, and a few others, but most Mackenzie crofts didn't run to a riding horse, and a bicycle didn't need to be fed or tended when you weren't using it. Their faces were glistening with sweat; it was no joke biking cross-country in thirty pounds of brigandine and helmet, with a quiver across your back and two more slung on either side of the rear wheel, but it beat marching for effort and speed both.

"The Grand Constable says you're to deploy there,

my lord," the Portlander courier said, pointing to the low crest ahead of them. "The Bearkillers and the contingent from the Warm Springs tribes will be on your right."

"Very well," he said. "You may tell Lady d'Ath that we'll hold the position."

And I don't like taking Tiphaine d'Ath's orders, either, he thought.

She had killed his foster daughter Aoife in the War of the Eye—with her own hands during the abduction of Rudi, back when she'd been Sandra Arminger's personal black-body-stocking girl ninja.

OK, that was war and Aoife was armed and fighting back. And now we're all allies. It still sucks.

The rest of the Mackenzie contingent set their bicycles on the kickstands, lining them up with the front wheels pointing west. The carts and ambulances and the healers set up nearby; everyone else followed him a thousand yards eastward, loping along at a ground-eating trot. Chuck reined in and waited until they were all within range and then raised his voice to carry; there was a trick to doing it without screeching.

"Mackenzies," he said. "The Prophet's men came onto our land and killed our own folk in Sutterdown last Samhain, when we'd never harmed them. When our dead come visiting *this* Samhain night, what will we tell them?"

"Blood for blood!" someone shouted. *"That we've taken the heads of them and nailed them up over the door!"*

A long growl answered from the broad semicircle of snarling painted faces, fists or bows thrust into the air in a rippling wave.

OK, I like the old stories too, but let's not get ridiculous.

The problem was that you could never be *quite* sure what the younger generation would take from the ancient tales. Chuck continued:

"We came here because we thought the Prophet's men might come and use Pendleton as a base against us, and his friend the tyrant of Boise."

Which would have been a bit *unfair to the old General,*

but fits his son Martin like a glove, he thought. *And probably a lot of these kids volunteered because they were bored with working on their home-crofts and because Lady Juniper asked it. I'm glad I don't have* Juney's *job, by the Horned Lord!*

He grinned at them and put his hands on the horn of his saddle.

"Well, it turns out they're both here—not just their men, but the leaders themselves, to be sure. Lady Juniper knew what she was talking about, eh? So there are more of the enemy than we hoped or expected, and that's war for you. Don't think of it as being outnumbered . . ."

"Think of it as having lots of targets!" someone finished the old joke, and there was a roar of laughter.

"That's not all we've learned," he went on. "We've had a letter from our tanist, Rudi Mackenzie—Artos himself himself, the very Sword of the Lady off on his quest to the sunrise lands."

That brought them all leaning forward, eyes intent.

"This prophet *scabhtéara* attacked him, yes, and set evil magic against him and his friends, and took his *anamchara* Mathilda prisoner. They scorn all other men, and all gods save theirs. But Artos walked into their camp at night, and brought her out for all their sorcerers or swordsmen could do . . . and when he left there were a fair number of them making their accounting to the Guardians, for the Morrigú was with him, and his sword her scythe, reaping men."

He paused, and said with mock solemnity: "Earth must be fed."

That brought more laughter, some a little scandalized, and another long cheer, with shouts of *Rudi!* and *Artos!* all rising into the racking banshee shriek of the Mackenzie battle-yell, stunning-loud from a thousand throats at close quarters. Chuck raised a hand to quiet it.

"The Lord of the Long Spear is with us, and the Crow Goddess. We're fighting for our homes, our kin, our Clan, and the land your parents spent their blood and their sweat to win," he said, just quietly enough that they had to strain to hear him.

"But Earth *must* be fed. Not all of us will walk away from this field. And this war won't be ended with a single battle. So listen to your bow-captains, stand by your blade-mates, and shoot fast, straight and hard!"

Their pipers struck up, leading the contingents to their places, the skirling drones pealing out the jaunty menace of "The Ravens' Pibroch." Behind them there was a faint *rat-tat-tat . . .* And then a shattering *BOOM!* Even expecting it, he had to control a start.

He'd read somewhere before the Change that a big Lambeg drum had about the same decibel level as the engine of a Piper Cub. Nothing else in the world today came close to massed Lambegs, unless it was thunder or an avalanche of anvils falling on rock. That was something Juniper Mackenzie had taken from her father's people, who'd been Ulster-Scots before they began the long trek West. This was the music they'd used to shatter their enemies' hearts and lash their own folk into the blood-frenzy.

BOOM! Then *Boom-boom . . . boom-boom-boom . . . boom . . . BOOM!* repeating over and over with a maddening irregularity. It wove through the piping until he could taste it at the back of his throat, like blood and hot brass.

He dismounted, handed off the reins, and walked a dozen paces eastward. That put him on the crest of a low ridge running north-south, with a long slope before them, a patchwork of stubble fields among the broader gray brown of bunchgrass and sage. It was good ground, as long as the sun wasn't in their eyes, and it was already too high above the horizon for that to be a real problem. It did gild the dust clouds that the feet and hooves of the advancing enemy raised, twinkling on spearpoints like stars through mist. A long ripple of comment went down the ranks of the Clan's archers. All along the front the bow-captains plucked out tufts of the dry grass and tossed them into the air to test the breeze; it was faint, but directly from the west.

Rowan planted the green flag with the Crescent Moon between antlers beside him. The Mackenzies waited in their three-deep harrow formation, a long slightly curving line like a very shallow S that followed the crest, each dun's fighters by the neighbors who would take home the news of their honor or their shame. He waited until they were set before barking:

"Plant the swine-feathers!"

Spread out like this they couldn't all hear his voice, but Rowan put the horn to his mouth and blew a series of long-and-shorts, the blatting snarl cutting through the rumble of an army shaking itself out into battle formation. Each of the Clan's warriors reached over their backs to a bag slung beside their quivers and pulled out a pair of yard-long ashwood shafts, tied together with thongs. There was a flurry of purposeful movement, and a long *snick-snick-clack!* as the metal collar-and-tongue joints were fitted together. That left every Mackenzie holding a six-foot pole with a long spearhead on one end and a narrow-bladed shovel on the other.

They jammed the shovel blades into the ground and hammered them home with boot-heels. The *shunk* of steel in dry soil sounded over and over again for a few seconds; when it was done a forest of spearpoints jutted forward, three ranks deep and slanted at just the right height to catch the chest of a horse. Then the whole formation took four steps back, and they had a barrier ahead of them that most horses would refuse to take— at least at a gallop.

He looked left and right while the clansfolk worked; northward was a battery of the Corvallan field artillery, their glaives stacked as they labored like maniacs with pick and shovel to pile up berms in front of their throwing engines. Beyond them the first of the Portlander infantry, leaning on their spears with their shields still slung across their backs.

In the distance there he could just make out Tiphaine d'Ath's banner, floating amid a forest of upright lances.

The First Armsman of the Mackenzies filled his lungs again:

"Make ready!"

The bows came out of their carrying loops beside

the quivers. Here and there some of the clansfolk stretched and twisted or rotated their right arms. From each contingent one trotted out to the front, planting a red-painted stick every so often out to three hundred yards—extreme battle range—to help the archers judge distance.

"Good open ground," Oak called to his father, grinning; he was leading the Dun Juniper contingent, nearest the standard, which put him within conversational distance. "Fine weather, the wind at our backs, and downhill. Praise to the Long Spear and the Battle-Hag!"

Chuck nodded back, matching the smile—but it was a conscious gesture for him. He envied the youngsters their calm acceptance of it all; there was still a touch of unreality to this, for him. As if he'd wandered into a tale . . .

Hooves thudded behind him. He glanced back; the carts with the spare arrows were already trotting along behind the Mackenzie line. Youngsters like Rowan— just a year or two too young to stand in the battle line— grabbed bundles and rushed them forward, planting them point down by the warriors' feet until each had three or four, and then poising ready to bring more as needed. A Mackenzie war-quiver held forty-eight shafts, but those were the chosen handmade arrows that each bought or crafted to suit their own fancy for precision work. These were from the stored reserves, and making them to the standard pattern was winter work, done as a part of the Chief's Portion that every dun paid from its crops and labor for the Clan's common purposes. All the heads were alike, too—narrow bodkins shaped like a metalworker's punch, of hardened alloy steel.

When the work was complete the ground around the clan's warriors seemed to bristle like the hide of some monstrous boar, topped with the gray goose feathers of the fletching.

Chuck took a sip from his canteen and spat to clear the alkaline dust of this dry Eastern land. Some of the others did likewise; more were lifting their kilts and taking a last chance to empty their bladders downslope towards the enemy—that always happened, for you went tight when danger approached. The bawdy jokes were as traditional as the harsh ammonia smell.

Horsemen cantered up before him, led by Winnemuca of the Three Tribes, and Eric Larsson of the Bearkillers with the ostrich-feather plumes on his helm making him even more of a steel tower.

Winnemuca looked as if he'd already seen some action; there was a sheen of sweat on his broad features, making the paint on his face run a little below the eagle-plumed steel cap—the design was black, with circles of white around his eyes.

"Whoa, that's *war*-paint," he said, looking at the crimson-gold-black-green designs that swirled over the faces of the nearer Mackenzies. "You white-eyes always go overboard with an idea once you steal it."

A few of the archers who could hear elevated their middle fingers in neighborly wise. Chuck grinned at him.

"The woad was traditional long before we decided to relocate, sure an' it was," he said, exaggerating the Mackenzie lilt that had become second nature over the years. "Along with scalping and head-hunting."

"No accounting for taste," the Indian said. Then he went serious: "They're going to be here soon. Light cavalry—Ranchers—they've got a good screen, but I saw a lot of them massed farther back, nearly a thousand horse-archers. Then the Cutter mounted levies, and then the Sword of the Prophet behind them, they've got bow and lance both. The Boiseans are over north, opposite the Portlanders, horse and foot—mostly infantry. And the Pendleton city militia in the center. Pikemen mostly, it looks like. We can't hold the Pendleton Ranchers off you much longer. Too many. Most of their cavalry is on this flank, but it looks like they're concentrating their field artillery in the center and the northern wing."

The three leaders looked at one another. The northern edge of the allied army was anchored on steep ravines, but the country southward was open and rolling, ideal for a horseman's battle.

"Well," Eric said to his son and Mike Havel Jr., who rode behind him with the snarling bear's-head banner of the Outfit on a staff that was also a very practical lance. "Now you're going to see how a fighting retreat is managed—and that's a lot more difficult to pull off than a pursuit."

He nodded to Chuck. "We'll hold 'em off while you get out," he said. "But you'll have to rake them hard first."

"Sethaz is going to regret ordering the horse in there," General-President Martin Thurston said, leveling his binoculars.

The long glitter of the swine feathers showed close through the lenses, and behind them the archers leaning on their weapons or squatting, waiting patiently or talking to one another—a few were even napping, amid the furze of arrows stuck in the ground. God alone knew how anyone could sleep near the savage music of the pipes and drums.

God, I'd love to have those longbowmen on my side! And someday I will, he thought, and popped a piece of the tasteless twice-baked hardtack into his mouth; there hadn't been time for breakfast, or even much sleep, and he chewed doggedly at the compacted-sawdust taste of it.

No time after that cluster-fuck at the Bossman's house last night.

His memory shied away from that a little.

And Sethaz' people act damned *odd, sometimes. Well, they're lunatics, but even so ... I thought Sethaz was a cynic* exploiting *fanatics ... maybe he's more sincere than that.*

"You think it's a mistake to attack?" his aide said. "About even odds—a thousand or so each. And they're light infantry; if the Pendleton cavalry can unravel them, the whole enemy position goes into the pot and we could bag them all."

"I've seen Mackenzies shoot," Martin said. "Two of them, at least. If they were within a couple of miles of typical, rushing a thousand of them head-on is a *bad* idea. Or maybe Sethaz *won't* regret it. The holy Prophet is sending our glorious local allies in first over there, I notice."

The Boisean command group were on a slight rise behind the line. Thurston's brown face was considering as the mass of Pendleton light horse finished sweeping their CORA equivalents out of the way and charged towards the Mackenzie archers. He took a deep breath, full of the smell of war—acrid dust, sweat of humans and horses, dung, piss, oiled metal, leather, dirty socks, the musk of fear and tension.

"Yeah, the wogs'll do to soak up arrows," the aide said, and a chuckle ran through the men around Thurston. "And if they get killed by the shitload, then afterwards there are that many less around to cause trouble."

"Those Cutter maniacs are polygamists, aren't they?" another said. "Lots of widows . . ."

The line of kilted archers was silent, and then a chant began—too faint to hear at first, but building until it rang clear even over the hammer of the drums and the noise of the hooves:

> *"We are the point—*
> *"We are the edge—*
> *"We are the wolves that Hecate fed!"*

Then a cow-horn trumpet snarled and blatted, and the chant stopped. Another call, and a thousand yew bows came up and drew, each arrowhead pointing halfway to the vertical as the yellow staves bent.

"Oh, notice the ranging stakes in front of each unit?" Thurston said. "That's clever, that's really quite clever."

The aide was from a prominent military family who'd supported his assumption of his father's power, and was beside Thurston because of it, but he was no fool. He blinked at the bristling unison of the movement, bringing up his own binoculars.

"They've got good fire discipline," he said. "I would have expected a fangs-out-hair-on-fire charge, what with the war-paint and the—"

He grimaced in a mime of ferocity, mock flapping his arms and making a movement that suggested jumping up and down; the traverse red crest on his helmet wobbled with the motion.

"—*wudda-wudda-wudda* stuff. It's like something out of ancient history."

"They had good instructors right at the beginning—British SAS men, and a Blues and Royals colonel, of all things. Right, the Pendleton horse are really starting to move."

The Pendleton men went forward in a body, calling out the name of their kidnapped Bossman as a war cry, not in any particular order but spreading out in loose clumps and clots around the banners of their ranches marked with brands. They rose in the stirrups as they came in range, loosing as they did—or possibly a little out of range, as the first shafts fell short of the glittering menace of the swine feathers. In every battle Martin had seen, someone overestimated how far he could shoot.

"Three hundred yards, two hundred and fifty—"

The first arrows from the Ranchers' bows were dropping on the Mackenzie warriors when an order ran down the harrow formation. It was too far to hear it, particularly with the drumming thunder of four thousand hooves an endless grumbling rumble between, but Martin had learned to read lips. His own followed what he saw through the binoculars, repeating softly:

"*Let the gray geese fly!* Wholly together—*shoot!*"

Despite his trained calm the General-President of Boise felt the tiny hairs along his spine crawl at the massed *snap* of waxed linen bowstrings striking the leather bracers on each left wrist. And beneath that a whickering, whistling sound. The arrows arched into the sky like a forest of rising threads, more and more, and still more—three more from each bow in the air before the first thousand struck. The whole Mackenzie line was a shiver of motion as the archers snatched shafts from the bundles at their feet, set them to the strings, drew and loosed in a single smooth wrench of arm and shoulder and body.

He focused on one bowman with a wolf's mask painted across his own face and mentally timed the sequence.

Three or four seconds per arrow. Christ, better than three hundred a second all up—call it twenty thousand a minute. Crossing the killing ground, even at a gallop . . . those saddle-bunnies are going to have to eat close to a hundred thousand *of those arrows!*

The narrow steel arrowheads blinked in a manifold ripple like sunlight on distant water as they reached the top of their arch and seemed to hang poised for a second. Then they turned and plunged. The whistle of their flight was much louder as they came down, and the air above was a continuous sparkling flicker as thousands more followed in wave after wave.

They can see and hear them coming, he thought. *Glad I'm not* there, *by God! Nor my men.*

The whole mass of charging horsemen faltered and shook as men sawed at the reins. Then the first volley *struck.* The noise was like a storm in the mountains driving hail or heavy rain on a shingle roof, but there was nothing in flesh or bone or the light armor of the range-country horsemen to stop the bodkins. The whole first swath went down, mounts dropping like limp puppets or tumbling or plunging and squealing and kicking in astonished agony, men falling out of the saddle or clawing at the iron in face or body or screaming as horses fell and rolled across them. The rising threnody of pain was loud even on a battlefield.

Those behind ran up against that wall of kicking flesh and halted, rearing, or slowed to pick their way between the bodies . . . and still the arrows fell out of the sky in a pulsing, hissing sleet. Three thousand of them in the time a man could count to ten . . .

The party around Martin was silent as the survivors turned and fled as fast as they could flog their horses; men followed them on foot, running or staggering or crawling. A mass of human and horseflesh lay where the arrowstorm had struck, some of it still twitching or writhing or screaming for its mothers . . . or simply screaming and moaning. Only when it stopped did you realize how loud the sheer rush of arrows had been.

"You know, sir, I'm sort of glad you wanted the northern part of the line," Thurston's aide said. "Even if the ravines are steep off there."

Martin Thurston grinned. "Courier! To the most holy Prophet of the Church Universal and Triumphant; I respectfully suggest that he try to work around their flank."

The party of Boisean officers chuckled. Martin went on: "Now, gentlemen, this allied army has three commanders—which means it's a disaster waiting to happen. But we *do* outnumber the enemy by two to one, so let's get to work. To your units!"

He looked to his front; there were the Portlander infantry, blocks of spearmen and crossbowmen, and beyond them the knights, sitting ready.

"Colonel Jacobson!" he said.

"Sir!"

The cavalryman was standing at the head of his horse. "You keep those lancers in play. I don't expect you to beat them, but keep them busy while we chew our way through their foot."

He saluted and vaulted into the saddle. Martin Thurston looked down at the solid disciplined ranks of Boise infantry, standing easy with the lower rims of their big curved oval shields resting on the ground. He raised his hand and then chopped it downward, and the signalers raised their *tubae*. The brass bellowed out the order *ready*; the men picked up their shields by the central grips, each holding an extra heavy javelin there too. Their right hands hefted the first pila, the long iron shanks sloping forward.

Then: "Advance!"

Two thousand men stepped off, an audible *thud* through the hard ground as the hobnails struck. Ahead of them the Eagle standard swayed, carried by a man who wore a wolfskin over his helmet, and along the lines the upright hands on poles that marked the battalions.

"The game begins," Martin Thurston said. Then: "Courier!"

His brain was busy with distances and numbers and contingencies, but behind that was an image of his wife and the son just born to them.

My son, he thought. *From sea to shining sea . . . and every bit of it will be yours!*

CHAPTER TWELVE

Knowledge waits beneath the snows
As flowers wait the spring
Chance some call such meetings
That bear fate as women bear a child—

From: *The Song of Bear and Raven*
Attributed to Fiorbhinn Mackenzie, 1st century CY

"The fever has broken," someone said.

Rudi Mackenzie opened his eyes, conscious of cleanliness and warmth and a faint odor of incense beneath the more familiar hint of woodsmoke ... pine of some sort. He was lying in a bed with brown linen sheets and blankets of some lustrous fabric that had the warmth of wool but less weight. Father Ignatius was standing at the foot of his bed, looking less drawn than Rudi remembered and in his dark Benedictine robe; beside him was a shaven-headed man in a saffron-colored wrap that left one shoulder bare, lean and middle-aged and wearing a stethoscope as well. And another man in the same odd dress, but far older—his flat high-cheeked brown face was a mass of wrinkles that nearly swallowed his narrow black eyes when he smiled, which he looked to do often.

The younger shave-head lifted Rudi's head and trickled water into his mouth from a cup with a spout. The young Mackenzie recognized a healer's bedside manner; he felt weak, but clearheaded ...

"I'm very hungry," he said, and was a little shocked at how faint his voice was.

When he tried to move the physician clucked at him, and Father Ignatius shook a finger—but he was smiling, obviously in relief. The shooting pain in Rudi's right shoulder was what stopped him; he looked down and saw that it was bandaged, and the wasted arm strapped across his chest. In a few moments another robed attendant came in, younger still than the physician, with jug ears on either side of his shaved white dome of skull and friendly blue eyes.

He carried a steaming bowl and a kettle and a cup on a tray, and Rudi gratefully accepted the smooth warmth of the bean soup. The tea was stranger, with salty butter added to the herbal infusion, but it made a welcome warmth in his belly, and eased aches he hadn't noticed much until they were gone. When it was finished he felt stronger.

"My thanks for your hospitality," he said.

The room came into clearer focus; the walls were plastered fieldstone, he thought, and undoubtedly whitewashed. One bore a colorful circle of abstract designs, a mandala, but none that his folk used. A small tile stove in a corner kept it comfortable.

"Where am I?"

"You are in the Monastery of Chenrezi, in the Valley of the Sun," the old man said. "Or in the old terminology, in the Rocky Mountains of western Wyoming."

His voice had a trace of another accent under the plains-and-mountain English.

"I am *Rimpoche* ... in your language, teacher ... here and my name is Tsewang Dorje. You are our guests, and you must rest and grow well, and your sister likewise."

Rudi's brows went up. Ignatius answered: "Mary was seriously injured fighting the Cutter scouts, but she's on the mend now too, God be thanked. They are excellent physicians here, and we are safe from pursuit for now, thanks to her and Ritva. Everyone else is fine, although Edain and the Princess have been haunting your bedside! What you need most now is food and rest."

The physician spoke: "The infusion will help you sleep and lessen pain. You should sleep as much as possible for the next several days."

Rudi nodded. The abbot smiled again and made a gesture of blessing with the palms of his hands pressed together, and everyone left.

"Thank You for the shelter of your wings, Lady," Rudi said into the silence. "And you, Wanderer."

There were glass windows in the side of the room opposite the mandala; double-glazed and aluminum-framed, obviously salvaged. They gave on a courtyard, where flagstones had been swept clear of snow, and a few trees stood in pots. Folk were at exercise there, some monks or nuns of Chenrezi, others more ordinary-looking, though the older ones who gave instruction all had their heads shaved. All wore practical boots and trousers and jackets, and some had helmets and practice armor of boiled and molded leather.

Must be cold out there, Rudi thought; their breath showed in white plumes, and the bright sunlight had that pale look that went with a hard freeze. From the length of the shadows it was in the afternoon.

Some of them were using quarterstaffs, thrusting and sweeping in unison or sparring with a clatter of wood on wood; others practiced with spears, or halberds, or swords much like the Eastern shete, or arcane weapons that looked like bladed hooks on chains, or bows. A half-dozen pairs drilled in unarmed combat, their movements fluid and sure, throwing and grappling and striking. He recognized some of the techniques, but others were strange to him. The focusing shouts—the exhalation from your center—were loud enough to be heard faintly through the thick walls of his sickroom.

Then a bell sounded, not quite like any he'd heard before, like the birth of an age of bronze in the crisp still air. All the shave-heads bowed to their partners and filed out, two by two, their palms pressed together and their heads bowed as they chanted. The sound lulled Rudi as strongly as the herbs in the tea he'd drunk, and he leaned back against the pillow and let his eyelids droop.

"You're not hungry?" Ingolf said, worried; his spoon halted halfway to his mouth.

Mary Havel was prodding *her* spoon at the turned-wood bowl that held her soup. Even without the bandage covering her left eye there wouldn't have been a problem in telling her from her sister Ritva's blooming health now. She looked pale, paler than winter could account for even in someone so fair, and her face was gaunt, showing the elegant bones beneath. And she moved slowly, with only a shadow of the fluid grace her sister still had.

"What I need is a *steak*," she said fretfully. "We've been here for weeks, and I'm not a leaf-eating rabbit. I want a roast chicken! Or a rack of BBQ lamb ribs with a honey-mustard glaze! Or pork chops with sautéed onions . . . or even *venison stew*, Lady Varda help us!"

"Stop!" her sister Ritva said. "Venison stew is starting to make *my* mouth water too!"

She and her sister laughed; at the others' looks, Mary went on: "Back in Mithrilwood, it's the staple diet for winter. We Dúnedain have a joke; when the sun rises in the east, it's an omen that we shall have venison stew for dinner. I never thought I'd get *nostalgic* for it!"

Ingolf laughed. Odard did as well; then his eyes narrowed, and he rose and left.

Mary smiled with them, but the tug at her eye wound must have hurt a little and the expression died. She'd been very patient with actual pain while she was really ill, but she wasn't a good convalescent.

"This will do," she said resignedly, and mopped up the last of the soup in her bowl with a heel of the loaf.

They were in the refectory the monastery kept for guests, non-novice students and the sick who were well enough to walk. It was a pleasant room, plain but comfortable, and well heated by the sealed stoves. Some of the older monks preferred to sit on cushions or mats, but the rest used benches and chairs, and nobody expected outsiders to do otherwise.

The food's actually pretty good, Ingolf thought, finishing his own. *But yah, I could use some roast pork with crackling.*

There was potato soup done with barley and onions, hard white cheese grated on it, warm dark bread and butter, pickled cucumbers, hard-boiled eggs and sauerkraut, and dried apples and berries. The young nun who had served it looked at Mary indignantly.

"Besides imposing a karmic burden, food which requires killing animals is unnecessary," she said loftily. Then: "And if you *must*, there are places in the town which serve it, when you are better. I admit that it is not wasteful, since we have abundant pasture."

"Prig," Mary muttered to herself as the girl moved away; she was about the Dúnedain's own age. *"Naeg nedh adel!"*

Ingolf's eyes went upward and his lips moved slowly; he'd been learning some Sindarin. It was fiendishly complicated, and the only two people in this part of the world who could talk it were right beside him, but he'd kept at it doggedly. It would have helped if they had some books, but the only material they'd brought on the trip was a small-print section of the . . .

Histories, Ingolf thought. *Think of them as the* Histories, *dammit. Mary takes that seriously.*

"There is pain in the . . ." he began.

Ritva grinned. *"Naeg nedh adel: Pain in the ass,"* she said. Then with concern as Mary pushed the bowl away: "You tired, sis?"

"Bored with being sick," Mary said. "I know I'm a lot better off than Rudi, but it's still a drag. We should be getting going!"

There were windows in the refectory, south-facing ones. It was getting dark already, and would have been even if the winter sun didn't set early. You could just see the powder snow the wind was driving at the glass, until one of the monastery staff went around cranking the shutters closed. Even when that was done the sound of the wind came through the stout log and fieldstone walls.

"This reminds me of winter at home," Ingolf said. "And that means we're not going *anywhere* for a good long while. You want to get caught in another blizzard?"

"It can be done," Mary said.

"Yah, and so can juggling sharp knives on horseback," Ingolf said. "A couple of hunters on snowshoes or skis, sure. Nine people? With *horses*? Big horses that need grain feed, some of them? We're lucky we didn't lose more getting here."

"I might as well go back to bed," Mary said with a martyred sigh.

"Something happened, didn't it?" Mathilda asked. "While we were in the cave."

"Well, I came close to dying," Rudi said, mock cheerfully.

Even that was hard when you felt as wretched as he did right now; in the daytime he was merely weak, but after dark like this, before sleep came, there were times when he felt as if the fever were back. An aching in every part of his body, not just the stabbing, itching ache of the healing wounds; as if he were utterly tired and at the same time too uncomfortable to rest. And when the simple comfort of the room was like a prison, wrapping him in tight bands from head to toe like a corpse trussed for the funeral pyre.

And that's when it's a struggle not to snap at people, Rudi thought. *Yet it's also when you don't want to be alone. The Mother's blessing on you,* anamchara.

Mathilda raised his head with a hand and fed him more of the bittersweet herbal tea. The low gutter of the lamp on the bedside table underlit her face, bringing out the strong contours, and highlighting small green flecks in her hazel-brown eyes. The acrid scent and taste of the liquid were comforting, and the heat relaxed him a little as it made its way down to his grateful stomach.

"Your problem is you're used to being Lugh come

again," she said severely, when she'd turned back from replacing the kettle on the stove. "And now you're not, for a while."

He rolled his head on the pillow and smiled a little at her. She looked a bit shocked, which meant he wasn't doing it as well as he'd hoped.

"I had a vision, *anamchara*," he said, and waited for a little, until the herbs took some of the ache away.

"Well, your family is prone to them!" she said, and smoothed a lock of hair back from his forehead.

"While we were in the cave," he said. "I thought I was dead for a moment, and on the trail to the Summerlands with the Dread Lord. Then I met—"

She swallowed and crossed herself when the tale was done.

"It *might* have been just a dream," she said.

His smile quirked a little. "I doubt it. But it made me realize something. Ignatius planted the thought in me, that night we rescued you, but now I know it's true."

"What?"

His eyes went to the shadowed rafters and planks of the ceiling. "That this journey's end is my own death," he said softly. "I am walking towards a sword indeed; and to take it up is to take up my own mortality. All our perils and struggle just bring the altar and the knife closer."

Matti took his hand. "We're all on a journey towards *that*," she said stoutly.

He shook his head slightly. "Let's not play with words, you and I, my heart. I'm the Sword of the Lady; my blood is my people's ransom, the price paid for their hearths and their happiness. That's my . . . fate, my weird. It's a hero's death, to be sure—but I'd rather it wasn't so *soon*. A hero's life makes a fine song, but the living of it is another thing altogether. It's one thing to risk your death in battle, or a hunt or even climbing a tree . . . it's another to walk a path with only one ending, every step a pace closer. Most men run from death . . ."

There was a long silence. Then her hand moved on his forehead again. "You could—"

Another pause. "I could what?" he said. He laughed faintly, and then stopped because it hurt. "Matti, I wish I could run off with you and start a farm somewhere, seeing your face every morning, and die at eighty-six with our grandchildren about us, and in between no worries but the weather and the day's work."

Her hand squeezed his. "Me too, Rudi. Oh, God, how I wish we could!"

"But I can't. My fate . . . *is.* All I can control is how I meet it—whether I can make it *mean* something."

"Your father's did," she said.

Rudi nodded. "But my father didn't believe in fate; he laughed at it and at the gods. He didn't know the story he was in—and I'm thinking that made it easier for him. I must walk the road with my eyes open, and renew my consent to it every moment."

Something splashed on his hand. He turned his head; she was holding his hand between both of hers, tears falling silently. With an effort he freed himself and cupped his palm against her cheek; she turned and kissed the palm.

"Och, darlin', all men are born fey," he said. "It's your part in this I regret even more. For I know now that a long life would be sweet with you, and if you and I are together, it will be to your sorrow."

Mathilda took a long breath. "I don't believe in fate," she said. "We make our own. Well, there's the will of God, but that's not the same thing."

Rudi sighed. *I have to tell her,* he thought. *But I don't have to work to convince her. Honor's not that demanding a mistress.*

"Right now the only path you've got to walk is the one marked *recovery.* Or *health!*" she said, and he could feel her pushing foreknowledge away.

"Now, that's true, and there's no doubting it." He closed his eyes.

Strange folk, Christians, he thought. Aloud: "Would you mind singing that song for me again?"

She nodded, and began; there was a quaver in her voice at first, but it strengthened into the soft melody:

> *"Oh, Ladies, bring your flowers fair*
> *Fresh as the morning dew*
> *In virgin white, and through the night*
> *I will make sweet love to you*
> *The petals soon grow soft and fall*
> *Upon which we may rest;*
> *With gentle sigh I'll softly lie*
> *My head upon your breast."*

Very quietly, he began to sing along with it, more a suggestion than real sound:

> *"... And dreams like many wondrous flowers*
> *Will blossom from our sleep*
> *With steady arm, from any harm*
> *My lover I will keep!*
> *Through soft spring days and summer's haze*
> *I will be with you till when*
> *As fall draws near, I disappear*
> *till spring has come again!"*

He closed his eyes and smiled. "Ah, that was a breath of home. Now tell me of *your* problems and worries, my heart's friend."

She laughed softly, that gurgling chuckle he'd always liked. Not even the fact that it was her mother's laugh could hide the warmth in it.

"*My* worst problem is boredom," she said. "I've been sparring—"

This time his sigh was pure sea-green envy. To *move* again!

"And reading in the library here, and talking with the monks, and sitting with Mary a little—she's recovering fast, now."

"How are the others taking it?"

"Pretty well. Odard . . ."

Rudi chuckled; as he did, he felt sleep coming over him, fading the world—the low *shsshs* of snow against the window, the muted howl of the wind, the low friendly rippling sound from the closed stove.

"Odard's not a bad sort," he murmured drowsily. "He's just a bit of an asshole at times."

His eyelids fluttered downward. He felt Matti bend to kiss him lightly on the forehead, but her last words faded away.

"Actually, the problem is that he's a lot *less* of an asshole these days."

Mary rose from the refectory table and wobbled a little. Ingolf stepped in, not reaching for her but putting his steadying presence close enough for her to grab if she had to. The corridor outside was a lot darker and colder than the dining hall; it was a relief to get to the room the two young women shared, which had its own stove. He helped her into bed and pulled up the blankets while Ritva opened the iron door, tossed in a couple of chunks of wood from the basket and then closed it and adjusted the flue. It was an air-tight model based on a pre-Change type, and it could keep the little room at something they all considered good enough—though he'd noticed back home that older people thought that range of temperatures a bit cool for comfort.

There was a heating element on top for boiling water, too. Ritva put the kettle on, and added herbs when it began to jet steam; the willow-bark tea eased the ache and itch of her sister's healing wound.

Time to do my bit, Ingolf thought, and took the lute from a corner and tuned it. *And hell,* I'm *bored.*

Winter was the stay-indoors season at home too, but there was always enough to keep the dismals at bay: making things, fixing things, looking after the stock, practicing with arms, some hunting now and then, and the Sheriffs and Farmers visited back and forth, having the leisure and the means for it. Sometimes they'd get sleds and go for a long trip down the frozen river . . .

And there's making music and telling stories, he thought with a wry smile, and went on aloud: "Like a song?"

Mary smiled and relaxed. "Something from your home," she said.

He started in on one: "The Wreck of the Edmund Fitzgerald," and then "Northwest Passage." Then he passed the lute to Ritva; she was only passable at playing, but had a fine singing voice, and she did one of the Dúnedain songs. He didn't get more than one word in three, but he had to admit that the language was pretty as all hell.

"Tell me more about Readstown," Mary said, when the tune—from something called the *Narn i Chîn Húrin*—was finished.

"Readstown?" Ingolf said, surprised. "Well, it's in the valley of the Kickapoo. The Injuns named it that before white men came there, and it means *goes here, then there.* That's one twisty river! Just about the right size for a canoe, most of it, but it gets bigger as it goes south and joins the Wisconsin. Sometimes the cliffs close in, and you're between these walls of red sandstone covered with moss, and other places they open out, and the fields go rolling away to the woods and hills and the forests—"

He could see it as he spoke; the flame of autumn on the ridges, the silk of the cornfields yellow with October; the smoke rising from the chimneys of strong stolid yeomen, the smell of the dark, damp turned earth behind the oxen in spring . . . the ache surprised him, and he was glad to fall silent.

Ritva was reading from the Histories—the Creation of the World, which was more interesting than the Bible version—when Odard came in.

They all looked up at him; a drift of cold air came in with him, and he was wearing his outdoor gear—quilted wool pants and a sheepskin jacket with the fleece turned in, and a hood with a flap that hid most of the face. Snow dripped off him as he triumphantly set the basket he carried on the table at the foot of the bed. It was wrapped in a thick blanket and tied with string; he couldn't get the knots undone and stood blowing on his fingers near the stove while Ingolf picked them free.

"Well, well, well!" the Richlander said, as a savory smell followed the unwrapping; there were a couple of heated bricks in there too, to keep things warm.

His mouth watered. He liked meat too, when he could

get it. The Kickapoo was good livestock country, the forests there were thick with game, and he'd been raised a Sheriff's son, after all, in a family who were lords of broad acres and many herds.

"BBQ pork sandwiches," the Portlander nobleman said. "*And* some fried chicken. *And* . . ."

He pulled out four beer bottles, pre-Change glass with modern wood-and-wax plugs.

"Not everybody's a Buddhist around here," he said triumphantly. "*And* not all the Buddhists are as pure about it as the monks and nuns. There were plenty of them at Ford's Cowboy Khyentse Bar and Grill down in the town."

"You must have been hungry, to go outside in *that*," Ritva said.

The window vibrated in its frame to illustrate her point, and there were trickles of cold air despite all the thick log walls could do. Odard peeled himself out of his integuments with an effort and then stacked them outside the door—the room was big enough for two beds, but not much more.

"They've got a pathway marked with poles and ropes," he said. "I wouldn't have tried it otherwise; Saint Dismas couldn't find his way through that, and it's getting worse. I'm not going to complain about all the rain in the Black Months back home ever again!"

There were plates in the basket too; they loaded one for Mary, and then dug into the rest themselves. Ingolf took a long drink; the beer went well with the rich spicy sandwich, and he'd missed both—they made a noble brew back home, and Sutterdown, Dun Juniper and Boise had all had maltsters of note. This was different, bitter with something that wasn't hops, but it was definitely beer and welcome after weeks of water and milk.

Mary managed to get one of the sandwiches down— they were little loafs split lengthwise—and a few bites of the chicken as well. The beer on top made her sleepy fairly quickly, and the two men packed up the remainder and stole out into the dim chill of the corridor as her sister tucked her in.

"Thanks, Odard," Ingolf said, and extended his hand.

The Portlander's brows went up, but he took it. "No trouble," he said.

"Hell it wasn't," Ingolf said, grinning. "It's the better part of a mile to the village—and you're not as used to this sort of weather as I am."

He considered the younger man carefully. The slanted blue eyes weren't as guarded as they usually were.

Funny. Most times when you've fought by a man's side and traveled with him, that's when you get to know him. Not with Odard. But this . . . this is a little surprising.

"Let's say I've had plenty of time to think," Odard said, as they walked back towards the male side of the monastery's guest quarters. "And plenty of distance and deeds to get some perspective on things back home."

"Yah," Ingolf said. "I had the same feeling after I left Readstown. It all seemed sort of . . . small, after a while."

"Did you ever consider going back?" Odard said curiously.

"Nah. I missed it—the place, most of the people—but it wasn't home anymore, after my father died."

"Ah," Odard said; there was nothing mysterious to him about the plight of a younger son, though he wasn't one himself. "I envy you. My father died in the Protector's War, when I was around eight. I don't remember him well."

Ingolf fell silent for a long moment, remembering the way his father had looked towards the end—the haunted set of his eyes, as his memories went back to the time right after the Change. His son didn't remember the terrible years well at all; he'd been around six, and all he could recall was how frightening it had been that the adults were so terrified. Readstown had been a little rural hamlet surrounded by dairy country and mixed farming. They hadn't been hungry . . . but there had been a fair bit of fighting with starving refugees. His home was just close enough to the cities that they'd have been overrun and eaten out if they *hadn't* fought, after they'd taken in every soul they could; he remembered his father cursing the Amish around Rockton because they wouldn't help, and the whispers about the raid ...

"Mine was ... a man who did what had to be done," he said.

Odard's mouth quirked. "So was mine." After a hesitation he said:

"You're sort of ... fond of Mary, aren't you?"

"Yah," Ingolf said, his gaze turning inward for a moment. "Didn't realize it, really, until she got hurt." He shrugged. "You were there when Saba died ... well, I realized when Mary came back that she could get hurt whether or not we were together."

Odard nodded and set a hand on his shoulder for an instant. "*I* realized that she might not be there to tease," he said. "The twins and I have been sort-of-friends for a long time. But on this little trip, sort of won't do, will it?"

They turned a corner—the monastery was really a series of buildings along the hillside, some pre-Change, some built since or heavily rebuilt, all linked together with covered walkways. From the thickness of the bracing timbers overhead, most of them got buried *deep* every winter. This time they nearly ran into Mathilda, probably returning from Rudi's bedside.

"Princess," Odard said, with that funny-looking bow. "How is he?"

"Better," she said, and made herself smile. "But still weak; he's sleeping now. That infection nearly killed him ... What's that?"

Ingolf offered the basket. "There's still some of the chicken left," he said.

"Mother of God!" she said, and her hand darted in. "Thass so guudf!" she went on, her mouth full of drumstick.

It was *good*, Ingolf thought. *The batter isn't quite like anything I've tasted before.*

"Thanks, Ingolf!" she said after she swallowed.

"Thank Baron Liu," Ingolf said. "He's the one who waded through the snow and back to get it."

Little cold drafts trickled around Ingolf's neck as he

said it. The stoutly timbered roof over their head was shingled and then covered in thick sod, but even so you could tell that the storm was building.

"That was good of you, Odard," Mathilda said.

He shrugged. "Mary's appetite needs tempting," he said. "And a very good night, Your Highness."

"You must not overstrain yourself," Dorje said.

"Sure, and I thought you Buddhists were given to disciplining the flesh," Rudi Mackenzie said. "Mind you, I haven't met many. And I'd go mad if I had to lie still any longer, the which would do my healing no good whatsoever or at all. I've enjoyed our talks, but I need to *move!*"

Dorje smiled as they walked slowly down the swept flagstones, their breath showing in white plumes in the cold dry air. Rudi judged he would have been egg-bald even if the monks here didn't shave their heads, and a little stooped, but even erect he would barely have come to the young Mackenzie's breastbone. There was absolutely nothing frail about him, though; he was comfortable as a lynx in the sheepskin robe and saffron overrobe and sandals despite the chill, and he was obviously suiting his pace to the convalescent's capacities. You could still see the shadow of the strong young mountain peasant in him.

The white Stetson hat had seemed a little odd at first, but by now he was used to it; doubtless it was an offering to the spirits of place.

"Here we teach the Middle Way," Dorje said. "When the Buddha first sought enlightenment he attempted fierce austerities of hunger and pain, but he found they did not aid him. The starving man and the glutton are both slaves to their belly's need; if the glutton is worse, it is because he is self-enslaved."

They came to a bench and Rudi lowered himself carefully to it; the wound in his back had stopped draining and was closing, but it was still sore. He thrust aside worry about the shoulder.

And Fiorbhinn could drub me with a feather duster right now, to be sure, he thought.

The pine-log pillars to their left had little lines and crescents of snow in the irregularities of the polished wood; beyond it was an open court, and in its center the image of a man carrying a white lotus—a wooden carving and none too skillful by Mackenzie standards, but the sincerity of it shone through nonetheless.

The land beyond fell away in terraced slopes to the valley floor below, with bleached barley stubble poking through the snow where the winds had eaten it thin. A frozen river shone like a swordblade in the bright sun, twisting away with a lining of dark willows and leafless cottonwoods. Beyond rose mountains, scattered with pine woods but bare blazing white at their peaks save where the dark rock bones of earth showed through. Smoke rose from a cluster of log cabins and frame houses in the middle distance, and a horseman was riding downward towards them. The snow of the roadway creaked under his horse's hooves, and the clank of a scabbard against a stirrup iron echoed; the whetted steel of his lance-head cast painful-bright blinks.

"I thought Buddhists were pacifists," Rudi said.

He took a slow deep breath of air leached of all but the ghosts of scent—a little woodsmoke and pine sap, and a hint of a sharp herbal fragrance—before he went on.

"As a general rule, at least. The which I am not, obviously . . . though if the world would leave me and mine at peace, sure, I'd oblige them gladly. But if a warrior's presence offends against your faith . . ."

"Obviously it does not," Dorje said.

"And I'm afraid that grateful as I am for your help, and your wisdom, you're unlikely to convert me!"

Dorje took the younger man's hand in both of his, turning it over so that the sword calluses showed:

"I have been assured by those wiser than I that a brave man, though he slay, and though he slay his many, is as a god in contrast to the men and women who are restrained from slaying only by cowardice. If the one who will not take life for any reason is higher on the Way than a warrior, then *they* are lower; just as he who fights for justice and to shield the weak is higher than he who fights for plunder or for pride."

He patted Rudi's hand before he released it. "I do not judge the necessities of your life or the karma you have chosen. But here, at least, you may be at peace for a little time."

It is peaceful here, Rudi mused. *It's nice to have time to stop and think for a bit, with all the . . . external things stripped away!*

As he did the sound of a bronze bell came through the cold air, still sounding a little strange; he knew now that it was because it was rung by a log hung beside it in rope slings, rather than by a clapper.

"I was raised to be a warrior, but I've seen enough of war lately that it disgusts me, so. Not so much the fighting, but the . . . waste of it, the things that are broken that should not be."

"You have chosen a hard path, my son," the monk said. "One that will test your courage; and the risk of pain to yourself and the death of your body are the least of its trials. But be sure, if you have courage it shall certainly be tested; because no quality in this universe goes unused. Walk the Way you have chosen in its fullness; when you have reached its end, you will find that it is the beginning of another path."

"You don't think killing is the worst of sins, then?" he said curiously.

Dorje sighed. "No; but considered rightly, it is . . . foolish. It is easy to kill. It is equally easy to destroy glass windows. Any fool can do either. Why is it only the wise who perceive that it is wisdom to let live, when even lunatics can sometimes understand that it is better to open a window than to smash the glass? But this world *is* mired in illusion, which is folly. As followers of the Way, we deplore the taking of life . . ."

Then he chuckled, slapping his knees. "Including our own! And more important, we deplore greedy or evil men taking the lives of those who look to us for instruction. There are few surviving pacifists in the world twenty-two years after the Change. A desire for peace does not imply submission to those who chose to be violent as their first resort."

He sighed again. "Yet if men were truly wise . . . Within our valley here, at least, there is little bloodshed."

"You rule here, then?"

Dorje's eyes sought the heights. "We were here—many monks, from many countries—for a . . . conference, they called it."

His voice turned dry: "If I remember correctly, the subject was to be *Buddhism on the World Wide Web,* with many learned panels on how the Internet might be used to transmit the Noble Eightfold Path. The hotel here gave us a reduced rate because the season for winter sports was nearly past. Then we experienced the . . . as one of our hosts put it . . . the 'mother of all service interruptions.' "

He chuckled again, though Rudi couldn't see why; but the young clansman knew a man in touch with the Otherworld when he saw one, he who'd grown up in Juniper Mackenzie's household. It took some this way, a bubbling current of joy.

"And the people here turned to you for wisdom after the Change?" Rudi said.

Certainly the ones I've seen are happy with their arrangements, the which would be unlikely if you were a bad man, to be sure. Also I still have some *confidence in my judgment, despite Picabo.*

"That most of us grew up scratching a living out of highland farms was more useful at first!" Dorje said. "And that hardship was nothing new to us. There were even yaks here! The Ranchers found our help useful, when their machines died, and many of the people here were tourists from the cities, or those who made their livings by serving them, and they were utterly lost. We helped as we could, and one thing led to another."

Rudi nodded. He'd seen before that . . . *unusual* folk had often had an advantage after the Change; his mother and her coven and friends not least.

"I have heard a little of your mother, the Juniper Lady," Dorje said. "Before the Change I studied your

Old Religion somewhat. It, ah, borrowed much from ours, and from the Hindus in the land where the Way was first preached."

"Meaning Gardner stole your doctrines like a bandit loose in a treasure house," Rudi said cheerfully; Juniper Mackenzie tended to shock her co-religionists with her frank assessment of the origins of their faith. "And from many others!"

Dorje made a *tsk* sound. "To say that you stole would imply that we *owned* the truths of the Way!" he said. "But the reverse is the case, if anything. Let the truths that Gautama Buddha first sought go forth and lead those who hear them towards the Buddha nature that all carry within, however they call it."

Rudi nodded; that was enough like his own faith's teaching of many paths to the same goal that he was easy with it. Then he smiled wryly, thinking of things he'd heard from Matti and her countrymen.

"You'll find Christians a little more proprietary about their doctrines, I think."

Dorje laughed. "Your Father Ignatius has been *extremely* polite," he said. "There is a young man earnest in his search for virtue, I think. Indeed, the greatest threat he will face is his own virtue, lest he become too much in love with it. He and the others have told me much of your journey and its purpose, and its enemies. We here have been troubled by the Cutter cult as well."

He looked up towards the eastern peaks. "That something extraordinary occurred on Nantucket has long been rumored. Fascinating!"

"It's more than that," Rudi said grimly. "The gods are taking a hand in these matters. Ah . . . I'm not sure how to put that—"

Dorje shrugged, in a manner that showed he'd been raised in the East.

"Are you familiar with the word *Bodhisattva*? No? These are beings who have achieved enlightenment, and with it great powers, but who from compassion for those still mired in illusion return to help them."

He indicated the statue. "That is an image of Chenrezi,

the Bodhisattva of Compassion. Who may be viewed as a god, an aspect of the Buddha nature, a personified idea, or a focus for meditation . . . and all these are true. This"—he pointed to a painting on the wall behind them, of a man with one hand held up in the *stop* gesture and the other bestowing a blessing—"is Amitabha, the Buddha of Pure Light, who dwells in the West and is of the element of Fire, and assists in overcoming fear."

"Ah . . . immortal, powerful beings who concern themselves with humanity, and I suppose the other kindreds . . . animals, the world in general . . . well, sure, and that sounds a good deal like a god to me!"

Dorje nodded. "We should not split hairs over definitions and forms of words."

Then he chanted, in a high reedy voice:

> *"If the causes are fully ripened,*
> *Buddhas will appear there and then*
> *In accordance with the needs of the disciples.*
> *The place and the time."*

Then he laughed, gleeful as a boy, and clapped his hands together: "But we do split hairs! We do! We split hairs so finely that often there is no hair, only the split! It is . . . what was the expression . . . a *professional deformation* of monks."

Rudi nodded, gathering his strength. *I'm as weak as a child,* he thought. *Worse! I had energy enough for two as a child, or so they tell me. Now I'm tired just from thinking.*

"Then what of devils?" he said aloud. "For I've met . . . things, forces . . . on this journey which I'd call by that name, sure."

"Oh, yes," the abbot said.

The glee leached out of his face, and he looked truly old for an instant.

"In the time of the Great Leap, when hunger turned good neighbors into worse than beasts, and later when the Red Guards came to burn our scrolls . . . then I saw how men could become devils and torment one another.

If mere men can do such great evil, how much worse are those with greater powers and insight, when they turn to doing devil's work?"

The black eyes held his, and the monk's voice went on softly:

"And only he who has by hard work conquered the devil in himself knows what a devil is, and what a devil he himself might be, and what an army for the devils' use are those who think that devils are delusion."

"No!" Master Hao said.

Edain wheezed fury at him from the ground where his shoulders had struck. The monk was at least thirty years older than the Mackenzie clansman, but he looked perfectly comfortable in his loose trousers and singlet, and even more comfortable within his skin. Edain and he were both of medium height, but Hao lacked the younger man's thick shoulders and arms; he was like a stripped-down anatomical diagram of a fighting man, with every muscle showing like a flat band of living oak under his ivory-colored skin. It lacked the ruddy-brown tint of the *Rimpoche*'s face, and there was a subtle difference in the facial structure; Rudi had the impression they came from different countries.

"No, you are fighting from anger!" Hao barked at Edain.

"When I'm trying to kill someone, now wouldn't it be strange if I weren't angry with the bastard?"

Rudi had been doing a slow, gentle series of exercises with a light fighting staff; today was the first he'd been able to do even that. The indoor practice hall was very much like a barn—from the smell, he thought it probably did duty as one from time to time—but the board walls broke the force of the wind, and the dirt floor gave good footing and was passable for falling. His right shoulder twinged again, and he let the end of the quarterstaff fall so that he could lean on it, gripping with his left hand.

"If you wish to defeat your enemy, you must first defeat yourself. Defeat your anger, defeat your hate, defeat your *self*. Then your moves will be pure . . . and you will *win.* Direct your *chi* energy; it is more important than your fists or your feet. You already have good *technique*, you are strong and fearless and young, yet this skinny old man can defeat you again and again. Consider this."

"Why didn't you say so, Master Hao? If that's what it takes to boot some head, sure and I'll do it."

He's saying he's so angry he'll overcome anger, Rudi thought. *My friend, I think in this case my mother would say your head is not firmly wired to your arse!*

Rudi kept quiet, nonetheless; help with throttled rage was precisely what Edain needed. What had happened in Picabo wasn't going to leave him anytime soon, or easily. Instead he began another of the series of exercises; some of them reminded him of Aunt Judy's methods. Patience, patience . . .

But I too, want to boot some head, he thought, and sighed. *And right now, I can't even try!*

It was going to be a long winter.

He racked the staff; a man beckoned from the pathway outside.

"The most holy *Rimpoche* Tsewang Dorje would speak with you," the man said.

His face was schooled to calm, but the censorious blue eyes were obviously rather disapproving that his superior was wasting so much time with this young outland infidel.

Rudi bowed slightly, keeping the smile off his face. He was reminded of a saying of his mother; that a fanatic was a man who did what he knew in his heart the Gods would do . . . if only They had all the facts of the matter. And it was a pleasure simply to be able to walk properly again. He was breathing a little hard when they ascended a final flight of stairs, but it was infinite relief after his lead-limbed weakness of a few weeks ago.

"Come in, come in!" the old abbot's voice said.

The sanctum was . . . the phrase that sprang to Rudi's mind was *pleasantly bare*, even to eyes accustomed to the flamboyant Mackenzie style. There were scrolls on a rack against one wall, and books on another, and an image of a Bodhisattva in a niche. A low desk and a mat were the only other furniture, except for a compact metal heating unit and a cushion obviously there for Rudi's convenience. The old man bustled about pouring tea for his guest; Rudi had come to actually like it with the salty yak-butter added. And it certainly helped keep you warm in this upland winter, where your body burned fuel as a bonfire burned wood.

"Thank you for spending so much of your time with me," he said, when Dorje had seated himself again. "Though frankly, there's little I can do but talk at the present!"

Dorje gestured at his own body. "When you reach my age, my son, you will find that talking and thinking are the pleasures that do not fade . . . although silence is still greater, and more lasting. As for the time"—he shrugged—"there is little pressing business until spring. If the gods have given us time to pursue wisdom, it is prudent to use it. Refusing such a gift brings no fortune."

Rudi nodded, collecting his thoughts. "Teacher—"

Dorje held up a hand: "Please. You can *teach* someone how to grow barley—I have done so. Wisdom is another matter. Concerning that nothing can be taught, although the learner easily can be assisted to discover what is in himself. Other than which there is no knowledge of importance, except this: that what is in himself, is everywhere."

Rudi grinned with a trace of impudence and quoted from the Charge of the Goddess:

"For if that which you seek, you find not within yourself, you will never find it without. For behold: I have been with you from the Beginning, and I am that which is attained at the end of desire."

Dorje laughed delightedly. "Yes, a . . . how shall I put it . . . *borrowing*."

"Or could it be that all who make wheels, make them round," Rudi said, and they shared the joke. Then he sobered: "But someone . . . Someone . . . has been *teaching* the masters of the CUT, I think."

"Yes," the *Rimpoche* said soberly. "And they are become the most knowledgeable fools on all the earth. A certain poet—and *he* was no fool—bade men take the cash and let the credit go. I find this good advice, albeit difficult to follow. Nevertheless, it is easier than what those men attempt who seek the aid of Malevolence. *They* try to take the cash and let the *debt* go, and that is utterly impossible; for as we sow, we reap. Men who sell their souls invariably make a very bad bargain."

Rudi shivered a little, remembering the eyes and the dead hands squeezing his throat.

"I've had more to do with the gods since I started this trip than ever before in my life, but I know less than I did when I started out! The more I'm told, the less I understand!"

"And knowing that, you know more than you did," Dorje said. "There is a saying of my people: that around the virgin daughter of a king are guardian walls, and before the walls are fierce men. So is it wonderful that God should cause His secrets to be guarded by ferocity, and that of many kinds?"

"The other side seems to get more help!" Rudi said, baffled. "Not that I'd take that aid if it were offered on a golden plate. Why *would* anyone do that to themselves?"

Dorje made that expressive shrug. "Why do men steal, and violate, and kill when no need drives them? And the lusts of the body are as nothing to the unmastered cravings of the mind. Subdue the body, and still the lusts of the spirit may consume you like fire. Death pursues life. Is there anything without its opposite? Can light exist without shadow? So, I tell you that when you seek to do the will of the gods, and help men rise through the cycles, your very inmost thoughts awaken hosts of enemies that otherwise had slept. As sound awakens echoes, so the pursuit of wisdom awakens the devil's guard."

"As above, so below," Rudi said, and his face went grim. "I have to fight them, then. But . . . *how*, that's the question!"

"I cannot advise you on matters of statecraft; not beyond this valley and its surroundings, at least. But I do say that if you are in league with gods to learn life and to live it you shall not only find enemies. You shall find help unexpectedly, from strangers who, it may be, know not why. Has this not already been the case?"

Hmmm, Rudi thought. *That it has. Sort of an equal and opposite thing.*

"And I have my friends," Rudi said; which was a comfort. "It's a lonely thing, having so much depend on you."

Dorje's chuckle was dry. "My son, when you have come to a decision between right and wrong, then act, not waiting on approval. If you do right it will add no virtue to the right that friends gave their assent beforehand. Be your own judge. But commit no trespass, remembering that where another's liberty begins your own inevitably meets its boundary."

"Can't we help each other, then?" Rudi said.

"Oh, most certainly! But though you strive in friendship, be that friendship as ennobling as the gods' good will, I tell you that each must enter one by one. But of the three, faith, hope and friendship, the last is not least. To him who truly seeks the Middle Way, the Middle Way will open. One step forward is enough."

"Then I'd like to ask your help," Rudi said. "For my comrade Ingolf. He was a prisoner of the Cutters for a long while, and I think they . . . did things to him. To his mind. Things that leave him vulnerable."

"Ah," Dorje said, leaning forward slightly. "Tell me more. With this, we may be of assistance."

"Father . . ."

"Yes, my child?" Ignatius said, controlling his breathing and suppressing a stab of irritation.

He bowed to the monk with whom he'd been sparring and returned the practice sword to the wall. Edain was trying another fall with the instructor in unarmed combat—who was *extremely* good—and Odard, Ingolf, the twins and Fred Thurston were taking turns at sword-and-buckler. He judged his own condition clinically; he was fully recovered in strength and flexibility from their time in the mountains, but still a little behind in endurance. It would be hard to build that again while the snow kept them inside.

And I am still disturbed in spirit by the things which we saw with the Cutters, he knew. *I must think and pray and meditate. But a soul in need is always a priest's task.*

He sat on a bench, and Mathilda joined him. "I've been reading in their library here," she said. "And . . . it's a bit odd."

"What is?"

"It's odd how much of it seems, well, *similar* to what the Church teaches. Not the devas and whatevers and layers of being and Western Paradises and everything, but the stuff you're supposed to *do*, and what's good and bad."

"No, it's not odd at all," Ignatius said. "It's only to be expected. Why do you think our pagan friends"—he nodded towards them—"speak of their god as dying and reborn, and renewing the land with his blood?"

"Well, that's just a pagan myth!"

"Exactly. But the Passion and Resurrection of Our Lord are also myths."

At her shocked look, he went on: "But they are *true* myths. Myths that have become history; not in some timeless land of legends, but in a particular place and a specific time."

"Then why should people like the Mackenzies or the Buddhists get the . . . the same answers as we do from something that was *real*?"

"Because those events are *so* real that they cast their shadow forward and backwards through all time, whenever men think of these matters at all. Even if they are mired in ignorance, they will see . . . fragments of the Truth, as men imprisoned in a cave see shadows cast by the sun. Likewise, all men derive their moral intuitions from God; how not? There is no other source, just as there is no other way to make a wheel than to make it round. In Scripture, He tells us directly what He wishes of us . . . but simply by being, by being His children in His world, we hear a whisper of the *logos*, the divine Word."

He saw her frown thoughtfully. "That makes sense," she said, then smiled; it made her strong-boned face beautiful for a second. "Thank you, Father."

"I can't take the credit for the thought, but if the words reach you, my child, then I'm doing my job."

He sighed. "I find this place both strange and familiar. It is interesting, and it makes me long for Mt. Angel. Marvelous are the works of God—"

"—but none so marvelous as humankind," Mathilda finished. "Thanks, Father. I'd better get back to Rudi now. He overdoes it if he's not watched."

"Thanks for the help, Fred. It's mad I'd go, gibbering and running into the woods waving my arms and crowing like a rooster, if I didn't get away from the women for a while. Well-meaning darlings that they are, my sisters and Mathilda both, the blessings of the Mother upon them."

Frederick Thurston nodded and took a sip of the chicory. He'd grown up calling it coffee, just like everyone else in the interior, though traders from the coast reached Boise a *bit* more often than they did this far into the Rockies, and the real bean wasn't to be had at Ford's Khyentse Cowboy Bar and Grill for any price.

Right now it was crowded here; Ranchers in from the long valley round about, farmers from the foothills, militiamen in from patrolling on skis, enough to combine with the big fieldstone fireplace to make it comfortably warm. The air was thick with the scents of frying potatoes and grilling meat, of rawhide boots drying by the fire and sheepskin coats steaming on their pegs by the door and beer and fruit-brandy, and someone had put a cup of it in front of an image in a niche he supposed must be Khyentse.

The owner paused by their table: "Everything OK?" he said.

"Mr. Ford, it's like a breath of home, so it is," Rudi said with that easy charm Fred envied. "The monastery is a splendid place, sure, but—"

The innkeeper grinned. "And I make my living off the 'but,' " he said, and passed on.

He was a lean gray man who must have been striking once, and the staff in stables and kitchen were mostly his children and grandchildren; Fred remembered someone saying the owner had built the place with his own hands.

It sort of reminds me of the time I managed to get away and do that bar crawl with that guard corporal, Jerry, he thought reminiscently—it had been just after his sixteenth birthday.

God, I thought Mom was going to have a cow! Particularly when she heard about the girls. I'm glad Dad didn't ream the guy out too *badly.*

His father had looked like he was halfway between being angry and laughing, fighting to keep the grin off his face as the course of the evening's dissipation was revealed, right down to the women's underwear found in their possession.

Not that his father had been one to coddle the children—

He squeezed his eyes shut for an instant, almost gasping as he saw that final glimpse again, Martin bending over Dad and—

No! he thought. *I can't go on reliving that! I'm headed the other way and Martin can keep.*

Instead he reached for his cup. Something clinked, and he saw Rudi Mackenzie pouring from a silver flask into it; he upended the oblong shape and shook the last drops free.

"There, that's the last of the Dun Juniper brandy. My friend Terry Martins Mackenzie makes it, and well he learned the art from his father, who was a brewmaster and distiller of note."

"Hey, I can't take the last of it!" Fred said.

"It's Yule, or nearly, the which is close to my birthday. The season for gifts—and you look as if you need it more than I."

The brown-skinned young man sipped. It *did* mellow

the harsh taste of the toasted chicory root, even more than the cream he'd laced it with.

"Yeah, you don't look like you're going to fold up and blow away anymore," he said.

Though you still look like shit, frankly, he added to himself. *Or like a ghost of yourself.*

He had trouble connecting the figure before him with the blood-spattered warrior who'd gone striding through the Cutter camp to rescue his friends like a God of War with men dead and crippled in his wake. Rudi Mackenzie was still far too thin, the flesh tight on his strong bones, and there were lines of strain around his blue-green eyes that hadn't been there before. Only the thick red-gold hair that fell to his shoulders was as it had been before. That and his smile.

"I'm feeling much better," the Mackenzie tanist said, with a flash of white teeth. "Which is to say, as if I'm only at death's door, not halfway through the Gate, screaming as my fingernails tear out while I grip the posts, sure."

"How's the shoulder?" Fred asked.

He'd be most concerned with his sword arm, in the other's place.

"I'm practicing more sword work with my left hand," Rudi said matter-of-factly.

Then he shrugged at Fred's wince. "It's not so bad; I'm ambidextrous anyway."

"Really?"

"Nearly. Slightly. It's important to keep a positive attitude, my mother always told me."

They shared a chuckle, and Rudi went on: "And the strength is coming back, slowly; I'll have enough in the right arm for shield work, and enough control. It's the range of motion I'm having problems with, though the exercises the monks have me doing help."

"They've certainly got some *good* weapons instructors here," Fred said. "I've been learning a lot . . . and I had the best trainers in Boise."

He shook his head. "Sort of odd to think of Buddhists having a military school."

"Well, a lot of the followers of the Old Religion also

had qualms about war training back before the Change, from what the oldsters say at times. But the survivors didn't," Rudi said. "From what the *Rimpoche*'s told me, there were monks of half a dozen different schools here when the day came, and some of them had always walked the Warrior's Way."

Fred frowned. "You know, it's odd ... but in a way, Abbot Dorje reminds me of my father. Which *is* odd because they're nothing at all alike—Dad went to church sometimes, but he was never religious, really."

A waitress turned up with their food; a loaf of brown bread, butter, a platter of plump aromatic sausages hot and steaming and sputtering juices from cracks in their skins, beets with herbs, cabbage, some strong-tasting boiled green that looked like spinach but wasn't, glistening slices of pan-fried potatoes. Weather like this gave you an appetite; he spooned some mustard onto the side of his plate, butter onto the cabbage, and dug in. Rudi did likewise, eating more slowly, as if he had to decide to take each mouthful.

"Well, they're both men who gave everything to what they did—and gave everything to their people," the clansman said after a moment. "Sure, and the *Rimpoche* reminds me of my mother, but that's a more obvious comparison."

"Dad talked about a government of laws and not of men a lot," Frederick said. "But you know ... I've been thinking as we travel, it means a lot what *sort* of men you have ruling. If they're the wrong people, no matter how good the laws are, they don't do much."

Rudi nodded. "Though good laws can restrain a bad ruler, somewhat, depending of course on the customs of the folk and the badness of the man.

"Or woman," he added after a moment, obviously thinking of someone and just as obviously not wanting to say who.

Mathilda's mother, Fred thought. *Who frightens everyone. Even Dad was cautious about her—everyone wanted him to fight Portland over the Palouse, but he agreed to split it with her. But Mathilda's wonderful!*

He blushed, and had the uncomfortable feeling that Rudi had followed his thoughts and was amused by them.

Hell, friends have a right to laugh at each other. We've fought side by side, and we are *friends. And we've got stuff in common, too. We grew up around rulers. That's something that most of us in this bunch have, and it's . . . different . . . to have people who really* understand *around.*

The waitress came back with two mugs of hot cider, pungent with something that smelled of berries. She put Rudi's down and gave him a motherly pat. The glance she gave Fred was anything but; he blushed and reached for some of the bread to mop his plate and ignored her disappointed sigh.

"If you're called to rule, you just have to do the best you can," Rudi said.

"But you need something to guide you," Fred said earnestly, the woman's smile as forgotten as the hunk of barley bread in his hand. "You need . . . something more than just finding money to pay the soldiers and keep the irrigation canals going and patrols to catch bandits."

"That you do," Rudi said. "Men are ruled by the visions inside their heads as much as by swords or castles or tax gatherers. Sure, and those laws your father mentioned, if they're to be anything at all it's a dream in the hearts of men, not just words on a page."

He sighed and watched the sway of their waitress' hips as she took the empty tray back to the kitchens.

"Not even the Foam-Born Cyprian with a rope tied to it, not right now, ochone, the sorrow and the pity," he murmured to himself, and then turned his eyes back to Fred. "A king is not just a war leader, or a head clerk. He's also a priest, he is; a priest of those Mysteries his people reverence, whatever they call them. And his lady a priestess."

The late dawn of Christmas Eve came bright and cold after a week of storms. Father Ignatius stopped at the top of the ridge and looked down over the roofs of the Chenrezi Monastery, the town below, the mist of driven snow that swirled along the surface of the frozen lake at the mountain's foot, and the distant ruins of a pre-Change settlement. The sky was bleakly clear from the mountain fangs eastward to those behind him; the one gilded with bright sunrise until he had to squint into them, the other still turning from night dark to ruddy pink, but otherwise bone white against cobalt blue.

So simple, so elegant, so . . . pure, Ignatius thought, inhaling air that smelled of nothing but itself and a little pine.

God is the greatest of artists! How good of Him to give us this world, and the chance to imitate Him by bettering it.

Wryly: *If only we did not mar it, and ourselves, so often!*

Then the sun rose a little more, and the light was like diamond on the fresh snow, with only a hint of green from the pine trees ahead. He climbed steadily towards them, eyes wide as the crystals sparkled and flew free to glitter in plumes from the branches. His head felt a little light—he'd been fasting for the past day or two, and had taken only a little bread and milk this morning. The light powder was knee-deep, but he had good stout laced boots lined with fleece, and quilted trousers of local make.

After a moment he found the place he wanted, a little clearing with a view down the mountainside and a convenient stump where a lodgepole pine had been pushed over by some storm. Snow hid the trunk, but the splintered base was thigh-high. He drew his sword and drove the point downward into the wood, so that the cross-hilt shape stood black against the sun, and looped his rosary and crucifix about it so that the cross clinked against the steel.

Then he knelt and began to pray, hands folded before him. The familiar words and gestures quieted his mind—which was one of their purposes. Some corner of his mind remembered what Abbot Dmwoski had said to the novices of his class once:

Silent prayer is the highest form. But God gives us a set

of steps for a reason—and you must tread every one of them to reach the heights. Better to stay on a step where you can keep your footing until you are ready, than climb too fast and fall. The Adversary can corrupt even prayer, if your pride gives him an opening.

"High is heaven, and holy," he murmured at last, his eyes on the mountain peaks and dazzled by the sun. "Lord, I seek to do Your will. Have I chosen rightly? Subdue my rebellious heart, Lord, which is full of fear and murmuring. I hear rumors of war in the West, of a great battle where my brothers of the Order defended Your Church and Your people from the minions of the Adversary. I have seen diabolism abroad in the land. Where does my duty truly lie? Free me of doubt, I beg. Make me Your instrument!"

Silence stretched like a plucked harp string, and the light poured down the mountains opposite like wine. He stopped the straining of his mind, seeking only to listen.

"Do not fear, brave *miles* of Christ," a soft voice said, a woman's voice, quiet but with an undertone like a chorus of trumpets. "For He is ever with you."

A shadow fell across him as the one who'd spoken approached, lit by the rising sun. He blinked his eyes in surprise as they adjusted; he'd come here for solitude, and if anyone else was near he would have expected a woodsman or a ski patrol. Then he could see her. It was a woman of . . .

I cannot say if she is young or old, or simply ageless, he thought, his mouth going dry. *No—*

"Who are you?" he whispered.

She was dressed in a simple belted robe of undyed wool, honestly made but the sort of homespun a peasant's wife would wear, or a village craftsman's, and her hands were work-worn. A long blue mantle rested across her head and shoulders, thrown over one shoulder to frame her features and the waving black hair. The face beneath it was olive-skinned, with a firm curve of nose and great dark eyes that reminded him of the Byzantine mosaics Abbot Dmwoski loved; a Jewish face, kindly and wise and a little sad. Her feet pressed the snow in sandals of goatskin, and a breath of warmer air came with her—air scented with lavender and thyme, a hint of sunny, dusty hillsides and hamlet fires of olive twigs and vine clippings.

"Under my father's roof, they called me the wished-for child. *Miriam*, in the tongue of my people."

Then he met her eyes, and cried out, throwing up a hand.

So bright, so bright! Like fire!

Like staring into the heart of some great star, burning in the vastness of space, like the sudden shock of being plunged into its furnace heart and transmuted as elements combined and died. Yet there was no pain in it, only a warmth that penetrated to every atom of his being, as if all that he was *shone* with it. The Light was knowledge; of his self, that showed him every mistake and sin and ignoble failing that had gone into him ... yet the light was still there, and had always been, would always be.

And yet she was the peasant woman he had seen, arms stretched a little toward him with the callused palms of her hands upturned.

"Do not be afraid, Karl Bergfried," she said again, using his baptismal name, and the tenderness in her voice was as overwhelming as the light. "You who have been Father in the spirit to my Son's children."

"Lady," he choked, the hand he had put between them slowly dropping to clasp his other, caught between terror and a rush of joy that was like all his homecomings at once, together with what he'd felt when he first raised the Host as a priest. "Lady—"

I am awake, he thought. *I am more awake than I have ever been.*

Every particle of snow, every roughness of bark or breath of air upon his skin seemed to *glow*. Time passed in a drumbeat of seconds, sounding as if its hooves would shake loose the mountains and break the sky, as if the stuff of existence itself creaked at the strain.

I am more myself than ever before, but I am faded to a shadow and the world is an image cast upon silver glass!

"Lady of Sorrows, Queen of Angels," he said, and tears ran down his cheeks, startlingly cold against the flushed skin. "I am not worthy—a miracle—"

Her lips curved. "And yet my Son's blood was shed for you, child of Eve," she said, the smile taking away the chiding. "And have you not been the instrument of miracle, the earthly bread and wine becoming His blood and flesh in your hands? Have you not granted forgiveness in His name?"

Ignatius nodded. "What must I do?" he whispered.

"You will be tested beyond what you can bear, unless you throw yourself upon Him and His love. In them is strength beyond all the deceits and wickedness you have seen; strength to put them behind you."

"Do I do right to follow the Princess?" he said.

"To whom did you promise obedience, under God?"

"To the head of my Order, and through him to the princes of the Church and the Holy Father."

The blue-mantled head nodded. "Humanity has suffered the fire from the sky, a punishment greater than the Deluge," she said. "But even in the Father's anger there is always mercy. And my Son is thrifty; He uses what is to hand. The young woman your earthly superior entrusted to your care also serves His purposes; guard her then in the trials she will face, with sword and counsel of the world and of the Spirit. In service to her you serve me, and through me the Most High. You shall be my knight, Karl Bergfried!"

She rested one hand on the cross-hilt of his sword; the other reached out and touched him gently on the brow, and the universe dissolved in song.

CHAPTER THIRTEEN

"*Right face!*" Martin Thurston shouted, as the Portlander knights loomed up again out of the dust to the northward; he'd learned *their* trumpet calls today. "Hold hard, the fighting Sixth! Prepare to receive cavalry!"

The battalion turned front and snapped its shields up as the Boisean tubae screamed, a motion like the bristling of a hawk's feathers.

"*Oooo-rah!*" the long guttural shout went up, as the soldiers of the Republic braced for contact. "USA! USA!"

"*Haro! Portland! Holy Mary for Portland!*" answered them from behind the couched lances and painted shields.

Even then, the war cry irritated him. They were fighting for their respective rulers, not for the putative mother of a hypothetical God. Though he supposed *Sandra, the bitch!* just didn't compare as a battle shout.

Centurions stalked between the ranks, and the optios in the rear braced their brass-tipped staffs against men's backs, firming the line and giving that little extra sense of solidity in the chaos and whirling terror that were a foot-soldier's view of combat. Pila jutted out between the locked shields, and the first rank knelt to brace the butts against the hard gritty soil.

Seconds later the lances struck, slamming through

the hard plywood and sheet-steel with huge *crack!* sounds, bowling men over or punching through their body armor. Shafts cracked across, pinwheeling up in fragments through the mist of powdered soil. More pila arched forward over the front rank's heads, and men pushed forward to take the place of the fallen, punching at the metal-clad heads of the horses with the bosses and steel-rimmed edges of their great curved shields, stabbing with their swords, trying to swarm the horsemen under now that they were halted. Men and horses alike were armored animals who cursed and struggled and bled and screamed, killed and died, blind with sweat and blood and the dirt churned up by the hooves and boots all the long day, voices croaking with thirst.

The knights' long blades and spiked war-hammers slammed down, and the destriers reared and struck with feet like milling clubs; the ugly crunching sounds when they struck the bodies of men were audible even through the huge scrap-metal-and-riot blur of noise. Here and there a mount went down, or a man, with a pila-point sticking from a joint in the armor or from the horses' vulnerable bellies. Martin watched as a dismounted knight swung his longsword in both hands, and three Boise troopers struck in trained unison, one to block the blade, the other two stabbing with the flickering speed of a shrike snapping its beak forward, probing for the weak points in the armor. Steel sparked on steel, and then the plumed helmet wavered and went down . . .

The oliphants shrieked again, a higher note than the brass horns the Boise men used, and the men-at-arms backed their horses and turned, cantering out of catapult range and then walking their mounts; infantry couldn't force horsemen to fight if they didn't want to. When they were a thousand yards away they turned and waited; he could see ambulances coming forward for their wounded, and—

Remounts. Goddamn them, they've still got fresh destriers ready! They must have been breeding and training them ever since the Change; it'd cost a fortune.

Boise's light horse were trying to re-form their tattered screen between his flank and the Portlander lancers. His head swiveled eastward, ahead. There his men had been steadily chewing their way through the Portland Protective Association's infantry, like a saw through hard wood ... but they'd had to halt while he refused the flank to take the attack of the heavy horse.

Now the enemy foot were backing, breaking contact, still with a disciplined bristle of spears over the kite-shaped shields; blocks of crossbowmen were between them, retreating by files. The men at the head of each rank of six fired their weapons and then turned and walked backwards to the end of the column, pumping the cocking lever set into the forestocks of their crossbows as they went. The man behind them shot and then followed, reloading as well ... Thurston's men crouched behind their heavy shields against the continuous flickering ripple of bolts; the sound was a steady *thock-thock-thock*; mostly the big shields stopped the short heavy missiles. Mostly, but a steady trickle were falling limp or screaming or staggering backwards towards the medics, and the Portlanders were too far away now for his men to reply with thrown pila.

He looked southward, to the section of the allied line on his left: the pikes of the Pendleton city militia wavered as they advanced, and he suspected that the glaives of the Registered Refugee Regiment at their backs had a good deal to do with the fact that they *were* still moving forward. A trio of six-pound iron balls blurred into them from the enemy catapults, bouncing forward at knee-height, and a whole six-man file went down screaming, their eighteen-foot weapons collapsing like hay undercut by a mowing machine.

A heavy *tung-tung-tung-tung* sound came through the screams, as one of his own batteries replied with globes of napalm, the burning fuses drawing black smoke-trails through the air and then blossoming into blurred flowers of yellow gold as they landed and shattered. The pump teams behind the field pieces worked like maniacs to drive water through the armored hoses to the hydraulic jacks built into the frames, and the throwing arms bent back against the resistance of the heavy springs.

The enemy catapults were already moving back, though—he could see their crews trotting beside the wheels of the field pieces. They'd hitched their teams, and were stopping only when the auxiliary pumps attached to the axles had cocked the mechanisms. Then they'd let the trail fall from the limber, slap a bolt or ball into the groove and fire and snatch it up again to make another bound backwards. A four-foot javelin from one of them went over his head with a malignant *whirrrt*, making him duck involuntarily. There was an appalling wet *smack* behind him; he turned and saw that the bolt had pinned the body of his dead horse to the ground.

Hooves thudded behind him. The messenger from his cavalry commander had a crudely splinted left arm, and her dark olive skin was muddy with pain and the exhaustion that grooved her face. She saluted smartly, though:

"Sir! Colonel Jacobson reports that he regretfully cannot slow any further charges by the Portlander lances. Sir . . ." Her voice changed. "Sir, they just have too much weight of metal for us to stop them. Not face-to-face without room to maneuver."

Thurston nodded. "Get that arm seen to, Sergeant Gonzalez," he said. "No return message."

Then he looked up at the sun. It was three o'clock at least . . .

And I am not *going to try to pursue in the dark, with the cavalry we probably have left.*

Another pair of horsemen approached . . .

No, goddammit, it's Estrellita Peters and her spawn, come to waste time I don't have!

They were both in breastplates and helmets, at least, and there were a dozen of their slave-guardsmen around them. The boy was pale but determined, gulping at his first exposure to the atmosphere of a battlefield—a cross between a construction site, an open sewer, and a neglected butcher's shop on a really hot day, seasoned with men sobbing or shrieking or calling for their mommas as their ruins were dragged back to the aid stations. The Bossman's consort was as calm with edged steel whickering through the air as she'd been in her own parlor greeting her guests. At least she wasn't trying to play General ...

"We are forcing them back, *Señor Presidente*!" she said.

Thurston nodded curtly. *And paying far too much of a butcher's bill for it,* he thought; the loss of every man hurt, and from his own ever-loyal Sixth doubly.

"We'll hold the field," he said, his voice a grim bark. "And they'll leave your territory. Now, if you'll pardon me—"

The boy spoke, and there was a disturbing flash in his brown eyes: "The Prophet has foretold victory!"

Thurston nodded curtly again. *And I could do the same,* he thought; for a wonder Estrellita showed some tact, and pulled the boy aside.

Martin went on: "Courier! Get south and find out what's the hell's happening on our left flank! And tell the Corwinite commander"—damned *if I'll be polite at this late date!*—"that unless he can turn their flank soon, a general pursuit is out of the question."

Then to his signalers: "Sound the advance!"

The tubae brayed like mules in agony, a long sustained note that meant *get ready* and then three sharp blats. With a unison that shook the earth the battalions stepped off, moving forward at a steady jog-trot, shields up and pila cocked back to throw. Astonishingly they began to sing as well, a raucous marching chant timed to the pounding beat of the advance:

> *"Yanks to the charge! cried Thurston*
> *The foe begins to yield!*
> *Strike—for hearth and nation*
> *Strike—for the Eagle shield!—"*

"By God, with men like these, I'll whip the Earth!" Thurston said, and drew his own blade.

It would come to that for the commanders, before the sun set.

"Plant the swine feathers!" Chuck Barstow Mackenzie rasped.

His voice was hoarse with the dust, raw with shouting. The signal blatted out, and the mass of kilted archers stopped their jog-trot to the rear. Each of them turned, jammed the shovel end of the weapon into the ground, backheeled it to plant it, and then took a few steps backwards as they reached over their shoulders for arrows—they were down to the quivers on their backs now, no time for spares to be brought forward. Westward the dimly seen ridge they'd abandoned suddenly quivered and sparkled; the sun was behind the Clan's warriors now, and it broke off the edged metal of the blades there, and on arrowheads.

"Let the gray geese fly—*shoot!*"

The yew bows bent and spat; this was close range, barely fifty yards. You could only just see an arrow from a heavy bow as a flicker through the air that close, and it was only a half second later that the first struck. Men and horses went down; and this time they reined around and fled, back below the swell of ground that would put them out of sight. Only a few kept coming towards the Mackenzie line, a handful of them screaming out:

"Cut! Cut! Cut!"

They galloped along the Mackenzie front, lofting arrows towards their foes and dying as picked shots stepped out of the Clan's ranks to take careful aim.

Chuck dismissed them from his mind. The ones who'd sensibly dodged back behind the protection of the ridgeline were the ones he was worried about; there were a lot more of them:

"Dropping shafts!" he shouted, and the bows went up.

Arrows glittered as they arched up and over the rise, discouraging any of the enemy from lingering. Off to the southward men were fighting and dying too—the Warm Springs tribes and the Bearkiller A-listers against the

Sword of the Prophet and the Cutter irregulars as they lapped around the flank like a rising tide creeping up a beach, a bit higher with each wave.

"Get ready to—" he began.

The impact was like a punch in the chest, or a blow from a hammer. He grunted and took a step backwards. Then the pain started, and he looked down to see the arrow standing in his chest; it had broken the rivets between two of the little metal plates inside his brigandine, just over the left branch of the Horns that cradled the Crescent Moon.

He grunted again, and this time there was a hot wetness in his mouth when he did; it leaked out between his teeth, and he could feel a gurgling as he sank to his knees and tried to take a breath. The pain got worse, pulsing out in waves from the cold center where the iron had pierced rib and lung. He blinked; Rowan was holding him, and Oak was there, bending over him with a look of astonished fury.

Why's the boy mad at me? he thought for an instant.

Then he forced the black wings back from the corners of his eyes for a second.

Important, he thought.

That was hard. His mind was like a movie in the old days, but one all put together from bits and pieces; Dad holding him up on his shoulders as he came home from his mail route, his mother, children, grandchildren, the look on Judy's face the first time he called the Goddess down to her, the overwhelming need to scream. A long slow breath was the hardest thing he'd ever done, ignoring the blood pouring into his ravaged lung for the sake of air in the good one. Things were beginning to fade, graying around the edges, and he felt himself falling as if the ground beneath his back was a hole into infinity.

"Get—them—out!" he said distinctly, coughing blood across the faces of son and foster son. Then: "Judy—"

Oak Barstow stood, his face contorted like something carved from blood-spattered wood, and his arms went

wide as he emptied his lungs in one long wailing shriek.
Faces turned towards him, shocked and pale.

"Retreat!" he called. "In good order!"

The archers turned and trotted away, leaving the irregular rank of the swine feathers. The bicycles were
near, now; the Clan's force threw their legs over the
bars, set feet to pedals and turned northeast, following
the dust of the ambulances and stores-wagons as they
pumped away in a column three ranks across.

Rowan brought up his father's horse, blinking in astonishment at the face, willing the still form to rise and
speak, to give an order, to say *something*.

"Get going," Oak grated, cuffing him sharply across
the back of his helmet, and heaving the body over the
saddle with one lift and wrench. *"Now!"*

That last charge was a mistake, Eric Larsson thought.

Men in the russet-brown armor of the Sword and
the patchwork harness of the CUT's Rancher levies
swarmed around him. Blades flickered, rippling in the
dying sun as the melee boiled around the stalled Bearkiller wedge.

*There's too fucking many of them and they don't give
up for shit.*

He smashed the broken stump of his lance over
a man's head and swept the backsword out. Images
strobed across his vision, targets and threats, everything
else blurred. The sword lashed down on the junction of
a man's neck and shoulder. Leather armor parted under
the steel and the edge drove halfway to the man's breastbone; muscle and gristle locked around it. He wrenched
it back with desperate strength and caught a shete on his
shield in the same motion, the curved bullhide boom-
ing under the stroke as the horses circled and chopped
with hooves and teeth, wild-eyed and as battle-mad as
their riders. Something else hit his thigh, but the armor
stopped it, and he stabbed into a familiar soft heavy resistance and heard an earsplitting shriek.

He wrenched his mount about and let that motion

drag the steel free. Time to go ... he looked for his signaler.

"Hakkaa Paalle!"

He didn't know if the war-shout of the Bearkillers came from his own throat or someone else's. A blow came at him out of the corner of his eye, and he whipped the shield around desperately. It was a man with a shaven head, leaking blood from a palm-sized graze where his helmet had been knocked off, his yellow goat-beard bound with golden rings and blue eyes glaring in a face inhuman with a rage beyond all bearing. A stylized wolf's head was painted across his lacquered hide breastplate, some Eastern Rancher's sigil.

"Cut!" he screamed, and struck with a war-pick whose haft was gripped in both hands, the horse moving beneath him as if it were part of his own body. *"Cut!"*

The long steel beak struck Eric's shield; the awkward angle of it hammered his arm back against him, and the spike punched through, through the shield and the armored gauntlet beneath and into flesh. He'd been wounded before, but the pain was enormous, a cold wash of astonishment that paralyzed him while the man wrenched the weapon free and stood in the stirrups for the killing blow. For a confused moment he saw something, a horse and a shield and a shining spear.

St. Michael— he thought. *Warrior saint, aid*—

"Hakkaa Paalle!"

This time he *knew* it wasn't him yelling; all he was capable of shouting right now was *Jesus, that hurts!* And thankful it wasn't *Mother, help!*

Bright metal speared across the side of the goat-bearded man's throat from behind; it carried the Outfit's banner, but the shaft below and the head above were an entirely practical lance. That was young Mike Havel Jr.; he recoiled desperately, bringing up the shaft of the banner to block the counterstrike of the war-pick. It worked, a little; the blunt back end of the terrible weapon smashed into the wood and bounced into the mail-shirt on the young man's side.

Eric let the ruined shield slide off his arm, but the jarring sent fresh waves up it and into his gut and balls, like a tooth being drilled but all over his body; the sword slipped from nerveless fingers. Then his own son Billy was there, an arrow drawn to the ear as he galloped past, perfect form with the recurve a single smooth C.

Thunk.

The bodkin punched into the side of the man with the war-pick, so deeply that the gray feathers were all that showed. Billy Larsson brought his horse up in a rearing halt; the beast pivoted like a cow pony despite the weight of an armored rider, and he snaked out the bow to catch at the reins of Eric's horse.

"The Mackenzies are out!" he shouted. "Let's *go*!"

"Sound *retreat*!" Eric snarled.

It was necessary. He still didn't like it.

Eric Larsson watched as the bodies were lifted onto the railcar. It was nearly dark, but flames underlit pillars of foul-tasting black smoke with flickering red where pyramids of boxed supplies had been torched to keep them out of enemy hands. A dozen Mackenzies were fitting their bicycles into the slots in the light-alloy car's surfaces, ready to pedal it up to speed, faster than anything a horse could do and far more enduring.

Others were already underway, stretching off towards the northeast along the rusty steel rails until they were moving dots against the flare of sunset. The CORA men and the bulk of the Bearkillers were a column of dust to the southwest, pulling back towards Bend and the passes of the Cascades.

"Mind if I hitch a ride?" Eric said, cradling the mass of bandages that was his left hand against his chest.

Every time he took a step, it was as if invisible cords inside the arm were stretched out and scraped with knives, all the way up his shoulder and into his chest. He knew a flicker of pride at the steadiness of his voice, but he certainly wasn't in any shape to get out of here on horseback.

Or anything else that requires more than lying on my back and whimpering.

The man overseeing the loading looked up; it was Chuck Barstow's foster son Oak. Smears of dried blood across his face looked black in the fading light, leaving his blue eyes like jewels of turquoise set in jet.

"Sure, and you're welcome, a hundred thousand welcomes," he said. "We'd none of us have made it out if you hadn't held them until we broke contact."

Eric waved the others forward; Billy was there, nothing but scrapes and bruises, memories of horror warring with the exhilaration of realizing *By God, I'm alive!* on his face. He was helping Mike Jr. along; the boy still had the broken shaft and the blood-clotted Bearkiller banner clutched to his chest. Getting onto the railcar without fainting occupied his next few moments. Then he realized whose body he was next to.

"Oh, shit," he said, looking down at Chuck Barstow's still face, relaxed into an inhuman calm beneath the blood; someone had closed his eyes. "I didn't realize—"

"He died well," Oak said, his voice harsh despite the musical lilt. "And he'll have company beyond the Western Gate before the last thread of this is woven!"

Chuck Barstow stood and breathed. For a long moment the sheer wonder of that was enough; and the air was like all the Willamette springs he'd ever loved, and warm scented summer nights amid the fields and the long wistful mornings of Indian Summer and a crisp autumn evening with the leaves blowing yellow about his feet thrown in. He was naked, but the feel of the grass on his bare feet was like a caress, and the forest floor was thick with white fawn lily and blue camas. Douglas fir towered over him, as majestic as redwoods, dropping their deep resinous scent into the still dim air. There was a thrill to it all, an eagerness for the day that he'd lost long ago bit by bit without even noticing it.

Motion drew his eyes. There was a meadow ahead,

hints of color and greenness amid a sunlight whose brightness was almost painful. Two figures came out of it, shadows at first, and then a woman and a wolf—the great beast was chest-high on her, and she walked with a hand resting on its ruff. The animal cocked head and ears and dangled a tongue like a red flag across bone-white fangs, its amber eyes amused.

The woman was Judy; as he remembered her from that first meeting, solid in her festival robe and three-colored belt, and beautiful. His own eyes went wide with alarm.

"No," she said, smiling at him, that smile that had made him feel like a boy on his first date for thirty years of marriage. "Time's different here. You came first, but I've been waiting."

He nodded. Somehow that made sense. The wolf made an impatient *wurrrff* sound and jerked its nose towards the meadow where light shimmered on flowers of gold. Judy extended her hand.

"Breakfast's ready," she said, and grinned as his stomach rumbled. "And Aoife's eager to see you again—you wouldn't *believe* the argument we had over who got to meet you first. Fortunately Liath talked some sense into her."

He took the infinitely familiar hand and grinned back at her. "Will there be gardens?" he said.

She nodded as she turned to lead him into the brightness.

"There's everything."

LARSDALEN, BEARKILLER HQ, HALL OF REMEMBRANCE
OCTOBER 31, CY 23/2021 AD

The great rectangular room fell silent as the food was cleared away from the long tables and the ceremonial drinking-horns set out, rimmed and tipped with gold and carved with running interlaced animal patterns. The central hearth beneath its copper smoke-hood flickered and boomed, for the night outside was cold and hissing with winter's rain. Light from that shone on the oak wainscoting between the tall windows, wrought in similar sinuous forms and hung with weapons and shields—round concave ones marked with the Bear, backswords and lances and recurve bows, and captured trophies and banners.

The fire scented the air, and the wax of candles from the wrought-iron chandeliers overhead, and the memory of the feast's fresh hot bread and the roast pigs and a dozen other dishes. Now military apprentices went their rounds with jugs of the wine from the Larsdalen vineyards and from elsewhere in the Outfit's territories, that the dead might be hailed in the drink grown on the land their blood had defended.

There had been a memorial mass in the Larsdalen church, and a *blót* in the Hoff that Signe had built years ago, and private rites in each family, but this was a ceremony they all had in common; both faiths accepted the arval, the grave-ale.

The feast hadn't been too somber despite the mourning; the Bearkillers remembered how their founder Mike Havel had joked with his comrades and his wife as he lay dying on the Field of the Cloth of Gold, scorning death. Most of those present believed that the spirit outlived the body, in Heaven or the halls of the High One or Hella's domain or by rebirth; and they and the minority of unbelievers all shared a faith that a man lived not one day longer than he lived, and that what mattered was *how* he met his end . . . or hers.

Strong bearded faces waited, and women no less fierce, many of them also with the brand of the A-list between their brows. Youngsters newly blooded were there, and the solid landholders of the A-list steadings, and representatives from the others of the Outfit; merchants of Rickreal, Larsdalen's craftsmen and engineers, and the commons from the Strategic Hamlets. The A-list's pride was that they were the first to fight, but they kept Mike Havel's law, that every member of the Outfit would defend the others at need, and to the death. The toasts ran up the tables; it was the custom for close kin to make them. Finally they reached the head table, the one that stood crossways to the others and centered about an empty chair.

No human sat in it tonight, but a sheathed backsword rested across the arms. The high back was draped with a bearskin cloak clasped with a gold broach, and above it was a helmet—the simple bowl with nasal-bar and mail aventail the Outfit had used in its earliest days, but with a snarling bear's head mounted on it so that the snout projected like a visor, and a fall of hide behind.

On either side were the seats for the war-leader Eric Larsson, and his sister Signe Havel who held the Bear Lord's power until his children were grown. They both stood, ending the toasts to the fallen with a collective tribute.

"I drink to our glorious dead!" Eric Larsson said, taking up his horn from its stand, and signing it with the Cross. "In the name of the Father, Son and Holy Ghost; may the blessed Virgin intercede for them, and my patron, St. Michael, and all warrior saints welcome them to everlasting glory, they who fell fearlessly for home and kindred; in Jesus' holy name, amen!"

There was a long murmur of *amen* from those who followed his faith. Signe took up her horn in turn and used her right fist to sign it with the Hammer; it was one of the set her grandfather had commissioned in a fit of youthful ethnic self-rediscovery eighty years ago, much copied since the Change by the Outfit's makers. With innocent eclecticism the craftsmen of the 1930s had included Northwest Indian symbols along with the Norse, but that was appropriate—she had a little of that blood too, after all.

Her voice rang out:

"I drink to our glorious dead. May they feast with the High One this night. May His daughters bear them the mead of heroes, and greet the new-come *einherjar* thus at the gates of Vallhöl:

"Hail to thee Day, hail, ye Day's sons;
Hail Night and daughter of Night,
With blithe eyes look on all of us,
And grant to those sitting here victory!
Hail, Aesir, hail Ásynjur!
Hail Earth, that gives to all!
Goodly spells and speech bespeak we from you,
And healing hands in this life!"

Then together the siblings raised the horns high and shouted: *"To our glorious dead!* And to all the Brothers and Sisters of the A-list, always first to fight! *Drink hail!"*

A hundred and fifty voices roared reply:

"Wassail!"

Signe looked at her twin brother with critical appraisal as they sat again; the stump of his left wrist was neatly bandaged, and he looked gaunt and pale but strong in black boots and pants and high-collared jacket; the doctors said it had been healing well, and he'd certainly been bugging the craftsmen for a whole range of hooks, blades, gripping devices and even a steel fist for when it was ready to hold a prosthetic.

The military apprentices moved along the tables, refilling for those who'd drunk deep. She was pacing herself, and had taken only a long sip, but it glowed in her stomach after the feast. Just enough to give the great room a glow as well. Her mouth quirked as she thought what the ancestress who'd had it built as a ballroom back in Edwardian days with a splendor of white silk hangings and chandeliers would have thought of it now.

Probably great-great-grandfather Sven would like it better, the old pirate!

That had been the man who came from a bitter little farm in Småland to the Pacific Northwest in the days when men like wolves snarling around an elk tore fortunes from the land with fangs of steel and steam. He'd started in a lumber camp and married the half-Tlingit woman who cooked for his bunkhouse; worked his way up to pay clerk, quit, made a minor silver strike in the

Idaho mountains, parlayed that into a fortune, bought this country estate to complement his town mansion in Portland ...

And his children went respectable in a major way, she thought.

His son married the daughter of a Lutheran pastor, *his* son the daughter of a Swedish-American engineering magnate, *his* son a Danish-German Milwaukee brewing fortune, and Signe's own father a Boston Brahmin of *Mayflower* pedigree so distinguished her teeth were permanently locked on her vowels.

And whose ancestors came from the Danelaw and were probably the descendants of Vikings themselves, she thought.

Luanne Larsson stood next, pride glowing on her dark comely Afro-mestizo face as she looked at her husband and eldest son and raised her horn.

"I drink to my son William Larsson, Brother of the A-List, who saved the life of his cousin Mike Havel Jr. on the field of battle!" she said, the Tejano-Texan accent still softening her voice. *"Drink hail!"*

"Wassail!"

Signe stood again, silent for a moment as she raised the horn, until all eyes were on her and the loudest sounds were breathing and the crackle of the fire on the central hearth. She inhaled the pleasant pungency of burning fir-wood.

"I drink to my son Mike Havel Jr., Brother of the A-list, who saved the life of *my* brother Eric Larsson on the field of battle at the risk of his life, shedding enemy blood and taking wounds. *Drink hail!"*

"Wassail!"

This time it was a roar. Mike Jr. flushed; he was seated at the high table for the first time, with the A-list brand between his brows still new enough to be raw.

He was too young for the standard Initiation, but there was an exception for valor in the field, and nobody had even whispered that he didn't deserve it, for saving Eric's life and for keeping the flag despite his broken ribs. They were still tight-bandaged beneath his jacket, but he grinned shyly and ducked his head. The banner hung on the carved oak wainscoting of the wall behind them, the snarling crimson bear on brown, the blood-stains on it just barely visible in the lantern light.

They cried the *Wassail!* again and again, until it turned into a chant: first "Hail! Hail! Hail!"

And then: "Lord ... *Bear* ... Lord ... *Bear*!" amid fists pounding on oak until the holders that carried the horns shook and the red wine quivered over the gold bound rims.

Signe felt the chant sing in her veins as it echoed through the great chamber. She leaned forward, sud-denly quivering-tense. Would he take it? She'd given him advice on what to say, but the boy had a mind of his own. The formalities would come later, but if her son stretched out his hand now ...

He stood, pale and looking older than his fifteen years. The noise died away to a breathing hush, like the tension in a great cat before it leapt.

"Brothers and Sisters of the A-list ... free folk of the Outfit ..." he said, and raised his horn.

"I drink to my father, Mike Havel, Corporal in the United States Marine Corps, Force Recon, who never turned his back on an enemy, or on a friend! My father, who stood between the Bear and his folk, who wrestled with Sky and Death itself on the day of the Change, who brought us from the far cold mountains to this good earth! My father, who built our walls and made our laws, who judged justly, who killed the tyrant Arminger with his own hands, whose blood was the sacrifice that re-newed the land. Hear us, Founder, lawgiver, land-father! We keep faith with you, Bear Lord! *Drink hail!*"

"Wassail!" came in a quivering roar that shook the very chandeliers overhead, until shadows swung gigan-tic on the walls.

Her son lowered the horn from his lips. He waited until silence fell again, then walked to the empty chair and laid his free hand on the hilt of the great blade that rested across its arms. His face was very calm; and it looked so much like the one she remembered there ...

"I'm proud to have shed my blood for the Outfit," he said, his voice steady and pure if still a little lighter than a grown man's.

He waited out the cheer that followed before he continued:

"And if our free folk hail me as Bear Lord when my time comes, I will take up my father's sword and the Bear Helm, and with it his drighten might and right. Then I will give you my oaths to render good lordship and take your freely plighted hold-oaths, that your might be mine and mine be yours. For the lord and the land and the folk are one."

Utter quiet fell, a tribute more complete than any roar; she could see tears on some faces, and slow nods of agreement from many more.

My son, my son! she thought, through a glitter of her own tears, and a pain that was also joy. *Oh, Mike, if only you could be here to see him now!*

The youth went on: "But first I must learn to fight like my uncle, Lord Eric, our war-leader—"

"Better than me, boy!" Eric said, grinning hugely. "I shouldn't have made that last charge—it was one too many. Your father always said I had to watch my temper."

"And I must learn to lead as wisely as my mother, Signe, Lady of the Bearkillers, whose forebears' blood won this land long ago. Until then, let them rule—and let me learn from them."

He turned to her: "I drink to Signe Havel, Sister of the A-list, whose wisdom saw the threat of the Prophet and the tyrant Thurston! *Drink hail!*"

"*Wassail!*"

Signe didn't drink the toast to herself, but the rush of pride was stronger than the wine could have been.

That's my boy! she thought. *He wants it, yes . . . but he knows* when *to take it. High Lord, Lady Freya, all kindly* alfar, *you've gifted him with brains and guts both!*

"I drink to our war-leader, Eric Larsson, who got us out of that cluster-fuck in Pendleton unreamed!" he went on. "And who gave his hand to smash down a wolf that ravened at our throats. *Drink hail!*"

"*Wassail!*"

Eric stood once more. "And I drink to my nephew, and my son, because without them you'd be drinking toasts to my ashes in a goddamned urn! *Drink hail!*"

As the shout of *Wassail!* rang out there was laughter in it, the high tension of the moments before gone.

It increased as the horn tilted back, and it became obvious that Eric was going to drain it or choke. Others did likewise; Mike and Eric's son William linked their arms each through the other's as they drank, laughing with the red wine on their chins. Fists and feet pounded in rhythm with the flutter of Eric's Adam's apple, dissolving in cheers as he pulled the horn away from his mouth, wiped the back of his great gold-furred hand across his bearded mouth and held it upside down to show that hardly a drop remained.

"And now . . . let's just drink!" he called.

DUN JUNIPER, THE FIELD OF FLOWERS
OCTOBER 31, CY 23/2021 AD

Juniper Mackenzie had planted flowers here on the slopes below the plateau many years ago, when this had been her winter retreat between the festivals and tournaments at which she busked for her living. Her great-uncle's grandfather had planted the gnarled apple trees, when this had been a working farm and the Mackenzie kin fresh from the Oregon Trail and the hills of East Tennessee. Even in the hungry days right after the Change they'd tended it, and in the years since the place of beauty had grown.

Now the flower beds and rosebushes spread along the slope to either side of the Dun's gates, the flowering vines climbing the stucco halfway to the frieze of painted blossoms and half-hidden faces below the parapet. Most of the blossoms were past now; a few faded slashes of color clung amid careful mulch and pruning, brought out by the old gold light of sunset on a day that had dawned with rain and was ending with a clear sky. There was a silty smell of damp turned earth and the musky scent of leaves and straw undergoing the slow decay of autumn.

And so many of them Chuck did the planting of, and we planned it together, the Chief of the Mackenzies thought.

Chuck had been Lord of the Harvest long before he was First Armsman. She remembered his face, that first year, when they started to dig the potatoes he'd planted.

And he scoured the Valley for seeds and cuttings for this garden so that we might have beauty as well as food, when he had the time between the ten thousand thousand other things . . . Thirty-two years I knew you, Chuck; more than half my life. Even before you married Judy you were a friend, and afterwards like the brother I never had, and you were there at my hand in all we built.

The meadows below the flowers were crowded. The voices of her people rang out, ending the ceremony:

> *"We all come from the Wise One*
> *And to her we shall return*
> *Like a waning moon,*
> *Shining on the winter snow;*
> *We all come from the Maiden—"*

Judy Barstow Mackenzie took the urn with her man's ashes as the song ended and walked down the rows of the garden, pouring them on the damp soil; her sons and daughters followed, spading the gray powder into the rich brown dirt. Beneath the hoodlike fold of the arsaid drawn over her head Judy's face looked . . .

Not older, Juniper thought; her friend was her age almost to the day, fifty-three. *But as if she's moved through sorrow and beyond it. Well, that's why we keen the dead.*

Her own throat was sore with it. There was a release

in the cries, as if your spirit was walking partway with the dead, a last look at the beloved before you committed them to Earth's embrace.

A little life came back into Judy's face as she finished; and then she looked around, a question on her face. *What now?* was as plain as if she'd spoken aloud.

As if in answer, her daughter, Tamsin, and sons, Rowan and Oak, and their mates reached out to touch her, and the grandchildren crowded around with their small bodies leaning against hers.

Life is the answer to life, Juniper thought, and spoke formally:

"Who among his close kin will speak the last words for Chuck Barstow Mackenzie, our brother?"

She was a little surprised when Oak stood forward. He bowed to her and turned to the folk assembled below—everyone in Dun Juniper who wasn't helping prepare the feast for the dead, and many from elsewhere in the Clan's territories as well, and a few from beyond. Chuck had been a well-loved man.

"I was an orphan of the Change," he said. "Younger than my daughter Lutra here."

He touched her head, and the girl turned her tear-streaked face up to him; the fingers were infinitely gentle on her brown hair.

"I don't remember anything much before then—just bits and pieces, and the fear and hunger as we all waited on the school bus and the grown-ups were gone. Chuck took me and my sister Aoife and our foster brother Sanjay off that bus. He and Mother Judy raised us; they're the only parents I know. Chuck was the one who took me out and showed me the stars and told me their names, and the plants and their names and uses, and held me with Mother when I was sick or afraid. He taught me how to hunt, and the rites of the woodland Powers. He taught me how to tend the land, and many others—he was a man of the earth above all, and there are thousands alive today who walk the ridge of the world because he could show them how to coax Earth into yielding Her fruits. He stood by my side when I was made an Initiate of the Mysteries. If I'm a man at all, it's his doing."

There was a long murmur from the assembled crowd. Oak raised his head and went on; tears glistened in his yellow mustache.

"He taught me spear and blade and bow; he fought for us all, and now like my sister and brother before him he's given his body to the earth that feeds me and my children, and his blood to protect them. His last words were *Get them out* and my mother's name."

The murmur grew louder and then died away again. Oak's voice rose for a long moment into one long wail of grief; then he spoke in words again.

"Lady Juniper, Chief of the Clan, Goddess-on-Earth, hear my oath!"

"I will hear your oath, Oak son of Chuck, whose totem is Wolf," Juniper said steadily. "By what will you swear?"

"I swear by Earth beneath my feet, by Sky above, by the Water in my veins and the Fire that is my life; by Brigid and Lugh and all the gods of my people, by the spirits that watch over the house-hearth and the byre and the field and the forest, and by Father Wolf who walked in my dream. And I call to witness that part of my father's soul that is not in the Summerlands, and the Chief of the Clan, and the folk of the Clan."

He bent down and picked up a pinch of the mingled earth and ash, and drew it across his forehead. When he continued his voice had the raw challenge of a bull elk's:

"Once I keened my father on the field where he fell. Once I have keened him here where we returned his ashes to Earth the Mother. I swear that when I keen him for the third time, it will be when his vengeance is won!"

Then he drew the little Black Knife from his knee-hose, and held out his hand as he pressed the point to the fleshy ball below his thumb. A line of red appeared, and drops fell through the darkening air to fall on the dirt, and a sigh went through the crowd.

"And if I fail in my oath, may Earth shun me, and Sky fall and crush me, and Fire burn me, and the Water of life that is my blood be spilled!"

A long silence fell, as Chuck's other children held out their hands and joined their blood to his.

"So mote it be," Juniper said softly, into the echoing quiet.

CHAPTER FOURTEEN

The hero knows, with every step
The fate to which he walks
Heart-glad he wins release from fear
And with it ransom for his folk—

From: *The Song of Bear and Raven*
Attributed to Fiorbhinn Mackenzie, 1st century CY

CHENREZI MONASTERY, WESTERN WYOMING
APRIL 15, CY 24/2022 AD

The fifty-pound sack of wet sand across his shoulders seemed to be pushing Rudi Mackenzie into the ground like a nail as he ran up the steep south-facing hillside. Sweat ran down his bare flanks despite the cool spring day, and he gloried in the play of muscle as his legs pushed against turf and rock like powerful elastic springs. The air was thin but so clean it made him feel as if he were washing his lungs by breathing it, pushing out all the poisons in his body with his breath and sweat.

Last year's grass was still matted on the ground, but new growth was pushing through it—the pink-tinged white of spring beauties, yellowbells, sagebrush buttercups. When he reached the sloping meadow they made drifts of rose and gold through the new grass; there was a spring, and he set the bag down and used his hand to cup the icy mineral-tasting waters; the snows were still there, only a little higher up the hillside.

Master Hao was the next to the plateau; he found Rudi in a handstand, slowly lowering himself until his nose touched the earth and raising himself to full arm's length again. Sweat outlined the monk's lean ropy muscles, stripped to the same loose pants that Rudi wore. A pole rested across his shoulders, carrying practice weapons and shields on either end, but despite his fifty-odd years he ran with an easy, springy stride that defied the weight of wood and metal and leather. It was as if gravity were a game, and he obeyed its rules only out of courtesy.

Rudi joined him in untying the bundles while the others arrived. Ignatius followed, which surprised him a little, but the warrior-priest had seemed very *focused* since Yule, even for a knight-brother of the Order. Mathilda came after him, giving Rudi a grin and a thumbs-up; the cleric had been pushing her hard, too. Odard and Frederick Thurston came in the middle, and then Mary and Ritva and Ingolf in a clump—the big Sheriff's son was matching Mary's pace and Ritva was instinctively working the rearguard's position, checking behind her every few seconds.

Master Hao stood scowling with his arms crossed as they stretched and then went through the tumbling and leaping that he considered an indispensable preliminary to training. Rudi had always been agile, but he'd never worked as hard on gymnastics as he had this winter. At last they finished with a long series of running backflips across the wet uneven surface of the plateau.

At least he's teaching us himself, Rudi thought. *That's a compliment, of sorts—he doesn't turn us over to the lesser instructors like beginners.*

"This," Hao said, throwing twin shetes—what he called butterfly-longswords—to Ingolf. "This—"

Rudi ended up with a longsword and buckler, to his relief; it was hard enough regaining skills with the hilt of his sword in his left hand, but learning an entirely *new* weapon like the sickle-blades on chains the monks favored was excruciating. Some of the group had taken to them like ducks to water, though; the twins loved them.

He faced off against Odard, raised his padded wooden blade in salute, and began. They both had round shields about two feet across—rather similar to what Bearkillers used, and calling for a quite different style from the four-foot-long kite shields Odard had trained on, and he wouldn't be used to facing a southpaw. Liu's sword was held above his head with the hilt forward, Protectorate fashion.

Rudi's blade looped out to strike at the knee, a hocking strike. Odard leapt straight up so that it hissed beneath his feet and smashed forward as he landed . . .

"*Feel* where your opponent's blade is to go!" Master Hao said ten minutes later when they backed away, panting.

His callused hand slapped the back of Odard's leather helmet.

"You think too much! You are clever, and you rely upon it. Then when your opponent does not do what your so-clever mind thinks, you are helpless—paralyzed!"

Now that *was clever. That* is *Odard's great fault as a fighter*, Rudi thought.

"And you!" Hao went on, turning on Rudi. "You are very fast again, you are very strong again, you have the instinct for the blade. On all this *you* rely—too much. You have pattern in your attack—too much. Even *good* instincts will betray you if you use them the same way all the time."

Odard's eyes went wide in apprehension as Hao picked up a quarterstaff and motioned him out into the open, flicking it back and forth.

"Come, clever man," the monk said, his face as impassive as carved beechwood. "Enlighten my stupidity."

Rudi grinned to himself and watched the others, rotating his shoulders and listening inwardly for the catch of pain in his right; it was fine . . . so far. Edain and Fred were in a shoving match, their shortswords locked at the guards and their shields tucked into their shoulders.

"Are you two men, or rutting buffalo?" Hao called, apparently not needing to look away from where he stalked in a circle around Odard. "Your aim is to hit your opponent, not to push him over like a dead tree!"

Edain let one leg relax and stabbed low. Fred almost caught it—he'd realized what the Mackenzie was about to do—but momentum drove him forward. The tip of the padded wooden sword struck him in the pit of the stomach; even with the tough rawhide of the practice armor the *thud* made Rudi wince slightly in sympathy, and the young man's brown face went gray behind the bars of the drill helm. He staggered backwards, whooping and desperately trying to cover himself; Edain slid forward, his face blankly intent . . .

"Enough!" Hao said.

The young Mackenzie stopped as if he'd run into an oak tree, shaking his head and blinking.

The staff spun in Hao's hands, and Odard was hopping and cursing and shaking his right hand as his practice sword flew free.

"The sword is not the weapon," Hao said to him. "The *hand* is the weapon; the sword merely extends it. Now you, Raven-man."

Rudi and the teacher bowed courteously to each other and faced off. Hao began turning the staff, hand over hand, the ends of the tough mountain ash blurring faster and faster as they made a figure eight in the air. After a moment he could hear the *whsssst* of cloven air as they moved. The Mackenzie tanist let his consciousness sink into the ground, grow into the air, knew the salt water in his blood and the fire in his nerves. Then he attacked, smooth and swift, aiming for the hands in the center of that blurring circle.

Crack.

The staff struck wood as it battered his sword away, flinging it high and wide; Rudi's eyes went wide even as he whipped his shield around to catch the other end of the six-foot length of wood with a hollow *boom* that jarred all the way into the muscles of his back. Only frantic effort brought his sword up in time to ward off a full attack.

"Think a little, Raven-man! Raw speed is less useful than anticipation. I am older and slower than you, but I block your attacks—by anticipation."

They circled again, blue-green eyes locked on brown. *It's true*, Rudi thought. *He started his block* before *I moved, just a little.*

Then, grimly: *Raven-man he called me, eh? Well, so I am.*

"Morrigú," he whispered. "Black-wing, Red Hag of Battles, be with me now!"

The world fell away from his vision; there was no pouring of something *other* into his self, but instead a focusing until there were only vectors, threats, targets—the ends of the staff, Master Hao's hands and face and feet. And the shadow of wings, bearing him up, and a huge joy in the play of weapon and muscle and nerve. He lunged again, long leg and long arm and long sword outstretched.

Crack.

This time the deflection was minimal, just enough, but the lunge left him overextended. He was moving with delicate precision, but so was Master Hao; the staff struck the wooden sword just forward of his fingers, nearly slamming it out of his hand.

Rudi drew on the certainty that flooded him, and turned the motion of the sword into a backhand slash. The same impulse drove his will forward like a spear's point. A shriek burst past his snarling lips, the Morrigú's own, the screaming that guided the birds of the Crow Goddess to their feasting upon the acorns of the unplowed fields of battle—whose yield was the heads of men. The blow might well have dished in a man's skull, even with the soft padding around the wooden practice weapon.

"Good!" Hao cried, and he was grinning now.

Only a blurring duck and whirl saved him, but more than the battering counterstrike of the staff made Rudi stagger. Then Hao struck again . . . and something struck with him, and the universe seemed to vanish in a blaze of white light. He backed, reeling, sword and shield moving in a desperate dance of defense.

"Good, good! But the hand is not the weapon—the *mind* is the weapon, and the hand only its extension!" Hao called, his words and breath in perfect unison with his motion. "Discipline your mind!"

Rudi did, baring his teeth and *thrusting* with his will. The sense that wood was flailing at him from every direction in a ceaseless cascade of motion died away, and he saw the staff floating towards the touch of his shield and sword, as if he and Hao danced in a dream. Now they were not fighting; they were priests of a ritual, all alone on a mountaintop, beneath a sky where ravens circled a single Eye . . .

A twinge brought him back to common day. He stepped back and looked around; the others were watching him, and blank-faced or wondering. Suddenly he felt a little tired, the good tiredness you felt after a day's work in the harvest fields. Hao looked at Rudi closely, then stepped closer and prodded at his right shoulder with a finger like a section of wrought-iron rod.

"Pain?" he said.

"A bit," Rudi replied—honestly.

"Then stop! Too much is worse than too little! The rest of you, continue."

Rudi sank back on knees and heels, hands resting on his thighs. Ingolf was sparring with the twins; Ritva was using her usual longsword-and-shield, but Mary had one of the local weapons, a length of chain with a ball on one end and a sickle-shape on the other—both wooden for this practice. In real combat, they'd be steel. The two young women spread farther apart than they usually had, too. The man from Wisconsin attacked first, using the twin dao-shetes in the whirling style the monks taught . . .

They're better balanced than shetes usually are, Rudi thought delightedly. *And that will give him an advantage once we've left here; the appearance is so similar . . .*

Ingolf attacked, pushing hard and circling around Mary's blind left side to maximize the disadvantage. Mary was turning her head regularly, and the chain slid out through her fingers to whip around one of the swords . . .

When they'd exhausted the possibilities of the match, Ingolf had been killed eleven times, Mary three, and Ritva only twice.

"You will run back to the monastery," Hao announced.

"You?" Rudi said; the monk usually did everything students did, backwards and carrying heavier weights.

"I will remain and give special instruction to that one," Hao said, pointing at Ingolf. "There is much to learn and he is not a particularly apt student."

Ingolf's ears flushed a little.

"Let's get on with it," he said grimly.

"Time to go," Rudi said a month later. "Although it's been like a dream here. A good dream, of peace and beauty and rest."

Dorje smiled. "Yet in leaving, you need not fear premature aging." At Rudi's bewilderment he added: "Classical reference."

The monastery had given them a tough light two-wheeled cart for their gear, and for the rest they were on horseback, with local ponies to replace the pack-animals and remounts they'd lost to hunger and accident and avalanche in the Tetons. The *Rimpoche* and several of the monastery's dignitaries were with them, and an escort of cavalry in the Oriental-style lamellar armor and flared helmets of the Valley of the Sun.

"You will find the people of the Wind River over the mountains"—Dorje nodded eastward—"friendly for the most part; they and the Shoshone and Arapahoe have been allies. Beyond that I cannot advise you directly; there are forces of the CUT in the Powder River basin, and many of the Ranchers there have submitted. Others still resist."

Rudi nodded, inhaling the scents of water, a sweetness of cut grass that Epona kept heading towards the side of the road to snatch a mouthful of, turned earth, horses sweating just a little in the spring's first really warm weather. The sound of hooves beating slowly on the damp earth of the roadway stirred his blood, but . . .

I'm a little sorry to leave, he thought, turning in the saddle for a moment to look up to the distant peaks of the Tetons, still snow-covered down to the tree line. *It's beautiful here, and I've learned much.*

"It's pretty, but sure and it would be a cruel hard place to farm," Edain said quietly as he rode beside him. "They'll have the spring planting finished by now, back home ... and it's a lot longer to the first frost, there."

May was a season of beauty in this high valley; even the sagebrush looked fresh, and the leaves of the aspen groves were uncurling and trembling in the light breeze. The lakes along the almost-vertical granite wall of the Tetons had finally melted; they reflected the high snow-peaks in stretches of azure blue as pure as the sky, ringed with reeds where snowy herons waded, and strings of yellow goslings followed the Canada geese. Wings were thick above; the meadows were ablaze with bright dandelion and buttercups, yellowbell lilies, bright pink shooting stars, mauve violets and purple lupins.

Ox-teams pulled plows here and there as farmers readied the last of their fields for buckwheat and other crops hardy enough to yield in the short time of warmth, the soil brown and moist behind the steel of the shares. Water chuckled in irrigation ditches; cowboys and shepherdesses alike armed and mounted followed herds of yaks, cattle, sheep and llamas dotted over the green immensity. Many of the houses scattered here and there in sheltered spots had turf roofs as well, and their dense green surfaces were dotted with flowers.

Many of the folk waved to the travelers as they rode past, or made reverence to the abbot of Chenrezi. The monks and the escort stopped where the road began its rise towards Togwotee Pass. The nine travelers dismounted, and so did the abbot and several of his chief followers. Some of them were wearing feathered headdresses like crimson-plumed helmets, and crimson cloaks, but *Rimpoche* Tsewang Dorje had only his usual rather shabby robe, hiked up a bit for riding and showing his skinny knotted calves, and Master Hao was in his usual singlet and loose trousers.

Ignatius bowed to the Buddhist cleric. "My thanks and that of my Order for your hospitality and help," he said. "This valley is indeed a holy place."

Dorje bowed in return. "I can see that you have found a measure of enlightenment here," he said.

For a moment, joy shone from the priest's usually rather impassive face. "High is heaven, and holy," he said. "Mountains have always turned my thoughts towards God."

"And you, my child, seem to have achieved a measure of rest," Dorje said to Mathilda.

She nodded, smiling and making the palms-together gesture of greeting and farewell the monks used.

"It's been nice, being just Mathilda," she said. "And I also thank you for your hospitality—and for your care for our friends who were hurt."

Seriously: "If ever I can do anything for you and yours—"

Dorje made a gesture of mild dismissal. "Hospitality imposes no obligation but its return. We ask nothing for it."

"You can't stop me feeling an obligation, *guru*, or fulfilling it. That's between me and God."

The abbot smiled, the smile that showed every wrinkle and made him look like a boy again. "I shall not seek to dissuade you from doing a virtuous deed," he said.

Then he turned to Ingolf. "We have given you a shield. Your own wounds only you can heal, however."

The Richlander nodded soberly. "I know."

Mary and Ritva were standing at the heads of their dappled Arabs side by side; Mary wore a black eye patch with the trees-and-stars of the Dúnedain embroidered on it. They bowed gravely to him, and he to them. Then he turned to Frederick Thurston.

"You, I think, were nearly of the opinion that justice was nowhere to be found among men save as a lie for fools, and that all was treachery in the pursuit of power," he said to him. "I hope you have learned better here."

Fred nodded soberly. "I wasn't really that bad, but I

could feel the temptation. Thing is, I've seen ... what that can lead to."

"Yes, and to only one place by many roads. But do not fall into an equal and opposite reaction. Though your path lead to a gallows or a throne, if you walk the Middle Way, you need not fear becoming that which you hate."

Then he moved on to Rudi. The Mackenzie extended his hand, and Dorje took it between both of his for a moment. They felt like sandpaper that had been worn very smooth, old and leathery and strong.

"You have been an excellent student ... for a *chiling* with an eccentric theology," he said.

"I regret having to leave so soon," Rudi said. His eyes went to the snowpeaks on the western horizon. "This is a good place for thinking."

"Regret is vain, and leads to attachment, binding us to the Wheel," Dorje said. Then he laughed again. "But I too have regrets. That I will never see the peak of Kanchenjunga again, or smell the wind that blows from the Roof of the World. Yet this is a good place to lay my bones."

Then he turned to them all, and spoke:

"Three men set forth seeking fortune. All three went by the same road. And the one found gold; another came on good land, and he tilled it. But the third saw sunlight making jewels of the dew. Each one thought himself the richer. Farewell. We shall meet again."

Master Hao turned to follow him, then stopped. "And we shall, as well. Some of you showed considerable promise," he added.

His flat voice was harsh as ever, but several of the party blinked. That was more praise than any of them had gotten in their months here. He astonished them even more by smiling slightly as he continued:

"We shall see how you implement what you have learned."

CHAPTER FIFTEEN

Archer, sage and swordsman keen;
Black-clad ones who hear the spirits of the trees
Young prince by kin betrayed
Princess from evil sire redeemed
Traitor's treason betrayed by honor of his own;
He leads them there to meet
Most ancient spirit of the land—

From: *The Song of Bear and Raven*
Attributed to Fiorbhinn Mackenzie, 1st century CY

"But the names you give the gods sound sort of weird," Frederick Thurston said.

They were all sprawled around the fire, eating or just resting before dropping off to sleep. Rudi flipped a well-gnawed rib to Garbh before he answered, and the half-mastiff caught it out of the air with a *clomp* of jaws like tombstones falling together in a quarry on a wet day.

"Well, then, you could call on Them in the forms they took to your ancestors," Rudi said. "*Mine* called on Brigid and Lugh and Ogma and the Morrigan, or at least a lot of them did, before the White Christ came."

Fred laughed. "I'd be sort of lonely, calling on the gods of the . . ." He searched his memory. "Yoruba? Ashanti? In Idaho, at least."

"That's not your only heritage," Rudi answered. "On either the spear or cauldron side. There's the matter of your name, to be sure."

"My name?"

Rudi grinned and leaned back against his saddle. "*Thurston* means *Stone of Thor.* English, I'd say—the Norse would have made it *Thorstein.* Thunor is how the old English said that One's name."

"Dad never said where it came from; we're from Maryland, though, far back. Might have picked it up there."

"And your first name is Anglo-Saxon, too, or German. An Anglo-Saxon being a German who's forgotten he's half Welsh, as the saying goes. It means *Peaceful Ruler.*"

"It does?" Fred said. "Well, I'll be damned. Where could I find out more about that?"

"Larsdalen, for starters," Rudi said, and nodded towards Mary and Ritva, who were combing each other's hair and rebraiding it. "Their mother, Signe Havel, is a priestess of that tradition—a *gythja*, a godwoman; she studied first with my mother, but took things in a different direction."

"Mom never could stand not being number one," Mary said. Then: "Not that she doesn't *mean* it, you know."

Edain Aylward Mackenzie had been silent during the talk of gods. Now he spoke:

"Someone's coming," he said

He jerked a thumb over his shoulder into the night, then licked his fingers and belched slightly. Rudi slid down and pressed an ear to the ground; Ritva and Mary rose, donned their war cloaks, and ghosted into the darkness.

"That's interesting," Fred replied, elaborately casual, and cut another slice off the buffalo hump. To himself he wondered: *How did he . . . hey, it's the dog. Not fair!*

He kept chewing. Bison weren't common in western Idaho, where he'd lived all his life until recently. It was the best meat he'd ever tasted, flavorful, meltingly tender—you could eat it like candy. The contrast with the flat wheat griddlecakes wasn't too great if they were fresh and warm, though.

He finished and stood, making sure his saber was loose in the scabbard. Edain came to his feet as well and strung his longbow. Then he rested his hand soothingly on Garbh's head where she pointed her nose northward into the darkness.

Fred looked over to where Rudi was lounging on his bedroll. The Mackenzie nodded slightly, and the young man from Boise raised his voice:

"You're welcome to share our fire."

There was silence from beyond the reach of the light, but that wasn't very far; the tough greasewood stems had sunk to a low reddish glow in the pit they'd dug through the thick prairie sod. The meat rested on a spit above the embers, with fat making them spit and flare now and then as it dripped from the flesh or out of the spray of fine bones. The smell of it and the wheatcakes and the pot of beans drifted into the prairie summer night, beneath the huge fresh scent of the grasslands. A kettle of chicory stood on three rocks, keeping warm enough for a slight plume of acrid vapor.

There was a moment of intense silence; the wind had died, and the moon was down, and only the stamp of a hobbled horse broke the quiet beneath the great dome of stars. Traveling the plains was a great way of making you realize how *big* this land was. They'd only covered a quarter of it, and it was more than half a year since he'd left . . .

Maybe Dad was wrong. Maybe it's just too big *to be all one country again. Meanwhile, let's keep our attention on whoever-the-hell this is . . .*

Fred went on:

"And in case you were wondering, there are two of us in back of you by now. Even if you're moving on, show yourself. And we'd be happier about it if you came in slow. Less chance of someone's fingers slipping off a bowstring that way."

"I'm coming in!" a voice called sharply. "I'm peaceable!"

Fred's eyebrows went up. That was a woman's voice; tight with control, and hoarse with strain and tiredness as well. Rudi sat upright, looking casual and relaxed to anyone who didn't know how fast he could move; he'd been pressing his ear against the ground.

"Only one horse anywhere near," he said quietly. "That's a good trick, Ingolf."

"Only works well when the dirt's dry and hard," Ingolf replied. "I learned it from a Pawnee scout when we were fighting the Sioux."

The slow clop of hoofbeats became audible. Then the slight jingle of spurs; the rider was walking and leading her horse. Fifty yards away the figure became vaguely discernible; the bright starlight was enough to show it was wearing a wide-brimmed hat. And to show the violent start as the twins rose like sections of the grass itself in their war cloaks. Starlight caught on the heads of the arrows ready on their bows.

"I said I'm peaceable-like, dammit!" the stranger said, in a strong range-country accent.

It was stronger and harsher than Fred's own; he'd grown up in Boise, which had never stopped being a city even when it shrank drastically. Out here where the largest settlements were generally a ranch home-place, speech had drifted faster and farther from the old world's standards.

"That's nice," Ritva replied. "A lot of people who might be dreadfully bitchy otherwise are peaceable with an arrow pointed at their briskets."

The stranger peered at her, and apparently found what she saw behind the arrowhead reassuring—which showed she was either overconfident or more perceptive than the usual run. She came on, looking around their camp as she approached. The two mules that pulled the cart were hobbled, dim shapes grazing not too far away; so were a dozen of the horses. The other nine were tethered to a picket line much closer, where they could be saddled quickly in an emergency; a heap of cut grass lay in front of them. Epona was neither hobbled nor tethered; she raised her muzzle from a doze at the scent of the stranger's gelding, snorted, and shut her eyes again.

There wasn't much else, except the sleeping bags

and saddles arranged around the firepit, though Fred noticed how the fire underlit everyone's faces, making them look a bit sinister . . .

And if I were a lone woman coming in out of the dark, I'd be a bit cautious, he thought, and tossed on a few more sticks.

The stranger dropped her reins and the horse stood; that might be good training, or it might just be exhausted.

Both, the young man thought.

It looked like a good horse that had been ridden too far and too fast, and there were silver studs on the bridle and breast-collar and saddle, and on the big tooled leather tapaderos that covered the stirrups. The silver was tarnished, or rubbed with mud, and the rest of the gear—coiled leather lariat, cased recurve bow and small round shield, checked shirt, leather breeches, boots, chaps, a quiver of arrows over her back on a bandolier—also looked good but hard-used. She had a shete and a bowie knife at her broad belt and a pair of soft leather gauntlets tucked through it; the buckle was worked steel, in the shape of a coyote's head.

The woman . . .

No, it's a girl. She's not thirty, the way I thought at first glance, Fred decided. *She's about my age or a little less, just dirty and dusty and falling-down tired.*

. . . looked around the circle of faces; Ignatius was out on watch, and the stranger's glance flicked at the twins and Mathilda for a moment longer. Which was logical; women along and armed made it less likely they were a bandit gang, slavers, or others of dubious character. Not impossible, but less likely.

She sighed and relaxed a little, tapping the wide felt hat against her chaps. Her face was narrow and straight-nosed beneath the trail dirt, and her hair was bound back in a single braid; it looked to be brown, perhaps with a hint of auburn, and her eyes were blue when the firelight flared a bit. He judged that her height would be about halfway between the twins and Mathilda; five-eight and a bit.

"Well, you're not Cutters, at least," she said after a second. "Nor friends of theirs."

"Emphatically unfriends of theirs, miss," Rudi said, standing. She blinked up at the height of him, noticed the kilt, and then looked over at Edain, a bit startled. "Still and all, are they on your trail? Your company is pleasant; theirs wouldn't be at all, at all."

"They were, but I lost them two days ago, I'm pretty sure." She took a deep breath. "Kane is my name, Virginia Kane, of . . . of nowhere in particular."

She seemed to relax a little further when nobody recognized her name. Rudi introduced himself, and then the others. Fred gestured at the fire.

"Help yourself. And there's water, a good seep in the slough over there for your horse. Barrel's full and we purified it."

"Yeah, my horse smelled the slough a couple of miles back," she said. "We're pretty dry."

She stopped to let Garbh smell her hand, watered and unsaddled her horse, rubbing it down and hobbling it before washing her hands and face in a little of the water and drinking cup after cup from the barrel on the cart. Then she dropped her saddle and bedroll in an empty spot, and came over to crouch by the fire. Her hands shook very slightly as she spooned beans onto a tin plate from her kit and cut meat from the hump with a clasp knife. Fred noted with interest that the little knife had been honed to a wire edge, and that she used it with a pulling stroke that showed experience. She piled the slices onto a couple of flat wheatcakes and wrapped them to make tubular sandwiches.

Despite that tremor of eagerness she didn't gobble, although she ate with concentrated intensity for a good fifteen minutes; she wasn't gaunt, so it had probably been only the past few days that she'd been missing meals. Fred judged she'd been well fed before that, but active—she had the lean hard look of it, though with enough in breast and hip to please a man's eye. When she'd finished she rolled a cigarette and poured a cup of the chicory.

Look at the hands, he thought—his father had told him that was the best quick way to read someone. *They're not soft, but they're not a working ranch-hand's either, or a servant girl's. Not enough battering, and that dirt's not ground into her knuckles and pores. And her fingernails are well trimmed. Plus tobacco is expensive.*

"Thank you kindly," she said.

Odard was lying against his saddle, idly strumming at his lute. He didn't look up from the instrument as he said:

"Left home in a hurry, *demoiselle*? Anyone after you that we should know about? Someone who might just kill any company you'd picked up . . . us, for instance?"

Her hand moved towards the hilt of her shete; then she unbuckled the weapons belt and set it aside slightly—though Fred noticed she didn't put it so far away that she couldn't draw the steel quickly.

"My . . . ranch that I was living on got taken over by the CUT," she said carefully. "By a couple of neighbors who'd gone over to the Cutters, at least; and there were Cutter troops around to back them up, a new bunch, not just their levies—Sword of the Prophet, regulars out of Corwin. I had to clear out fast; the Cutters don't live like human beings, if you ask me, and it's worse for a woman. That was in the Powder River country, north of Sheridan."

That didn't mean anything to most of them. Ingolf whistled softly. "That's a long way to come on one horse, miss," he said.

Virginia looked at him; her eyes narrowed slightly, noting the difference in accent between him and the others who'd spoken. His Wisconsin rasp wasn't much like her twang, but it was a lot closer than Rudi's lilt or the archaic Portlander dialect or the way Sindarin influenced the way the twins sounded.

"I had a remuda," she said. "But they were after me. I had to push my horses hard, and leave a couple that foundered or went lame."

"And are you heading anywhere in particular?" Rudi said.

She looked at him, visibly considered, and said with a trace of bitterness:

"Mister, it's more a matter of headin' away from anywhere those maniacs is likely to go."

Then she yawned; her head drooped, until she pulled it up with a jerk.

"You can put your bedroll over here on the girls' side," Mathilda said. "And tell us more about it in the morning."

> "... Guide me and guard me this day and all days
> By Your grace, with harm to none,
> Blesséd be!"

Rudi lowered his arms as the disk of the sun cleared the eastern horizon. The plain there was nearly featureless, though it was rising ground and rolled very slightly more than the flatness behind them. Even a slight roll here was deceptive, making you think you could see farther than you could. Was that the slightest trace of blue irregularity on the northeast the Black Hills, or was knowledge born of maps fooling him?

Hard to tell, he thought. *It's tricky to measure distance here by eye. And who knew the sky could be so ... big?*

Dawn and evening were the best hours on the plains, he'd found; for a few long moments it was a mystery of brown and green and blue, of long shadows and enormous distance. The morning was cool, and for an instant there had been dew on the grass, but the great cloudless dome of blue all around them augured for a warm day. Grass ran in rippling calf-high waves to the edge of sight, still green in early June, with only the occasional big sage or white-blossomed yucca bush, but with a thick scattering of flowers yellow and pink and blue. A herd of pronghorns flowed past in the middle distance; prairie dogs whistled from a town whose little conical hillocks scattered the land ahead, and then they dove for cover as a golden eagle soared by on seven-foot wings, its shadow flowing ahead of it.

"Ah, you guys aren't from around here, are you?" Virginia said carefully.

Rudi turned from where he and his sisters and Edain had been making their morning prayer; Fred Thurston had joined in. A bit to his surprise, Ingolf had joined them too, standing beside Mary, though he hadn't actually recited the Salute to the Sun with them.

"No, we're from the Far West," he said. "Except Ingolf here, and he's been all the way West to our home."

Ignatius was looking a little unhappy about Ingolf, but too polite to say anything in public, and he was sticking close to Mathilda anyway—since Yule, he'd been like a goose with one gosling around her. Odard was with them, of course; *he'd* been getting more pious lately.

"You mean from that valley near the Tetons, over past the Wind River country, where they've got the funny religion and all the weird fighting tricks?"

"We passed through there," Rudi said, grinning. "But we're from farther away than that, and *our* religion is even funnier than theirs!"

The ranch-woman went on, still carefully: "Yeah, the skirts look . . . a little strange. No offense."

"We're from Oregon," Edain amplified. "And these aren't skirts, they're *kilts*. We're Mackenzies—everyone wears them in our clan."

She smiled at him, revealing even white teeth. "Except the women?" she said, nodding at Mary and Ritva, and Mathilda, all of whom were in pants.

"We're Dúnedain, not Mackenzies," Ritva said. "We wear pants, or robes. All the Mackenzies wear kilts . . . well, the older women wear arsaids, sometimes. Mathilda there's a Portlander Associate—women where she comes from wear skirts all the time, except her, she gets a special break. And Father Ignatius is—"

"A Roman priest, yeah," she said, inclining her head politely to him; he had his Benedictine robe on over the rest of his clothes. "Some of us are . . . were . . . Catholic. I'm a Baptist, myself, more or less."

Fred Thurston came over to Rudi as she went to gather her gear.

"She's some Rancher's daughter," he said quietly, his face serious. "An important Rancher; probably a Sheriff."

Rudi suppressed a smile. "It's a bit obvious, isn't it? She hasn't the manner of an underling."

"Or the gear of one," Fred said. "That's expensive horse harness—not just the silver, the workmanship—but it's her working tack, not something kept for special occasions. It's a good horse, too. People like that have a hard time disappearing." A grin: "I did!"

Rudi nodded. "Which means that she might be worth the trouble of pursuing, and draw enemies on us," he said thoughtfully. "Hmmm. See if you can draw her out."

The son of Boise's first ruler went over to get his cold meat and beans. Breakfast was leftovers from last night; buffalo hump was so succulent that it still tasted good cold, and the flatbread was only a little stale. Garbh gnawed on some ribs, delighted to get them raw and with all the meat still attached.

"I'm from Idaho, myself," Fred said in friendly fashion.

She gave him a long considering look. At least she wasn't acting like he was a kid; even as the President's son girls his own age had tended to treat him that way, when they weren't obviously trying to get to his dad through him.

It's a bit of a relief to be just another guy, he thought.

"Boise?" she said.

"Yeah."

Her eyes narrowed. "We heard some rumor that they've thrown in with the Cutters."

"Some of them have," he said bleakly. "That's . . . a lot of the reason why I left."

Her smile was broad and genuine. "Hell, this outfit here might as well have WHS for its brand, for *We Hate Sethaz*! I wouldn't mind slapping that iron on a maverick. Or a Cutter's butt."

When they'd finished breakfast he tossed the remains of the hump to Garbh. They still had most of the young yearling they'd killed two days ago, but it wouldn't last long in this weather unless they made a drying rack; nine people could eat a deer down to the bones and hooves easily enough before it spoiled, but not a yearling bull buffalo dressed out at six hundred pounds of meat.

Rudi looked after them as Fred took her to look at the remounts, talking animatedly; he smiled tolerantly. The girl was pretty—in a strong-boned, strong-willed way—and they were both young.

Her own horse obviously needed a few days' rest at least. Rudi was wondering whether it would be worthwhile to stop and jerk some of the buffalo—he hated the thought of waste, though of course the buzzards and coyotes had to eat too—when Ingolf came riding in from his early-morning circuit.

"Visitors," he said, and gave Virginia a hard look.

"What direction?" Rudi said. "How many?"

"At least twenty, from the sound, you betcha. From the east."

"Well, boggarts bugger us and the Dagda club me dead," Rudi said in annoyance, controlling a prickle of alarm; that was where they were headed. "Backtracking would be . . . risky."

Everyone looked at Virginia Kane. She'd *said* she'd lost her pursuers, and there had been no sign of any until now, but . . .

"She came in from the west," Fred pointed out. "Not from the east."

Virginia nodded. "Cutters wouldn't loop around through the Lakota country, I don't think. You're already over the Seven Council Fires border. The Cutters are crazy but not crazy-stupid."

"Gear up, everyone!" Rudi said. "Mistress Kane, put your saddle on one of our remounts—your horse isn't going to be fit for much anytime soon."

It was twenty-two riders, when they could see the approaching party. They were spread out over a fair stretch of the grassland, taking their time to swing around the prairie-dog town and drawing in at long bowshot away from the nine—now ten—travelers. Two of them rode on, coming closer with arrogant confidence.

The which they're entitled, since they outnumber us nearly three to one and this is their land, Rudi thought.

Back home, there was usually somewhere to take cover, and you could place yourself by a swift glance at the mountains.

Here . . . *And it's like a bug on a plate I feel, hereabouts. Waiting for the fork to come down . . .*

"Sioux, all right," Ingolf said out of the corner of his mouth. "Don't put their backs up—but don't let them think they can push you around, either."

"*This* porridge is just right, as the ill-mannered girl said when she wandered into Father Bear's house," Rudi said quietly back; he kept his hands carefully free of his weapons, but his skin prickled with an awareness of where they were.

The two men pulled up halfway between the parties. Rudi and Ingolf walked their horses out to meet them; when they were in speaking distance he raised his hand palm out.

"*Háu kola,*" he said, and used one of the phrases of greeting Ingolf had taught him. "*Lay he hun nee kay washte.*"

"Yeah," one of them replied, the older of the pair. His tone was as pawky as his words. "And the top of the beautiful fucking morning to you, too, kilt-boy."

Both the Sioux riders were in fringed buckskin trousers, beautifully tanned and supple; their hair was parted in the center and hung to either side in braids wrapped with leather thongs. The younger wore nothing else save pants, boots, the skin of a kit fox around his neck and a feather in his brown hair with a red dot on it. He carried an odd-looking standard, with a curve a bit like a shepherd's crook on the end, lined with eagle feathers; the red flag attached to it had a device of seven white tipis grouped in a circle.

The other wore a long buckskin tunic as well, dyed yellow above and red below, with beads and quillwork and bone tubes in rows on the chest, and a steel cap that mounted a headdress of bison hair and horns. Both had bows in their hands, shetes at their belts, lariats and shields slung at their saddlebows. The man in the steel cap was in his forties and darker than his follower, with a few strands of gray in his raven black hair and lines in his big-nosed, high-cheeked brown face. He had a pair of binoculars in a case as well.

All the men behind them were well armed; a few had short lances as well as bows and blades, or stone-headed war clubs; all the ones Rudi could see were young but in their full strength, and looked wiry tough. Several wore leather breastplates, probably tough bison hide, one had a mail-shirt, and all of them had light helmets at their saddlebows. Many had battle scars as well, sometimes proudly picked out with red paint. He *hoped* the tufts of hair on the lances and shields were just tufts of hair— horse hair, for example, or buffalo.

And not hair *hair.*

A herd of remounts followed them, with a few near-naked youths in breechclouts riding about to keep them bunched. The herdsmen were mounted bareback, but the grown warriors had good Western-style saddles.

"We're just passing through," the Mackenzie said.

The older Indian's eyes went to the buffalo-hide pegged on the side of the wagon to dry, and to the quartered carcass hanging from the rear of it.

"Passing through, eating our *tatonka*," he said. "You know, we're sort of sensitive about armed white-eyes coming on to our land without permission, making themselves at home and killing our buffalo. Call it an ethnic quirk."

Rudi spread his hands over his saddlehorn in a peaceable gesture, and smiled.

"We didn't know it was a herd beast," he said.

"It's *not* a herd beast," the Indian said—Rudi noted uneasily that he hadn't introduced himself yet, either, or used any formula of hospitality. "We *herd* cattle and horses and sheep and llamas, not buffalo and pronghorn and elk and deer. Those are game, and all the game on the Lakota nation's land belongs to us and our brothers of the Seven Council Fires."

"There seemed to be quite a few of the buffalo. We're ready to pay for it, sure, and you can have the hide and the meat if you'd rather."

"Thanks a lot for offering to give us back our own," the Indian leader said. "Last time round, we said: *Sure, it can't hurt, there's a lot of buffalo and water and grass, let 'em take a little now and then when they're passing through . . .*"

He paused for effect and held up a mock-admonishing finger: "And that turned out to be a *very bad mistake*. Fool me once, shame on you. Fool me twice, shame on me."

He looked at them, carefully scanning each individual; all the travelers had their fighting gear on. The Portlanders hadn't brought the latest articulated plate suits because they were too difficult to get into without a squire to assist, but Odard and Mathilda and Ignatius all had full knee-length hauberks with greaves and vambraces and kite-shaped shields, twelve-foot lances in their hands with the butts resting on the stirrup-irons. They'd even had time to put the barding on their destriers; Rudi hadn't bothered with Epona, calculating that the extra weight would be more burden than it was worth out here where a horse had room to run as far as its legs would take it.

The Indian finished the once-over and went on: "So unless you're looking for a fight, why don't you just turn around and go right back the way you came?"

"Well, we'd be seriously inconvenienced if we did," Rudi said. "First, because we're heading for the Far East. Next and more important, because the Cutters would kill us all if they caught us, do you see, and there are so wretchedly many of them in that direction"—he pointed westward over his shoulder—"the pity and the black sorrow of it, ochone, ochone."

The younger man grunted, and the older's black eyes narrowed.

"We're at peace with the Church Universal and Triumphant," he said. "And we're not supposed to take in refugees from their territory."

But he said it as if the words made his mouth hurt. His companion grunted again and spat on the grass, then unexpectedly spoke:

"We're not supposed to harm their missionaries, either. But it's funny how many of them fall off their horses and break their necks or get run down by stampeding herds."

Hooves sounded behind Rudi. He looked over his shoulder and swore silently; Virginia Kane was pushing her borrowed mount up beside him, and herself into a negotiation that wasn't going so well. She raised her hand in the greeting gesture and spoke herself:

"*Wacantoognaka,*" she said unexpectedly. "*Oun she la yea.*"

The Indian's eyes went wide. "Virginia? Christ, you've grown!" he blurted.

"I remember you, *lekší Whapa Sa,* even if I'm a woman now."

"What about Dave?"

"My father's dead," she said shortly. "The Cutters killed him. It was supposed to be outlaws . . . but I never thought they'd stand by the terms of the peace treaty. And they weren't going to let *me* inherit!"

"Damn. He was a good man. Yeah, of course *you* can have sanctuary. Dave Kane was my blood-brother, and we don't forget."

"And for these people too; they took me in and fed me without asking anything for it just because the Cutters were after me."

The man studied her face. "Yeah, I'll stretch it that far. Sorry, *tonjan*—you're welcome in our camps anytime, but I know it's hard."

"I'm just glad Mom didn't live to see the Cutters take over Skywater."

He sighed and said a phrase that Rudi hadn't heard before and couldn't even render into syllables in his mind without repetition. The swift-rising, slow-falling sounds of Lakota were pleasant, but the strangeness to an English-speaking ear made Gaelic sound like a first cousin.

Our lady guest must have learned some of it early, he thought.

Virginia relaxed slightly; she didn't have any trouble

following it. "Thank you for accepting my friends as guests, Uncle Red Leaf," she said formally.

The Sioux leader nodded to her, edged his horse closer and extended a hand to Rudi.

"John Red Leaf, Kiyuska *tiyospaye* of the Ogallala and the Lakota *tunwan*," he said resignedly as they shook, then smiled. "Also BS in Range Science from SDSU, class of 1998. This is my son, Rick Mat'o Yamni—Rick Three Bears. Welcome to our land, oh sacred guests, yada yada yada."

Three Bears looked faintly scandalized, at a guess because of his father's irreverence, but shook hands as well. The Mackenzie clansman sympathized; he'd had the same experience with people who'd grown up before the Change. Sometimes they had no idea of what to take *seriously.*

"Rudi Mackenzie, tanist of the Clan Mackenzie," Rudi said politely. "My sept is Raven. Many thanks for your hospitality. We're from Oregon. Well, most of us."

"Ingolf Vogeler, of nowhere in particular," Ingolf said.

Virginia looked at the warriors behind Red Leaf. "Kit Foxes, Uncle John?"

"Yeah, I'm *akicita* chief right now. We're out patrolling the border."

"I . . ." She looked at Rudi, and winced slightly.

She's going to be franker with her uncle John than she was with us, Rudi decided. He smiled and inclined his head to her. *And I wouldn't be blaming you,* moi glic caileag.

"I *think* I lost the ones who were after me. Vince Rickover decided right at Dad's funeral that it was time I had *protection* . . ."

Red Leaf nodded. "Figures. Wants to marry you to get the land, right?"

She nodded. "But there was a unit of the Sword at his place, the Bar Q—they were what gave him the nerve to move on us. My people would have fought, and we could handle the Bar Q easy enough, but trying to fight Corwin would just get them and their families killed, so

I took some horses and ran for it. I *think* I lost them, but . . ."

"But we'd better push it hard," Red Leaf said. "The damned Cutters' idea of a peace treaty is that it means whatever suits them from moment to moment—which is sort of unpleasantly familiar, though at least they didn't promise to leave us alone while the sun shone and the grass grew."

Pushing it involved turning and riding a little north of east without losing any time about it, which was the way Rudi's band had been going; the pace was a lot harder, though. The Mackenzie didn't object.

If the people with the local knowledge think it best, it's best, he thought. *Especially as this Red Leaf has survived all the time since the Change.*

As he thought, the Sioux leader spoke: "So, Rudi Mackenzie, are you guys refugees, traders, or what?"

Rudi thought for a moment. "What," he said. "Very much *what*."

"Oh, crap," John Red Leaf said four hours of walk-trot-canter-trot-walk later. The Sioux pointed to a circle of vultures in the sky ahead. *"Again."*

He flung up his hand. The Lakota and Rudi's party had been riding along more or less in a loose clump, shifting as people wanted to talk; now they came to a halt, with the loudest sound the endless *sshhhh* of the wind through the ankle-high green grass. Virginia, he noted, had been accepted by the warriors as if she were everyone's younger sister, chaffing with them—in English and in scraps of the older tongue, which she spoke as well as anyone in this band, Red Leaf included. These folk seemed to use it about the way Mackenzies did Gaelic, which was to say mostly for emphasis and the odd word for flavor, but rather more so since there were quite a few actual speakers.

It's an odd language they'll be speaking in a few generations, he thought.

The prairie rose and fell, rose and fell in long swales; it was hot now, enough to make Rudi unpin his plaid and fold it into a saddlebag, and it leached out the land until everything looked like a green-brown vacancy, with only the occasional sagebrush for visual relief.

"You know what that is they're circling?" Rudi said, cocking an eye at the buzzards.

"I've got a strong suspicion. Same as last week . . . oh, well, we can water there."

"And my folk can change out of their armor, so they could,"

"Yeah, it looks heavy," Red Leaf said. "Sort of inconvenient, having to stop and get in and out of it, I'd say. With our gear you can be ready to fight anytime."

"It is a bit of a nuisance, I'll grant. But worth it in a stand-up fight, the which is more common where we come from."

The Indian nodded. "I can see that. Less room to run and dodge out on the West Coast."

The whole group proceeded cautiously. More buzzards rose from the ground as they crested the low rise. The two buffalo ahead were very dead, mostly eaten and buzzing with flies; from the smell it had been a couple of days ago. The bones and heads lay near the edge of the muddy little stream—it would dry up later in the summer, but for now it still held a slow trickle between banks of grass thicker and greener than that on the uplands to either side, with a few cottonwoods just coming into leaf. It also made the ground soft enough to hold prints; you could see clearly where the ambushers had pounced from the cover of a clump of rabbitbrush, and the splashing, thrashing fight it had been until two young bulls were brought down.

Epona danced a little nervously until Rudi ran a soothing hand down her neck. He swung to the ground, looped up the reins from her hackamore, and turned her loose; the big black mare mooched a few yards upstream and dipped her muzzle into the muddy water, being naturally too intelligent to drink down current from a body. He looked at the ground more closely, and caught a faint rank odor, like a neglected catbox. The killers had been messy feeders, too, even before the birds and coyotes had gotten to work. Several of the broad-winged scavengers were circling resentfully overhead, waiting for the irritating humans to go away and let them get back to serious eating.

Even in the midst of his annoyance, Red Leaf gave Epona an admiring glance.

Sure, and she's a better introduction than a friendly dog, Rudi thought.

Red Leaf dismounted in turn, and handed his horse over to one of the teenagers in breechclouts; the Sioux war-party had little apparent discipline, but organization seemed to appear like mushrooms after rain when they needed it. From what he and Virginia had said, the Kit Foxes were a brotherhood devoted to defending the tribal borders, and also a social club that organized everything from dances to marriages and acted as a police force besides.

"I'd say that's a tiger's prints," Rudi said, squatting for a moment and tracing the great plate-broad pugmarks with a finger. "But you don't have tigers hereabouts, I'm thinking. And there's at least four different animals, and tigers don't hunt in packs."

"No," Red Leaf replied. "We've got plenty of lobos these days, some grizzlies just lately, but no tigers. We *do* get goddamned *lions*, of all the crazy things, the past few years. They follow the buffalo north from Texas and New Mexico when the snow melts; now I hear some of them are wintering in the Black Hills. They breed like rabbits; only rabbits don't have fangs and claws and four hundred pounds of attitude."

"It doesn't look as if they'll take more than you can afford," Rudi said.

There was a herd of several dozen bison not half a mile away, a bachelor herd of bulls cropping at the new grass, and shedding their winter coats. That made them look tattered, but they were plump and healthy. He could see pronghorns from here as well, and some horses that were probably mustangs, and elk, mule deer, cattle that were probably also at least half-feral. When the travelers startled waterfowl out of the little stream, their wings had made a momentary thunder.

This was a spare land compared to the Willamette, but next to some of the deserts Rudi had crossed since he came east of the Cascades it swarmed with life.

Red Leaf glared at him. "It's the principle of the thing!" he said. "And they go for horses and stock as well. People too, if they get a chance, probably."

This Red Leaf was well named; he could use some time in Chenrezi Monastery, Rudi thought. *He's a frustrated man, and lets that make him angry. Or to be sure, a spell with Aunt Judy...*

"Sure, and it's not *my* fault," he pointed out.

"You white-eyes were always importing things. Starlings and tumbleweeds were bad enough, but *lions*?"

Rudi chuckled. "You could scarcely expect the ones running those ... what were they called, Father? Seifert Parks?"

Ignatius came up, telling his beads with his left hand and looking around with the mild intelligent pleasure he showed at any new thing.

"Safari Parks, I think, Rudi. Those are lion prints? Fascinating! There's an empty ecological niche here for an open-country predator that can take down full-grown bison, I suppose, since the extinction of the American lion ten thousand years ago. They must be gradually adapting to the colder climate."

"... those *Safari Parks* to know the Change was coming," Rudi pointed out.

"My Order's information is that dozens of species have naturalized themselves and are spreading rapidly—giraffe, camels, ostrich, emu, baboons, rhino of both varieties, eland ... no elephants, alas. And of course tigers over much of the continent—"

Immigrants all around. And speaking of white-eyes ... the Mackenzie thought.

He cocked an eye at Red Leaf's followers as they attended to watering their horses and the remount-herd. About a quarter of them looked much like their leader;

broad square strong-jawed faces, narrow-eyed, high-cheeked and big-nosed, with ruddy-brown complexions. A third wouldn't have suggested Indian at all as far as appearances went, if it weren't for the braids and feathers and fringes—there were several blonds and one tall, skinny narrow-faced young man with milk-white freckled skin and hair the color of new copper, come to that. The rest were every variety in between.

And Red Leaf's son Three Bears looked suspiciously lighter than his father, too. Folk had moved about a good deal almost everywhere after the Change, settled where they could and mated as inclination and necessity dictated, with little time or attention at first to spare for the old world's notions of who was what.

The which it would probably not be tactful to mention, he thought. *Sure, and there are enough Mackenzies who have similar delusions about being the ancient Gaels themselves. In the long run, believing makes things like that near-as-no-matter true.*

"And I'm part-Indian myself," he added. "One-eighth, to be precise about it; one-quarter, for my father."

Red Leaf snorted. "Cherokee, I suppose? Damn bunch of mutts."

"No, Anishinabe. Ojibwa," Rudi amplified, before he caught Ingolf's covert shushing motion.

A ringing silence fell. Red Leaf said: "You ever wonder why we're called *Sioux* by the *wašicun* . . . you guys . . . oh sacred guest?"

"No," Rudi said politely. "I know that you call yourselves Lakota. It means *friends* or *allies,* doesn't it?"

"Yeah; because we're the only friends we've got. *Nadewisou* is what the Anishinabe called our ancestors—Sioux is what the English made of the French try at saying the Ojibwa word. Like what we called telephone tag, when I was a kid, only through three languages."

"Ah, now, isn't that curious, and it's always good to learn new things. What did the word itself mean?"

"*Nadewisou?* It means . . . oh, something like *treacherous little rattlesnakes.* It's not a compliment. We weren't so fond of them either."

"Ah, well, I won't be usin' it, then," Rudi said cheerfully.

Red Leaf laughed, a little unwillingly. "You don't faze easy, do you, Rudi Mackenzie?"

"Not so that you'd notice, John Red Leaf," Rudi said. "There's no point in it, as far as I can see."

When they were out of quiet-conversational range of any of the others, he went on:

"Who's Virginia Kane?"

Red Leaf sighed and reached into a pouch and rolled himself a cigarette; when he'd flicked his lighter he passed the smouldering twist to Rudi, who hid a smile at the thought of the last time he'd shared tobacco with anyone—if it counted when you were dreaming, and the other party was a god. He took a puff, coughed slightly, and handed it back.

"She's Dave Kane's daughter," Red Leaf said, and looked sideways at Rudi's face. "Big wheel in the Powder River Ranchers' Organization, the PRRO—"

He pronounced it *pee-double-r-oh*.

"—and he and *his* father helped us a lot right after the Change—helped us get going, and brought his men to fight on our side when some folks decided that land was just plumb wasted on Injuns, and we backed him up a couple of times when the PRRO's politics got dirty. Or bloody."

"And it's the truth a man should stand ready to fight for his friends," Rudi acknowledged. "And stand between their friends' families and their enemies, if it's needful."

Red Leaf nodded. "There was a rumor he was part Lakota, but I don't know if that's true; he was a good friend for certain, but a bad man to cross. Anyway, after that we were tight with him and the PRRO—the Southern Lakota at least; we visited back and forth, did some trading, that sort of thing. And that kept this part of the country fairly peaceful, which was damned useful when we were fighting the States . . . the Midwesterners. We got a little overambitious in that direction back when things were still up in the air, thought we could take over our old stamping grounds in the Red River country since

Wakantanka had given the white-eyes the grandmother of all wedgies."

"It didn't work, I presume?" Rudi said.

I know it didn't because Ingolf fought in that war, the which I will not mention either. It's a diplomat I'm becoming, or a shameless equivocator, if there's a difference.

"Nah, too many Norski farm-boys with pikes and Swedes with axes in the way. Even with all the, ah, volunteers from here and there we had joining up with us back about then, they outnumbered us bad. We *should* have gone after the Cutters while they were still small potatoes, but that's my perfect hindsight talking. They weren't a problem then and who wanted western goddamned Montana anyway? Only a Cutter or a Crow would take it on a bet."

"And so Virginia has a claim on you because of her kin?"

Red Leaf looked unhappy. "Yeah, but that's not what's activating my ulcers."

"What is, then?"

"Now that Kane finally got chopped by the Cutters, it means everything but the southern fringe of the Powder River country will be under Corwin's thumb. We were fighting them ourselves until about a year ago, up north of the Black Hills in what used to be Montana—frankly, we got beat, though we hurt 'em bad; we offered the Kanes sanctuary as part of the deal at the end of the war, but they were just too damned stubborn. Now the Prophet's boys might start in on us again if we shelter her ... but we *can't* turn her over. It wouldn't be right. How'd she end up with you?"

"Rode in last night, hungry and dry and about to keel over, and her horse in worse shape than that," Rudi said. "All we did was give her a meal—of your *tatonka*—and a place by our fire. And just as a matter of interest, the Cutters are fighting in the Far West right now, and might be a little shy of starting up their war with you, so."

I seem to be developing into a collector of disinherited princes, just as Ignatius warned me, Rudi thought whimsically; underneath that was a slight chill. *Well, the*

Rimpoche warned me that I'd be collecting friends and *enemies the way a dog does fleas in summertime.*

"This is above my pay grade . . ." Red Leaf said.

What does that mean? Rudi thought. *Is that a Sioux saying?*

"Above my level of responsibility, I mean. I'd better—"

"*Ky-ee-ky!*"

The Indian's head snapped around. One of his scouts came galloping in from the westward, waving his bow over his head. He drew rein beside the chief and gabbled details.

The Sioux boiled into motion, tightening girths and checking weapons. After a moment, Rudi's band did likewise.

"*Hokahe!*" Red Leaf shouted. "*Let's go!*"

CHAPTER SIXTEEN

From sunset to sunrise in flight
The Gods are hammering out
The hero from the man—

From: *The Song of Bear and Raven*
Attributed to Fiorbhinn Mackenzie, 1st century CY

"Damn," Red Leaf said. "They outnumber us by quite a bit."

The Sioux and their guests had stopped at the top of a rise. The pursuers had halted a mile and a half farther back, near the little stream, and they were watering their horses. Rudi leveled his own binoculars and rough-counted, being careful to distinguish between warriors and remounts. He pursed his lips thoughtfully.

"Eighty or ninety," he said. "Twenty of them are Sword of the Prophet, from their gear. The others are cowboys."

"Yeah, locals from the Powder River spreads that've gone over to the CUT. Three-to-one all up, bad odds. And they wouldn't have come this far onto our territory if they weren't ready to fight. I'm really worried about the Sword; I've run into them before. Those guys are nuts. They *want* to die for the Prophet, and they like killing for him even better, and they won't give up for shit—we learned that in the war we just had."

"You're not telling me anything new, so," Rudi said dryly. "I think I recognize their commander and he's been chasing me since last Lughnasadh, or nearly, and over better than a thousand miles of rough country . . ."

"Lughnasadh?"

"The summer harvest festival. Call it a little less than a year. Any chance of reinforcements from your folk?"

"Not much, but let's do what we can. No point in keeping all the remounts . . ."

He shouted. "Hey, Wolf Paws, Brown Bear!"

Two of the youths riding bareback trotted over. "Take four horses each and get to the *hocoka*. Tell 'em where we are and how many of the *wašicun toka* there are after us, and tell 'em to hurry."

They looked slightly mutinous, and he barked: "*Hokahe!*"

The youngsters turned and went, fast—*get going* was evidently what *hokahe* meant.

While they did the rest of the Sioux put on their war gear, which in most cases simply meant transferring their metal-strapped leather helmets from the saddle-bow to the head, and adding a few feathers to them, kept carefully wrapped against need. The covers came off their shields, revealing designs painted or pyrographed or picked out in feathers and beads on the tough bison hide—a buffalo's head, zigzag lines to represent thunder and lightning, a bear's paw, a dragonfly, eagles or falcons, deer, cougar, lions and patterns of dots to show hailstorms. One had a whole stuffed weasel attached to his.

The men were cheerful, laughing and joking with one another as they took a few seconds to paint their faces, usually simply a few bars of black or yellow, though one did his face with red on the right side and yellow on the left. Edain had managed to get the more complex Mackenzie war-paint on—his was a stylized wolf's face—and it attracted some admiring comments.

"Most times of year there would be bands scattered all through here, but this is the season we get together and do the social thing. We're about a half day's hard ride from the nearest *hocoka*—that's a big encampment," Red Leaf said to Rudi as the band rocked back into motion.

"Any chance of running into a patrol?" Rudi said through the drumming of hooves.

"We *are* the patrol. Wolf Paws and Brown Bear ride light, they can gallop all the way. They'll get there soon."

"But if we tried it, our horses would fall down dead."

"You got it, not to mention the time we'd lose switching saddles. Once they get there ... gathering a warparty big enough won't take long, but getting it back to us ... that'll take a bit longer."

"And the Cutters will be upon us earlier," Rudi said.

"Yeah, looks like their horses are fresher, dammit, from the way they ate up the ground behind us. Either that or they started out with a lot of remounts and they're abandoning them as they founder. Which means they're really, really determined."

Rudi sighed. "We'll leave you then. They're probably after us, and they'll let you go."

"You fucking well *won't*, kilt-boy! Virginia's my *tonjan*, my niece—Dave Kane was my blood-brother. And we're not going to let them ride onto our land and do as they please! We spent four years fighting them to a draw, well, nearly to a draw, and we're not going to roll over and show our bellies now."

Rudi nodded, honor satisfied. Red Leaf went on: "I'll organize us into a column of twos. That ought to help ... a bit, and there's a sort of convention we've got here ... If we can just keep them off until dark ..."

He pulled his horse to one side and began to shout orders.

Wish we'd had time to change out of full armor, Rudi thought; it would slow them and tire any horse they rode. *On the other hand, they'd probably catch us anyway, and we may last a little longer in our gear.*

The column kept to a steady canter. Disconcertingly soon, the enemy came over the rise behind them at the same pace, but a little faster. They spread out as Rudi watched over his shoulder, working themselves into a loose crescent pointed towards the Sioux. The horns of it began to creep up on either side; when they advanced far enough, they could stab inward and surround the smaller band.

Now I am commencing a serious annoyance with these people, Rudi thought. *If they persist, it's soon I will be angry.*

"Ah, *shit*," Red Leaf said. "They've got a lot of spare gear, see? They're driving their remounts along saddled with the stirrups tied up on the horn. Makes it faster to switch horses, but it's expensive if you're abandoning the ones that've been ridden out. Someone back there *really* has a hard-on for us. But I know a trick for that too."

The sun grew hotter, and Rudi sweated under his brigandine and war gear. When Red Leaf gave the order he switched to a remount and rode it bareback, with Epona pacing beside him unburdened, saving her endurance for later; the others did the same. The roll of the land grew a little steeper, and the blue on the horizon was definitely hills. They splashed through another seasonal stream, and then onto a flat upland where the Cutters came up on them faster . . .

Just about long—

One of the russet-armored Sword troopers rose in the stirrups and drew, his bow pointed halfway to the sky for maximum range.

—bowshot, Rudi thought.

The first arrow twinkled towards them and landed with a dry *shunk* in the dirt not far behind the last of the Sioux. The second was never shot; a Rancher whose saddle glinted with silver in the hot sunlight rode close and cut the man's bowstring with the head of his light lance. Suddenly unstrung, the powerful recurve bucked and twisted, and the trooper clapped his hands to his face.

Does that smart? Rudi thought, grinning to himself. *Ouch!*

The relentless pace of the pursuit faltered as a furious argument broke out between the Rancher and his men and the soldiers from Corwin.

Virginia left her place beside Fred for a moment.

"That'll be Vince with the fancy saddle, the son of a bitch always did like to show off. *He* needs me alive. At least for a while—and if he did catch me, he'd wake up dead sometime soon. But they won't be spraying arrows at us long distance, not when one might hit me."

"That's good news," Red Leaf said as the argument among their enemies died down. "Three arrows beat one, pretty much. And that'll make them keep their distance—there's no reason we can't shoot at *them*. Hey, though . . . didn't I hear Vince was already married?"

"He's a Cutter now. They can have as many wives as they want. He *is* a bastard, too—was even before he went over to the enemy."

As she spoke a young cowboy spurred out from among the pursuers. He shook his bow overhead and screeched a challenge.

"I was hoping for that," Red Leaf said. "They're going to challenge us to one-on-one fights. It's one of our ancient traditions here, both sides of the border."

"Ancient?" Rudi said.

"Yeah, ten, twelve, maybe even fourteen years old—immemorial antiquity, as my Classics teacher used to say. They figure they can't lose, since they outnumber us; we'll get whittled down until it's safe to charge us. OK, Black Elk. Get him!"

Others shouted encouragement too:

"Hoo'hay, Lakota!"

"It's a good day to die!"

"Nail his balls to the barn door!"

Both parties slowed a little. *A way to let the younger men prove themselves,* Rudi thought; that made sense. And . . . he grinned.

That commander of the Sword of the Prophet must be trickling steam from both ears, and his nose, not to mention his arse, he thought happily. *Here he's caught up to us after month upon month of chasing, and now the locals won't let him just shoot us full of holes. But there's not enough of his men to ignore their sensibilities, that there is not. Most of them must be scattered elsewhere, looking for us.*

It was worth bearing in mind for the future. No man was ever *really* just an instrument of another's will; everyone had their own purposes.

Then the grin died. The two young men had galloped towards each other, standing in the stirrups and shooting as fast as they could. Red Leaf swore under his breath as the Sioux rocked back in the saddle, an arrow standing in his body. The cowboy cased his bow and pulled out his shete; the curved blade glinted in the sun as he swept past the wounded man, and the Indian toppled to the earth. The victor reined in, a showy flourish as the agile quarter horse reared and milled its feet, and sprang to earth.

"Yes!" Red Leaf said, as the crumpled form suddenly lashed out with a knife. Then: "Damn, it didn't work! But you tried, Black Elk!"

The cowboy skipped backwards, then stabbed with his shete. He left it standing in the body as he bent; there was a flash of knife blade, and then the man stood again, dripping scalp in one hand and knife in the other, shaking them aloft and screaming his triumph.

Mathilda swore and reined out, sliding the knight's shield from her back.

Red Leaf spurred ahead of her. "No!" he said. "If you interfere, they'll do a massed charge. We *want* to spin this out!"

Rudi nodded grimly. The whole thing made a certain sense; battle customs often did. Not every fight was to the last man standing. This was something halfway between a tournament and an all-out fight to the death. The winner stripped Black Elk's body of weapons and grabbed the reins of his horse, riding back with his trophies and his loot.

Both war-bands had slowed down to a trot, halting altogether during the duels; the horns of the Cutters' crescent were level with the forward part of the Sioux formation. By tacit agreement they went no farther, as long as the Indians didn't refuse the challenge.

"It's our turn," Red Leaf said, looking down the line of his men. Every one of them raised his voice, asking for the honor ...

He waved to one. "Go for it, Jimmy."

Jimmy was slender, dark, and looked young, probably younger than he was, and he was naked to the waist except for the kit-fox pelt that marked his membership in that warrior society.

Hmmm, Rudi thought. *He also looks quick as a weasel.*

The young warrior nodded soberly at the chief's call, sliding his round shield onto his left arm and taking a two-foot stick from his belt, one with a feather at the end.

"He's toast, *itancan*," he replied, and rode back along the Sioux column with a whoop.

"Challenger gets choice of weapons," Red Leaf said. "Sorta."

A cowboy spurred out to meet Jimmy. He had a metal-strapped leather breastplate, and a helmet like a steel bowl topped with a horsetail that bobbed and fluttered with the motion of his gallop; there was a letter Q with a diagonal slash through it in white on the dark brown bullhide of his shield. He cased his bow and drew his shete, which showed what Red Leaf had meant by *sorta*; evidently no bows were used if the challenger started with an impact weapon.

The two horsemen met in the field between the war-bands. Rudi didn't think the life and death of brave men should be just a show . . . but he *was* a warrior by trade, and it was frustrating not to be able to see the details. The men came together with the combined speeds of their horses, screaming their war cries, and there was a tangle as the Cutter's blade chopped down. Rudi's breath caught for an instant as the shete flashed . . . and then Jimmy was past, shaking his stick in the air and whooping, and the Powder River man was reeling backwards in the heavy Western saddle, pawing at his face with both hands.

A groan that was half growl went up from the ranch-hands and their patron; the Sioux gave a high shrill cheer—one that contained the banshee Mackenzie shriek, and shouts of *Haro!*, *Richland!*, *Lacho Calad*,

Drego Morn! and *USA!* as well as Father Ignatius' more restrained *Good!*

Red Leaf grinned like a wolf. "They're about to find out Jimmy's other name."

"Which is?" Rudi said, his eyes still glued to the two small figures.

"*Many Coups*. In the old days sometimes they'd just whack someone with a coup stick and leave them to swallow the humiliation, but we're more practical now."

Jimmy Many Coups brought his pony around in a tight circle, dust spurting up from under its hooves. He ducked under a wild swing of the cowboy's weapon—Rudi guessed that the first stroke had been a blinding slash across the eyes—and struck again. The shete pinwheeled away from a broken hand, and the stick jabbed. The cowboy fell. This time it was the Sioux who screamed triumph and led his enemy's horse back with the captured weapons across its saddle, waving the fresh scalp to an admiring chorus from the other Sioux:

"*Ohitike!*"

"*You* rock, *Jim!*"

"*Ohan, Many Coups!*"

"*Dude! That* so *does not suck!*"

The deadly game continued as the sun crept past noon. Father Ignatius punched his opponent neatly out of the saddle with his heavy lance, then dismounted to offer the dying man absolution. Which, to the visible fury of the Sword of the Prophet, he accepted. Rudi nodded to himself; not all the folk the CUT had overrun really accepted its teachings. The Sword troopers kept to their solid disciplined block, but an hour later the Sioux had lost five men and their opponents seven.

Then:

"I'll take this one," Rudi said. *Because honor demands it,* he thought. *We can't let our hosts do all the fighting for us.*

Epona turned beneath him, so responsive that he didn't need to conciously think of directing her.

"So, so, my fine lady," he whispered, smoothing a hand down her sleek neck.

Sweat ran on it, and she wasn't as young as she'd been . . . but she wasn't too tired, either. Rudi guided her past the little two-wheeled cart; it had kept up so far, and Edain was driving it, being the worst horseman in the group.

"Show them how a Mackenzie fights, Chief!" he said.

"I'll show them how the Morrigú wards her own," Rudi replied grimly.

He reached for his sallet helm and settled it on his head. The steel dome had a flare of raven feathers in holders at either side; the helm and the smooth semicircular visor were graven with feather patterns inlaid in niello, and the curve of the visor was drawn down in a point over his mouth like a beak. He'd switched his sword to his right hip, but he used that hand to pick up one of the lances in the wagon bed.

It'll do, he thought, hefting it. *Better than trying to use my left; I haven't had enough time to get the memory into the muscle there.*

He snapped the visor down with the edge of his shield, and the world shrank to a narrow horizontal slit. Then he tensed his thighs and Epona came up to a canter; he halted in the space between the two bands, tossing the lance up and shrieking the Clan's battle-yell. There was a hesitation; the cowboys had already seen that these twelve-foot lances were something entirely again from the light spears some of them used. Even if they didn't recognize the brigandine that armored Rudi's torso, they could see that he had a knight's four-foot shield, plate shin guards and vambraces, and mail-sleeves and mail covering on the outer sides of the leather breeches he'd pulled on beneath his kilt. Fighting a steel tower on a tall horse was simply outside their experience . . .

After a few moments one pulled out of the slow-moving crescent mass, coming forward at a hard gallop. The Rancher's man left his round shield over his back and his shete at his belt, but he didn't use his bow either—evidently he was going to stick to the rules that far. Instead he unlimbered the coiled lariat from his saddlebow and held it out to one side, spinning the lasso vertically as his horse rocked up to a gallop.

"Well, friend, at least you're being different!" Rudi called.

Epona drifted forward, her long legs moving in an easy canter. Rudi kept the lance sloped up as long as he could; it protected his head from a cast of the rope. Only in the last fifty yards did he bring it down and clamp his thighs tight against the saddle and brace his feet. Both war-parties roared as the horses headed towards each other at full tilt, their combined speed closing at seventy miles an hour. Rudi could see the taut grin on the cowboy's red-bearded face, and the flexing of his greasy leather coat as his right arm moved in wider and wider circles. The foot-long lance-head pointed at his chest didn't seem to bother him at all.

An instant later Rudi found out why. The plainsman threw himself sideways—for a moment the Mackenzie thought he'd jumped out of the saddle altogether, and then he saw that he was crouched down with one knee around the horn.

The spectators roared again, this time in admiration at the feat of horsemanship; the lance-head punched through the space where he'd been, and the cowboy brought himself back into the saddle with a snapping flex of leg and body. Rudi turned Epona with desperate speed as she felt the appeal of his body and pirouetted with a speed astonishing in a horse her size. The noose settled over his head nonetheless, and over his left arm, pinning that and his shield to his shoulder.

The lance was already falling as he released it. He grabbed the lariat instead, the braided three-quarter-inch rawhide rope clamped tight in the soft chamois of his gauntlet's palm. Then he set his feet in the stirrups and hauled; Epona reared, adding her weight to the grip. Pain flexed deep in his shoulder despite all the healing, but the cowboy hadn't quite had time to snub the end of the lariat to his saddlehorn.

It ripped through his hands instead, and his horse

staggered sideways as the force of the tug was transmitted through the rider's body and the grip of his legs. The man lurched to one side, the easy centaur grace of his seat on the quarter horse destroyed for a moment at the shocking force of it. Then he drew his shete, setting himself. Rudi's shield was on his left arm, the one he used for the sword now; he didn't attempt to juggle the weapons. Instead he pushed in close.

There was a *thud* as Epona's shoulder struck the cow pony. There wasn't enough momentum to pitch the lighter horse over, but even so the big black mare's more than half ton of weight made it stagger again, sinking back on its haunches. That spoiled the overarm slash aimed at Rudi's head; he smashed his shield up and the curved steel-rimmed upper edge caught the blade near the guard. That tore it from the cowboy's grasp. And in that instant, Rudi made his right hand into a fist and punched the metal-shod mass into his face. Bone and teeth snapped and the man's eyes rolled up, but even three-quarters unconscious his superb horseman's reflexes kept him in the saddle.

The cow pony whirled again, turning on its hind legs and coming down moving; Epona sped the gelding on its way with a hearty snap in the buttock and bugled a challenge at the plainsmens' mounts, dancing lightly sideways with an unmistakable air of satisfaction. The Sioux gave a collective groan of disappointment, but Rudi wasn't too displeased that his opponent had survived. The Powder River men halted, several of them easing their comrade out of the saddle. However unwilling, the troop of the Sword had to do likewise until their allies were ready to move on.

Mr. Lariat won't be fighting anytime soon, not with his face rearranged so thoroughly. And he was a brave man, and clever. That trick nearly worked.

The Mackenzie did take a moment then to dismount and recover the lance—it was a product of Isherman's Weapons Shop in Bend, a thousand miles west as the crow flew, considerably more as humankind had to travel, and replacing it would be difficult. It was a combination of Epona's tossed head and the drumming of hooves and the shout of outrage from the Sioux that warned him.

It was a Cutter who charged, grimly silent as he drew his bow to his ear. At that range, armor probably wouldn't stop a hard-driven shaft, and the Corwinite's bow was thick with sinew and horn; his upper body hardly seemed to move at all, despite the plunging gallop of his horse, and the narrow point of the arrowhead grew until it was like the head of a spear. He was taking no chances.

Anticipation, some corner of Rudi's mind thought.

Nobody could dodge an arrow at this range, but his body was already moving. The *snap* of string on bracer and the *bang!* as the curved steel of his helm shed the point were so close together that they blended into one sound. The impact on the steel covering his head felt like a blow from a club and white light flashed through his brain, but his hands brought the lance-point up then—too quickly for the horse to be able to follow its natural instinct against running into an obstacle at speed. The sharp steel bit, and Rudi was thrown backwards by the impact. The butt of the lance struck the hard ground as he landed flat on his back, pinned for an instant by his gear. Momentum drove it deep into the horse's chest, and then the ashwood snapped across two-thirds of the way from the point.

He rolled frantically to avoid the falling, thrashing body of the wounded horse; its huge astonished scream seemed to propel him like a giant's hand. He used the movement to flick himself erect, his sword coming out. The Cutter had been thrown clear as his mount went down; the lacquered-leather armor and padding protected him a little, and his horseman's instincts for a fall even more, and he managed to stagger erect and draw his blade as Rudi charged with sword in hand.

Ting.

The blades met, sparking as flat met edge, then slid down and locked. Rudi's right hand clamped down on the Cutter's left as it reached for his dagger and they strained against each other, motionless for a long moment except for the shifting of their feet as they shoved like rutting elk locking horns in the fall. His enemy's face filled the vision slit in the clansman's visor, dark gray eyes, flared nose crossed by a white scar, tuft of brown beard. There was no fear in those eyes even as his arms bent back under Rudi's inexorable strength, simply a cold intentness.

The shete slipped backwards and the Cutter released it and clawed for Rudi's face beneath the visor. The pommel of Rudi's sword clubbed down on his upper arm, and the limb went strengthless despite the tough leather armor. The smaller man staggered back and went to one knee, freezing as the point of the Western long-sword flashed to rest just below his chin. The world grew brighter as Rudi used his free hand to push up his visor, but the sword stayed precisely where it was, delicate as a surgeon's scalpel, a tiny trickle of blood sliding down from where it dimpled the weathered, stubbled skin of the other man's throat. The rank-smelling sweat of agony beaded the Cutter's face.

"What's your name?" Rudi said.

The other man showed a little expression; surprise, and then an iron pride.

"Major Peter Graber, third battalion, Sword of the Prophet of the Church Universal and Triumphant, tasked with your destruction."

"Well, it seems to be working out the other way round, I'm thinking," Rudi said dryly. "Despite your sticking to my arse like an importunate tick this last long while."

"Kill me, then," he said. "My lifestream will join the Ascended Masters, and yours will be dispersed in the Outer Dark."

Rudi's wrist moved, and the blade flicked off the man's helmet.

"It's easy to kill," he said. "As easy as smashing glass. Any fool can do either. And dying is even simpler. Living well ... now that, my friend, is a more difficult matter. Think on that when you wake up."

"Kill me!" the man said, lunging up against the point, before the sheer agony of his broken arm stopped him.

Rudi smiled. "No," he said, and flicked the flat of his sword sideways.

Bonk.

The stroke was precisely judged, though you could never tell exactly what a head injury would do; at the least, Major Graber would have a set of bad headaches. The man slumped down bonelessly. Rudi sheathed his blade, whistled, caught Epona's bridle as she was about to step on the man's face accidentally-on-purpose—that would rather spoil the lesson—and swung into the saddle. As he trotted back to join his comrades he worked the right shoulder.

Just a little twinge, he thought. *Not bad since I was using it to ten-tenths, as old Sam Aylward puts it. But Master Hao was right; too much is worse than too little. I'd just as soon rest it now.*

He looked back. The Sword troopers were grouped around their officer. Probably splinting his arm, at a guess, and it was a mercy to him that he'd be unconscious during the process of getting the armor off, though he wouldn't thank Rudi for the head he'd have when he woke up.

"But somehow I don't think they're going to give up," he said as he drew in beside Red Leaf.

Mathilda leaned over in her saddle to give him a hug and a kiss—always awkward beneath a raised visor, and Epona shouldered her horse rudely. The beast was a big rawboned grey destrier, but it was thoroughly in awe of the alpha-mare, and shied. Mathilda was still laughing as she lurched and took a moment to regain her seat.

"Is that beast your horse, or your wife?" she said.

"I think she has her moments of doubt," Rudi replied.

Red Leaf looked back, and Rudi did as well. The cowboys had left the Sword men to tend to their commander. Even as he watched they legged their horses up from a trot to a canter, and then a gallop. The Sioux did likewise.

"You counted coup there pretty good. But I don't think they're in a mood for playing now," Red Leaf said grimly.

*   *   *

The Sioux fanned out at Red Leaf's command, unlimbering their bows and ready to shoot over their horses' rumps when the pursuit came in range. The cowboys brought their shields up, and most of them drew their shetes; they intended to cross the killing ground and come to handstrokes. A dead Virginia Kane was of no use to their leader at all, and evidently their discipline was good enough to take the risk. A little rise ahead hurtled towards them . . .

Suddenly Red Leaf whooped. "The land's fighting for us, Kit Foxes!" he said. "*Pispizah!* Prairie dogs! Keep going! *Hokahe! Hokahe!*"

They topped the rise. The land fell away before them, a slope as gentle as the other side . . . and it was dotted with the neat round mounds of a prairie-dog town. The little ground squirrels were mostly gone underground at the noise of the hooves; a few lingered, standing erect with their paws dangling and noses up, but they whistled shrilly and vanished with a flicker of black-tipped tails as the whooping mass of riders bore down on them.

"Epona, protect Your daughter!" Rudi shouted, invoking the Horse Goddess for his mount.

Only blind luck—and for some of the Sioux, superlative horsemanship—would decide who got through, and whose horse would step in one of those hills as it galloped. He heard a cannon bone snap with a crack like a breaking lance-shaft, and a cut-off scream of equine pain. A glance over his shoulder showed Virginia Kane down, lying stunned just beyond a horse with a broken neck. A Sioux was down too, the tall red-haired young man. Both managed to get to their feet, and then Fred Thurston and Mathilda had both turned back.

"Shit!"

Rudi began to do likewise, then reached for an arrow instead; it would take too long for him to do them any good directly. Thurston leaned far over with his right arm extended and crooked; whoever his father had kept to teach his sons horsemanship must have been a rodeo star of former times. The Powder River Rancher's daughter turned and ran five steps in the same direction, then grabbed the young man's arm and bounced upwards, landing neatly astride the horse behind him. Rudi's eyes went wide; he'd have tried the same thing, and counted his chance of bringing it off no more than even.

Red Leaf shouted again, and swung up his bow. The Sioux halted their horses, turned, and drew their recurves to the ear, lined up just beyond the edge of the dangerous ground. Hooves thundered from beyond the ridge, and dust smoked above it. Rudi's eye sought Mathilda; she hadn't the strength to duplicate Thurston's feat, and her target was heavier as well. Instead she slugged her destrier to a halt by the red-haired Sioux and held it plunging while he scrambled up, steadying him as he put a foot on her stirrup and swung around pillion.

The big horse would need a moment to get up to speed, as well—it was carrying twice the usual weight, and its own leather-and-steel barding.

And the cowboys were over the rise, yipping and whooping as they saw their foes halted. They didn't notice the prairie dogs until they were well into the town and the first of their horses went over in a whirling tangle of equine limbs and crackling bone. A galloping horse *couldn't* halt quickly, not even a cow pony of quarter horse breed, and the fighting men of the Bar Q were more tightly bunched than their opponents had been. Their greater numbers left them unable to dodge even if they'd known what was coming. Some sawed at their reins anyway, and half a dozen pairs of horses collided and fell even without putting a hoof down a burrow. Many of the rest halted with horseman's reflex overcoming warrior instinct, and those behind them had to pull up or run into them.

And then the Sioux bows began to snap, the first volley lashing out at fifty yards and into the milling confusion of the enemy formation. More screams followed. Some of the cowboys *did* make it through at a gallop; one stood in the stirrups and poised a spear to drive into Mathilda's back, or the Sioux riding with her. Rudi cursed and wheeled Epona, but there were too many of the Sioux in the way . . .

A gray-feathered arrow went *through* the space between Mathilda's head and her passenger's, brushing the fletching against the back of her head and his nose. The cowboy froze with the light lance poised to thrust, looked down at the goose fletching that had blossomed against the leather breastplate, and toppled like a cut-through tree. Then Mathilda was with him, grinning under the raised visor of her helmet, but with her face gone pale.

"Thanks!" she shouted at Edain.

The young Aylward stood with his longbow on the bed of the cart, shaking the long yellow yew stave overhead and screeching the shrill ululations of the Mackenzie battle-yell. Then he reached over his shoulder for another shaft.

The redhead and Virginia Kane slid down and did creditable ten-yard sprints to the remount herd, vaulting onto the bare backs of the spare mounts without breaking stride. The Sioux wheeled their horses and followed, and some of the cowboys were among them as they went up another long swale. The clash of steel on steel sounded, and the flat *bang* of a blade hitting the bison-hide surface of a shield, along with the thunder of hooves. More and more of the Bar Q men followed as they pulled themselves out of the tangle and picked their way through the dangerous ground; Rudi had hoped they'd be discouraged enough to quit, and from his expression Red Leaf was equally disappointed.

The land here wasn't quite as table flat as it had been an hour earlier; the foothills of the Black Hills were nearer now, and Rudi could see the first dark mantle of the pine forests that had given them their name. The mule-drawn cart was bouncing just ahead of them as they crested the ridge and plunged downward towards a shallow hollow with a little blue water in its lowest part. Garbh rode the lashed-down cargo beside her master, and it was her bristle and roaring growl of challenge that alerted Rudi. That and a rank musky odor, like tomcat magnified a thousand times . . .

Then the whole cursing, shrieking, slashing mass of Sioux and cowboys were down the slope at full tilt . . . and the lions were starting to their feet from among the grass and the shade of the single cottonwood tree. His mind froze for an instant, just long enough to note that they were very large, about as big as most tigers he'd seen, and a little shaggy compared to the old pictures.

"Urr-urrh-*oooouurrrghhhHHHHHH*!"

One of the big black-mane males roared, a sound that shattered even the battle frenzy, and sent well-trained horses into bucking, bolting panic as they realized what they'd been forced into. Edain's mules bolted themselves, galloping in a flat-out frenzy with their teeth showing yellow, ears laid back and eyes bulging; clods of the hard high-plains dirt flew from beneath their hooves. The younger clansman dropped flat and gripped the ropes that held the cargo down as the light vehicle bounced shoulder-high and threatened to tip over at any moment. His other hand pinned Garbh beside him, and she barked in a long continuous quasi-howl.

A tiny form squalled as the hooves and wheels passed over it—tiny in comparison to the adult lions, though despite its kitten spots it was the weight of a moderate-sized dog already. The pride had been on the verge of flight, but the sound drove the lioness mad; she leapt, and a Sioux and his horse went down as nearly four hundred pounds of parental fury struck, swinging paws the size of dinner plates with sledgehammer force, claws out and ripping, her fangs sinking into the man's shoulder and shaking him the way a terrier would a rat until he came to pieces.

That sent the other lions leaping among the mounted humans; there were four adult males in their black-maned prime, and twenty females only a little smaller and far more savage with cubs to protect. Red Leaf's horse jinked to the right and his son's to the left as one of them landed and whirled in a circle, lashing out with

paws like knife-edged rams moving so fast that they
were tawny blurs. The older man's mount recovered and
galloped on, despite his attempts to slug it to a halt, with
five bleeding grooves down one haunch. Three Bears'
pony skidded on the dry dusty earth and went down on
its left flank with a hollow boom like a struck drum as
its ribs hit the soil.

The young Sioux tried to leap clear, and almost made
it. At the last instant his foot caught a little in the stirrup, just enough to slam him down beside his mount and
send him rolling. The lioness landed on the pony, her
paws gripping its head as her jaws closed on its throat
by reflex in the throttling bite that the big cats always
used on their larger prey.

Epona wore no bit; and even now, she responded to
Rudi's urgent hands on the hackamore and reins, rearing to a halt. Rudi leapt to the ground; it thudded up
through his boot-heels, but he kept his footing in a
bounding lope that slowed to a halt just by the bruised,
bleeding form of Rick Three Bears. A snatch, and the
Indian was over his shoulder.

He turned. The lioness had both forefeet on the dead
pony not fifteen feet away. And it was snarling at Epona,
showing teeth like yellow-ivory daggers, its face wrinkled into a bloodied mask of ferocity. Rudi whistled, and
the great black horse turned and trotted towards him.
That apparent flight triggered the big cat's reflex, and
it sprang.

Epona's head was over her shoulder, and her hind
feet lashed out with precisely calculated force. The cat's
spring turned into a tumble as it saw the paired horseshoes moving, but even its speed could only turn it sideways in time to receive the massive *thump* of impact.
The big predator flew squalling, landed with another
thump, and began to limp away with one foreleg held up
against her breast, and no further interest in the fracas
except to get as far away from it as she could.

Rudi fought down an almost hysterical laugh as Epona
floated towards him, head and tail high, feet tapping out
puffs of dust as they touched down, and pride glowing

from every line of her. He heaved the younger man's limp form over the saddle and ran on, holding on to the stirrup leather to steady himself—even for someone of his size and long legs, running in sixty pounds of armor was no easy thing.

Red Leaf was waiting for him; his wild-eyed horse made a final circle against the ruthless pressure of the reins and then submitted.

"Look! Look!" he shouted after one swift glance at his son, pointing eastward. "The cavalry!"

Rudi looked. Seventy Lakota were pouring down into the hollow. Foam from the mounts' dripping jaws coated their forequarters and the legs of the riders, but shetes and spears and bows waved in the warriors' hands. The cowboys and the lions seemed to pause for an instant, then fled in all directions, like a spatter of water on waxed leather. The rescue party was in no condition to pursue; as Rudi watched and panted like a bellows against the constriction of his armor one of their horses went down by the hindquarters in a limp collapse.

Sure, and I feel like doing the same, Rudi thought, leaning against Epona and panting like a dog.

"The cavalry to the rescue!" Red Leaf said, as he lifted his son down from the saddle, pulled the stopper from his water bottle with his teeth and held it to the young man's mouth.

Then: "Well, sorta."

Rudi nodded, wheezing. *My own folk?* he asked himself.

A quick survey showed them all—except Edain, but the mule cart was small in the distance by now, and it would keep going until the mules recovered their nerves or dropped dead. He closed his eyes for a long moment, then pulled his canteen from Epona's saddlebow; he took off his helmet, filled it, held it for the mare's slobbering muzzle and then rinsed out his mouth with the last swallows. There was blood in his mouth from a place where he'd cut the inside on his teeth, an injury he hadn't noticed until now.

Now it stung like fire under the salt-iron taste, and he

probed gingerly at it with his tongue. Luckily the teeth all seemed in order; he doubted there were any first-rate dentists within reach.

As he looked up Virginia Kane came to them; Fred Thurston was by her side, looking at her a little oddly. He saw why when she held up a dripping scalp of her own; it was one shade lighter than her sun-streaked auburn-brown locks.

"Vince Rickover," she said with satisfaction. "Guess he's goin' to be along to *protect* me after all."

She looked at the bloody lock of hair. "Leastways, part of him will be."

Rudi blinked. *Remind me never to press an unwelcome suit with this one!* he thought.

Just then Mathilda came up. Their eyes met, and they both smiled. He would have laughed, but his mouth hurt too much.

Then: "What's *that*?" he blurted, looking down at the squirming bundle in Mathilda's arms.

Epona looked at it too, and bared her eyeteeth, rolling a great dark eye and sidling a little, snorting through wide red nostrils.

"Stop that, you big baby," Mathilda said to her. "It's just a kitten."

Then she held up the cub, all head and eyes and huge paws absurdly disproportioned to its gangly little body. "Isn't it adorable?"

The three-week infant turned and tried to sink its needle fangs into her hand, then recoiled when they met armor.

"Good thing you've got a first-rate pair of mail-gloves, *moi brèagha*," Rudi said.

Suddenly he needed to sit, but . . . he looked around.

Is there a spot nearby without bodies on it, or at least blood?

CHAPTER SEVENTEEN

Dead cities cry laments
For children grown strange
For a world that died in birthing
Children it could never know;
Beneath the winter's grass
New blossoms wild and fair—

From: *The Song of Bear and Raven*
Attributed to Fiorbhinn Mackenzie, 1st century CY

Ogallala hocoka, Western South Dakota
June 3, CY24/2022 AD

"Wake up, people! Get up and wash your bodies, drink a lot of water, make your blood thin and healthy!"

The crier was shouting at the top of his lungs and beating on an iron triangle as he walked; now and then someone would stick their head out of a tent and shout back at him, usually something unfriendly and sometimes involving invitations to do things with horses, sheep or his mother. Rudi Mackenzie woke, yawned and stretched beneath the comforting buffalo-robe. Most of the aches and scrapes from yesterday's running fight were fading, though some of the bruises would have to go through the gamut of colors before they left him. Still, that was familiar enough; if you fought, you got thumped, and counted yourself lucky to have no more.

The welcome was nearly as strenuous as the fight! he thought.

It flickered through his memory in bright shards; the great ring of fires, the excited crowds pushing forward to hear Red Leaf's impassioned description of the action, the discordant wailing from the womenfolk of the fallen in the background. Louder chanting and nasal song from the throng, drums throbbing, cheers around him as the victors showed their captured horses and weapons and the grisly personal trophies and boasted of their deeds.

And then Red Leaf had gotten to the part where Rudi beat the Cutter officer and saved Three Bears from the lion: hands lifting him out of the saddle, pounding him on the back, pulling him into the whooping, whirling, stamping, screeching, leaping delirium of the scalp-and-victory dance, until he could scarcely stagger to his bed.

He sat up and ran his hands through his hair as the crier outside called his message again, winced as he hit a tangle, then searched for his comb. The tent where he and the other men of the party had been put up was something new; he'd expected tipis, and there had been a few in the encampment, some of them huge. But most of the dwellings were like this one, a round barrel shape twenty feet across on a wheeled platform, the walls five feet tall and topped by a conical roof rising a little higher than Rudi's head in the center. The structure was an interlaced pattern of thin withes crossing one another in a diamond pattern and lashed together with thongs; the outside was covered in neatly sewn hides treated with some sort of glaze to make them waterproof, and from the look of it the interior could take a quilted lining as well in cold weather. The floor was plywood covered in rugs.

Everyone was stirring; Rudi took down a canvas water bottle from a peg and obeyed part of the herald's injunction. The more he looked around, the more he was impressed with the neat economy of space; their weapons, armor and other gear were all stowed overhead on racks that folded down from the ceiling, for example, and the middle of the tent had a ceramic plate inset to mount a stove in cold weather, with a space for a flue running up to a hole in the central peak. Light came from actual glass windows set in the latticework walls, and there was an unlit lamp on a shelf over the door; the interior smelled of well-tanned leather and faintly of smoke.

"Rise and shine, men!" he called, as he rolled up his bedding and lashed it to the wall with the thongs provided.

Groans and grunts answered him; like his mother he was always cheerful in the morning, and it had always mystified him why some people resented it.

Why waste the day? There's things to be doing! *But sure, you can't convince the sleepyheads.*

He slipped on his kilt instead and picked up his shaving kit; Ingolf joined him, and they ducked out of the door—thoughtfully leaving it open to the bright early-morning sunlight and cool air. A pillow thrown by Odard, who was *not* cheerful in the mornings, bounced off their backs.

"Whatever's cooking smells very good indeed," Rudi said; it involved frying and, he thought, onions. "Odard will crawl out when it penetrates."

Men in breechclouts were walking past; the two travelers jumped down from the wagon platform and joined them at their friendly invitation.

Seen by daylight the *hocoka* was a great horseshoe of the tents-on-wheels, with an opening to the east and the tent doors facing inward; their white exteriors were painted in colorful geometric patterns, or stylized birds and beasts, or what looked like murals. Some of the larger ones had words inset in the decorations: at a glance he saw LIBRARY and CLINIC. Rudi estimated at least a hundred and fifty of the dwellings in all, not counting two huge conical tipis flanking the entrance and another, even larger and colored red, in the center of the open space. Smoke drifted from cookfires, mostly under sheet-metal tubs on legs or Dutch ovens, and the intoxicating smell of brewing chicory was strong.

And I'm even beginning to like the taste.

The interior of the great encampment had been trodden to bare dust, but grass was soft beneath the soles of his feet when the crowd left it. Around was a view of mile upon mile of rolling green splashed with drifts of the delicate white-pink prairie rose, taller purple cone-flower, scarlet western lily and yellow wild sunflower. The ground dropped off to a fair-sized river southward, and the Black Hills showed clear to the north, but most of the horizon was like a bowl dropped over a world of infinite spaces.

A roped-off enclosure not far away held the ready-use horses, and herds of horses, red-coated cattle and off-white sheep dotted the landscape. Outside the circle of living-tents was a vehicle park, wagons of every size and shape and description, from ones that wouldn't have looked out of place on the Oregon Trail to cut-down pickup trucks and converted mobile homes.

Red Leaf waved, then came over as they walked down to the water. "Men bathe here," he said. "Women over there, and stock water below that."

Rudi nodded; Mackenzies didn't have much of a nu-dity taboo in their communal bathhouses, but other folk were more prudish, he knew. There were a good three or four hundred in the crowd who dove into the water and splashed around with much horseplay, from boys just a little too old to join the women down to the few elders; his mind automatically noted that well over half were fit to bear arms, and looked as if they could, too. A lot of them had brought their weapons to the riverbank, within easy grabbing range, even though it was obvious nobody expected real trouble.

He swam in the cold water, scrubbed with soap and sand, cautiously around the sore spots, shaved with his straight razor, and headed back for the tent.

Should I try growing a beard again? No, still too patchy.

The warm dry air had the last of the water off his skin by the time he'd gotten back . . .

And I'm a little reluctant to put the old clothes back on. Well, we'll have time to wash them—

There was the first surprise; their clothes had been

taken away to be cleaned and repaired, and new outfits set out for all of them—his consisted of buckskin trousers with buffalo-hair fringes down the seams flanked by colorful quillwork, and a linsey-woolsey tunic bleached creamy white with bands of beads in geometric patterns along the sleeves and in a triangle at the neck.

Mathilda and his sisters and Virginia Kane came back from the women's section of the river; they'd been decked out in dresses that had capelike upper sections, with rows of shells across the yokes, flowers and birds along the hems, belts with hammered silver conchos, and moccasins done with a buffalo-hoof design; some of Red Leaf's female relatives sat with them, dressing their hair in local style. Others headed for Rudi and the others with combs in their hands and determination in their eyes; Odard's bowl crop, Father Ignatius' neat tonsure and Fred Thurston's short cap of wiry fuzz defeated them, but Rudi and Ingolf and Edain soon had twin braids fur-wrapped, albeit rather shorter than the local fashion.

Rudi's had two long raven feathers tucked in. "Sure, and the Raven is the bird of my sept," he said.

The girl doing his hair nodded. "And she's the bird of the battlefields. These are for the two coups you counted yesterday. And this"—she added an eagle feather—"is for saving my brother's life."

He stood to buckle his sword belt, and the girl—she was about fourteen—glanced up at him with an unconscious sigh, clasping her hands together. Out of the corner of his eye he caught Mathilda looking at him with a pawky raised eyebrow. She mouthed *peacock* at him, and he replied with a silent *you're another!*

"My, my, don't you all look fine," Red Leaf said, when the work was done.

He poked a finger at Rudi: "You know, you're a dead ringer for a guy on the cover of one of those *Sweet Savage Romance* books I saw before the Change. There was this Swedish . . . woman . . . who used to haunt the powwows, she read 'em by the cartload; thought she was the reincarnation of an Indian Princess. We called her Princess Yumping Yimminy—"

Rick Three Bears grunted; probably because the massive bruise along his flank and the left side of his face made talking painful. He rolled his eyes and made the effort anyway:

"Dad, nobody's interested in what happened before the Change—at least, not right before. Let's go eat. Mom got up before dawn to start breakfast and she'll have a cow if anything spoils."

The visitors kept their faces polite, as was fitting for guests; Rudi suspected it was with a bit of effort.

Because each of us has thought exactly the same thing about our own oldsters, haven't we now?

From the wry smile, Red Leaf knew what they were thinking; he led the way to his own extended family's quarters, located in the place of honor near the *hocoka*'s entrance. His household had a set of five of the round platform-tents, with the sides rolled up to the roofline for better ventilation on the fine early-summer morning. The *itancan* introduced his wife, Sungila Win—a matronly lady a little younger than he, presumably named Fox Woman for her hair, with pleasant green eyes—and their four children, from one barely walking, stumping around in a moss-stuffed hide diaper, to Rick Three Bears' early twenties; his wife, *his* two children, his widowed sister and *her* three children and *their* spouses and infants, four young cousins and a brace of servant girls (who ate with the rest), and a couple of guests.

Evidently an *itancan*-chief was expected to keep open house.

Fair reminds me of home and the Hall, it does, Rudi thought, accepting a plate from Three Bears' mother. *What does Aunt Judy call it? A mispocha?*

"Sure, and it's a delight this hospitality is," he said, as they settled cross-legged around a low folding table that made a complete circle of the biggest tent. "I thank you for the trouble."

"You saved my boy Rick," Fox Woman said flatly.

Rudi blushed a little, made the Invocation, and applied himself to the food. The women had been busy with three portable stoves, and not in vain; there was frybread, lamb sausages redolent of garlic and sage, grilled walleye fillets fresh from the river, done with butter and pecans and steaming white and flaky on the fork, and plates of buffalo-hump hash and scrambled eggs savory with herbs and wild onion. While they ate, and drank the chicory and rose-hip tea and talked, Rudi leaned closer to Ingolf.

"You seem a little reserved, my friend," he said.

Everyone else is happy as crickets; nobody's trying to kill us, for starters, which is a pleasant change from yesterday and too many days this past year. Edain saved two lives with a close shot, which is something he needed *to do . . . but* you *are a bit grim.*

Ingolf chuckled. "Yah. Thing is, back when I was your age or a bit younger I spent *years* when the worst nightmare I had started with waking up in a Sioux camp. I nearly crapped myself this morning for a second, before I remembered the circumstances."

Rudi's brows went up. "Well, I suppose these folk can be bad enemies. Though they think there's nothing too good for a friend, I'd say, from how they've treated us, the which makes me think well of them."

"Yah . . . you know how the Anishinabe called the Sioux *the rattlesnakes*?"

"I'm not likely to forget," he said, wincing a little with remembered embarrassment. "I should have noticed you were signaling me to shut up . . ."

"Well, that's not the only name the neighbors had for them."

"Oh, so?"

"Yah. *The torturers* was a favorite too."

"Ingolf!"

He looked up as Mary called. "Come on, let's have a walk. The girls say there's going to be some all-female do later."

The party broke up. Three Bears and some other younger men captured Edain and demanded that he show them his longbow in operation, with Odard and Frederick in tow and Virginia following, elaborately casual. A collection of grave older men and women took

Father Ignatius away to spend the day administering sacraments; there were evidently a fair number of Catholic Christians in the *hocoka*, but a shortage of clergy.

Red Leaf looked a little surprised when Mathilda automatically joined him and Rudi.

I don't think women are much put upon here, Rudi thought. Certainly his host's wife and daughters hadn't been shy about offering opinions—they'd been strongly in favor of the men hunting down and killing all the lions, for instance. *But I get the impression war and politics are men's business, at least formally.*

"Ah . . ." Rudi said. "We didn't have time for formal introductions beyond the basics. This is Princess Mathilda Arminger, heir to the throne of the Portland Protective Association. Which is—"

"Yeah, I've heard of them," Red Leaf said. "Knights in armor . . . which after yesterday sounds a lot more credible. I've also heard that they're at war with the Cutters now; that all you Westerners are. Them and Boise."

Rudi nodded gravely, and Mathilda made a gesture of stately politeness, like the beginning of a curtsey.

"OK, I see your point. C'mon, I'll show you both around the place."

They strolled around the great circuit. Children and dogs followed them, but the people were mannerly; there seemed to be a code of conventions about when and how you could step within a family's section of the encampment, and for that matter who could speak to, or even notice, whom. Red Leaf pointed out the public facilities—the school-tents (in recess right now), the armories, the big tipis that were used for meetings of the warrior societies starting with his own Kit Foxes, the women's societies like the Tanners and Virtuous Women—

"Or so they claim," Red Leaf observed sardonically.

"Oh, Mathilda's as virtuous as you'd care to see," Rudi said blandly, and suppressed a yelp as she prodded him cruelly in one of the bruises on his ribs.

Some of the dwellers were setting out goods—weapons, tools, household gear, a vast array of leatherwork—

including a few traders from towns like Newcastle that had coal mines to fire their foundries. There were craftsmen at work as well: women spinning and weaving, a blacksmith with a portable forge, carpenters making the latticework frame of a tent, a saddler tooling intricate designs into the flaps of a silver-studded masterpiece.

"Fewer than I'd have expected, though," Rudi said. "From the abundance of well-made things."

"Ah, you noticed," Red Leaf said. "Yeah, we spend a lot of time in winter making things, when we're split up in our cold-season camps."

He nodded at two men a few years younger than himself. "Those guys are talking a big livestock deal."

Farther out from the *hocoka* men and a few younger women were practicing with arms; shooting at marks on the ground, and from the saddle at targets or at hoops of rawhide thrown to bounce and skip. Others picked pegs out of the ground with light lances, or speared hide rings held on the ends of poles, or cut and parried with shetes and used lariats.

Rudi grinned as one young man stood on the saddle of his galloping horse, dropped to one side with his hand on the pommel, vaulted over to the other flank and then bounced back up as if he were on a trampoline, doing a handstand on the saddle before flipping himself down again.

"Not bad, eh?" Red Leaf said proudly.

"Not bad at all."

Which is true enough, he thought. *They're fine shots and better than fine horsemen. Only middling with the blade, though, at best.*

Two youngsters brought them saddled horses. "Let's go up somewhere high and private," the *itancan* said.

"Your folk have done well by themselves," Rudi said.

They hobbled their horses, then sat and looked downward at the bustling activity as they shared a cigarette—from here you could see things kept at a sensible distance from the *hocoka*, like the butchering ground well southward along the river, downstream. The smoke of the cookfires was a faint tang from here. The scent the noonday sun baked out of the prairie was like lying in a haymow, with a spicy undertone and the grassy-earthy smell of the horses.

Mathilda coughed a bit as she handed the cigarette back. "I know this is an acquired habit," she said. "But why would anyone acquire it? And the old fo—ah, people who were around before the Change say it's bad for you."

Red Leaf gave a slight shrug and a smile. "It's sort of a religious thing here," he said. "Like sweetgrass. Besides which, the weed's so expensive these days you can't have enough to kill you."

He sighed and looked at the butt, then carefully ground it out; Rudi had noted that all these plainsmen were *very* careful about fire.

The last of the smoke blew away; the air had a hint of ozone to it as well, alien to someone raised in the well-watered Willamette but not disagreeable. And under that huge sky even the bustling *hocoka* looked tiny, an anthill among the vastness.

He's friendly because I saved his son, and because we fought with his band, Rudi thought. *This is a man who takes honor's obligation seriously. But also, I'm thinking, he's interested in us because he knows we're not just travelers. And that what we are could serve his people's need; which is also the honor of a Chief.*

"Yeah, we've done pretty well," the Lakota *itancan* went on. "Sure as hell better than most people did after the Change. Of course, when you're already flat on your face falling doesn't hurt as much. And we were way the hell away from anywhere urban. Unless you counted Sioux Falls as a big city."

Evidently he considered that funny, for some reason; probably a local joke, even a pre-Change one. Rudi went on, remembering things his mother and the other older Mackenzies had told him:

"And I imagine that a lot of your folk were more ready than most to believe that something *had* happened. Their spirits not being comfortably settled in the way things were before the Change, so. One of *our* founders said . . . what was it . . . *When the going gets weird, the weird get going.*"

"Ah, you're not just tall, handsome and quick with a chopper, eh, kilt-boy?" Red Leaf said with respect. "Yeah, there was that. It'd been one damned shafting after another for us since my great-great-granddaddy's day, when we lifted Custer's hair. Not that the son of a bitch didn't deserve it . . . Everyone else around here was knocked flat mentally in 'ninety-eight—*their* happy time was over, but they didn't want to admit it. A lot of *us* thought it was time to rock."

"We in the Willamette are the only place we know near a big city where *everyone* didn't die. And most did, so," Rudi pointed out.

Mathilda nodded. "There were more than a *million* people in Portland," she said. "My father and mother managed to get a couple of hundred thousand through alive. Nobody here . . . nobody east of the Cascades . . . was *that* badly off."

Red Leaf lay back on one elbow and handed them a skin bag from his saddle. "Yeah, the Ranchers got back on their feet after a while, doing the *Lonesome Dove* and Kit Carson thing. But a lot of us Lakota saw the Change more as opportunity knocking and *landed* on our feet. We knew what we wanted to do and we went and did it."

"And when you know that, and others don't, they'll follow your lead," Rudi said, and took a drink.

After a moment he looked down at the *chagal.* The liquid within tasted faintly alcoholic, and very slightly fizzy. The rest of the taste was something vaguely related to sour milk; as if you'd poured beer into what the hearth-lady of some farm left out for the house-hob. He took another swallow for politeness' sake and handed it to Mathilda; if he was going to suffer, why shouldn't she?

"Damn right," Red Leaf went on. "Though there was a fair bit of argument over what sort of opportunity it was. I mean, we couldn't *really* go back to the old ways."

"I remember my father complaining about that," Mathilda said. "He *did* want to go back to the old ways— the new ones having failed. But it was impossible. The people were different."

Red Leaf nodded. "Yeah, by 'ninety-eight it'd been five generations since we followed the buffalo; a lot of things we had to dig out of books and experiment with, or set up relays of people to learn from some old geezer who was the last one who knew it, or find a hobbyist, all the while not starving to death in the meantime. Would you believe it, there were even people on the rez who'd never butchered an animal or ridden a horse? *Lakota* who'd never ridden a *horse*! And finding people who knew how to make things like bows . . . Jesus."

"And they more precious than gold," Rudi said, remembering Sam Aylward.

"Damn right. And for another, just between me and thee and don't tell Three Bears I said so, the old days weren't all that great. They probably beat the hell out of living in a leaky mobile home on the rez and dying of diabetes or crawling into a bottle of bad whiskey or just plain what's-the-use, or even running a casino, but I and a bunch of others realized we'd have to make something new—with the best of the old, sure, but new. And including things like germ theory and books. You can carry books around in a wagon—printing presses too, for that matter, and microscopes."

"I'd noticed the tents weren't exactly tipis," Rudi said.

"The *gers*?" Red Leaf laughed. "That one was my doing. There was this guy from Mongolia at South Dakota U while I was there. Name of Ulagan Chinua—it means Red Wolf—he was studying how we managed our grasslands, some sort of State Department foreign aid thing, and he actually built a *ger* out of stuff from Home Depot—"

That required a minute's explanation, though Rudi had once helped strip the last useful goods out of a burnt-out shell with that name on the front.

"—and lived in it just off campus. A bunch of us used to hang out there and drink *airag*—"

He held up the leather bottle.

"What's *airag*?" Mathilda said; to Rudi's surprise she took it and drank a long swallow. "It's not bad. Sort of like small beer."

"Fermented mare's milk," Red Leaf said. "Red Wolf home brewed it; his mother sent him the starter culture by Federal Express. We'd swig it and swap stories about Crazy Horse and Genghis Khan or talk about girls and horses and football ... I really miss football ... It's too weak to get really blitzed on, and it makes milk easy to digest for us non-palefaces. Something about breaking down the lactose."

"What happened to Red Wolf?" Rudi asked curiously.

"I pretty well dragged him back to Pine Ridge with me about Change Day plus six; the poor brave bastard was going to try and ride a horse back to Mongolia via Alaska, but I talked him out of it. He married my *t'ankši*, my kid sister, as a matter of fact. Died three years back on a buffalo hunt—those bulls will hook you if you're not careful. But he was *real* helpful. Nice guy, too."

"I'd guess *his* people did well after the Change."

"I'd be surprised if they didn't, from what he told us about the place. Anyway, tipis are *drafty*; there's all that waste space above your head. A *ger*'s easier to heat, it doesn't blow over in storms, and if you put it on wheels all you have to do is unhitch the horses and you're there, wherever there is. And we had to get out of those shacks and trailers or freeze, with no more gas. Took a couple of years, but we managed."

He pointed; a family were leaving, their two *gers* drawn by half a dozen horses each and a wagon following along behind; two more were coming in, heading for the banners of their *tiyospaye*—clans—and being directed by the camp marshals.

"Moving around makes more sense here than trying to stay in one spot where you eat the land bare; in the winter we spread out in the sheltered places along the rivers or in hills, and in the summer we get together to swap and trade and socialize and talk politics. We're really stockmen now—we grow a few gardens here and there, we put up lots of hay, we mine the ruins and make stuff, and we hunt a fair bit, but there aren't enough buffalo to keep us fed. Not even now, and we've got a couple of million as of last summer's count. Back right after the Change, not a chance; plenty of cattle, though. You can live pretty well in this country, if you know how and you're careful and you've got enough acres."

"The real problem being the neighbors," Rudi guessed.

The Indian sighed. "No shit, Sherlock. Not the Fargo or Marshall people and the other Staters. We can live with them—they're not short of farmland anyway. When they do get crowded they'll move East. It's the Cutters."

"Who are mostly cattlemen too," Rudi observed.

"And we've got a lot of good grazing country; but even that wouldn't be too bad without that crazy religion of theirs. Yeah, a little raiding back and forth with the Ranchers, some horse-stealing... that keeps the younger guys on their toes, and keeps life from getting dull. But Corwin wants everything and they want you body and soul. And there are a hell of a lot of them nowadays. We Lakota can put thirty, forty thousand men into the field, max. The Cutters can do three or four times that."

The young man and woman from Oregon winced. "The Protectorate... my country... has about four hundred thousand people," Mathilda said.

"And the rest of our area... the realms that come together at the Corvallis Meeting... about as many again," Rudi added. "All of us together could probably match their numbers in war, or nearly."

Red Leaf cocked an eyebrow. "But I hear Boise has thrown in with the Cutters, made an alliance at least. That kicks up their numbers even more. We're not afraid of the Cutters, exactly, but we sure don't want to take 'em on by ourselves again. Once bitten, twice shy."

Rudi smiled. "Now, those numbers of theirs are a

shame and a pity. But it isn't necessarily so that if you fight them you must do so alone."

Red Leaf nodded slowly. "We haven't had much luck with alliances," he said. "Virginia's dad aside. We'll talk about this more later. Right now, there's some things planned for later today."

"So this ceremony is OK?" Mathilda asked, feeling a slight flutter of nervousness beneath her breastbone.

Father Ignatius nodded. "It's more a civil matter than religious in our sense, strictly speaking," he said. "I've questioned the Catholics here. In fact, there would be no problem with even a priest taking part. God is no respecter of either persons or names—Dieu or Gott or Kyrie or Adonai or Wakantanka. He *is* the Great Spirit whose pity we ask. If this helps you direct your thoughts to Him, or to Our Lady or your patron saint, there is no harm in it."

The women's sweat lodge was surrounded by a square of leather panels on poles. Two older women stood at the east-facing flap with their arms crossed and stern expressions on their faces. Mathilda swallowed and ducked through. Within was the dome-shaped lodge, set directly on the earth, with a door made of a hide flap, facing eastward. The fire was ready, and the rocks were already starting to glow and crackle . . .

Rudi blinked into the dimness of the men's sweat lodge. It was made of sixteen willow poles bunched to the four points of the compass and covered in buffalo skins; the last of the hot rocks had just been handed in held between wooden paddles and dropped into the pit in the center. The roof was no more than four feet high at the tallest point, and it was crowded with the five men of his party, plus Red Leaf and Three Bears and the *wicaša wakan*, the Sacred Man, the shaman sitting at the end of their circle by the entrance. Naked bodies crowded to either side of him. It was already hot; there was a smell of sweat and earth and scorched rock and leather, of the tobacco and sweetgrass already burned, of the sage padding beneath them.

"*Yuȟpa yo!*" the Sacred Man cried, in a cracked elderly voice.

The flap was thrown closed from the outside, and the darkness became like hot wet cloth over the eyes. The stones hissed as the shaman sprinkled water on them. The eight men cried out together:

"*Ho! Tunkašila! Ho, Grandfather!*"

The shaman's voice rose in nasal chanting prayer, directed to the four points of the compass; the sprinkling and response was repeated, and each time it finished the men called out "*Hau!*" together.

The rite was strange, but Rudi could feel the power in it. A calling had been made, and Someone had answered. Sweat poured from his body, and with it he seemed to feel all impurity leaving him; the darkness was absolute, but he could *see* with a clarity he'd rarely had before outside dreams. He stilled mind and heart, breathing in deeply of the scented steam, drawing it down into the depths of his self. Something glowed in the darkness . . .

A command, and the flap was thrown open. He gasped and shuddered, his skin rippling as the cooler air flowed in, and with it a little light. The old shaman grinned at him with his wrinkled eagle face, and the dipper was passed around. The sip he took was like wine . . . like the *spirit* of cool white wine, and when he poured a little over his head the chill came like a breath off the glaciers of the Cascades.

"*Mitak oyas'in,*" he murmured as he'd been instructed, and passed on the dipper to Odard beside him.

The Baron of Gervais was looking very pale, he thought; beyond him Father Ignatius had a secret smile on his face as he stared into the heat quaver over the rocks—almost the look a man might have when he contemplated his beloved.

I wonder how Matti is taking it, he thought. *And I wonder if the women's rite is much different.*

The thought flitted through his mind without leaving any tracks; it was as if something within—the part that carried on a conversation with itself and watched itself in endless contemplation—was being lulled to sleep. Then the shaman cried:

"Yuȟpa yo!"

Darkness fell once more. He was falling with it, like a particle drawn in by the breath of a beast larger than the Earth. He tumbled through the dark, and panic started to build up, and with it consciousness of the sage beneath him and the others around. Rudi took a long breath and released it, letting his heartbeat slow, letting awareness of everything but the steam hissing up and the wailing chant vanish.

"Ho! Tunkašila! Ho, Grandfather!"

He sank again, but this time it was a spiral glide—a dance, where his feet moved through a mist of stars. He could *hear* thoughts roaring by him, buffeting at him like storm winds against a man on a mountaintop. It was exhilaration, like a perfect stroke with the sword, like the kiss of danger, like the exultation of rising above fear.

Light glowed again. It took shape—

The flap opened. He felt as if he could laugh aloud, but there was no impulse to actually do it. Instead he took the water, sipped, poured a little over his head.

"Mitak oyas'in."

Darkness fell again, and he danced with stars. Flaming curtains walled creation; beacons shone across endless skies. But he was not alone; the others were with him; Edain's earth solidity, Ingolf's elk strength, the priest's joyful stillness that vibrated like a single harpstring, Odard's sharp-flavored complexity, Fred's young eagerness. Distantly he knew he was slapping his hands on his shoulders and thighs; when he cried *Hau!* at the end of a prayer it was as if the breath left him in a plume of silver light.

The cycle repeated. *The sword is a mind,* he thought. *The sword is my self. The sword is a song that They sing through me.*

Light returned; the light of common day, but it was shining *through* him now. He became aware of the shaman's high call:

". . . but the one eye which is the heart, *Chante Ishta*. We give thanks to the helper, may his generations be blessed. It is good! It is finished! *Hetchetu welo!*"

The men turned and paced sunwise, the shaman leading them out of the lodge, each stopping to purify their hands and feet over the fire of sweetgrass. Rudi blinked; hands led him gently to the edge of a leather tank on poles, and he scooped cold water over himself. With each shock of coolness he could feel himself sinking down into his body once more, but that was good as well. That was where he belonged, and there were things that must be done before he walked amid the sea of stars again.

And I could use dinner, he thought suddenly, grinning.

The helpers handed them their clothes. The shaman looked at him.

"You're one strange white man," he said. "I wasn't sure if my nephew was being smart about this, but he was right. You've got some important *wakan* people looking after you, Strong Raven. Your friend Swift Arrow"—he nodded at Edain—"has a Wolf; and White Buffalo Woman is with the Father. But you, you've got Mica—Coyote Old Man—nosing around, and not just him. That can be really good or really bad . . ."

Rudi bowed gravely, and made his own people's gesture of reverence, as he might have to an antler-crowned High Priest in the sacred wood.

A crowd stood outside, a blaze of feathers and beadwork and finery in the light of the setting sun; a shout of *"Hunka! Hunkalowanpi!"* went up. Red Leaf and his son led them proudly to the great tipi which had been pitched nearby—this was no *ger*, but in the ancient twenty-eight-pole conical form, the hides snow-white and drawn with pictograms. His wife and the women of Rudi's party were there as well. Suddenly Red Leaf and Three Bears seized Rudi by the shoulders and thrust him within; he staggered past the doorway, nearly colliding with Mathilda and then the others as their hosts pushed them through. An earthen altar stood in the center of the tipi, with a buffalo skull and a rack that held the sacred pipe. Two wands decorated with horsetails and feathers stood in the rack; another was speared into the earth, with an ear of corn on it.

Beside him Virginia Kane drew a sharp breath. *"Hunkalowanpi!"* she said.

"And what would that be when it's up and about?" Edain murmured.

"It's the *making-relatives-ceremony*. Red Leaf must have been *really* impressed with you guys. You're about to be adopted."

The platters went around again. Ritva contemplated a cracked marrow bone, decided not to, and belched gently.

"So, the big one with the brown beard is your guy?" one of the Lakota girls asked her.

She was Red Leaf's sister's daughter, and her name was Winona—which actually turned out to be a Sioux name, and meant something like *First Female Kid*—but she looked a little different from her uncle, her eyes much narrower and more sharply slanted, and her nose nearly snubbed.

"No, he's my sister Mary's," the Dúnedain said. "She won the toss when we flipped for him. I *still* say she cheated."

Everyone laughed. There were a couple of dozen of young Ogallala women within earshot, watching the men dancing in a way that involved hoops, drums, flutes, chanting and some extremely acrobatic maneuvers, and the feasting was at the stage Dúnedain called filling-up-the-corners. The drink was mainly herbal teas and the vile, and vilely weak, *airag*, but there was beer and some just-barely-passable wine in jugs as well. She took a mouthful of frybread; one of the stews had enough chilies to pass for *hot* even in Bend.

And all of these girls are just as curious as I would be in their shoes . . . or out of them.

"I did not cheat!" Mary chided. "You just have *no* skill in coin-flipping, Ritva. Anyway, I won paper-scissors-rock for him, too! Plus, I had to catch him all on my own."

"Hell, I always said you should make 'em chase you until you catch them," Virginia Kane said.

"Or until they catch you and you scalp them," Mathilda said dryly.

I don't think she likes Virginia much, Ritva thought. *Don't worry, Matti, Rudi will always love you best. Though you're driving him up the wall, poor boy . . .*

There was another laugh at that, but there was a trace of uneasiness in it, and the glances Virginia got were halfway between admiring and apprehensive.

"That's nice dancing," Ritva said.

"Oh, that's nothing. You should be here for the Sun Dance—the costumes are gorgeous."

"So, your fellah is the tall, good-looking one with the hair like a sunset?" the teenager said to Mathilda, returning to the subject with terrier persistence.

"Ah . . . well, we're very good friends."

That produced more giggles. "I'd like to be his good friend too," one young woman said.

"Oh, looks aren't everything," another said. "He might be one of those I-am-a-buffalo-bull types, bone clear through the head."

Mathilda bristled, and Ritva smiled as she went on: "Well, he's smart, too, and a fine swordsman"—her blush went up to glowing-coal levels at the laugh *that* got—"and a good hunter and he has a wonderful singing voice!"

"But can he cook?" one asked teasingly.

"He'll get a chance to hunt," another said. "The *itancan* says the buffalo need trimming."

That brought a bit of a groan. Ritva raised her brows. "You don't like hunting?" she said.

"The men get all the fun, and we get to do all the work."

We'll see about that! Ritva thought.

CHAPTER EIGHTEEN

Blood yields life, the land's deepest gift
Is taken and given—

From: *The Song of Bear and Raven*
Attributed to Fiorbhinn Mackenzie, 1st century CY

PRAIRIE, WESTERN SOUTH DAKOTA
JUNE 10, CY24/2022 AD

"It's different, seeing so many together," Rudi said quietly. "They're impressive enough one by one, but it's something else here."

The rise they were on was a hill only by prairie standards, but it gave them a good view. The bison were in clumps and straggling groups and lone individuals, grazing their way across the rippling plain and working gradually northward; the grass was fetlock-high before them, and cropped to an inch or less behind. The morning sun cast their outlines eastward, until the shape was like cloud shadow moving over the plains.

And as you raised your eyes there were more, and more, and more . . . almost to the edge of sight. The wind was from the south, and it brought the scent of them, like cattle but harsher, a wild musky smell. Birds flew about the great animals' feet, snapping up the insects they stirred; a twenty-strong pack of wolves hoping to cut out a calf had sheered off to the westward when the mounted humans arrived. Several pair of golden eagles swept the sky above, seven-foot wingspans tiny with height, waiting for the herd to flush something bigger. As he watched, one of them folded its pinions and struck like a bronze-colored thunderbolt.

Rudi mentally drew a box, rough-counted the buffalo within and multiplied.

Eighty or ninety thousand head, he thought. *I don't think I've ever seen that* many *of anything breathing but birds in one place before.*

He could feel his hair starting to bristle; the low rumble of their hooves was like a vibration that echoed in the tissues of his lungs and gut. And he could *hear* the sound of their feeding, nearly a hundred thousand pairs of strong jaws tearing at the Western wheatgrass, needle-and-thread and sagewort.

"Pretty, aren't they?" Red Leaf said, looking down at the mass of moving muscle and bone and horn and smiling with delight. "Never thought I'd see anything like it when I was your age, except in a movie. This is a cow-calf herd—cows, calves, yearling and two-year bulls. The big herd bulls mostly stay away until the rutting season, in another couple of months."

"*Awesome* was more the word I was thinking, not *pretty*," Rudi said. "And so many! Weren't they rare before the Change?"

"There were a couple of hundred thousand around, on ranches mainly," Red Leaf said. "And they can double every three years, if there's room, even if you harvest a third every year—you just take the bulls. They only need one for every twenty or so cows. There's another herd twice as big as this a few miles north; millions altogether."

Mathilda blinked. "Do they go away in the winter?"

"No, they just scatter a bit. Storms that'll kill half the cattle on a range don't even bother 'em—they don't freeze and they can get at grass through any ordinary snow."

"Why hunt a lot of them now, then? Why not a bit at a time when you need them?" she asked.

Red Leaf nodded. "We do take a few every so often, for fresh meat; and we have a winter hunt, for robes—

that's when the hair's best. But this is the best time of year to make pemmican; you dry the meat, grind it up to powder and flakes, mix it with melted fat and pour it into rawhide parfleche bags. It'll keep for three, four years if you're careful. It makes great soup base, with a little dried onion."

Mathilda nodded gravely in her turn; she'd tasted the results. Rudi had the same thought: pemmican was convenient and nourishing, and that was about all you could say for it.

Red Leaf raised a brow and waved at the prairie. "I know what you're thinking. But this has been a good year; good rain, good grass—third good year in a row. Sure as fate, though, we get bad droughts every so often. Sometimes for years at a time. Then most of the herds will die, cattle and *tatonka* both, or we have to slaughter everything except some of the breeding stock to let the grazing recover faster. So we keep a couple of years' food on hand. That way after a dry-year dieback we can harvest less. Then they'll breed back faster."

Mathilda nodded thoughtfully. "Very sensible," she said.

"Pemmican isn't hump steak by a long shot, but it beats starving to death," the *itancan* said. "Which is what the *wolves* do when the rains fail."

He waved, and Rudi's group gathered close, their horses' noses in a circle; the young men and a few of the young women of the *hocoka* who'd be going on their first hunt closed in around them. His first words were to the outsiders.

"OK, now you're *hunk-ate*, you're entitled to take part in the hunt. That doesn't mean you *have* to do it. These aren't cattle; they're wild animals, and big ones. You come off your horse once they start moving, or your horse goes down, you'll have to be scraped up with a shovel. Even guys who've been doing this for years get killed sometimes. Understand?"

They all nodded; Rudi kept his face sober, but he felt a grin bubbling up beneath it, like the ones that were splitting Edain's face, and Fred's. Odard was looking politely interested; he might not have gone if the other men hadn't, but he was going to enjoy himself anyway. The only male of their party not here was Father Ignatius, who'd politely excused himself to continue hearing confessions and celebrating masses; and to consult with the *hocoka*'s physicians about replenishing their medicine chests; and to the brain-cracking labor of putting their reports in cipher.

And none of the girls was going to back down if the others didn't, either. They wouldn't have been here if they were the types who could back down from a dare, even an unspoken one.

Mathilda and Virginia don't seem to have hit it off. That's a pity; they're rather alike, in some ways.

Red Leaf nodded, then spoke a little louder to include the Sioux youngsters: "OK, here's how we do it, and don't you roll your eyes while I'm talking, Mato Kokipapi. The bears may be afraid of you, but *tatonka* ain't. You've helped your folks with their cattle since you could ride, right?"

"Sure, *itancan*," the young man in question said.

"Well, there's a good goddamned reason you haven't been allowed on the buffalo hunt yet and how heavy a bow you could pull is only part of it. *Tatonka* aren't cattle. You can get 'em moving but you can't head them off. We love *tatonka*, but remember that the Buffalo People don't love us; we're just like the wolves or the damn lions to them. They don't care if you yell and wave a lariat in their faces. If you get between them and where they want to go they'll smash right into you and dance on you, and they'll hook you or your horse if they can. You keep behind them or alongside . . . but not too close."

He pointed, obviously taking the opportunity provided by the newcomers to force the Lakota youngsters to listen to what they'd already heard many times; that one more time that could save a life. Even with the mounting excitement Rudi recognized the manner. Sam Aylward and Sir Nigel had the same technique of patient repetition to drive essential lessons home in resistant young skulls.

"Now, everyone see those guys?"

A dozen mounted Sioux were easing their horses into the herd on the southern fringe, careful not to spook any of them. The animals moved away from them, but slowly; sometimes a ring would form, the bearded horned heads looking inward. A few of them blatted in surprise when the riders approached and lumbered off, or bellowed and pawed the earth, but most put their heads down and began grazing again almost immediately. The men were mostly older, in their thirties or even forties, and they were lofting balls of fleece at the odd buffalo here and there. When one struck a gout of pink dust went up, staining the beast's hump.

"Those are the Choosers. They've been marking the ones you *don't* shoot for a couple of days now."

Ah, Rudi thought. *They're picking the young bulls that* won't *charge or make threat displays. Selecting the most even-tempered ones.*

The *itancan* continued: "Don't go near the cows with calves, or the young females. When the herd starts to move, the mothers will drift to the inside anyway, so stay towards the rear and the outside. The *other* reason we have the big hunt now is that they start breeding in July, and *Iktomi!* they get mean! What we're after is the yearling and two-year bulls and the barren cows. Give them an arrow through the lungs or heart, and then sheer off. Finish them with the lance later when they're down. Start when you hear the call and *stop* when you hear the call for that."

Rudi nodded, and there was a murmur of agreement from the others. The Sioux dismounted and gathered in a murmuring circle around a small fire of sweetgrass; Red Leaf was waving it with an eagle-wing fan. Rudi made the Invoking sign, raised his bow above his head and murmured his own hunter's prayer:

"Forgive us, brothers, and speak well of us to the Guardians; thank you for your gift of life. It won't be wasted. Horned Lord, witness that we take from Your bounty in need, not wantonness. Guide the spirits of those we slay home to the fields of the Land of Sum-

mer, where no evil comes, until they are reborn through
the Cauldron of Her who is mother to us all. This we
ask, knowing that the Hour of the Hunter shall come for
us too at the appointed time, for we borrow our bodies
from Earth for only a little space, and Earth must be
fed."

Then they moved out, bows in hand and hunting
lances in the scabbards behind their right elbow; the
weapons had seven-foot shafts and a vicious head like
a double-edged butcher's tool. Rudi was riding one of
Red Leaf's trained buffalo ponies, though Epona and
the rest were with the remount herd. The animal was
smallish for someone his height, but it had a deep muscular barrel and a bright intelligent eye, and it had done
this for five or six seasons. They rode south down the
long slope, across the front of the great mass of bison
and down its western flank with a thousand-yard wide
space on their left, until they were behind the herd and
the Choosers rejoined them.

Those were Red Leaf's most experienced hunters, and
each of them took a selection of the first-timers under
his care; other men worked alone, or in family groups,
and there were seventy bows in all. The *itancan* himself
kept his son and his new relatives with him, as well as
Frightens Bears and a few others. The older hunters
were steady and intent, their faces grave; Rudi took a
deep breath and focused, pulling up strength from Earth
below and down from Sky above.

They fanned out and walked their horses forward.
The noise of the herd grew steadily as they approached
it, the grunting of mothers to calves the loudest sound.
Rudi blinked as he realized that the deep rumbling beneath it was tens of thousands of ruminant stomachs,
then grinned in delight for an instant. That would be a
wonder to tell his grandchildren!

"When you get within twenty yards, they start moving
away," Red Leaf said.

The chief's recurve came up and he drew smoothly
to the ear. The four-edged triangular head slid back
through the cutout of the bow until it rested just above

his left knuckle. The buffalo ahead of him was a two-year-old male, big and turned dark brown but without the muscled hairy massiveness of the great herd bulls. It sped up a little as his horse approached, giving a look over its shoulder and then moving up to a trot that looked clumsy and lumbering but started to draw away from the hunter.

"So shoot . . . *now*!"

The snap of the string against his bracer and the wet solid *thunk* of the arrowhead merged with each other. Beneath that Rudi could hear the crack of a rib parting under the impact of the steel. The arrow vanished to its fletching against the beast's flank, and a bawl of astonished agony cut across the lowing and stomach-grumble of the great herd. The young bull galloped then, blood fanning from its nose and mouth as it groaned; a thousand yards later it stumbled and went down as its left foreleg collapsed under it.

Rudi came to himself with a start as the other bows snapped, distracted by the primal dance of life and death. A yearling threw its head up at the smell of blood not ten yards away; he clamped his legs on the barrel of his horse, judged the moment . . .

Snap. The arrow's flight had the sweet inevitability to it, as always when you were going to hit the mark. It struck the buffalo high on the right shoulder and slanted down, vanishing completely within the body cavity. The beast stiffened and raised its tail, started to gather itself for a leap forward and collapsed.

"Kiy-ee-kiy!"

The shout rose from three-score throats as the hunting party signaled their agile ponies up to a gallop, and the alarm ran through the herd like a wave across water—the ambling progress suddenly turning to milling chaos, and then to headlong flight. The sound of its passage changed from a grumble to a roar to a thunder like the hammer of a god striking ten times a second, as twenty thousand tons of weight pounded the hard prairie soil through three hundred thousand hooves. Dust spurted upward, and suddenly he was riding through a mist of it, with great hairy rolling-eyed shapes looming up out of nowhere.

One came close; it had the pink slash on its hump, and he ignored it. Now he was deeper into the rearward fringe of the herd, with the black-brown shaggy humps plunging up and down on either side of him. A head jerked sideways, and the black curved horn missed his foot by inches; his arrow was already on the way, and cracked into the beast's spine. It fell, and another rammed into it from behind and went cartwheeling.

"Kiy-ee-kiy!" Rudi screamed exultantly himself; twitched an arrow out of the quiver and shot again—

When the recall sounded he coughed dust out of his lungs and spat brown. A swill of water from his canteen came out almost as soil-stained; he could feel the dust gritting between his back teeth. He coughed again, rinsed his mouth once more, then took a long lukewarm swig. The hunt had been brief—he'd spent the same amount of time stalking a single deer in the Cascade forests many a time. And none of the humans had been hurt badly, though Frightens Bears was flushed and embarrassed because Red Leaf had had to pull him out of a tight spot, and his friends were giving him new names—Craps His Pants and Tatonka's Trampoline were popular. The herd had swung well away eastward, and it was slowing as the pursuit ended and the smell of blood fell away.

There were smells aplenty around the Sioux hunting camp with its wagons and bustling scores, and plenty of work left to do. Nothing in either was unduly strange to someone who'd been born among farming folk who also hunted for the pot; Rudi had helped butcher livestock and dress game all his life, and so had his friends.

"Except the *scale* of the thing," Rudi muttered to himself, as he turned his exhausted pony over to a youth.

The great bodies were scattered back over miles, until they dwindled to black dots against the flower-flecked tawny-green grassland. Horse-drawn sleds of salvaged sheet metal with upturned fronts like toboggans were already at work, dragging the carcasses back. Rudi walked over and joined in as a team of men heaved a thousand-pound body onto one of them, then moved on to the next as a woman led the horses away, leaning into their collars; after he had his breath back it was enjoyable enough work except for the flies. Soon his whole body gleamed with sweat in the hot sun as he labored stripped to his breechclout.

At the camp the bodies were skinned by the women— that seemed to be considered female work among the Lakota, their curved knives flashing with unerring skill—but help in turning the bison from one side to another was appreciated. Then they were hoisted up by the hind legs with hook and rope and chain on tripods of stout wooden poles or metal rods, aided by pulleys at the top. The gutting and cleaning went swiftly with over a hundred hands at work with knife and hatchet, cleaver and bone-saw, but there were over eight hundred of the big beasts.

The first few bison to be broken up were surrounded by rings of hopeful camp-dogs, but there was enough offal to spare that they soon wandered off in a daze of bloated ecstasy. Garbh had quickly established herself as alpha-female and got the best bits; he saw her lying on her back not far from where Edain was working, feet splayed in the air and belly rounded, tongue lolling over her fangs as she made faint moaning sounds.

"Eight hundred and twenty-two!" Red Leaf called, as he walked through—the most senior hunters didn't have to do anything more. "Good work! Plenty of pemmican for winter, plenty of hides for tipis and harness and clothes!"

Call it two hundred tons of meat when they're dressed out, and much else of use besides, Rudi thought. *Now, that* is *a good day's work!*

The scores of the individual hunters were chalked up on a board hung on one of the wagons. Rudi's had been very respectable—seven—but Red Leaf had gotten fifteen, and his son Three Bears twelve. Edain, listed as Swift Arrow, had scored nine, the highest of all of the newcomers; he'd been using his longbow, possible on horseback when you were shooting directly to the left.

You know, I'd like nothing better than to pass a summer with these folk, Rudi thought. *It's a pity that we'll be moving on soon.*

The butchering teams worked steadily at their messy, bloody task, stopping only now and then to sharpen tools on whetstones and drink water carried around by youngsters. The area stank and attracted hordes of flies, but everyone was in good humor; there was a lot of teasing between the men and women, some of it as bawdy as anything Mackenzies did, though most of *that* was in Lakota. The entrails were turned inside out and scraped, put aside for a dozen uses; horns were carefully stacked, to be turned into everything from drinking vessels to strips on the bellies of bows; the valuable sinew that ran down beside the spine was bundled up. Most of the tongues went into barrels, to be salted down as delicacies for months to come.

Others gave the hides a first scraping and then scattered salt on the flesh side and stacked them high in bundles on wagons. The *crack ... crack ...* of axes on bone sounded as the skulls were split for the brains that would be used to tan the leather. Bones and hooves would make glue, or handles for tools; from what Red Leaf had told him, there was a use for everything, right down to cured stomach linings making good canteens. Of course, that didn't mean that every part of every beast was used, but most were.

The meat itself was sliced into long narrow paper-thin strips; those were dumped into tubs and pulled over to the racks. Others had cut back long shallow trenches in the turf and lit fires in them, low and smoky with sage; over those were erected the knock-down drying racks of wire mesh. The meat was rubbed with salt and powdered herbs and laid carefully in long rows, in the first stage of preservation.

Still other fires were lit for cooking. A number of young calves had been killed inadvertently—mostly knocked down by the near stampede. Those were split open and butterflied and set to grilling over the coals, with a cook using a long-handled brush to slather sauce on them from a keg. Tongue and hump meat went on beside them, and young girls carried around skewers of grilled tongue and kidney and liver. Rudi paused for a moment to take one; the rich taste of the organ meat spurted over his tongue, just short of burning-hot, incomparable when taken fresh in the field like this.

"That's the hunter's share," the girl said. "Seven *tatonka*! And on your first hunt, too."

"Tasty!" Rudi said, grinning at her; she was about the age of his sister Maud, twelve or so. "And done just right. Have a bite."

She did, then looked at him. Her eyes went a little wider as she took in the scars; the distinctive puckered arrow-marks on his shoulder and lower back, the long white marks of blades on his arms and legs and along the left side of his jaw. It was a remarkable collection for a man his age, and one who wasn't crippled by it either. If you knew anything about the matter, which nearly everyone in a Sioux camp did, it implied that the people who'd given him the scars were mostly worse off—fatally worse.

"You must be a *great* fighter!"

He took the skewer back and bit off a lump of kidney, chewing with a solemn, considering look, and said:

"Well, I'd be lying if I said no." Then he grinned and winked at her. "But I prefer hunting to fighting, and also dancing and wine and song and talking to pretty girls."

She laughed, flushing to the roots of her ash-blond hair, and dashed away. Rudi tallied on to a rope and helped hoist up another carcass, heaving with half a dozen others as the pulley clattered. Butchering hundreds of tons of buffalo took a lot longer than hunting them. By the time the late-summer sunset came Rudi could feel the tiredness down in his bones, the way you did at the end of the wheat-harvest back home. And the brief shower under nozzles attached to a wagon bearing a water-tank was inexpressibly welcome.

The night-camp was well away from the butchering

site, though relays of guards would be posted through-out the hours of darkness around the racks; he could hear the song of the coyotes already, and fainter with distance the deeper, fiercer sound of the lobo packs sig-naling to one another. The smell might bring bear or lion as well, which was a good reason to get a little distance before you slept. The water and fuel carts were there, but nobody needed a tent tonight.

"That was . . . interesting," Odard said, as they settled down around Red Leaf's campfire. "It's certainly *not* like shooting cows, which I thought it might be. Not in the least!"

Airag tasted better after you'd been drinking it for a week or so, Rudi found. It had a dry flavor beneath the first snail-squeezing impression, and it went down pleasantly with plates of hump steak and slices of juicy buffalo tongue. He took a swallow, upending the leather bottle with the bulk of it supported on his right elbow in the local style, and managing to avoid spilling any over his chin. Then he passed it on to Ingolf.

Mathilda sighed. "I'm having a great time. Things are less . . . complicated here than they are back home."

Fred Thurston nodded, but Virginia Kane thumped him on the shoulder.

Now, they *are getting on well indeed.*

"No, it ain't," she said. "You're just seeing part of it, and with an outsider's eyes, too."

Rudi sighed agreement, despite Mathilda's glare; still, even if it was disappointing, it was better to shatter the illusion.

"Matti, if someone were a guest at Castle Todenangst, they might think that *your* life was nothing but balls and hunts and hawking and tournaments and listening to the minstrels."

"This isn't like that," she replied. "This is work-ing life. And even the festivals at home, you're always looking out for some plot or intrigue or conspiracy or something."

Red Leaf was on the other side of the fire from them. He could still hear, and he chuckled:

"Nah, this is more of a working *vacation*; more interesting than sitting on your horse looking up a cow's ass, at least. And we've got our politics and problems, same as anyone else—and not just the Cutters. You folks haven't been around long enough to get a handle on them, is all. Plus, you're seeing the best time of year. Hunkered down in a blizzard, things can get sorta stressful, nothing but the same faces for weeks on end. I think that's why the old Lakota had a lot of those rules that look silly when you hear about 'em—not looking at your mother-in-law, and that sort of thing."

Rudi finished up the last spoonful of beans and roasted buffalo sirloin tips. He'd put away a lot of it, and felt an impulse to curl up on a warm rock for a week or two.

It's a good thing I'm not prone to constipation, he thought. *This diet would bring it on, sure and it would.*

Ingolf poured himself a cup of chicory from the tin pot that rested across two stones in the firepit; he could drink it past sundown and not stay awake, which he claimed was the result of overdosing on the stuff in his career as a paid soldier and salvager. Mary was leaning against his shoulder, blinking into the embers of the fire with drowsy contentment while Ritva plucked out a little wandering tune on Odard's lute.

The man from Wisconsin spoke, his voice a deep rumble:

"Yah, I've been to a lot of places from Oregon to the East Coast and back, and I've yet to find one where life is simple. You might think some plow-pusher's is, but you get close enough to see the details and it's got just as much going on beneath the surface as a Bossman's court. Mind you, there are Bossmen and then there are Bossmen. Des Moines—"

He shrugged. Unexpectedly, Ritva spoke:

"I agree with Matti, a little. A lot of things depend on size. Things *are* simpler when there aren't so many people."

She grinned. "Not necessarily *better*. Sometimes Mary and I would go on long winter hunts just to get away from Stardell Hall. There's that point where if you hear

Aunt Astrid correcting someone's pronunciation of the Sindarin pronominal verb endings *just one more time* you're going to start screeching and do something nasty with a hatchet."

She bent her head and began playing seriously, and she and Mary sang a duet. Rudi lay back against his saddle, watching the occasional spark drift upward towards the frosted sky. Matti's hand stole into his and she squeezed forgiveness for the momentary disagreement. He squeezed back, pleasantly aware of the solid warmth of her and the herbal wash on her hair, something the Lakota women made from sunflower oil and boiled-down flowers.

Then the twins started a tune he knew and he joined in with his strong baritone:

> *"A shadow in the bright bazaar;*
> *A hint of gold where none should shine—"*

More of Red Leaf's people drifted over, listening quietly.

> *"—her gold flanks heaving in distress;*
> *Half woman and half leopardess;*
> *From either side—nowhere to hide—*
> *It's time to fight or die!"*

CHAPTER NINETEEN

The faithless often treachery suffer;
Ill-will will evil mar
Luck is the gold of the Gods
And open-handed they bestow
To the hero whose courage earns—

From: *The Song of Bear and Raven*
Attributed to Fiorbhinn Mackenzie, 1st century CY

PRAIRIE, WESTERN SOUTH DAKOTA
JUNE 11, CY24/2022 AD

He dreamed of drums; drums that beat softly in the distance, and they woke him. His head had slipped from the blanket rolled around spare clothing that was his pillow, and his ear was pressed to the ground.

Hooves, he realized. *Many.*

He coiled erect, the night air cool on his naked skin and his sheathed sword in his right hand, his left on the long leather-and-wire wrapping of the hilt. A shape moved in the darkness, and he drew a handspan of the sword, moonlight and starlight glittering on the honed edge and the intricate damascene patterns in the steel.

"It's me," Red Leaf said. "Someone's coming from the *hocoka*, fast and at the wrong time."

Rudi sniffed the scents—dew, the stale ash odor of banked campfires. Then he cocked an eye at the heavens; no moon, and the stars had moved to—

"Three-quarters of an hour to dawn," he said. "You're right; they must have left not long after midnight."

Traveling in the dark is somewhat dangerous, even if you know the ground. They wouldn't have done it unless it was an emergency.

Ingolf was already awake when he began nudging his foot; Mary turned over and opened her eye as well. The others woke silently, except for a slight groan from Odard. They rose and dressed quickly and quietly, putting on the light war gear they'd brought with them, swords and bows, helmets and shields. By the time they were finished and had tied up their bedrolls Rick Three Bears had their horses and remounts cut out of the herd.

The whole Sioux party were awake and ready not long after, moving their wagons into a circle, the warriors ready to fight and the youngsters and women within—not that they weren't armed as well, and prepared to do whatever they had to. Even then, Rudi was a little impressed.

I wouldn't like to have to fight these people, he thought. *Doubly so not on their own ground. It would be like trying to hit a ghost with a club—and sure, you'd have to grow eyes in the back of your head, too.*

One of the perimeter scouts came trotting in on foot—it was hard to be inconspicuous on horseback, even for the lords of the High Plains.

"Horseman and a cart, *itancan*," he said.

"There's more behind them, by a couple of miles," Red Leaf said grimly. "Big party."

"I'm sorry if we've brought this on you," Mathilda said steadily.

Red Leaf made a single fierce gesture. "It's our land! Nobody comes on Lakota land without our leave, and nobody attacks our guests on our land!"

There was an answering growl from the crowd of his people. He pointed to six, all young and slight-built, and spoke rapidly in a mixture of English and Lakota.

"You get going," he said at the end. "Tell 'em we need everyone, and fast, and to pass it on."

Then he turned to Rudi. "That'll bring a couple of

thousand of our *zuyá wicaša* here, but that'll take a while. You'd better get going."

Rudi winced slightly; that meant abandoning their extra gear. But needs must ...

The sound of hooves and wheels came out of the darkness; the sky was just beginning to pale eastward, but the western horizon was still purple-black.

"It's me, Father Ignatius!" the priest's voice called.

He pulled up the two-wheeled mule cart; his horse was tethered to the rear of it, with the stirrups looped up over the saddlehorn.

"Two hundred of the Sword of the Prophet are approaching, according to the scouts around your *hocoka*," he said succinctly. "They're looking for Rudi and the rest of us."

"Right," Red Leaf said. He turned to Rudi, then pointed: "See that star? Keep it directly ahead of you until full daylight, then turn north and you'll hit the Black Hills. That's better than heading straight east— flat as a plate thataway."

Then he hesitated. "And the big herd is in that direction too; the one we hunted yesterday has probably joined it. It'll be moving north, pretty well, this time of year. Get across in front of it and it'll cover your tracks. Then you can turn north while they're trying to find you."

"How long would that take?"

Red Leaf smiled, or at least showed his teeth. "That's the main southern herd. How long does it take a quarter million of the Buffalo People to go by? And what's left of a trail after they've crossed it?"

"Right," Rudi said. He swung up onto Epona's back and leaned down to shake hands. "Lord and Lady bless you and yours, my friend."

"*Wakantanka* walk with you, Rudi Mackenzie, and all of you."

"I'd have liked to spend a summer hunting with your folk, and seen the Sun Dance. Maybe someday I can, and you and Rick can come to Dun Juniper for the Lughnasadh festival."

Red Leaf spoke a phrase in Lakota, then translated, first literally, and then the meaning: "*On the hillside. Someday, maybe.*"

Then he looked around for his son: "Rick, you go along until they're on their way—"

The young man looked a little mutinous at leaving when a fight might be coming.

"You forget what you owe Rudi?" his father asked. *"Hokahe!"*

The troopers of the Sword rode in disciplined silence despite the disconcerting vastness of the morning prairie and the subliminal knowledge of what the Sioux preferred to do to trespassers. Most of them were from mountain-and-valley country, only a few from the Hi-Line of central Montana, and they felt helplessly exposed here where the horizon merged into the slowly lightening sky.

Major Graber ignored the sensation, and the pain in his left arm, with equal indifference; he kept in mind that it would weaken his shield work and that he couldn't use his bow properly, and he would adjust his actions accordingly. He was here to command anyway, not fight with his own hands if avoidable.

And there was nothing wrong with his nose. The abattoir reek of death mingled with an ever-stronger hint of smoke, and of cooking meat. Drying-smoking racks . . . and yes, there was a plume silhouetted against the lighter eastern sky. He squinted into the sunrise that edged a few clouds there with crimson and faded to pink and then green and blue above, as the last stars guttered out behind him.

The smell and clutter as they rode through the Sioux hunting camp offended him, but . . .

What can you expect from savages who know not the Dictations? he thought, remembering the ordered neatness of Corwin with pleasure.

The new Seeker had arrived from the capital with reinforcements when they returned to the Bar Q ranch. That had been very fortunate . . .

Then he glanced quickly aside at the Seeker. The man had arrived *before* any message could have gotten to Corwin that he'd found the trail again. All they would have known from his dispatches there was that High Seeker Twain was killed in the Teton foothills last fall, and that he intended to work through the mountains and resume the search in the spring. Even that would have been lucky ... and there was no possible way the Hierarchy could have known how his own first foray across the border had ended.

But the Seeker had been there at the ranch, waiting— with troops who must have left *weeks* ago to make it through the wilderness and the passes.

Graber swallowed. *The Ascending Hierarchy commands all power,* he thought. *Doubtless he commands the Seventh Ray. That is an amethyst on his wristband.*

His own service was with the Fourth Ray, as the diamond on his personal amulet showed; that was under the Master Serapis Bey, and hence largely physical. The Seeker might even be an adept of Djwal Khul, who ruled communications of all sorts.

Dalan is *different from most Seekers I've seen.* Usually they were thin or gaunt; this one was stocky-muscular. *But the eyes are the same.*

He wrenched his mind back to the present, despite the thin film of sweat on his forehead. His was to obey. That he didn't *like* Seekers was between him and his conscience and the long wrestling with the emanations of the Nephilim that any soul must undergo.

There were no Sioux working around the drying racks, though the low fires under them still smoldered. A dozen wagons had been drawn up in a circle on a nearby rise, and between them he could see spears and the twinkle of arrowheads. That would be the noncombatants—not that they wouldn't fight if need be, of course. A good sixty Sioux warriors were drawn up a little way off, armed with bows and shetes and hunting-lances. Few of them had any body-armor beyond shields and steel caps, but they would fight like cougars, as he knew from painful experience.

Graber swung his fist aloft, and the formation halted, spreading out into a two-deep staggered line, bows in hand and the butts of the lances in the scabbards. Seeker Dalan spoke:

"They are not here. Close, but not here."

"Can you be more precise, honored Seeker?"

The square face with the flat black eyes turned back and forth, frowning. "No. I am ... resisted. A shadow is drawn."

He put his hands to the sides of his head; the sleeves of the robe of dried bloodred he wore fell back, showing arms encased in black leather guards striped with narrow steel splints.

"A woman? Or is it a buffalo? And a raven ... the blockage is not so complete as when they were in the Valley of the Sun, but you must rely on the physical. For now."

He felt relief at that, and reined out towards the mounted Indians. The Seeker followed; he had to admit the man was fearless, not like many of the red-robed ecclesiastical bureaucrats Corwin bred, who always put him in mind of the maggots that had writhed in a dead raccoon he'd found under the floorboards of his home two summers ago.

A man rode down to meet them, though he stopped well within bowshot of his own position.

"Hau kola," Graber said, raising his right hand in the peace gesture as he drew rein.

The Indian was a dark middle-aged man, muscular and heavy-featured, with a little gray in his braids; a full-blood from his looks. He wore a steel helmet with bison horns and fur, and a fox pelt over his colorful war-shirt. There were scalp-locks down the seams of the arms, more than was comfortable to contemplate; he'd have fought in the long indecisive struggle between the Church and his nation.

He didn't return the gesture, or speak at all.

Bad, Graber knew. *But, then, I expected that.*

"We're here after some fugitives, *itancan* Red Leaf," Graber said, guessing at his rank and remembering the briefing files. "Under the Treaty of Newcastle, the La-kota *tunwan* agreed not to harbor refugees from our territory or to hinder our recapture of such criminals."

The black eyes were chill as they rested on him. "Under the Treaty of Newcastle, the Church Universal and Triumphant agreed to recognize our sovereignty. Last time I looked, sovereign nations didn't have to let other countries send troops onto their soil uninvited. You invade us, the war starts up again and from what I hear, you folks are busy out West."

Damn those rebels to the Void! Graber thought.

"These criminals are under the personal ban of the Prophet," Graber said softly.

"Remind me why I should care what the Crackpot of Corwin thinks."

Graber felt himself flush at the blasphemy; rage came off the Seeker like heat from a closed stove in winter.

"You deny that there were fugitives here?" Graber said, his voice still flatly unemotional.

"Nobody here but my relatives," the Indian said, baring his teeth.

"He speaks truth, but with intent to deceive," Seeker Dalan said. Then: "There! There!"

He pointed north and east. The impassive face of the Sioux didn't move ... but Graber was experienced at reading men's eyes. Their lips lied, speaking or smiling, but the pupils never.

"We will pursue," he said. To Red Leaf: "Don't get in our way, and none of your people need be hurt."

The Sioux leader raised his hand, and his folk began to draw their bows. Graber smiled thinly, and raised his own left hand—despite the savage twinge of pain that shot into the joint. The long formation broke into motion again, advancing and reaching over their shoulders for arrows in a sinuous unison like a tiger uncoiling from sleep.

"I have two hundred men, *itancan*," he said. "We outnumber you four to one, and my men are in full armor. If you fight me at close quarters like this, I will lose perhaps twenty dead, including any too seriously wounded to ride. We will kill you all, and it will take less than ten minutes. Then we kill all the women and children in this hunting camp. Then we will proceed on our mission."

"None of you would leave Lakota territory alive!"

"Words cannot express how much I do not care, as long as my mission is fulfilled," Graber said flatly. "Or as long as I die in the pursuit of it."

A boast would have rung false; the Indian was no fool. Graber's eyes never left his. After a moment, the Sword commander nodded curtly and reined his horse around.

It will take them some time to assemble a war-party that outnumbers us sufficiently. We have that long.

He remembered blue-gray eyes looking into his, and a pleasant lilting voice speaking:

It is easy to kill. Any fool can do it.

"Shite," Rudi said in exasperation.

Maybe it wasn't a good idea to stop long enough to put the gear on pack-saddles, he thought. *But if we'd kept the cart, they'd be a lot closer. And we're going to* need *that equipment, later.*

The sun was well up now; his binoculars showed the wink of its light on lance-heads southeastward. Far too many of them and far too regular to be Sioux; and besides, the Lakota didn't use nine-foot lances or russet-colored armor, as far as he knew.

But the Sword of the Prophet do, *the creatures.*

Ritva rode towards them and reined in, pointing eastward in the direction she'd come. "The buffalo are there, Rudi. You would not *believe* how many. But . . ."

"But?"

"They're moving north, and picking up speed. It looks like something spooked them. We'd better hurry if we want to get across the front of them—if we don't, we'll have to wait on this side. It is *definitely* impossible to get through that herd while they're moving."

"Shite," Rudi swore again, this time with more feeling.

He couldn't see them yet, but he thought there was a haze of dust in that direction. And even when the ground looked as tabletop flat as it did here, he'd learned that distances were deceptive—the slightest roll or fall of the ground could hide anything shorter than a hill even if it was only a few miles off.

"No," Three Bears said. "It's good. If we can get across the herd before the Cutters catch up, I mean. It'll take hours—maybe a whole day—for them to pass. If we're on the other side, we might as well have mountains in between."

Ritva nodded vigorously.

"Then *go*," Rudi said. "Ingolf, you and Mary take lead. Three Bears and I will bring up the rear; we're the best mounted archers. *Now*."

The Easterner nodded grimly and legged his horse up to a hand gallop.

Rudi wished briefly that he had time to switch to Epona, but he'd been riding one of the remounts to spare her. It was a good beast, but not quite fifteen hands—and even riding in kilt and shirt, he was a little heavy for it. It was sweating already, the musky scent strong under the dust and crushed grass of their passage. Usually being six-two and built like a cougar was an advantage, but sometimes . . .

Three Bears cut out two more for them as the remount herd went by, with Edain and Virginia and Fred driving them forward. The pack-saddles some of them carried had only about half a rider's weight and wouldn't slow them much.

Ahead, Ingolf signaled and the travelers turned sharply east of north, moving in a compact mass with the remuda of remounts in the middle. Rudi shifted his balance forward, and the well-trained animal stretched its legs, head beating up and down as if to set the pace. He looked over his shoulder, and the enemy were visible to the naked eye; as he watched the ant-tiny dots seemed to swarm, and then some of them were pulling out ahead of the others.

"How many do you make it?" Rudi called over the rising rumble of the hoofbeats, as a covey of quail burst from the grass ahead of him; he gentled the horse instinctively as it started.

"Ten or fifteen pulling away from the others," Three Bears said, nodding at Rudi with his brown braids flying in the wind of their passage.

They'd both had the same thought: the Cutters knew they couldn't catch the smaller, better-mounted group all at once. Two hundred mounted men could only proceed at the speed of the slowest mounts, and in a group that size there would always be some slugs, especially if they'd been taking horses where they could get them. So they'd sent their best riders and beasts on ahead to push their quarry into tiring their horses.

"It's going to be close!" Rudi shouted back.

The Indian grinned; he was a young man, after all, younger than the Mackenzie, and of a warrior people. Then he turned in the saddle and shook his bow in the air.

"*Kye-eee-kye!*" he screamed. "Hoo'hay, *hoo'hay*! The sun shines on the hawk and on the quarry!"

Rudi bared his teeth too; he wasn't an oldster yet, either, and the Clan wasn't shy of a fight, and it was a bright summer's day with a good horse beneath him. His spirits lifted, seeming to fly with the long stride of the valiant mount between his legs. He added the saw-edged wailing ululation that Mackenzies took into battle.

Then he settled down to coaxing as much speed as he could out of the horse, short of the all-out dash that would set its lungs foaming out. The Cutters *were* pushing theirs to the uttermost; they could fall back and let others take up the sprint if they had to. And the buffalo herd was just coming into sight eastward.

"Cernunnos!" he blurted as it did.

There's miles *of the things!*

He could *hear* them, even miles away and on a galloping horse, a fast drumming rumble that struck at his face and chest. Too far to see individual animals, even ones as big as buffalo, but the great black-gray mass seemed to undulate, like waves on the sea. The forefront of the herd was a spray of dots; as they got a little closer he could see that they were the big ton-weight herd bulls, their massive heads down and the great shaggy humps rising and falling. At rest or walking they would look clumsy and slow, but now they were moving as fast as a horse could, or a little faster, their mouths open and lines of white foam falling from their tongues, everything lost but the need to *flee*.

"Going to be close!" Three Bears said again.

Rudi looked behind, over the head of the remount on its leading rein. The foremost Cutters were much closer now, and foam *was* slobbering from their horses' mouths and clotting on their forequarters. Probably none of the Corwinites was Rudi's size or weight, but they all had their war-harness on, which more or less equalized things. As he watched one of the ones at the rear fell away, his horse shaking its head and stumbling. The three in the lead rose in the stirrups and drew. Their upper bodies hardly seemed to move at all as their horses galloped . . .

"Uh-oh!" Three Bears called.

"I know what *uh-oh* means!" Rudi replied.

"It means *we're fucked!*"

They both hunched down in the saddle. Wearing helms and with their round shields slung over their backs, they presented a minimum target. His back crawled a little as he waited for the *whipppt* of arrows.

And since that fight after Picabo, I've been just a little more nervous of that sound.

It came, but faintly. He looked around; the last shaft hit the ground as he watched, about ten yards behind them. Rudi clamped his thighs on the saddle and twisted, bringing up the bow. The recurve was a masterpiece from the best bowyer in Bend, and the long muscles of his arm coiled as he drew to the ear. Then *loose*, and the snap of the string on his bracer, the slam of the recoil, the shaft seeming to slow as it arched out at the doll-tiny shape of the pursuers.

Three Bears whooped as one of them ducked, and his horse took a half-step sideways in a puff of dust as an arrow landed between him and the Mackenzie. They fell back a little as Rudi sprayed three more shafts towards them as fast as he could draw, but hitting a moving target from a horse at better than two hundred yards was more a matter of luck than skill.

"Cernunnos!" Rudi grunted again as he looked forward.

The herd was much closer, and closing fast; the beasts were running straight north, and the travelers were angling to cut across their front. That *might* be possible; Ingolf and Mary were already past the first of them. The noise was much louder now, and the dust-cloud turned the morning sun into a swollen red orb. Looking back southward they stretched to the end of sight—and you could see a *long* way on the plains; it was as if a carpet of running bison extended from here to the other end of the world. The angle gave him a view across the front of the herd, where the mass frayed out into individuals, and it was half a mile to the other side.

The noise was stunning, and growing with every stride, building to a roar like all the waterfalls in the world, the sound of a million hooves hitting the soil as a quarter-million buffalo stampeded in blind fear and fury. He could smell them too, dung and piss and the hard dry stink of their bodies, like oxen working in the sun but wilder, and the rank exhalations of their panting breath. It took an effort of the will to keep angling towards them; his gut was convinced that it was insanity, that they could pound down mountains and turn him into a paste mixed inextricably with the flesh of his horse.

Whipppt!

An arrow went by, not ten feet to his left, and then three more followed it; the last was uncomfortably close to his horse's haunches. He turned and shot again himself, and one of the pursuers went down in a tumble of man and horse—he must have hit the mount.

"Sorry, brother horse!" he called, and then whooped laughter as the Cutter staggered to his feet only to topple face-first on the grass.

This is immortality! he exulted. *I'm immortal because I could die in the next second!*

Three Bears shot too; he rode twenty-five or thirty

pounds lighter than Rudi and his horse was pulling ahead, turning across the front of the herd.

Thock!

The arrow hit Rudi's shield with an impact like a blow from a club; there was no pain beyond that, and a quick glance showed it standing in the bullhide like a weed sprouting from dirt. The narrow point showed just under his armpit, dimpling through the felt glued to the inside of the shield.

Rudi twisted and shot again. That let him see the Cutter shaft hit his horse just behind the saddle, as well as hear the wet sharp slap of it. He kicked his feet free of the stirrups instantly, dropping the bow and planting both hands on the saddlehorn as he swung his body over and down, hitting the ground running as the horse fell over on its side.

Momentum was too much for him; he went down head over heels, but an acrobat's training gave him a little control as the hard ground battered at his body and snapped the leather strap that kept the shield on his back. It went flying as he tumbled; the arrows scattered from his quiver in a spray like oracle sticks tossed for a divination and his sword hilt hit him under the armpit with a thump that sent agony running through the arm and down his torso. Then he was on his feet again, long legs pumping.

The remount's leading rein had snapped as his horse fell; it was slowing down as he vaulted onto its back, bare except for the saddle-blanket left on. That made it rear and bolt ...

Too late!

A single glance to his right showed that the head of the dense-packed buffalo herd was past him; where Three Bears was he couldn't say. All that existed eastward was a wall of flesh, rising and falling as it ran; his horse was doing its valiant best, but it was sliding backwards along that rampart of hair and horns and mad rolling eyes. The Cutters gave a shout of triumph as they closed in, casing their bows and tossing their lances up into the overarm stabbing grip. They'd be within range in seconds. They didn't even have to kill him themselves—just keeping him in play until the rest of them came up would do nicely.

Do me, *nicely,* Rudi thought.

There was only one thing to do, save that it was utterly mad. Rudi wrenched at the reins, forcing the unwilling horse closer to the buffalo. A Cutter trooper was almost within killing range now, raising his lance over his head, his face a mask of effort as mindless as the glazed eyes of his horse. The six-inch head of the lance glittered through the dust, light breaking off the honed edges and needle point.

Rudi gathered his long legs beneath him against the back of the horse, waited until the next heave of the mount's back was rising beneath him, and *leapt.*

For a moment he was soaring through the air, and he could see the goggling of the Cutter's eyes as his thrust cut empty space. Then he landed and his hands gripped the hair on a buffalo's hump, closing with convulsive strength. His feet dragged painfully; he bent his knees and drove them down in the trick-rider's leap, matched with the thrust of his arms.

He bounced up out of the dust, and then he was astride the buffalo's back behind the hump, looking leftward as the Cutter troopers rode not ten yards away, lances poised and utter disbelief on their faces.

And none of them can shoot at me, unless they're left-handed, he thought, fighting down a crow of laughter—a mounted archer could only shoot forward and back and to the left.

He rode with his knees braced high up to keep them from being crushed between *his* buffalo and the one to the right, leaning forward with the curly mass of the hump inches before his face. If it had been at rest the beast would have bucked him off or crushed him by rolling, and then stomped and gored him in short order. Now it virtually ignored him, intent only on the blind flight that was carrying it northward nearly as fast as a railcar with half a dozen men pedaling madly. The musky smell of it filled his nostrils; he turned his head left and grinned at the Cutters as they ever-so-gradually began to slip behind.

Somewhere deep within his mind a voice wailed, *What next?*

Right now in this instant of time he was thoroughly enjoying the look on their faces, the lances held as if they simply could not believe they were to be denied that first deep, soul-satisfying stab. And Major Graber had the expression of a man with an insect dancing on his eardrum and no way to get at it.

Then one of the troopers gave a cry of raw frustration loud enough to be heard even through the thunder of the bison stampede and threw his lance. The weapon wasn't made or balanced for casting, but it landed point-first in the rump of the buffalo bearing Rudi anyway. He pulled his feet up even as the forequarters started to go down and jumped, letting the motion of its body fling him skyward.

No good landings in sight, he thought, a crazed memory of piloting a glider into a wheat field near Portland running through his mind's eye.

The buffalo he'd left tripped, and the one behind it rammed helplessly into the prone shape kicking on the ground. Seconds later half a dozen of the beasts were piled in a heaving mound ten feet high, and the stream behind parted on either side of it. Rudi landed with an impact that half winded him; for a moment he was half across the next buffalo, slipping as its pounding motion threw his body down the slick right side, wet with foam from its lungs and slimy with the mud it had made of the dust in the animal's thin summer coat. He locked his hands in the thicker hair on its hump, and then nearly fell as a patch came off in his hands where it was still shedding.

"Dagda's dick!" he swore, the world lurching down towards the pounding hooves.

His feet struck the ground. He ran as he would by a horse when he was doing tricks, bounding, touching down only once every six feet, working his hands into the curls of coarse hair. They cut at his fingers like wire, even through the hard callus, and he made himself relax the death grip a little; he would need all the strength of his hands, if he lived more than a few seconds longer.

Then the animal bawled with a different note than its panting fear. An arrow had struck it not far from where his hands gripped, slanting downward into the hump. He risked a quick backwards look; the Cutters were just barely visible through the dust, and they'd fallen back twenty or thirty yards—enough that they could shoot forward and have some chance of hitting him, if they were very good shots and rode like centaurs.

"The which they do," he snarled.

Blood was leaking down towards his hands. He let his feet hit the ground again, pushing up off the buffalo's hump as he leapt like a high jumper in the Lughnasadh games. To the Cutters it must have appeared as if he'd popped up out of the dust like a man on a trampoline.

This time the soles of his moccasins came down on a buffalo's back, the surface heaving beneath him like an earthquake. He crouched in the same motion and sprang again before the checked leather of his footwear could slip against the slick hide, and landed two beasts over. He let his feet slide apart and came down on his buttocks astride the bison, hands once more sunk in the thick hair on the animal's neck; it stuttered in its stride and crab-jinked, bruising his leg against the beast beside it, but not quite hard enough to do more than set up a ripple in the great flow of animal flesh.

That gave him an instant's time to look back. Graber had managed to get his horse almost level with Rudi, and the lance was in his hand. But thirty feet separated them, an impossible cast with something not meant to be thrown, and with the awkward positioning. Rudi raised his own hand. Instead of throwing the spear the officer of the Sword raised his weapon in what was almost a salute, then turned his horse away to the west.

Leaving me to the tender mercies of tatonka, Rudi thought.

Escaping from the Sword had been one thing. Escaping from the escape was likely to be more difficult . . .

Because I can't get off while they're running, but when they stop running, they'll notice I'm here and kill me, he thought.

The dust was thick in his mouth, even though he wasn't far from the front of the herd; he coughed and spat, coughed and spat, blinking eyes that felt as if ground glass had been rubbed under the lids. Ahead of him the rumps of bison rose and fell, rose and fell, looking absurdly tiny compared to the huge hairy shoulders, but shoving the massive bodies forward with graceless efficiency. And looming up through the dust, a rock—twelve feet of jagged gneiss, one of the bones of the earth that sometimes stuck through the thin skin of the high-plains soil.

Rudi's buffalo was headed straight for it. *I'll pour out a bottle of whiskey for you, Coyote Old Man,* he thought, raising his legs until they were along the buffalo's back. *Just no more of your jokes, now, you hear?*

He turned his feet in, frantically trying to dig in with the toes. Then the world shook with a *whump* as the buffalo struck the rock and staggered sideways; another as it rammed into the animal on that side, which promptly tried to hook its horn into whatever had hurt it. Rudi could feel his stones trying to crawl up into his belly now; the beast he rode was staggering, and there was nothing he could *do . . .*

A horse loomed out of the dust, pacing the buffalo; he realized it must have been in the lee of the rock, where the stampede parted around it.

Rick Three Bears rode it, leaning low over the neck as he urged it up to speed, death closing in all around and on his heels.

"Hey, Strong Raven!" he screamed, just barely audible through the cataclysmic noise of a million hooves, his streaming braids framing a wild grin. "Room for two on Big Dog here!"

Rudi waved back the circle of faces as he staggered forward and then collapsed to his knees. A hand held a canteen in front of his face; he drank, spat, coughed, drank more and coughed again convulsively, dust-colored water shooting out of his nose. His stomach heaved with a sick dropping sensation, and he swallowed acid at the back of his throat. When he raised the canteen again, his hand shook so badly that the horn mouth rattled against his teeth.

Breathe in. Breathe out. Ground and center.

He struggled and controlled his diaphragm. Behind him Three Bears was talking:

"Jesus Christ, I've never seen anything like it—we'll have to rename him Rides Mad Buffalo—"

"Rudi, Rudi, are you all right?"

That was Mathilda's voice; he could feel her hands on his shoulders. He concentrated, and her face came into focus, the big hazel eyes soft with concern.

"Anamchara," he croaked, and fell forward into her embrace.

"Are you all *right*?" she asked, her hands stroking his hair.

Another shuddering breath, and he felt a little control come back. "Apart from feeling like I'm going to puke, the which would be no return at all to you for your care of me, I think I am," he said.

Amazingly, it seemed to be true; he felt stiff and bruised, and he'd be sore as a graze tomorrow—and he had more than a few of those—but nothing was damaged.

Mathilda rose, helping him up. He stood, panting, and took a real drink of the water, giving her a squeeze around the shoulders with his left arm. He held his right out to the *itancan*'s son, and they gripped forearm to forearm.

"We're even," he said to Three Bears. "In fact, I'm in your debt."

The dark face was flushed now too; the memory of those moments was coming out, and it was harder to bear than the doing had been.

"Shit, they were only going to kill us, not eat us like the lions!" Rick said, his own voice a little shaky. "Brother," he added.

Rudi nodded gravely. "You'll be wanting to get back to your father and family, brother," he said. "But I'm thinking we'll be meeting again."

"Yeah, and we'll be fighting Cutters together again," Three Bears said.

Then he looked west. Half a mile away the herd was still streaming by. "I'll head back when the Buffalo People get out of the way!"

CHAPTER TWENTY

Wide is the land, and high under heaven
Many the folk, their gods and ways;
All Artos would see, and with them take counsel
Wisdom win from friend and from foe—

From: *The Song of Bear and Raven*
Attributed to Fiorbhinn Mackenzie, 1st century CY

BIG SIOUX RIVER

WESTERN BORDER, PROVISIONAL REPUBLIC OF IOWA

JULY 25, CY 24/2022 AD

"I could use a watermelon," Ingolf said, as the whole party slowed their mounts. "Kept nice and cool in a well. You cut it open with your bowie, and then that first bite into a big slice, crisp and sweet, with the juice just dribbling down your chin—"

"You're not *helping*," Mary said, and slapped him on the back of the head.

"It's not the heat, it's the humidity," Rudi added, and wondered why Ingolf laughed.

"Welcome to the Midwest," he said.

Mary groaned: "I'm sweating like a horse. I can't tell where my sweat stops and Rochael's begins anymore."

"You still smell better than she does, honey," Ingolf said, and reached over to pat her dapple-gray Arab on the neck. "Though she's mighty pretty, for a horse."

Ritva snorted. "I don't mind sweating, but it doesn't

seem to be doing me any good—I'm still just as hot, only sticky too. Is it like this all the time?"

"Only about half the year. The other half's freezing cold and snows like hell," Ingolf said. Then he shrugged: "Actually there's a month or so of good weather in spring and fall, but we don't like to admit it."

They'd been ambling through farm country; now the land dropped away to a river valley, wooded with hickory and oak and cottonwood and spanned by a pre-Change metal bridge. Beyond it just past the immediate floodplain was a small walled town; rumpled hills rose gray-blue-green above the flats a few miles away eastward. Rudi could see several children sitting on the eastern bank, fishing or playing with a dog, their sun-faded tow hair bright against the dark earth. One of them rose and waved at the travelers, then turned back to his rod as the float on the string dipped below the water.

The stream was about medium bowshot across. Close to the middle a bald eagle's talons struck the water and punched up a burst of spray. The great black-and-white bird flogged itself back into the air with a fish twisting in its talons.

"Good luck to see an eagle striking," Odard said, and Edain nodded.

"Slow down here by the fort. They're likely to be a might testy about travelers," Ingolf said, and Rudi raised his right hand to signal the others.

"A testy man with a napalm shell on his catapult is not someone to offend," he agreed.

More quietly, Ingolf went on: "And the Bossman has reason to be offended with *me*," he said. "Remember, he paid my Villains quite a bit to go get that stuff for him from the dead cities."

"Not your fault Kuttner was working for the Prophet."

"I don't think so, and you don't think so, but the *Bossman* may not agree. Tony Heasleroad didn't strike me as being the forgiving sort."

"There's your friends," Rudi said.

"Yah. They've got pull. I don't know how *much* pull, not after years. We *could* go north through Marshall and Richland."

"And take months extra time. I lost us too much, when I was wounded and got us stranded in the Valley of the Sun. Things aren't going well back home. We *must* get that Sword, my friend."

Iowa held the western bank of the river where the bridge crossed; from what Ingolf had said, the Nebraska folk accepted that with sullen acquiescence. A strong fort of concrete reinforced with steel stood beside the road where the land started to dip to the wooded river valley; it was a rectangle with corner towers, and two more by the gatehouse. A dry moat—mostly dry, with puddles and mud at the bottom—surrounded it, filled with rusty sharpened angle iron and barbed wire and smelling of stagnant water and waste, and the drawbridge was down. From the gatehouse flew a flag with three broad vertical stripes of blue, white and red; when a puff of breeze lifted it for a moment, he could see an eagle in the central panel clutching a scroll in its bill, but the words were too small to read.

A swinging barrier came down to block their passage on the bridge as the party approached, and from behind the rusty metal an armed man shouted:

"Halt!"

Rudi duly halted, letting himself sink backwards in the saddle to signal Epona. He waited patiently, wiping at his forehead with his sleeve; she tossed her head, thumping at the gravel-patched asphalt with one hoof and flicking ears and tail against the flies. He'd packed his jacket and folded his plaid with his blanket roll behind the crupper, but his linsey-woolsey shirt was sticking to his back and sides and making patches black with sweat. Sitting the saddle in the grilling sun in a powerful cloud of human and equine perspiration and assorted insects wasn't pleasant.

"I would be *sooo* glad to sit somewhere shady and have lunch," Mary said. "Something besides beans and bacon and corn bread, too."

Ingolf smiled reminiscently. "There used to be a place in Hawarden"—he nodded towards the town on the other side of the river—"that did a great pepperoni pizza. And they made a fine beer there, too."

"I'd like to have a *bath*," Mathilda commented. "And get some pumice to sand the calluses off my backside. How long have we been in the saddle now?"

Virginia snorted, as befitted a Rancher's daughter who'd ridden before she could walk, but then admitted:

"It's a powerful big country; I never realized how big. I thought there was a lot of the Powder River range, but it's like a little corral compared to the rest."

"I didn't realize how much . . . muchness . . . there was either until I left home," Fred replied. "We'd been on the trail for a hell of a long time before you joined up, Virginia, and then since then . . . From the way Mom and Dad talked, I'd always thought it was a lot smaller. The maps don't tell you the half of it and the old books are useless. Worse than useless—they give you the wrong idea."

Father Ignatius nodded: "In your parents' youth, it *was* smaller. At least in terms of how long it took to travel across it. It wasn't a surprise to me intellectually, but then the Church has to communicate all around the world. We *know* how big the planet has grown. And it's still a shock when you experience it in person. My admiration for the couriers the Vatican sends out from Badia knows no bounds."

"Yeah, but Mom and Dad always sort of gave me the impression that America was a *country*, like Idaho. It's a *world*."

Rudi kept one ear on the byplay, but most of his attention on the fort; there were men moving on the ramparts, and a hot bright blink of sunlight on edged metal. Then a trumpet sounded, and a platoon's worth of troops double-timed out of the open gate of the fort with a bristle of polearms. Ingolf inclined his head towards them:

"Some bored officer's playing at soldiers because he can," he said. "This is a hardship post for guys someone

in Des Moines doesn't like. Most of what trade there is
goes through Sioux City, farther south."

The men were in full gear, jointed two-piece breastplates, arm-pieces and thigh-guards of polished steel,
helms shaped like the old American army headgear, and
metal gauntlets. The ones here all had either sixteen-foot
pikes or something that differed from what the Willamette country called a billhook only in detail—a chopping blade on a six-foot pole, with a spike on top and a
cruel hook on the back; short straight-bladed footman's
shetes hung at their waists.

Ritva spoke softly: "I saw something move behind
the firing slits on the north tower. Murder machine. And
there are crossbowmen on the crenellations."

Odard nodded. "If they're just going through the motions, they're going through all of them."

Rudi took off his bonnet and fanned himself with it.
He gave the pikemen a look of pity; they were only the
length of their own weapons away, and he could see how
red their faces were. At a guess, someone had rousted
them out from their midday meal or the siesta after it.
Though to be sure doing that occasionally was good
training; here he suspected that it was sheer frustrated
spite. A minute or two later a pair of men strode down
the sloping roadway from the fort.

Ah, the one in the lead is in charge, Rudi decided.

If the soldiers' armor was polished, his was blinding
with a luster possible only with chrome steel, and his
shete was the long curved horseman's model.

I think this is a man who stands on his dignity. He dismounted, signaling the others to do likewise. *As he'll be
resentful if I look down at him from the saddle.*

He couldn't help being six foot two and he was cursed
if he'd slouch, but fortunately the Iowan officer was only
a little shorter, and his helmet with its tall horsehair
plume made up the difference. As the man approached,
he muttered to the one beside him.

"Oh, all right, Sergeant."

"Thank you, sir. Stand at ease! Helmets off!"

There was a rattle and thump as the polearms were

grounded and leaned against shoulders. The soldiers were unexceptionable young men; big, muscular and fair-skinned for the most part with a country-boy look as if they weren't long from the plow, their hair cropped close to their heads and their faces shaved. Rudi gave them a professional glance and decided that they were strong and used to hard work, well-enough drilled, and certainly splendidly equipped. But probably not very experienced. Nobody had dared to challenge mighty Iowa lately.

No reason to think they wouldn't fight well, given good leaders, he decided. *But this man isn't the one to do it, I'm thinking.*

The officer had a small yellow mustache and pale green eyes set a little too close together and an expression of permanent discontent.

"I'm Captain Schlenker, Iowa National Guard," he said, his tone suggesting that the name should mean something.

Which, hereabouts, it may, Rudi thought, with an expression of polite interest.

"In the service of His Excellency Anthony Heasleroad, Governor, President Pro Tem for Life of the Provisional Republic of Iowa, the Sheriffs' Choice, Protector of Farmers and Vakis, Bossman of All Hawkeyes. You can stop your merry band right there until you've answered a few questions."

The Iowan had a flat harsh accent much like Ingolf's, one that turned the vowels in words like Mary and marry and merry into the same sound. It sounded much less agreeable in his mouth than in their companion's.

"So, who are you people?" he asked less formally.

Rudi introduced himself. "We're travelers from the Far West, sir," he said.

It didn't hurt to be courteous on someone else's land. "Traders?"

"It may be, if we find anything to buy in Des Moines, which is where we'll be heading, to see the remarkable sights of the city, so far-famed it is," he said.

Schlenker's eyes narrowed. "We don't allow armed vagrants to wander around Iowa," he said.

For the first time he seemed to pay real attention to the party. Rudi had left his sword slung at Epona's saddle, but there was no point in trying to conceal that they were well armed, or the quality of their horses. With Mathilda and the twins and Virginia they were slightly implausible as a bandit gang . . . but they looked as much like that as anything else, and it wasn't absolutely unknown for women to take up that trade. Or for genuine traveling merchants to indulge in a little banditry on the side, if they saw an opportunity.

Sure, and Mary's smile would look more reassuring without the eye patch.

They certainly didn't have the wagons or pack-animals you'd expect of serious traders, and it would be ridiculous to claim they were traveling across the continent for the pleasure of it.

"We're well able to provide for ourselves, sir," Rudi went on. "If there's a regulation for posting bond, in gold shall we say . . ."

According to Ingolf there wasn't, but the officer's face brightened at the diplomatic offer of a bribe. When he still hesitated, Rudi continued:

"And we'll be staying with a friend near your capital, a Farmer and Sheriff. A Colonel Heuisink, with whom you may check if you'd be wishing it."

That brought a definite change in attitude.

"Let's get into the shade," Schlenker said. "Sergeant Morrison! Bring them into the fort. And pull a watermelon and some beer out of the well."

> *You asked what land I love the best*
> *Iowa, 'tis Iowa,*
> *The fairest State of all the West,*
> *Iowa, O! Iowa,*
> *From yonder Mississippi's stream*
> *To where Missouri's waters gleam*
> *O! Fair it is as poet's dream*
> *Iowa, 'tis Iowa.*
> *See yonder fields of tasseled corn*
> *Iowa, 'tis Iowa,*

Where plenty fills her golden horn
Iowa, 'tis Iowa,
See how her wondrous prairies shine.
To yonder sunset's purpling line
O! happy land, O! land of mine
Iowa, O! Iowa.
And she has maids whose laughing eyes
Iowa, O! Iowa.
To him whose loves were Paradise
Iowa, O! Iowa
O! Happiest fate that e'er was known.
Such eyes to shine for one alone,
To call such beauty all his own.
Iowa, O! Iowa
Go read the story of thy past.
Iowa, O! Iowa
What glorious deeds, what fame thou hast!
Iowa, O! Iowa
So long as time's great cycle runs,
Or nations weep their fallen ones,
Thou'lt not forget thy patriot sons
Iowa, O! Iowa

The song rang out in children's voices as they climbed down from the railway; it came from a frame building not far from the depot, where a choir was apparently practicing. As the travelers unhitched their horses from the rearmost wagon the eight- and nine-year-olds spilled out clad in shorts and T-shirts, mostly barefoot in the warm summer afternoon. They came running down the dusty street to watch as the passengers disembarked, with the dust motes glowing golden in the slanting beams of the westering sun.

"All out for Valeria!" the conductor cried, walking down the line of cars and flourishing her speaking-trumpet. "Refreshments available in the station building! Train will embark for Des Moines in one hour!"

"What a surprise," Mathilda said, as they stretched and rubbed parts affected by the hard bench seats and Garbh growled at a village mutt that went into a dancing, barking frenzy until a boy pulled it away. "Another hot, humid, hazy day!"

"Could be worse—" Rudi said.

"—could be raining," Edain finished with a tired grin.

He nodded towards clouds on the eastern horizon—which were very visible, flat as the land was. They towered into the sky, black at their base and shading off into a froth like thick whipped cream at their summits, with the topmost heights starting to glow gold as the sun sank westward.

"Or hailing and storming," he added; they'd had enough time to realize how undependable the weather was here.

The station was a small four-square brick building, with a stable and paddock to one side where the spare teams were housed; the train's driver and his assistant led their tired beasts there to be turned over to the ostlers, and began assembling the replacement. The travelers clustered around the pump to one side of the station, taking turns to work the worn hickory of the handle. Once the trough had been filled and their own horses were dipping their muzzles into it the humans held their heads beneath the flow and drank heavily from cupped hands—the deep tube wells here were generally safe.

Rudi sucked down another draught of the cold, slightly mineral-tasting liquid, then splashed some over his head and brushed the long red-gold locks back, enjoying the momentary coolness in his sweat-itchy scalp.

"Gods of my people, you *always* feel like it's time for a shower here!"

"Welcome—" Ingolf began.

"To the Midwest," the rest of them chorused.

Valeria was a town so small that any Mackenzie dun would have made three of it, but the streets were crowded right now. Most of that was a convoy of big six-wheeled wagons drawn by huge gray horses much like those that pulled the train, just finishing loading from a series of warehouses of pre-Change sheet metal by the side of the railroad track.

Same breed, but better horses, Rudi thought, admiring

their glossy spotted coats and hooves the size of dinner plates, thick arched necks and flared nostrils, the muscle that rippled in their massive haunches and flanks. *Well tended, too.*

A man came around one of them, talking to someone behind him, then froze as he saw Rudi and his party.

No, he's looking at Ingolf, Rudi thought, as the man walked slowly towards them, eyes wide with wonder.

Then he drew himself up, coming to attention. He was in his mid-twenties, Rudi's age, or nearly. A little shorter, a bit under six feet, but broad-shouldered and slim-hipped, with short auburn hair and blue eyes and a wide, snub-nosed face; that was emphasized by the small blob of scar tissue on the very end of his nose. Most of the little finger of his right hand was missing, and a bit of the top of the next digit.

Moves well, Rudi thought. *Good balance.* His eyes went to the wrists and shoulders, and the swing of the walk. *Strong, and quick with it, but there's just a shadow of a hint of a limp in the right leg.*

His clothes were plain but good quality; knee-boots and indigo-blue denim trousers with a horseman's leather inserts on the inner thighs. The trousers rose to a sort of bib with shoulder straps; he had a green linsey-woolsey shirt beneath that, a silver-studded belt with a shete, bowie and tomahawk around his waist, and a billed cap on his head. The bib overalls and cap were what farmers wore in Iowa; rather confusingly, here-abouts *Farmer* seemed to mean about what *Rancher* did in central Oregon. Or *knight* in the Association territories; a landed gentleman, or at least a member of the ruling class.

He faced Ingolf, came to attention and saluted briskly. "Corporal Heuisink, reporting for duty, Captain Vogeler, sir!" he barked.

Ingolf frowned like a thunderstorm. "Sloppy as a hog in a wallow, as usual, Heuisink! You're not on your daddy's farm down in Iowa now, by God!"

Both men burst into roars of laughter and fell into each other's arms, hugging like bears, dancing around in a stomping circle, pounding each other on the shoulder and back. Then they held each other at arm's length, each examining the other with wonder.

"Jack, you miserable son of a bitch!" Ingolf said, and mimed a punch to the face. "You couldn't get a message to me in Hawarden? You know how long we waited in that lousy oozing chancre on Iowa's fat ass, eating overpriced pizza and listening to ourselves sweat?"

The other man pretended to stagger. "You expect the heliograph net to work out *there*, you ignorant cheesehead?" he said. "There's a surface-mail letter on its way!"

"Ignorant? I left Readstown because I had to. *You* were the one who thought that being a hired soldier for those cheapskate dickheads in Marshall was going to be an *adventure.*"

"I ended up in deep shit, far from home. That *is* adventure."

Rudi laughed aloud; only someone who'd *had* adventures knew how true that was, though it wasn't the whole of the matter. Mary cleared her throat.

"Why is it that when men play, they always play at hitting and insulting each other?" she said.

Ingolf turned with his arm around the younger man's shoulders; he was laughing, and his battered, craggy face was more relaxed than Rudi had seen it.

Younger, in fact, he thought; as if the brown beard and scars had been removed. *A lot of the time you forget he's only five years older than I.*

"Mary, this is Jack Heuisink, who was dumb enough to run away from a perfectly good home and enlist in Vogeler's Villains back when we were fighting the Sioux War, up north in Marshall."

"I was a teenager," Heuisink said defensively. "More . . . hormones . . . than sense."

"I kept him alive long enough to come to his senses, which happened about the time he put his right hand in the way of an Injun tomahawk headed for my noggin."

"Good as new, what's left of it," Heuisink said, flexing it. "Gave me a decent excuse to come home, too."

"Jack, Mary Havel, my intended."

Jack's eyes went wide; his eye skipped from the patch to her face, down to her feet and up to the braided yellow hair. They also skipped to the worn hilt of her longsword, and the gear on the dappled Arab behind her, and then widened a little as he realized that Ritva was identical to her—except for the missing eye and the scar.

"Pleased to meet you, Miss Havel," he said, and shook hands. "Ingolf always did have more luck than he deserved."

"I keep telling him that," Mary said, smiling.

"He's not the only lucky one," Ritva said, and introduced herself. "And if you play dice with her, use your own."

That turned into a general exchange of names. Heuisink's hand was hard and strong in Rudi's; he could see the same instant calculation in the other's eyes as they measured each other—*this one is dangerous.* Then the Hawkeye looked along the line of travelers.

"Well, you've assembled another prime bunch of plain old-fashioned cutthroats," he said to Ingolf when the introductions were done.

"Even if they're prettier than we were on average," he added gallantly, with a slight bow to the twins and Mathilda and Virginia.

"Rudi's ramrod of this outfit, besides having the misfortune to be my future brother-in-law," Ingolf added. "I'm number two."

Heuisink's eyes went wider. "Where's Kaur and Singh and Jose and the others? Everyone wondered what the hell happened when the Villains didn't make it back from that crazy salvage trip to the East Coast. Hell, we thought you were all dead and eaten by the wild men."

"Everyone but me *is* dead," he said; the pleasure of the meeting leached out of Ingolf's face for a moment. Then he took a deep breath and pushed away grief with a visible effort: "Christ, it's years ago now. I haven't forgotten, though; and we're here to get some answers, among other things."

Heuisink grunted as if he'd been belly-punched. "Jesus, all of them?"

"Backstabbed by that little shit Kuttner . . . and that's something we need to talk to the Colonel about. But that's old news. The latest is we're here from the West Coast. Oregon, by God!"

That brought a silent whistle. "You *are* one traveling son of a bitch, Ingolf. How'd you get through the Sioux?"

"We spent a while in a *hocoka,* as a matter of fact."

The younger man ostentatiously craned his neck to look at the back of Ingolf's head. "And you've still got your hair?"

"Not only that, you're now addressing Iron Bear, adopted member of the Kiyuska *tiyospaye* of the Ogallala," he said. "Mostly courtesy of Rudi here, and Miss Kane."

"That I have *got* to hear about."

"How's the family? And Cecilia?"

"Dad's fine and meaner than ever, Mom's fine, my brothers and sisters are all fine—Louise got married to Sheriff Clausen's son Hauk over by Dubuque this May—and Cecilia and I just had a kid, a boy this time—"

"Congratulations!"

"—and young Ingolf is doing fine and crawling like a maniac, driving her and the nursemaid crazy. The farm's fine, our *vakis* are fine, and let's get the hell home! Man, we've got some serious talking to do! *And* drinking!"

He turned to his men: "Mitch, hightail it back to the house and tell my father we've got guests, Ingolf among 'em."

The man climbed into the saddle and trotted away down the road that led north from the little town. Heuisink turned to the rest of the travelers and waved.

"Let's get your traps on the wagons. Our house is your house, and any friends of Ingolf's are friends of ours! Stay a week, stay a month, stay as long as you damned well please."

Ingolf said his friends here were well-to-do, Rudi thought. *They must be, to have nothing but smiles for ten hungry guests!*

The land near Valeria had been intensely cultivated in small orchards and large gardens by the townspeople, the rows of lettuce and carrots and potatoes, sweet corn and onions and turnip greens against dirt black as coal. Beyond that was shaggy common pasture for their beasts, and then more of the same.

A ride always seems longer in open country like this, Rudi thought, as they turned off the road and under a tall timber gate with a hanging sign:

Victrix Century Farm
est. 1878. Colonel Abel Heuisink, prop.

Then beneath that, in different lettering:

Emergency Evacuation Center
and Registered Farm #21,726

"Almost home," Ingolf's friend Jack said. "This is my family's land, from here on."

Rudi's brows went up slightly; all he could see *was* land right now, rippling with grass sometimes chest-high on a horse, no houses or even tilled fields.

"What's the significance of the number?" he asked.

"Oh, that's our farm number ... back at the Change, every farm that could keep going got a registration number, 'cause all the farmers were sworn in as deputies and Justices of the Peace to handle the evacuation. Last count I heard, there are ..."

His eyes went up in the gesture of a man remembering a number: "Fifty-two thousand four hundred and thirty-two Registered Farmers in the Provisional Republic of by-God Iowa. Dad's a Sheriff too, of course ... It's about another two miles to the house; that's square in the middle of our land."

The size of a Baron's fief in Portland, Rudi thought. *Not much compared to a lot of ranches—but this isn't sagebrush where you need five acres for a single sheep, by Brigit's Sheaf!*

"It's a fine stretch of country you have," he said sincerely.

The whole of Iowa was apparently laid out in squares a mile on a side with roads along the edges, and would probably look as geometric as a chessboard from a balloon or glider. That distance meant the Heuisink property must be at least two square miles, and probably three or four . . . which was very big even by local standards. Rudi looked around himself. Grazing stretched on either side as they entered the estate, but it was neatly fenced, with old-style posts and barbed wire, or in places by bristling hedges of multiflora rose.

Herds of black hornless cattle moved over the fields, their glossy hides tight with good feeding, and horses—some massive Percherons, others tall long-legged beasts that reminded him of Epona—as well as square-bodied sheep, still looking a little naked as their fleeces grew back from the spring shearing. There were herds of black-and-white pigs too, looking like giant moving sow-beetles as they ranged belly-deep in pasture; he could hear them grunting and snuffling as they fed. Occasionally animals of all varieties would wander over to a pond dug in the corner of a field to drink, or to a trough kept full by a skeletal windmill.

The younger man nodded with obvious pride. "None better in the state, and my family have held it since my great-great-grandfather's day; well, parts of it, at least. All of it's useable, too. You go a couple of days' ride north and half the country's gone back to swamp again, but ours is naturally dry."

"This looks to be as good for pasture or grain as you could want," Rudi agreed with perfect sincerity.

Though I might say something of the sort even if I weren't sincere at all, he thought, smiling to himself.

You couldn't go wrong complimenting a man's horses and cattle or his land. He *didn't* add that he thought it as boring a stretch of the Mother's earth as he'd come across, barring some that were even flatter.

I've seen enough prairies since we left home that they don't bewilder me anymore. At first he'd had a subconscious conviction they weren't moving at all, even when he knew they were. *I still miss having something to measure distance by—woods, hills, mountains in the distance.*

The land here wasn't really *flat*, not compared to some of the tabletop country he'd seen and—endlessly—ridden across. It had a very slight roll to it, enough that vistas opened out and closed in again, though slowly. There were few trees, only a clump of oaks and hickories and poplars here and there or a row along the edge of a field, and apart from the cottonwood and burr-oak groves along the banks of the odd slow-moving trickle of creek they all looked to have been planted by human hands rather than the will of the Mother. The grass by the side of the road was sometimes high enough to nearly hide the view beyond, though.

They rode at the pace of the wagons, which were loaded with heavy goods, brick and tile and tools and bolts of cloth and boxes that might be anything, and big bevel and wheel-gears strapped on top of one, machinery for some sort of mill. Besides the teamsters there were six mounted guards in crested helms and mailshirts, armed with shete and bow; Heuisink had introduced them as *our National Guard security detail*.

Rudi mentally translated that as *my father's household troops*.

"Chief?" Edain said quietly, pulling his horse in beside Rudi's when the Iowan noble drifted ahead to Ingolf's side.

"Yes?"

"This is good land," he said, and offered a clump of grass with clods of earth attached that he'd stopped to cut out of one of the fields by the roadside. "You could plant bootlaces here, and by Brigid's Cauldron it would come up bootlaces!"

Rudi hefted the clod as they rode, and rubbed some of

the black dirt between his fingers and smelled it. It was full of fine roots, and compressed easily like sponge cake when he squeezed some between thumb and forefinger, the good crumb structure keeping it moist days after the last rain. The scent was rich and almost meaty, as much like well-rotted mulch as soil. He touched his tongue to it, and the taste was neutral, without any acid sourness or alkali bitterness either.

"You're right," he said, dusting his hands off and spitting aside. "As good as any I've ever seen. Easy to work, too, I'd think. They do have a mortal lot of it here, don't they?"

There was fine farmland in the Willamette Valley, but not fifty thousand square miles of it in a solid block. That was more ground than everything from Bend and Sisters to the ocean and from the Columbia to the old California border south of Ashland, desert and mountain and dense Douglas fir woodland and the whole Willamette put together.

"And all this bit here belongs to Ingolf's friend?"

"Since that sign," Rudi said.

Edain shook his head, frowning. "That's not right," he said. "Not decent, by the womb of the Mother and the blood of the Corn King! One family shouldn't have that much."

"My friend, it's in total agreement I am," Rudi said; Mackenzie crofts differed a bit in size, but not even the wealthiest had much more than one family could till with a little help at harvest. "But mentioning it wouldn't be very tactful, if we're to be guests. We need this man's help. Also we're outlanders here."

Edain nodded and dropped back, half scowling as he looked around at the land about, half in sheer sensuous enjoyment of it; for it was a sight to delight the eye of someone who'd worked the earth since he could toddle, the thick pell of life on it promising food in plenty for man and beast.

Heuisink was obviously bursting with curiosity and even more eager to drag Ingolf away for reminiscence and questions, but he made a determined effort to be polite; he dropped back to talk with Rudi and the others every few minutes.

"The house is another half mile ahead of us."

"Fine stock," Rudi said, as a stallion went pacing along the roadside fence, brown hide rippling and neck arched.

"Dad was a breeder even before the Change," Jack Heuisink said proudly. "Pedigree stock. We've won State Fair blue ribbons three times in the past five years."

"Handsome beasts," Rudi acknowledged. "I don't think I've seen finer."

Though I was more impressed yet by the pasture; and the fact that your herds can't keep up with it. For all their feeding, it's stirrup-high out there in places.

After a while they came to cultivated land in big square fields; he rough-estimated four or five hundred acres. The wheat and oats and barley had all been reaped, and green clover was poking up through the blond stubble. The flax looked about ready to pull, the last of its blue flowers gone by and the plants chest-tall and browning, and there were low-growing rows of sugar beets. Some of the other crops were odd to his eye. Back in the Willamette maize was a garden vegetable, grown to eat boiled or to be canned in mason jars or pickled with tomatoes and onions in relish.

Here there was acre after acre of it, the heads just tasseling out now and casting a faint haze of gold over the distant part of the green block. The stalks were nearly as tall as a mounted man; you could look down endless rows, and the clatter of the leaves made a strange rustling sound that surged and died with the wind. More fields were growing some bushy plant.

"What's that?" he asked.

"Soybeans," Heuisink said, surprised. "You don't have them? They're mighty useful."

"I've heard of them," Rudi said. *Mostly from my mother, who hates tofu with a passion.* "The climate's not right for them in our country. Or for maize either."

The younger man laughed. "It's hard to imagine farming without beans and corn!"

Then he inhaled deeply and smiled; an overpowering sweetness marked a hayfield, where five horse-drawn mowers in a staggered row cut knee-high alfalfa and laid it in windrows to dry. The workers waved their hats at young Heuisink, and he returned the gesture with his billed cap.

"Pretty good year, so far," he said with satisfaction. "No blight on the alfalfa, either. What do you grow out there?"

"Alfalfa, to be sure. Wheat and barley, oats, potatoes, orchards—"

He and Rudi talked crops and weather for a little while—another topic of conversation that was good almost anywhere, since life itself depended on it. When they came in sight of the *house*—evidently he meant the whole settlement by that—Rudi blinked a little in surprise. There were some of the things you'd expect; turn-out pasture for dairy cattle and working stock surrounded by board fences, a couple of big orchards—apple, pear, cherry—which looked young, but flourishing, and a twenty-acre tract of garden truck. Some of the early apples were starting to turn ripe, glowing red through the green leaves.

But . . .

"There's no wall!" he said.

No sign of defensive works at all, not even the earth berm and barbed wire a farmstead in law-abiding Corvallis territory would have. The settlement looked obscurely naked without it, like a man fully dressed save for his missing kilt. Every single Mackenzie dun had a good log palisade around it at the least, with a blockhouse at the gate—Clan law required it.

Jack Heuisink nodded pridefully. "We have order here in Iowa! And have since the Change—or nearly. Well, we've got an emergency fort we keep up with the neighbors, over there about a mile, but we don't *live* in it, the way I hear they do in some places. We just keep it maintained and stocked."

And sure, I suppose it is *a prideful thing not to need walls,* Rudi thought.

It showed how strong Iowa was on its borders, and how well patrolled inside them. He'd noted that few men or women went armed here, too, unless they were warriors by trade.

But on the other hand, things can change. And they can change much faster than the time needed to build a wall. Whereupon the memory of pride, my friend, would be no consolation as you sat in that fort and watched your home burn, at all, at all.

Ingolf had dropped back into hearing range. "You've also got Nebraska and Marshall between you and the Sioux, Jack," he said dryly. "And Richland north of you, and Kirkville south. *They've* got walls around their settlements, you betcha. And there's the Mississippi between you and the wild men eastways, and you've got a river-navy for that."

"Well, yeah, Captain," he said. "But things here never did go to hell the way they did in a lot of places."

He turned to Rudi: "Dad says there was just so much damned food around that folks here had to make a real effort to starve; silos and elevators in the towns, bins on the farms, trains and trucks stopped on the roads and rails stuffed with grain. Things got bad enough, but there are almost as many people in Iowa now as there were before the Change."

"I can believe it," Rudi said. "I'd never imagined that there could be so much good land in one place."

"And it was all cultivated then—corn and beans, beans and corn, right out to the horizon, land that's pasture now or not used at all," the younger Heuisink said. "Lots of cattle and hogs, too, though they kept them penned up so tight a lot died before Dad and the others could get them out to the fields. Still, there was plenty left once they got things organized."

"And until the Change it all fed tens of millions far away who did *not* survive," Father Ignatius said, and crossed himself. "Madonna, intercede for them. *Kyrie eleison. Christe eleison.*"

The two younger men looked at him. *Now, that's true, but I wouldn't have thought of it,* Rudi mused.

"Yeah, we were lucky, Padre," Jack said gravely.

"Then you would do well to add wisdom to it, my son," Ignatius said. "For however much luck God sends, sinful man can—"

"—manage to screw the pooch somehow or other," Odard cut in.

Then he made a graceful gesture of apology when the priest frowned at him; Mathilda stifled a giggle. Ignatius looked stern, but he had to fight to keep one corner of his mouth from quirking up.

And he's no older than Ingolf, Rudi thought.

"That is one way to put it, Baron Gervais. Ah, we have arrived," the priest said.

The core of Victrix Farm was a tall house, three stories of white-painted clapboard with a shingle roof and wraparound verandas at ground level and above. It was flanked by two others much the same, looking as if they'd been put in since the Change and joined by roofed galleries, and all set amid lawns and flowerbanks behind windbreaks of tall old trees; evening's shadows flickered across the white walls and graceful windows, and a yellow lamp-flame lit in one of the upper windows as they watched.

The great barns and sheet-metal sheds, the silos and granaries, workshops and corrals were downwind to the east, and a substantial village lay on either side of the road southward. The cottages were smaller but mostly frame and white-painted like the house, obviously built of materials salvaged from the dead suburbs and stretching back in short lanes on either side of the road that led to the master's dwelling, shaded by trees that looked about a generation old. A few houses converted to storage sheds were of lime-washed rammed earth, relics from the years of resettlement; Rudi estimated the hamlet had room for two hundred people, give or take and assuming the normal three or four children per household.

A bit fewer than you'd expect from the cultivated land, he thought, in the quick estimate any farmer—or warrior—could make.

This Victrix place had around four hundred acres of plowland and lea, not counting rough pasture; and apparently excellent equipment to go with the fine fat land—reapers, disk-plows, mowing machines, hay balers, cultivators, and threshers—so they probably produced a hefty surplus as well.

Children and dogs were playing in the lanes, or working at chores with the chickens and turkeys and gardens and homes. Field workers were walking in, or riding bicycles home, or dropping off from a couple of wagons fitted with benches, and he could see a woman putting pies to cool on the ledge of a kitchen window. Smoke rose from chimneys, and a smell of cooking food filled the air along with the homey scents of any village; his stomach growled—it had been a long time since a not-very-good lunch. The folk he could see looked well fed, well if roughly clothed, and not overworked; they greeted their lord's son with easy courtesy.

But less of bowing and forelock-knuckling than you'd see in, say, Barony Gervais, he thought dryly, as the wagons headed off towards the storage sheds and the guardsmen to their homes.

Besides the homes the village had a schoolhouse shuttered for the summer and flanked by a small reading-room-cum-library, a bakery, a butcher's, a tavern and two small shops selling sundries, a smithy, a leatherworkers' shop and a carpenter's, a clinic and doctor's office, two churches with spires, a baseball diamond with bleachers, and a drill field with an armory attached where the local militia's gear was stowed. It had a sign that read NATIONAL GUARD SPECIAL RESERVE.

"And we've got piped water to all the vaki houses now," Heuisink said, pointing to a row of great three-story windmills that turned briskly with a metallic groaning noise and poured their yield into earth-walled water tanks. "Plus hydraulic power for grinders and so forth. And a swimming pool for the vakis, not just one for the house."

He spurred ahead to carry the news of their arrival. "Vakis?" Rudi asked Ingolf when he'd gone.

"What they call the work-folk here," Ingolf said. "From *evacuee*; you know, city folk moved out to the farms, what they call refugees most places. Though the Heuisinks treat theirs well—they all get a share in the crop and what the Colonel sells of the farm, and they can run stock of their own on the pastures. A lot of these Iowa farmers still just give vakis their rations and a little pocket money, the way they did when all they could do was hoe a row if they were pointed at it and shown how."

Odard and Mathilda nodded—the Portland Protective Association had done something much like that before the War of the Eye forced reforms on them, although under the newfound aristocracy that Norman Arminger had created from his Society cronies and gangster allies, rather than the pre-Change owners of land. Edain snorted quietly, voicing his feelings on *that* matter, but then the Mackenzies—meaning mainly Juniper Mackenzie and her friends—had split up their land into family units as fast as the refugees had learned the skills they needed. Sam Aylward had been a farmer's son in England, too.

Ingolf shrugged. "Don't use the word in front of the Colonel, by the way; he doesn't like it. They're bigger than most even here in Iowa, of course. Back home in Richland, the Farmers and the Sheriffs need their refugees to back 'em up come a fight, of which we've had a fair number, so they rent them land of their own and don't try to make them work full-time on the Farmer's fields. Here . . ."

"You'd be pretty silly to try and treat cowboys bad. You wouldn't see 'em for dust, if they didn't just shoot you," Virginia Kane said. "In the Powder River country we never allowed any of that slavery nonsense the Cutters have. Though I've got to admit, some refugees did end up doing chores on foot around the ranch house all their lives, if they couldn't learn to be useful with the stock. Not most of 'em, though, and surely not most of their kids."

"Yeah," Fred Thurston said. "But a ranch isn't like a

farm, Virginia. Dad left the Ranchers pretty much alone back home in Boise, but he made people who owned big crop farms split up their land as soon as people could handle it—had to use troops to make 'em do it, sometimes. And he used the army to bring land under the furrow, then settled guys on it after they'd done their three years. He wanted to keep hired workers expensive and scarce, and for everyone to serve in the army and then the militia."

"I don't think your brother, Martin, will necessarily continue those policies," Father Ignatius said thoughtfully.

"No," Fred replied, his lips compressed. "But I will."

"We Dúnedain don't do much farming at all," Ritva said with satisfaction. "Something I've *never* regretted. We do Rangers' work, and we hunt."

Mathilda sighed. "We Armingers don't farm either," she said dryly. "But we need the peasants or we don't eat—and neither would you Rangers, unless you didn't mind no spuds and bread with the venison, and nothing but buckskin to wear. You just do it at second remove."

"One more thing," Ingolf said, his voice dropping as much as it could and still carry to ten riders. "Colonel Heuisink's first wife and the kids he had with her were in New York on a visit when the Change hit. He gets sort of out-of-sorts if it's mentioned, even now. Or at least he did when I met him before, and I doubt he's changed."

They all nodded; that sort of thing was common enough among their elders. The pain of never knowing what happened to your kin was made worse by the grisly knowledge of what had *probably* happened to anyone caught in the big cities, which started with quick death by fire and violence for the lucky and went downhill from there. The stories brought back by explorers from Oregon who'd probed into California were still enough to chill the blood, and they'd heard Ingolf's tales of what lay in the death zones of the East Coast, where scattered wild-man bands still lived out their grisly game of hunt and dreadful feasting.

Grooms came to take their horses when they drew

up on the curved graveled driveway before the house;
Rudi had the usual minute's trouble persuading Epona
that the stranger wasn't someone she should hammer
and bite. When he looked up, Colonel Abel Heuisink
was walking down from the veranda.

The master of Victrix Farm was about the same height
as his son, but older than Rudi had expected—in his six-
ties, with only a fringe of cropped white hair around
a bald dome. His spare frame was erect and vigorous,
though, and his eyes bright as turquoise in a seamed,
tanned face; he wore the usual bib overalls and cap of a
Hawkeye gentleman.

"A pleasure to see you again, sir," Ingolf said.

"Always a pleasure to see the man who hammered
some sense into my boy Jack, Captain Vogeler," the
older man said. "It was more than I could ever do."

"You couldn't put him on the latrine detail for a
month. *That* helped."

The master of Victrix turned to take in the rest of the
party, blinking a little at Rudi's kilted height. When he
shook hands it was a brisk no-nonsense gesture.

"Come on in," he said. "Plenty of room at dinner."

Showered and in his set of clean clothes, Rudi felt much
more human. The room he'd been given was larger than
his at home in Dun Juniper, with a window that over-
looked the gardens behind the house; it smelled pleasantly of rose sachets, and there was even a shelf of books
above the desk, and the luxury of a private bathroom. The
floor was interesting; he recognized broad heart-of-pine
planks, worn but beautifully fitted—they must have been
there since the house was built a century or more ago.

Our host's kin are old in this land, he thought. *Good
for folk to have roots.*

A servant girl knocked at the door. "Dinner, sir," she
said, poking her head around it and smiling with her
yellow-brown braids swinging on either side of a freckled face.

"In a moment," Rudi replied, made a last adjustment
to the lie of his plaid, and walked out.

Dinner was to be served on a screened-in veranda at the rear of the house, pleasantly open to the breeze as the sun set on this hot summer's day, with a view of a rose garden blossoming with white and crimson, and a stretch of lawn with a swinging chair. Garbh was out there beneath a huge oak that had a tractor tire slung from one branch by a rope, gnawing on a bone and surrounded by several cautiously curious local dogs.

Rudi's nose told him what awaited the humans just before his eyes could.

Now, don't be drooling down your plaid, Rudi Mackenzie, he told himself. *You must do the Clan credit among strangers!*

A cold roast suckling pig lay at one end of the long table in brown-glazed glory on a slab of carved oak, with an apple in its mouth; a sirloin of beef rested at the other, pink at the center where a thin slice had been shaved away. Between them were breads and hot biscuits and yellow butter, salads of greens and cherry tomatoes and onions and peppers and radishes dressed with oil and vinegar, potato salad with its creamy whiteness flecked with bits of red, deviled hard-boiled eggs with their yolks replaced by minced ham forcemeat, platters of fresh boiled asparagus, cauliflower and eggplant baked with cheese, sautéed mushrooms, glazed carrots . . .

Well, so much for being afraid we'd impose, Rudi thought, and wrenched his attention away for the introduction to his host's wife, Alexandra, and his daughter-in-law, Cecilia.

"Padre, will you do the honors?" Abel Heuisink said to Ignatius; from the crucifixes, Rudi assumed the family were Catholics.

They all bowed their heads, and then the pagans murmured their own graces, which got them startled glances.

Mrs. Alexandra Heuisink must have been around twenty at the Change; in her early forties she was still very attractive, in a full-figured way which her cotton dress showed to advantage, and it was obvious where Jack had gotten his reddish brown hair. Jack's wife, Cecilia, was dark-haired and quietly pretty with very pale blue eyes; her children were apparently too young to sit at table. Besides the married daughter off towards Dubuque, the other children were Jack's twelve-year-old younger brother, George, agog for the travelers' tales, and sisters, Andrea and Dorothy, quiet and grave at first with so many strangers present; they were about two years apart, alike enough with their russet ponytails to be twins at first glance.

Rudi gave them an account of the buffalo hunt with the Sioux, and got wide-eyed wonder; Virginia Kane told a story of Coyote Old Man, and got a laugh.

"I wish I'd been with you!" George burst out, when he'd heard a bit more of the band's passage.

His father gave him a stern glance, and his elder brother an exasperated one; obviously having run away to soldier in a free company himself undermined any prospective words of wisdom to a youngster with his head fermenting full of romantic yeast. Rudi grinned at the boy.

Time to deflate his enthusiasm a wee bit, he thought. *No danger of doing it too much, not with a spirited lad like him. Heroing is something fate and duty inflict on you, boyo, not a grand game you seek out for the fun of it.*

"Not while we were holed up in that cave, and my sister"—he nodded towards Mary—"and I were like to die."

"Did it hurt?" the boy asked with ghoulish enthusiasm; no normal lad that age really believed in agony and death.

I did, Rudi thought. *But then, I met them earlier than most.* Aloud he went on with malice aforethought:

"It wasn't that so much, as not being able to go to the latrine by myself, and having to be swaddled and cleaned like a baby."

The two younger girls made disgusted faces, and George looked as if he'd like to; he also went thoughtful for a while.

"*This* hurt," Mary added, tapping her eye patch. "But that wasn't as bad as knowing I'd never get it back."

Jack winked at Rudi behind his sibling's back, and the two elder Heuisinks gave him slight, silent, grateful nods.

He didn't let conversation interrupt his eating more than he had to until well into the meal. It concluded with apple and cherry pies and ice cream with walnuts, and then the children were sent off; Cecilia shepherded them away. The two blond maidservants cleared the table, and everyone moved to softer chairs around a low settee where they set out a pear brandy much better than the indifferent wine which had accompanied the meal, and real coffee in an old-looking silver service and bone-china cups.

"Thank you, Francine, Marian," Alexandra Heuisink said. "That'll be all."

The girls looked a little startled, but went. Alex went on to the group:

"They're perfectly trustworthy, but what you don't know, you can't blab."

Abel nodded: "I'm not in as good odor with the current Bossman as I was with his father."

"Dad's head of the Progressives," Jack explained, nibbling a biscuit. "He's the Vakis' Friend—sorry, Dad, but that's the word people *use*. Anthony Heasleroad's a Ruralist."

"Anthony Heasleroad is a Heasleroadist first, last and always," his mother said, as she poured the coffee. "And his father was a strong-arm artist who got into office by what amounted to a coup d'etat. *And* murder, in my opinion."

"We did what had to be done, 'Zandra," her husband said. "I know your father was a good man—"

"—who had a convenient accident," she replied. "He was also the legitimate Governor, and *he* wouldn't have tried to make the position hereditary."

"Yeah. But he *would* have let us be swamped instead of closing the Mississippi bridges. We certainly couldn't afford a civil war then, things were too close to the edge. We all saw what happened in Illinois. And we don't *want* one now."

"Maybe Tom Heasleroad was a necessary evil, but damned if I can see why Tony's necessary at all."

"He's got the State Police and the Ruralist Party on his side, Mom," Jack pointed out. "It's *necessary* not to get sent to the mines for sedition and violating the Emergency Legislation."

"True," his father said. He turned to the travelers. "Sorry, but if you're going East, some of this local politics is relevant."

"Some of it sounds unpleasantly familiar," Fred Thurston said. Virginia Kane nodded beside him.

"Do have some coffee. We get a little these days," Mrs. Heuisink said, taking some knitting out from a basket beneath her chair. "Just recently."

"The coffee's the only thing we've had that didn't come from Victrix Farm, apart from some of the spices," her husband said proudly, relaxing from the tension of a moment before.

"It's a fine estate, sir," Rudi said. "I've come all the way from the Pacific Coast and haven't seen better, and few to equal it. Though of course it must have been finer still, before the Change."

"You folks still use *farm* for the holding a man who works the soil cultivates, don't you?" Abel Heuisink said.

"Yes. Well, we Mackenzies say *croft*; they say *farm* in Corvallis and the Bearkiller territory and *virgate* in the Portland Protective Association."

Abel Heuisink smiled a little sourly. "Before the Change, Victrix Farm actually *was* just a farm in that sense of the word, though a pretty big one—a lot more of it was cultivated, too. Cash grain, mostly. My family and six or seven men handled it all with some contract work now and then, and I could have done with fewer if I hadn't bred show stock as a hobby. Then it turned into a refugee camp. And now it's more like a town than a lot of Iowa towns were, back then."

Rudi nodded wisely; he knew that folk had been thin on the ground outside the cities before the Change.

It seems unnatural, but then, things were *unnatural in the old times.*

"All that machinery," he said. "With so few hands to eat the produce, it must have been a gold mine!"

"I kept it as a loss leader," Heuisink said. When Rudi's eyebrows went up: "As a tax write-off. That meant . . . in those days, we were taxed on our incomes. If you had a business that was making a loss, you could balance that against other income and pay less."

Baffled, Rudi blinked, thinking of the rich fields outside.

"How could land like this *not* pay? People had to eat then too, and to be sure there were so many of them! And with machines to do the work, you could sell nearly all of it."

His host chuckled. "Farmers used to ask themselves that question all the time. The short answer is that there were a lot of people between us and the hungry mouths, and *they* made the profit."

As a nobleman used to paying levies and to making them on his vassals, Odard's thoughts were a little different:

"How could the Crown know your income to tax it, my lord Heuisink?" he said. "I mean, the old American government. Did they send clerks around to assess your fields?"

"You told the government what your income was," he replied. "And I'm not a lord, young man."

Odard gave a charming smile and spread his hands. "You are by the way we'd reckon things in the Portland Protective Association's territories, sir. I'm a Baron myself back home; perhaps you'd say *Farmer* here. But about that . . . income tax, did you call it?"

"Most of my family's income came from stocks and bonds, investments."

The travelers nodded; all of them at least knew what those were, in theory, except perhaps Virginia Kane. Seeing that they'd followed him that far, Heuisink went on:

"The law required you to report your total income every year."

"And people *actually told* what they had, Lord Heuisink?" Mathilda said, her cup halfway to her mouth.

"That's more power than my mother has as Regent of the Association, by Saint Dismas! It's hard enough to collect the mesne tithes and the tallage and corvee and the salt tax!"

"You had to tell, or the IRS would get on your case, young lady. Believe me, you didn't want that to happen."

"Ah," Odard said wisely. "Rack? The steel boot? Pincers? Not," he added piously, "that we Associates do that sort of thing anymore. Not much."

Their host looked at him sharply, obviously wondering if he was being mocked and then looking even more startled when he realized the younger man was perfectly serious.

"Worse than that," he said. "Audits. But as you say, Mr. Mackenzie, it's good land . . . and that's what matters now. Thank God I didn't let my accountant talk me into selling it and putting all the money in Intel stock! His son actually keeps my books here now."

He poured himself a brandy and leaned forward. "But it's *your* story I'd like to hear." A glance around. "From the introductions, you can all tell me things about parts of the country we hardly hear rumors from these days. So, Mr. Mackenzie . . . Unless you'd like to start, Captain Vogeler?"

Ingolf looked at Rudi, who gave a fractional nod.

This all started with you riding into Sutterdown, with the Prophet's men waiting for you and everyone all unknowing, he thought. *Unless it really started with that prophecy Mother made at my Wiccanning . . . or with the Change . . . or the creation of the universe, so!*

Ingolf knotted his big hands for a moment, considering, and then began:

"Well, Colonel, you know we . . . my Villains and I . . . got sent East, heading for Boston, going on four years ago now."

The magnate nodded. "Waste of resources, but young Tony was set on it. Not that I grudged you the contract, though that offer of a job is still open."

"Yah, but I had my people to think of. And he sent

Kuttner along with us. Well, Kuttner had—said he had—secret orders from the Bossman that we pay a visit to Nantucket ..."

Heuisink sat quietly while the story spun out, and fireflies glittered like captive stars in the gardens outside, and some sort of cricket shrilled. The others began theirs when Ingolf left off with his arrival in Sutterdown ...

By Ogma the Honey-tongued, that was more than a year ago! Rudi thought.

When they'd finished, a long silence fell.

"Well," the master of Victrix said at last. "If I didn't *know* you were a reliable man, Ingolf Vogeler, I'd toss you all out on your keesters right now. Even so, I'm dubious."

"It's a wild tale," Rudi agreed. "But our *enemies* seem to believe it, so."

"Yeah, and that's one more reason to take it seriously ... most of it, at least. This cult out West has ambassadors in Des Moines now. At *court*," Heuisink added, using the term wryly for some reason.

"Oh, court intrigue is something we're used to," Mathilda said helpfully.

The others nodded. Abel Heuisink looked at them and sighed.

"Sometimes I think I've lived too long."

CHAPTER TWENTY-ONE

Oath-sworn band were sundered
Held in bonds of adamant and iron
Hostage to compel Artos, high-hearted lord
Would he save companions dear
Or would revenge be his arval-gift to them?

From: *The Song of Bear and Raven*
Attributed to Fiorbhinn Mackenzie, 1st century CY

"Well, Victrix Farm may not have a wall," Rudi
said softly. "But Des Moines most certainly
does, the awe and wonder of the world, to
be sure!"

The Heuisink family had traveled openly to the capital in their private railcar, pedaled by men of their own
household and faster than a mount could gallop; Rudi
and his party were coming in discreet anonymity on
one of the plain horse-drawn trains that plodded along
the steel way. That gave them plenty of time to watch it
approach. They'd seen the skyscrapers first, of course,
but those were farther away on the west bank of the
Des Moines River, and fewer and smaller than those of
Portland or dead Seattle. Those grew from dots on the
horizon to stark height as they passed through the last
ring of truck-farms and villas, where only the marks of

roadways showed where suburbs had been before the Change.

Finally they could see the raggedness of the great ruined outlines, where some had burned and half collapsed in the chaos after the Change, and others had been mined for metal, disassembled from the top down. Then the golden dome of the state capitol caught a gleam of the afternoon sunlight on this side of the river, and the city walls approached across the flat open ground kept bare for defense.

There was a twenty-foot-tall outwork with towers every hundred yards, then a wet moat half bowshot broad and flowing like a slow river, and rearing above it on the inner side a wall twice the height of the first. Its towers were sixty feet high or more and staggered so that they covered the gaps between those on the outer wall. Many of them bore tall windmills, creaking and groaning as their metal vanes turned.

Probably pumping up reservoirs for hydraulic cocking systems, Rudi thought, as an observation balloon tethered to one tower was winched down. *Whoever built this didn't miss a trick.*

The construction itself was concrete and steel, though faced with salvaged stone; he suspected a welded web of construction girders inside poured mass-concrete. The ramparts had crenellations overhanging it so that murder-holes could be opened to drop things straight down, and they were topped by an outward-sloping metal roof that was definitely *not* thin sheet.

More I beams, welded into a solid mass. Like the gates of Larsdalen. And the wall around Mt. Angel is taller, and built into the side of a hill four hundred feet high. But the size of this!

The wall stretched out of sight, curving away to the northeast and southwest towards the river. As he watched gaslights flared up along it, a long ripple like a wave across a lake; that showed the thick steel shutters of the firing ports in wall and tower.

"That is . . . a large city," he said mildly.

Ingolf snorted. "Sixty square miles within the circuit of the walls, more or less. A hundred and twenty thousand people, not counting transients. I wandered around bumping into things like some Rover from the Hi-Line the first time I came here."

Edain cursed softly. *That* was nearly twice as many people as the whole of Clan Mackenzie—about as many as the Mackenzies and Bearkillers put together, and this was only Iowa's *capital city*.

"Tarnation," Virginia Kane said; she'd never seen a city at all, until she came to Iowa. Then, quietly: *"Fuck!"*

Fred Thurston chuckled. "You said it."

They all nodded; cities in the old days had been much larger, of course, but those were the distant times of wonder that none of them had seen. This was *now*, in the ordinary, prosaic world of the Change.

A sharp rank smell grew stronger as they approached; not anything organic, but a chemical tang Rudi had never experienced before. It made his eyes water a little, as well, like smoke from an invisible fire.

"Coal smoke," Ingolf said. "Coal and coke. They bring it in by rail, and by barge on the river from places like Carbondale."

They'd been talking in low tones; now they fell silent as the train clattered over the bridge that spanned the moat, a slow *click ... clack ...* sounding beneath the steady pound of the hooves. The gate in the wall ahead was just large enough to pass the two tracks of the railway; within was deep shadow for the length of the passage through the wall, but looking up Rudi could just make out the teeth of multiple slabs of metal that could slide down to close it and lock into girders driven deep into the ground below.

"Now, that's a mite excessive," Rudi said mildly. "One alone would make the gate stronger than the wall."

Somebody in charge of this realm wanted a very *strong redoubt. The cost, even for Iowa!*

Rudi blinked as the train pulled through the thickness of the wall and into the open ground beyond. The streets were brightly lit by the incandescent mantles of the gaslamps spaced along the streets, and more inside the buildings. Northward he could see the high gilded dome again, but with a suggestion of more walls around it—the Bossman's palace, no doubt.

Palaces and forts he'd seen before. The buildings on either side of the railway line were something else again. Corvallis had a few water-powered factories, and so did Portland; even Sutterdown had mills for sawing lumber and breaking flax.

Here there were solid miles of them— tall brick chimneys trailing black smoke, a hot glare of molten metal and trails of sparks as a great cupola furnace was tapped into the molds, glimpses through huge but grimy glass windows into stretches of whirling overhead shafts and belting driving machines and figures attending them— here if people wore overalls the garments were filthy, soiled, covered much more of the body, and were entirely practical linen canvas, not expensive cotton symbols of gentility. The noise was shattering, snorts and grunts like gigantic pigs as mechanisms gulped air, blurring roars from furnaces and drafts, the tooth-hurting squeal of metal on metal, stamping and grinding.

Roads and railway sidings wove among the factories; oxen and horses and men pulled and pushed loads of ingots and coal and timber in, shaped metal out. Rudi recognized some of the products—cloth he supposed came from power looms . . .

He snapped his fingers. "*That's* what was bothering me. Back at Victrix Farm, you never heard any looms thumping! I suppose everyone in Iowa buys from here?"

"Everyone near Des Moines," Ingolf said. "If I were a Farmer or Sheriff here, it'd make me nervous having to buy in everyday stuff like that, but you have to get out near the frontiers to find much home-weaving, here."

Several of the others nodded thoughtfully. "I wonder why we don't do that," Ritva said. "We have spinning mills, or at least they do in Corvallis. Granted most people weave when they don't have anything else to do, but it's still pretty tedious."

"It only pays if you've got a lot of people close together and with cheap transport so they can buy the stuff, and a lot of water power," Fred Thurston said. "Dad tried to set up something like that, but it had to be subsidized with tax money all the time, so he shut it down—something for later, he said."

"It's a matter of market size, to be technical," Father Ignatius said.

Rudi kept an eye on the factories. More goods poured out, turned cylinders and pistons for hydraulic machinery, gears, crankshafts, chains, cast-iron pipe. Others were entirely mysterious . . .

"Tarnation," Virginia said again softly. "It's like something out of an old story. Like magic."

"How the Cutters would hate this!" Mathilda said, grinning. "They get upset when they see a clock, and there's a *hell* of a lot more than gear turning gear turning something here!"

"How *I* hate this!" Edain said, and coughed. "The stink's worse than it was outside the walls. Sure and it's like being trapped inside a chimney!"

"You're right about that," Rudi said; his sinuses and throat already felt a little raw, as if he were coming down with a cold. "It's sweating hot, as well. How a man could work next to a furnace in this, only the Gods know. Why don't they put it outside the walls, the way most places do a tannery or soap-boiling?"

"Because the Bossman and his cronies all have shares in these, and they don't want them risked outside the defenses . . . and it's easier to control things in here, too?" Odard said.

Ingolf gave him a wry look. "Right on both counts."

Odard is clever, Rudi thought. *But sometimes he lets you see the way his mind works.*

"There's *power* here, though," Fred Thurston said. "Dad tried to get as many factories going in Idaho as he could. Said the old Americans won a lot of wars because they could produce weapons cheap, fast and plenty."

As if to illustrate the point a load of armor was pushed out of one of the factories on carts with little wheels, breastplates and tassets stacked in bundles according to

size and tied securely together. The train they rode slid
onto a siding, behind one loaded with bundles of raw
flax. The team pulling it stood with their heads down,
utterly spent; grooms bustled over to lead them away.
Rudi frowned a little. Horses weren't machinery, and
Epona—the goddess his horse was named for—didn't
like it if you treated them as such. He hoped they'd get a
good rest and some mash, and have their hooves seen to;
the roadbed of the railway would be hard on them.

A squad of armed men waited when the passengers disembarked, most clutching their bundles of
belongings.

"State Police," Ingolf said quietly. "Don't get them
riled. They're the Bossman's own sworn men."

The squad looked more like soldiers to Rudi. They
were in light horseman's armor, mail-shirts and helms
over blue-gray uniforms, and they carried shetes and
glaives and crossbows with an ingenious crank mecha-
nism built into the butt rather than the forestock lever
used in Oregon. They also looked tougher and more
alert than the border garrison the travelers had seen
outside Hawarden weeks ago, and a little older.

Their commander had officer's insignia on his sleeve,
and he was a pug-faced man in his forties with cropped
blond hair and a face that looked like it had been forged
in one of the factories.

"All right, you miserable vakis," he said, after the passengers had jumped down on the crushed rock of the
roadbed.

Sure, and that's a safe enough assumption, Rudi
thought.

The other passengers were dressed in the same sort of
clothes Rudi and his friends had been given; shapeless
coarse-woven linen and linsey-woolsey. Most of them
were fairly young, more than half were men, and they
all looked as if they'd grown up doing hard labor of one
sort or another, and not getting all that much for it. All
their possessions were in the shapeless bundles they carried, and those were mostly small.

The Bossman's retainer went on:

"I am Captain Edgar Denson of the Iowa State Police, Department of Public Safety, and I am going to tell you the rules. You want to live here, you have to work and pay your way, and this is a damned expensive place to live; no matter what Mom and Dad told you, the streets aren't paved with gold—just horseshit, like anywhere else. You don't have a Farmer to pick you up and kiss it better if you stub a toe. You can get rich here—or you can end up starving. It's up to you. Begging is forbidden within city limits. Vagrancy is punished by six months at hard labor. Theft is punished by six *years*' hard labor. Armed robbery and murder are punished by *life* at *really hard* labor—but life's only a couple of years, in the mines. Understand?"

"Yes, sir!" the would-be townsmen chorused raggedly.

"Now get going. That building over there is the hiring hall—you can pick up some day-labor there. Move! Not you lot," he added.

Rudi sighed. He hadn't expected to slip in entirely unnoticed. You could dress like a local, but that was far easier than *looking* like one, to anyone who saw past appearances.

"You're foreigners from out of state, right?" Captain Denson said.

"Yes, sir," Ingolf replied; they'd agreed that he'd be the one to speak, having both more experience and a less conspicuous accent.

"And those are weapons, right?" the state trooper said, jerking his helmeted head at their suspiciously elongated bundles.

"Yes, sir. Nobody told us they were illegal."

Denson grinned, an expression with a little too much tooth to be pure enjoyment.

"They aren't. *Wearing* them in the streets is illegal. *Using* them except in self-defense is illegal. And remember we don't have capital punishment here. Being dead doesn't hurt. You planning on hiring out for guards in salvage companies? That's mostly in Dubuque and Keokuk."

"We've been out West. We *do* have enough money to keep us for a while."

"Spend it wisely."

"Here's the money," Tancredo said. "See, not a penny missing." He pushed a ledger across the table to Ingolf.

"You have the most *interesting* friends, sweetie," Mary observed, as he studied it.

Ingolf winced slightly and bent more closely over the paper. Rudi hid a quick smile. On the one hand, his half sister and the man from Wisconsin seemed genuinely fond of each other. But . . .

But if we didn't *have the same blood-father, I still wouldn't want her or Ritva for a lover. The Maiden knows they're fair women, and smart and funny and good loyal friends in their fashion. But.*

The man who called himself Tancredo shrugged and spread his hands.

"I've thought of it as more of a business relationship," he said dryly.

Ingolf picked up his pipe and puffed a cloud, possibly as camouflage. That habit was much more popular here than in the Far West, and about a quarter of the people in this riverside dive were puffing away at pipes, or cigarettes, or rather vile little twisted black stogies; a blue haze hung under the rafters, and the sparse gaslights glowed through it as through fog. From the smell, not all of it was tobacco by any means. The harsh smoke and spilled beer and—from the alley out back—stale piss were the predominant odors, with frying food a close competitor. The plates of catfish in corn batter and fried chicken and fried potatoes had been surprisingly edible.

Ingolf's . . .

Acquaintance, Rudi thought

. . . had brown skin, about the same shade as Fred Thurston; that and the tight curls of their black hair were the only things they had in common. Tancredo was in his early thirties, shortish, slender, with an easy smile that seldom reached the upper part of his face, and restless hands that tended to make short abortive moves towards his knives, of which Rudi had spotted three, besides the one worn openly on a belt covered in steel plates. He wore a crisp cotton shirt and a sleeveless leather jerkin, and denim pants and good boots; he also had a gold ring in one ear, and several more on his fingers.

"Ingolf was big in the salvage trade for a while," Tancredo said. "A salvager needs . . . unofficial contacts . . . if all the profits aren't going to go on 'fees' and graft. I'm as unofficial as it gets. Hell, my daddy was unofficial too—didn't think it was a good idea to get shipped out of town after the Change and spend the rest of his life hoeing corn for some hick and stealing watermelons and eating fried chicken, sho' 'nuff."

"You don't like fried chicken?" Fred said curiously; he had a plate of bones in front of him.

"Classical reference," the man replied. "Anyway, Ingolf, old buddy, what you want?"

Ingolf flicked his eyes to Rudi. The Mackenzie spoke:

"We're heading for the East Coast; indeed we've an urgent errand there, which has waited too long."

The image of the Sword floated before the eyes of his mind, like an itch he could not scratch.

More haste, less speed, he told himself. *Impatience makes mistakes.* His voice was calm and friendly as he went on:

"The fastest way to do it would be by water, up the Ohio. Something big enough to handle ten people and their horses, but no more, as far as the head of navigation."

Tancredo nodded, elaborately unimpressed by the fact that they were heading so deep into the death zones.

"You want that done officially? Or unofficially? Because *that*," he added, "would be very expensive."

"We hope it can be done officially," Rudi said. "We have friends at court, and they're trying to get us permission, or at least an audience."

Tancredo smiled, and this time it reached his eyes. "Ingolf didn't get a great fat wonderful hairy deal from his *official* friends the last time. Anyone relies on the Bossman *deserves* what he gets."

"It wasn't the Bossman who finked on me," Ingolf said quietly. "It was Kuttner. And Kuttner wasn't working for Anthony Heasleroad, whatever Tony thought."

"But we agree with your basic point," Rudi said. "I'd be saying that this was insurance, so to speak. If we get the official permissions we wish, then you've gained a legitimate, official profit as a respectable businessman. And if we don't, sure, and you'll be getting a much bigger unofficial one."

Tancredo's left eyebrow went up; then he grinned. "Now let's talk prices and details."

They did, though most of the party stayed quiet; Father Ignatius was off talking with the local archbishop. Rudi finally agreed on a figure with a slight wince; they'd started out with a good deal of money, but this was a major chunk.

But to be sure, once we're east of the Mississippi, money becomes moot. It'll be what we can find or take, there.

"Man, you're talking a *ship* here," Tancredo said after the bargaining had gone around in the usual circles for a while. "That's a *capital asset*. And you'll be taking it places where it very possibly ain't coming back, and do you think I could get insurance? No, I could not."

Rudi sighed and reached over the table to shake the local's hand and seal the bargain—he refrained from spitting on his palm first, that not being a rite used much in these lands. The Iowan stretched out his own hand and shook.

And Garbh looked up from where she sat at Edain's feet, growling slightly and looking at the door. It burst open. A draft of cooler air came with it, into the fug of the big room.

"Freeze!" a voice bellowed; one Rudi recognized. "Iowa State Police!"

Captain Denson stood in the doorway, a bristle of billhooks behind him. "Rudi Mackenzie, Ingolf Vogeler, you and your companions are under arrest in the name of Bossman Heasleroad!"

There was a moment's silence, then a murmur of mingled anger and fright. That grew to a roar as Tancredo stood and signaled before turning and walking quickly away; that took just long enough to block Rudi in the booth's inner seat. The man behind the long bar at one end of the room reached below the scarred surface, and the gaslights died. Blackness filled with screams and the crash of tables being overset; the stink of spilled drink filled the air, choking-strong.

"Sherwood!" Rudi called, clear enough to carry to all his own party.

He stood as he did so, turning and reaching for the sword belt looped over the partition between this booth and the next. His teeth bared in the darkness, and he forced his breath to come slow and deep. You took a risk, and sometimes it paid off—

Lights speared into the common room; the troopers had mirror-backed Coleman lanterns with them, and the incandescent mantles glared into his eyes. He moved his hand away from the hilt of his sword—slowly—and raised both palms shoulder-high as the edged metal of the billhooks rammed close, a circle of them poised to thrust if he moved. The men holding the polearms were shadows, outlines backlit by the second rank carrying the lights, but he could see a gleam of flame on chain mail. A third rank of State Police were behind those, facing back with their crossbows leveled.

Rudi put up a hand, as if blinded. That let him look around; Ingolf was still across the table from him, and Odard and Mathilda were in the same frozen reaching-for-the-sword motion as himself. He let out a silent sigh of relief when he saw that Mary and Ritva were gone, and Fred and Victoria and Edain with them. Edain's quiver had been snatched free of the hatrack in such haste that a gray-fletched arrow had spilled out, and it still spun on the littered brick of the floor.

"No need for trouble," Rudi said mildly to Denson. "It's your lord we came to see, after all."

"Yeah, no trouble," Ingolf said mildly. "Just a word to the wise, Captain, these folks"—he indicated Odard and

Mathilda—"are VIPs back home. Whatever the Boss-man has against me, he won't be happy in the end if they get roughed up."

"We'll see," Denson said; his shete was drawn, and he used it to reach over and flick their sword belts to his waiting subordinates. "Secure the men. The woman can come along peacefully if she feels like it."

The Bossman's palace was certainly magnificent; the grim massiveness of the citadel built around it since the Change didn't obscure the high dome gilded with genuine twenty-four-karat gold leaf. Neither did the evening's darkness; a golden lamp atop it and four more at the corners made it gleam above the marble and pillars of the great building. The gate passed them through with password and countersign and displays of ID cards, despite Denson and his men being known to the detail there. Under his anxiety, Rudi rather approved—procedures were like habits, and good ones tended to keep you alive, and keep the enemy from putting one over on you.

Inside the walls, lawns and gardens filled the giant rectangle; he suspected that the stables and barracks and so forth wcrc on the eastern side, behind the showpiece.

Though perhaps right now I should be worrying about the location of the dungeons, he thought.

Square in the center was the palace. The middle block had four smaller domes at its corners besides the great gilded piece in the middle, and two smaller but still large buildings to either side had copper-covered domes of their own. The entrance was up a long stone staircase, under a portico of six eighty-foot marble columns with a triangular sculptured portico above. Guards snapped to attention, grounding their billhooks with a stamp of metal on stone. Inside a broad corridor led to the rotunda, with the inside of the dome soaring nearly three hundred feet above; two more hallways gave off to north and south as they approached it. There were polished red-marble columns with gilded finials, floors of shimmering stone in geometric patterns, murals show-

ing ancients breaking the prairie sod, meeting in stiff
archaic costumes and hats like stovepipes, fighting with
strange, powerful weapons. And it was not a ruin, but
the heart of a living realm; guards stood at corridor en-
trances, gaslights shone brightly, and clerks and officials
and courtiers in archaic suits and ties or the more modern bib overalls stood in clumps or bustled officiously by
with files even past dinnertime. There was a smell of wax
and polish, not the cold abandonment he'd felt in other
pre-Change structures.

Sure, and I'd appreciate it more if I weren't tied up,
Rudi thought.

The State Police had cuffed their hands before them;
they'd also thrust batons between their elbows across
their backs, which was painful and allowed two men to
steer them by gripping the ends.

Ground and center, ground and center, Rudi thought,
breathing deeply again and imagining his anger flowing
out with the air.

It didn't, but it did recede; he couldn't afford to be
angry right now. Mathilda was striding along with her
head up, as if she were in Castle Todenangst; Odard had
his lips pursed, as if at some social solecism, and Ingolf
just looked blankly watchful. He blinked when they
stepped into a great rotunda, the oculus of the dome
above them and a great staircase leading up to a second
story; above the stair was a huge and well-done if surreal
painting of goddesses floating around a covered wagon,
holding books, seed and various objects he supposed de-
noted their sacred functions.

Not what I'd have expected of a Christian land, he
thought.

Mosaics of iridescent glass glittered above it. The
carved and jeweled throne itself was at the foot of the
stairs; he saw Mathilda's mouth quirk. That was *precisely*
the location her father had picked for *his* throne in the
great hall of the Portland city palace—what had once
been the Central Library on Tenth Street.

*The men who would be King tend to have similar
tastes,* Rudi thought.

"*That's* new," Ingolf murmured. "His old man used to meet people in the Governor's office."

The State Police troopers gave the pole between his elbows a warning shake, making his boots skid on the marble tiles. Rudi's breath hissed as he saw who awaited; beside the usual crowd of toadies and flunkies and officials and guards and general reptilia you'd expect around any monarch, a man in the dried-blood-colored robe of a CUT High Seeker stood below the dais to the left; and the Cutter officer who'd pursued Rudi and his friends into the Sioux country was beside him.

Peter Graber, that was the name, Rudi thought. *And I'm less glad to see him here than I was riding a mad buffalo, sure and I am.*

The Heuisink father and son were on the other side; not under arrest, but looking very unhappy, in a stone-faced way.

The State Police detachment and their prisoners came to a halt; the bodyguards around the throne were in the same gear, but two of them slanted their bills across each other in an X to bar the way to the ruler's chair. Captain Denson came to a halt, saluted smartly, and bowed:

"Your Excellency, we are reporting with Ingolf Vogeler and his associates, as ordered."

It was then that Rudi gave the occupant of the throne a careful look. Anthony Heasleroad was in his mid-twenties, and a hair under six feet. There was muscle on his frame, under a budding plumpness that had just begun to obscure the line of his jaw and thicken his middle under the blue-silk bib overalls. His short hair was sandy blond, and his eyes pale blue, in a short-nosed face with a cleft chin; a strong face, the Mackenzie thought, but not a good one. He leaned one elbow on an arm of his throne and reached out with the other hand into a bowl of chocolate truffles and ate one while the silence stretched.

And that's a boast, too, Rudi thought. *Mrs. Heuisink said that only a ship or two a year reached here from the Caribbean.*

When he spoke, the Bossman had a smooth well-modulated voice. "I gave you a hundred thousand dollars' worth of equipment and cash, Vogeler. Where is it?"

Ingolf's guards forced him down on his knees. "My people and I got to Boston, and we collected most of the stuff on the list you gave me, Your Excellency," he said. "But you also sent Kuttner with me, and I trusted him as your man. He was working for the Church Universal and Triumphant; they ambushed my Villains in Illinois, and as far as I know the goods are still there. Of course, that was years ago now. They dragged me all the way to Corwin, tortured me, held me prisoner, and if I hadn't escaped, I'd be dead now—and that's not for lack of their trying since."

The Cutter priest looked as if he were about to explode, his face flushed red; the dead flatness of his eyes was more vivid by contrast. Graber stood motionless, his hand near the vacant place on his belt where his shete would rest, but his eyes were never still and his body was poised ready for action. The ruler of Iowa spoke languidly:

"Yes, yes, Sheriff Heuisink has been entertaining us all with his stories of assassins, plots, exiled princesses, mad monks, battles in Idaho . . ."

The Bossman leaned forward. *But I still didn't get what I paid for, Vogeler.*

"I'll fetch it for you, Your Excellency . . ."

"Fool me once, shame on you. Fool me twice, shame on *me*—"

Rudi took a deep breath and stepped forward; his guards were too startled to do more than grab the ends of the rod, and he wasn't trying to move any farther.

"Your Excellency, if I might be of assistance? You've a right to be displeased that your expedition to rescue the beauties and glories of the time before the Change was brought to naught, sure and you do, by the Gods. But it wasn't my comrade Ingolf's fault; it was the Prophet and his lackeys and spies—"

"Lies!" burst out of the Cutter priest.

Anthony Heasleroad's hand swung out, the finger

pointing at the High Seeker; he didn't bother to look around. He smiled slightly at Rudi as he spoke to the man who'd interrupted him:

"First and last warning." Then to Rudi: "It's all he-said-they-said, isn't it? This is amusing, but it'll turn boring if it's like a court session."

"Then let me fetch your goods, my lord. Keep Ingolf here, if you will, as security for it."

Quiet fell again, and Heasleroad gave a sidelong glance at Colonel Heuisink as he thoughtfully ate a chocolate-covered cherry.

"What do you say, Sheriff?" he asked the master of Victrix Farm.

"Our intelligence has nothing good to say of this Western cult, Your Excellency," the older man said carefully.

"Oh, they've been fighting the Sioux—who are *such* a nuisance and have been for years," the Bossman replied.

Then he clapped his hands together. "I think I'll take you up on that . . . what were you called?"

"Rudi Mackenzie, tanist of the Clan Mackenzie," Rudi said. "Your Excellency."

"There can be only one," the Bossman said, and laughed; it was more like a giggle, and for some reason Colonel Heuisink shot him a glance.

"Yes, only one. You may go and get my artworks. If you have them in . . . oh, shall we say one month . . . you and the others may leave. If not . . . well, breaking a contract with the Bossman is treason, isn't it? And we all know what treason brings."

Rudi forced himself not to lick his lips. A month wasn't too long for a well-found party to get to where Ingolf's wagons had been left. The weather wouldn't have disturbed their cargos much, from the description; the goods had been tightly sealed in metal boxes, under tight-strapped canvas tilts on Conestogas whose bodies were mostly steel. The problem was that the local inhabitants might well have been busy at them.

"Your Excellency, that's a bargain," Rudi said calmly. "Now, if you'll give the order for the release of my friends and our goods and gear, we can be about your business."

"You can go wherever you want, you mean, as soon as you're over the Mississippi," the Bossman said, a slight jeering note in his voice. "No, no, there can be only one. I said *you* can go and fetch the treasure."

He looked speculatively at Odard and Mathilda. "These and Vogeler will be safe enough here."

"Look after Matti, Odard," Rudi said softly a week later, and held out his hand. "This is going to be hard on you all, but hardest for her, I think."

"I will," Odard said seriously. His grip was firm for the brief shake. "I'm going to get all the help I can, too."

Rudi Mackenzie nodded and swung into the saddle. Epona danced sideways half a dozen steps as she sensed his tension, and the hooves beat hollowly on the pavement of the bridge. He made his face calm as he nodded to Mathilda; her face held an iron pride, but her eyes were reddened and slightly swollen.

"Did you see the follower?" she asked in halting Sindarin.

"Am I blind?" he replied, and gave her a brief grin.

Captain Denson of the Iowa State Police was standing near her; a full mounted troop of his men were on either side.

"Tell the Bossman that I'll be back as soon as possible," Rudi said politely, gathering up the leading rein of his packhorse.

Denson grinned like a shark. "Most of the wild-men over there aren't cannibals anymore," he said. "Or at least so they say."

Rudi nodded again, and gave a last look at the walls of Dubuque, and the spire of the cathedral rising over them.

"Guard my soul-sister," he murmured quietly to it. "Brigid, be at her side; Dread Lord, be their shield."

He took a deep breath of the air, full of the damp warm river scent, silt and greenery, then signaled Epona up to a fast walk. The bridge stretched ahead, a mile or more of embankment and concrete piers, the center section suspended on cables from a horseshoe-like arch of steel truss beams.

A galley went by underneath as he rode, the oars stroking the blue river water into foam in centipede unison; he could hear the drum of the speed setter faintly through the rush and rumble of the current past the footings of the bridge. The eastern shore loomed ahead, wooded hills like those behind him ... but the only buildings were ruins, and a single small fort flying the Iowan flag.

I'll be back, he thought. *And Mary and Ritva and the others are there now, and they can act without my holding their hands, can they not?*

Eyes were probably watching him from those hills, looking at his gear and horses. He shrugged and sat taller in the saddle; that straightforward greed was easier to deal with than the treachery of princes and the unsleeping hate of the Prophet's men and their demon lords.

"And sure, I'm looking at *them,*" he said softly; Epona's ears flickered back. "The savages, and the foes behind me too. And if they'd stand in my way ... well then, the worse for them!"

NEW IN HARDCOVER

from

S. M. Stirling

THE SWORD OF THE LADY

Rudi Mackenzie has journeyed far across the land that was once the United States of America, hoping to find the source of the world-altering event that has come to be known as The Change. His final destination is Nantucket, an island overrun with forest, inhabited by a mere two hundred people who claim to have been transported there from out of time.

Only one odd stone house remains standing. Within it, Rudi finds a beautifully made sword waiting for him—and once he takes it up, nothing will ever be the same...

"NOBODY WRECKS A WORLD BETTER THAN S. M. STIRLING."
—*New York Times* bestselling author
Harry Turtledove

Available wherever books are sold or at
penguin.com

THE SUNRISE LANDS

by S. M. STIRLING

A generation has passed since The Change that rendered technology inoperable around the world, and western Oregon has finally achieved a degree of peace. But a new threat has risen in Paradise Valley, Wyoming. A man known as The Prophet presides over the Church Universal and Triumphant, teaching his followers to continue God's work by destroying the remnants of technological civilization they encounter— and those who dare use them.

Available wherever books are sold or at penguin.com

S. M. STIRLING

From national bestselling author
S. M. Stirling comes gripping novels of
alternate history

Island in the Sea of Time

Against the Tide of Years

On the Oceans of Eternity

The Peshawar Lancers

Conquistador

Dies the Fire

The Protector's War

A Meeting at Corvallis

The Sunrise Lands

The Scourge of God

"FIRST-RATE ADVENTURE ALL THE WAY."
—HARRY TURTLEDOVE

THE ULTIMATE IN
SCIENCE FICTION AND FANTASY!

From magical tales of distant worlds to stories of
technological advances beyond the grasp of man, Penguin has
everything you need to stretch your imagination to its limits.

penguin.com

ACE
Get the latest information on favorites like
William Gibson, T.A. Barron, Brian Jacques,
Ursula K. Le Guin, Sharon Shinn, Charlaine Harris,
Patricia Briggs, and Marjorie M. Liu,
as well as updates on the best new authors.

ROC
Escape with Jim Butcher, Harry Turtledove, Anne Bishop,
S.M. Stirling, Simon R. Green, E.E. Knight, Kat Richardson,
Rachel Caine, and many others—plus news on the
latest and hottest in science fiction and fantasy.

DAW
Patrick Rothfuss, Mercedes Lackey, Kristen Britain,
Tanya Huff, Tad Williams, C.J. Cherryh, and many more—
DAW has something to satisfy the cravings of any
science fiction and fantasy lover.
Also visit dawbooks.com.

*Get the best of science fiction and fantasy
at your fingertips!*